Book Two of

A WOLF IN THE SUN

A novel by

Coltrane Seesequasis

KEGEDONCE PRESS, 2025

September 2025

Published by Kegedonce Press
11 Park Road, Neyaashiinigmiing, ON N0H 2T0
Administration Office/Book Orders: P.O. Box 517, Owen Sound, ON N4K 5R1
www.kegedonce.com

Printed in Canada by Sinix Media Group
Art Direction: Kateri Akiwenzie-Damm
Design: Chantal Lalonde Design
Cover art by: Chantal Lalonde and Lauren Lavictoire
Author's photo: Michelle Quance & Tracey Biel

Library and Archives Canada Cataloguing in Publication

Title: The threads of time / a novel by Coltrane Seesequasis.
Names: Seesequasis, Coltrane, author.
Series: Seesequasis, Coltrane. Wolf in the sun ; bk. 2.
Description: Series statement: Book 2 of A wolf in the sun
Identifiers: Canadiana 20250223813 | ISBN 9781928120513 (softcover)
Subjects: LCGFT: Novels. | LCGFT: Fantasy fiction.
Classification: LCC PS8637.E44548 T47 2025 | DDC jC813/.6—dc23

For Customer Service/Orders
Tel 1-800-591-6250 Fax 1-800-591-6251
65 Quarterman Road, Unit 1, Guelph ON N1C 0A8
Email: orders@litdistco.ca

We acknowledge the support of the Canada Council for the Arts which last year invested $20.1 million in writing and publishing throughout Canada.

We would like to acknowledge funding support from the Ontario Arts Council, an agency of the Government of Ontario.

For Anneke Siemers,
Emma Etchells Foisy,
Terri Kulak,
and Suryia Seesequasis,
your comments, feedback, and suggestions
were paramount in making these pages see the light of day.
Once again, thank you for helping me
bring Silversong's journey to life.

Coltrane

MAP OF THE NORTHLANDS
(The Mortal Realm)

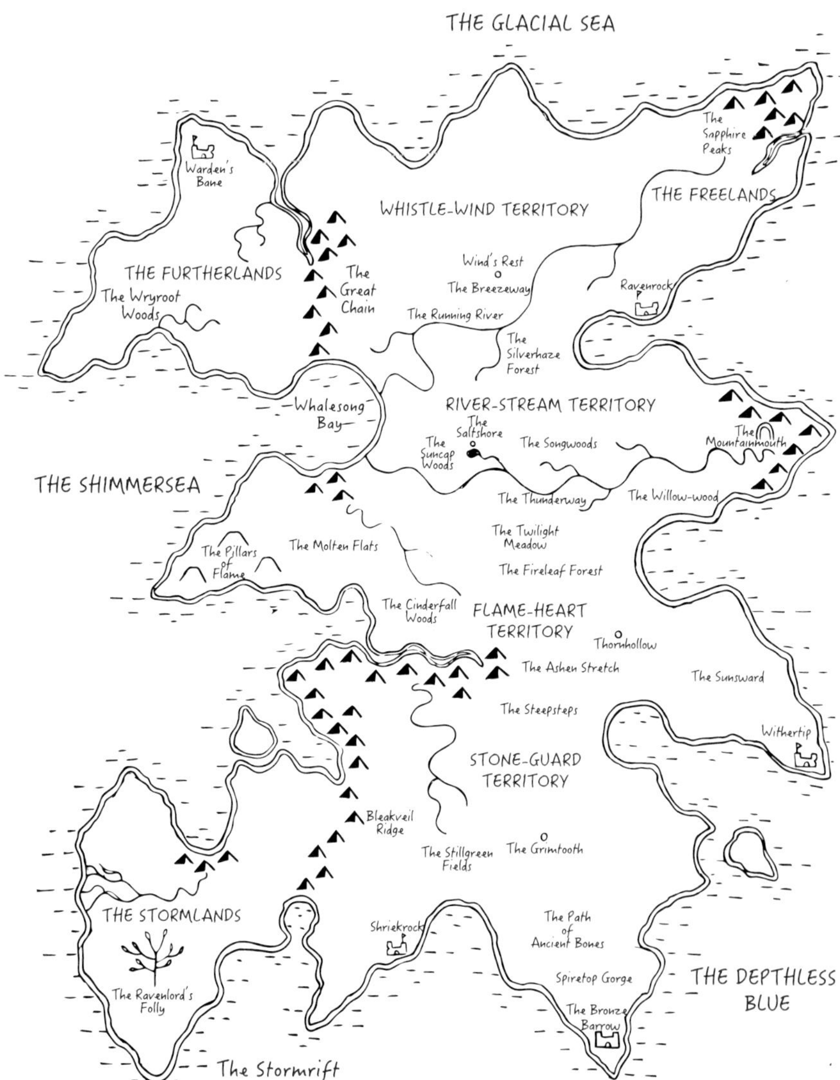

Table of Contents

PROLOGUE

Crimes of the Heart

Rime prowled through the forest of the enemy under the cover of darkness.

It wasn't the gentle, tranquil darkness of a clear night nor was it the natural, waning darkness of a passing storm. This darkness spread across the sky like a rotting tumour and seemed to mock the idea of daylight ever returning. It came from a place of hatred and despair, a place corrupted by the undying spirit of a monster, a monster who now lived within Rime's very being.

He carried this curse wherever he dared tread, ever on the brink of succumbing to the same blind rage that turned the once noble Forest Father into the Fallen Titan. The struggle of maintaining control over the vile fiend within him was beyond exhausting, made worse by the recent… complications. He had to anchor himself to his own hate, or he would be swept into the hatred of another and lose his sanity.

His anger pulsed in harmony with the Fallen Titan's—an oozing pustule close to bursting. He imagined his paws squishing the bloated growth, and out flowed all the negativity and pain contained within it. Thunder rumbled within the black clouds.

"Should've killed the silver pup," he growled. "Shouldn't have let the master spare him."

Lightning brewed above as falling specks of frost smothered the blood-red leaves of the shivering white trees. The victory of the exiles would've been assured if Ironwrath had consumed the piece of time… if he hadn't foolishly allowed it to be stolen from him.

The briefest thoughts of betrayal took root. Instinctively, Rime's mind retreated to an old memory. He closed his eyes, and the familiar landscape of the Furtherlands unfolded before him, transporting him back to a time when his greatest concern wasn't the monster within, but the one that lurked in the darkness. He stood helpless in front of a great deer wreathed in shadow, its antlers sprouting from its malformed skull like twisted branches, its gaping mouth displaying an array of fangs sharper than shards of ice. A chill ran down his spine as he recalled offering himself to the fiend at Ironwrath's command. He remembered the terror shaking him to the core, tempered only by the exhilaration coursing through his veins as the Fallen Titan's spirit sank into his body. The shock, the pain, the fear… he would carry the effects of it all to his dying day and perhaps even beyond.

The unnatural strength and endurance that came after the ordeal were but small rewards in comparison to the burden of bearing the Fallen Titan's soul. He would never be rid of it. Not unless he found a host willing to let themselves be infected by the wretched monster, but who would be crazy enough to accept such a foul blessing?

None are strong enough. None are hateful enough.

Ironwrath had chosen him to be his instrument of terror. Rime would wreak havoc on the Four Territories and deliver them the reckoning they rightly deserved! This curse was his alone to suffer; only he could properly wield it without falling into raging madness.

The fallen leaves decayed in his wake. He strode onward, keeping an eye out for sentinel activity. Staying ahead of the enemy was paramount especially upon learning that the Warden still lived. Rime had never known anyone more zealous and ruthless than her, including Ironwrath.

Silversong would be on his way to the River-Stream den by now, and if Ripper was to be believed, he was in the company of Swiftstorm and Greyhail—two thorns Rime had thought were long since plucked from his hide.

"Fallen Titan take them," he grouched, stepping on an unlucky caterpillar and feeling it pop under his weight.

Every scout report brought worse news. The latest was that River-Stream and the scattered remnants of Whistle-Wind had joined forced to combat Ironwrath. Never would Rime have believed that two rival territories could set aside their differences to pursue a common goal, and the Warden had allowed it too! Even if the alliance was only temporary, its mere existence contradicted many of Rime's beliefs.

The flood of doubt began. *Is the master wrong? Is unity between the Four Territories possible without drastic change forced upon them?* He shook his head and laughed.

No, of course not. Their alliance is tenuous at best. The Wolven Code they so dearly cling to ensures their downfall. The division and distrust it encourages is our advantage. Even the Warden can't control a legion of wolves who see their closest allies as potential threats. Who knows, maybe we won't have to apply any pressure at all before they break.

A smooth, melancholic howl ripped through his thoughts. His ears perked up, and his eyes widened at the tragic, familiar song. Memories of a brighter past fought the shadowy present and vaporized the miasma of hate choking his heart. A bitter lump formed in his throat as he crept toward the sound, drawn to it like a bee to sweet nectar, unable to even think of his mission much less his purpose as an exile.

The Fallen Titan raged and thrashed inside him, trying to shake off the tide of Rime's softer feelings. The fiend screeched and bellowed, but untamed hate couldn't vanquish its nemesis. Rime wrapped the shadow of the monster in pure light as he approached the edge of the forest. His connection to the Fallen Titan changed somehow, shifted as if by a massive wave. No longer was it a constant struggle for dominance between the two. Now Rime was fully in control.

The chaotic snowfall let up, and the black clouds loosened their grasp on the sky. Glowing edges spidered across the horizon. Life bloomed anew over Rime's trail of decay, and the looming darkness faded to a grey veil as he padded away from the woods. He came to a slope and beheld a scene he remembered perfectly from his youth.

The heavenly howling resonated from the centre of a still meadow. Determined to reach its source, Rime wasted no time descending the slope and sneaking through the sea of violet flowers. Prickly thorns nicked him, but he refused to flinch. He would gladly suffer any pain for his pursuit. He picked up the pace, impatience winning over caution as the voice called to him.

He was young again, daring and gallant without shame or fear. He was Tiderunner, corporal of River-Stream, and there was someone he desperately needed to see.

He stopped at the heart of the meadow. There she was, oblivious to his presence, immersed in her own howling as the sun's tender rays reached through the thinning clouds in an attempt to touch her. She was still as pretty as the flickering stars themselves. Her scent reawakened a surge of blissful memories as Rime stepped delicately forward. He wouldn't allow anything to ruin this moment.

She sang the final deep notes of her song and sighed perhaps in yearning, perhaps in regret. She looked pained by something, as if she'd hoped for another voice to answer her lonely tune.

A sudden breeze flowed through Rime's coat and carried his scent to her. His breath stopped itself short of a gasp.

She turned around and yelped when she spotted him. Her shadow-touched fur hardened into spikes, and her flame-coloured eyes expanded until it looked like they would pop out of her skull. She crouched and remained on the brink of baring her teeth.

Waves of joy forced a smile to creep onto Rime's face. "Hey, Cindersky."

CHAPTER 1

The Warden

Sunlight pushed through the breaking clouds to illuminate the shocked faces of the wolves staring at Silversong.

"YOU WHAT?!" Hazel and Palesquall barked at the same time.

Swiftstorm and Greyhail exchanged a look of concern for Silversong's sanity. Frostpaw stayed put a few steps away from the others, eyes bouncing between Silversong and the ground.

The piece of time turned within Silversong's body as he watched a stray hummingbird hovering over a blue flower. He tensed the winding threads only he could see, wrapping them around the small creature and freezing it midair. Removed from the currents of time, the hummingbird stayed still as if encased in ice. A cool breeze gusted through the woods and carried on its trail an array of broad leaves. He captured those too.

Gasps came out of every mouth save Frostpaw's. Silversong cleared his throat and repeated himself. "I swallowed the piece of time before the Heretic could claim it, and now I have its powers."

Palesquall nosed one of the leaves frozen in time's embrace, moving it through the air, through the threads. "Whoa."

Whoa was right. From Silversong's perspective, it looked like Palesquall was pushing a small island through an ever-flowing river. Even after consuming the piece of time, it proved an immense struggle to understand its workings. None of the things Silversong could now do should be possible, and yet they were. He fought to keep a headache at bay. He needed to study the weapon more. He needed to master it if he had any hopes of defeating the Heretic once and for all.

Swiftstorm's wide eyes remained locked on him throughout the display. "Brother..."

Silversong turned to his sister, and the swell of joy warming his heart influenced the invisible threads rotating around her. If he squinted at them, he could make out glimpses of her potential futures. They branched out and revealed wildly different fates, good and bad. Piecing together all the circumstances leading those outcomes would require substantial concentration. The weapon, aged and used as it was, wouldn't be as easy for Silversong to manipulate as it had been for its previous wielders.

Tiny thorns pressed into his brain, and he flinched, letting go of the tightened threads and allowing them to resume their course. The hummingbird glided from one flower to another, oblivious to its previous entrapment, and the once stilled leaves drifted downward much to Palesquall's disappointment. Silversong padded to his sister and bathed in her scent, nuzzling her concerned face. She smelled of home, of family, of something that should never have been lost.

Greyhail watched him close by, eyes lit by the glint of opportunity. "We must get you to the Warden as soon as possible. She needs to know exactly how this weapon functions."

Hazel studied the freed leaves. "Why must you keep plunging into dangerous situations, Silversong? Palesquall told me all about your audience with the Empress of Spiders, and now you go and steal the weapon she revealed to the Heretic?!"

His sister failed to conceal a shiver. She'd obviously heard about Silversong's *exploits* from Palesquall too.

Wait until you learn about all the other dangers I faced.

Silversong thought it best not to mention his other audiences with equally murderous Titans. "Look, I—"

"Can you see the future?" Palesquall prodded. "Can you let me know when I'll finally be promoted to lieutenant? I'm looking forward to bossing Hazel around all day."

Hazel nudged him on the cheek. "In your dreams, gullwit."

"You can freeze objects in time," Greyhail's tail swished in a controlled manner. "But what else is possible, I wonder?" His suppressed excitement was almost unnerving.

"Can you go back in time?" Swiftstorm's whine carried the weight of deep regret. "If we can stop the Heretic before he uses Rime to break the Great Chain—"

The wolves hurled a swarm of questions at Silversong, and it quickly became impossible to keep track of them all. Within him, the piece of time stirred, urging him to tie its threads around every yapping mouth.

Frostpaw, who'd stayed silent so far, barked loud enough to frighten a soaring eagle. "That's enough! Silversong can answer all your questions once we're safe at my den. Speaking of… shouldn't we get there before an army of wolves departs to the Mountainmouth?"

The startled wolves all turned to the River-Stream lieutenant, realizing they'd gotten carried away. Silversong smiled his thanks to Frostpaw, but his new friend only returned a blank stare as though they hadn't just faced death itself together.

Before Silversong's mood could be dragged down further, Greyhail spoke up. "You're right. We'll have all the answers we need in due course. Let's keep moving."

They maintained a trotting pace through the waking forest as summer's heat boiled away the final wisps of a foul storm. Silversong remained at Swiftstorm's side, reminiscing about younger days before the Warden had separated them. It was his way of blocking out the gossip about his new powers.

"I hope it wasn't too difficult for you when the Warden chose me to become a sentinel." Guilt trickled into his sister's tone.

Bitterness flooded Silversong as he tried to stamp out the memory of howling his sorrow following Swiftstorm's departure. "The Warden could've at least given us more time to say goodbye to you. Mother and father tried pretending they were all right for my sake, but I saw through it. For the following seasons, we couldn't even mention your name without wishing we'd done more to stall the Warden from taking you away."

Swiftstorm lowered her ears and head. "I'm sorry. I also remember the awful feeling of leaving Wind's Rest. The crushing weight of knowing I might never see you all again haunted me for a long while." She sighed, and Greyhail licked her face as a gesture of comfort. "Good thing I had you there to distract me," she teased, earning her a smirk from Greyhail.

Silversong stared at the passing ground, at the ants battling for measly crumbs under the shade of the trees. "No. I'm the one who should apologize. It must've been way harder for you being separated from all your packmates. I can't even imagine how scared I would've been if I'd taken your place. I don't think I could've survived all the challenges you've faced."

To his surprise, his sister only laughed. "You were one of the reasons I became the sentinel I am today, Silversong, mother and father too. Without you three, I would've been food for the exiles by now." Silversong tilted his head, his confusion met by a tender smile. "All throughout my training, I had your encouraging faces ingrained in my thoughts. The need to protect those I loved far outmatched the pain of every hardship I suffered. Even though it was unlikely, I had faith I would see you all again. I knew everything would by all right in the end."

Silversong returned his sister's smile. "Looks like you were right." The piece of time vibrated as if in warning. The threat of chaos and destruction was still out there, but he put aside his worry for now and enjoyed his sister's company while Hazel and Palesquall laughed about something.

"Your sister is one of the strongest sentinels I've ever had the pleasure of knowing," Greyhail grunted at Swiftstorm's other side. "She's saved me more times than I can count. There's a reason the exiles fear her. It's the same reason the Warden chose her. She'll do anything to defend the Four Territories, even if it demands the ultimate sacrifice."

My sister is the best sentinel ever! Silversong beamed, tail wagging and chest kindling a happy heart. Another future flashed in the threads surrounding her. Like a chilling wave, it doused the tender flames. The vision passed too quickly for him to make out many details, but he could've sworn Swiftstorm had been smiling and staring lovingly at someone as she soaked in a pool of her own blood.

Swiftstorm must've caught on to Silversong's concern. "Hey, is something wrong?"

At the front of the group, Frostpaw halted. "Someone's coming." Tail going stiff, he sniffed the air some more.

Silversong dismissed his vision. Brief as it had been, it was probably among one of the more unlikely outcomes. Still, he had to be careful. He wouldn't let any harm come to his sister. Especially not now that he had the power to save her.

Anxiety bubbled in his core as he studied the new scents drifting his way. They clearly belonged to wolves, some strong and tangy, others more mellow and sweet, but they all brought a sense of familiarity he couldn't quite explain. They reminded him of his sister, and of the one who took her from him all those seasons ago. He honed his focus and attempted to search the near future for answers.

"It's her." Greyhail tensed.

Swiftstorm's ears perked up in alert, stopping the trotting wolves.

"We stopped," Palesquall yipped obliviously. "Why've we stopped?"

"Use your nose for once, bug-brain," Hazel snapped. "I think it's the Warden."

Palesquall finally caught on to the unmistakable presence of approaching wolves. "Oh."

Silversong padded up to Frostpaw, who took one look at him and backed off. It was like Silversong's heart had been strangled by thorny vines. Why was the lieutenant suddenly so scared of being close to him?

Did I do something to offend you? Silversong frowned, but Frostpaw refused to meet his gaze no matter how intensely Silversong stared. *It's like you're pretending I'm a complete stranger all of a sudden.*

Before Silversong could confront the lieutenant, the new scents intensified, and a shuffling in the nearby bushes announced the newcomers.

Swiftstorm dipped her head to whisper into Silversong's ear. "If she wanted to, the Warden could've snuck up on us, and we would've been blind to her approach until she was directly in front of our eyes. She can be silent as a butterfly."

Silversong wondered why the piece of time hadn't warned him about the Warden's approach. It seemed the weapon chose what to reveal and what to withhold at random.

There must be a way to make it more precise. Maybe it just needs to get used to me.

Greyhail flicked his tail beside Swiftstorm. "Despite her age, the Warden is as fierce in battle as she is cunning. Don't for a moment underestimate her power, Silversong. She can make the toughest Chiefs whimper in fear if she thinks they're acting out of line. I've seen her reduce the meanest of exiles into sniveling mongrels, and never has she tasted defeat in battle."

Greyhail's embellishment of the Warden certainly had an effect on Hazel and Palesquall. Tucked away behind Swiftstorm, their tails shook against their bellies. Frostpaw froze where he stood, every strand of fur lifting like a quill.

Out of the shadows she came, fur so white not even the snows of winter could compare. Her gaze swept over them all as more sentinels appeared behind her, battle-hardened and showing not an inkling of emotion. The Warden's stance was elegant yet deadly, as though she could spring into action at a moment's notice. Her pale eyes descended on Silversong, devoid of kindness. Staring at a ghost wouldn't have been as unsettling! An icy chill trickled along his spine as he recalled the first time he'd seen her. She was as intimidating then as she was now. If anyone could beat the Heretic in a fight, it was her. Silversong would bet his life on it.

The Warden's voice, deep and smooth in spite of her age, cut cleanly through all lesser sounds. "You are Silversong, are you not?"

"Yes, ma'am," Silversong answered instantly, pouring all the respect he could muster into his tone. Her station demanded as much. He tucked his tail as far as it could go but met her gaze confidently. How would she react when he revealed his triumph over the Heretic? Would she see him as a threat?

"I thought so." The Warden's tail swished slowly as her escort of sentinels surrounded his friends, forming a perimeter in case of an attack. Although they were deep in River-Stream Territory, the Warden plainly wouldn't take any chances where the Heretic was concerned. "Swiftstorm has mentioned you on countless occasions, and after hearing about your recent *endeavours*, I grew eager to finally meet you."

Silversong gulped as the weight of all he'd done crashed onto his shoulders. "I, uhm…"

"Ma'am," Swiftstorm came to his defense, "we found him earlier this morning, and we were on our way to the Saltshore in hopes of intercepting your army before they—"

"It's curious how fate rewards those faithful to the Wolven Code." The Warden craned her head skyward, and even the clouds seemed eager to flee her stare. "I had a feeling something was amiss, and so I delayed the advance of my army until I could be sure no threat would hinder our assault on the Mountainmouth. I set out to join your scouting party, and here we are, siblings reunited, a wayward lieutenant found safe, and the Heretic thwarted for the time being. An accurate assessment, is it not?"

Silversong gasped, and the golden circle lurched in his belly. "How did you—"

"After you've interrogated as many wolves as I have, you'll learn to piece together clues in a very accurate manner." The Warden's voice was constant like a creek—no, a river—that carved through earth and stone without pause. "If I hadn't learned of exiles willingly giving themselves to the Fallen Titan's corruption in an attempt to wield it against us, the Heretic would've launched his assault on the Four Territories before the Wise-Wolves even gave you your name. He would've succeeded too, but I stalled their invasion for as long as I could. Unfortunately, I failed to predict just how powerful the Heretic's prized lackey had become in his mastery over the corruption. An oversight that shall haunt me to my dying day."

The Warden let her confession burrow into the ears of everyone present. "Now, our current situation is made rather obvious. Your eyes wouldn't be as confident as they are now if my nemesis had claimed the weapon he sought, so either you prevented the Heretic from consuming the piece of time, or you beat him at his own game and ate it yourself. I'm willing to bet on the latter, judging by your untroubled scent, not to mention you're emitting a subtle aura I can't quite describe. I'll also venture to say that the Heretic isn't fully vanquished, or you would all be far more jovial."

Frostpaw shifted from paw to paw, eyes darting between Silversong and the Warden.

The leader of the sentinels let out a quick grunt, making Frostpaw flinch. "Your unlikely ally is as afraid of you as he is of me, or should I say, he's afraid of the thing inside you."

The lieutenant made no sound, so the Warden took this as confirmation. Silversong wasn't convinced. There was another reason for Frostpaw's fright. Another reason why he refused to stand near his friend.

Silversong thought about explaining his actions now before the anticipation got too high, but the Warden allowed none of it, barking a declaration. "You'll reveal to me everything about your journey once we're all gathered at the Saltshore and no sooner. I'll escort you there to save time. These old bones need the exercise." She raised her head high to address everyone. "Take heart, my wolves, my soldiers. Stay true to the Wolven Code. Condemn those who break it, and we'll overcome any obstacle. Move out!"

The sentinels howled in unison and began their stride toward the River-Stream den. Hazel and Palesquall pursued them submissively, as did Frostpaw. One look from Swiftstorm was all it took to get Silversong moving, but the uneasy sensation gripping his insides slowed his pace.

Condemn those who break it. Silversong and Frostpaw had broken many rules in the Wolven Code. But surely the Warden would forgive their infractions after they'd achieved so much.

Doubt plagued his thoughts. He closed his eyes and tried forcing the piece of time to reveal the inevitable outcome of his code-breaking. He cursed under his breath. As if to spite him, his own anxiety had beckoned a sheet of opaque fog to hide the future. He needed a clear head to properly use the weapon. He would have to try again later.

He clenched his teeth at the acknowledgment of another threat to the Four Territories. This one was far more sinister and hid in plain sight, masquerading itself as a blessing when in truth it was a curse constricting the freedom of every soul. A chain preventing the wolves of the Four Territories from becoming their strongest selves.

Silversong lifted his eyes to the Warden—the embodiment and enforcer of the Wolven Code.

CHAPTER 2

The Saltshore

Using the piece of time to its fullest extent required a clear mind. This fact was becoming increasingly obvious to Silversong as he hastened through the trees on his way to the Saltshore. Somehow he still couldn't clear his brain of worry. The more he tried, the more he failed, and the angrier he got… and the angrier he got, the more the winding threads resisted his attempts to wield them.

He wanted to tie them in a knot out of pure frustration and force them to reveal what was in store for him and Frostpaw at the River-Stream den. The Warden would spell trouble, that much he could accurately guess, but how much trouble?

He squinted at the circular reach of the piece of time. It radiated outward from his stomach—a perfect spherical *aura* a few tail-lengths in size, comprised entirely of tiny rotating threads only he could discern.

Stupid golden circle. He growled at his stomach without a care for how many eyes glanced his way. *Do something! Show me how to get on top of this!*

As if in answer, the piece of time shuddered. Splintered futures flashed in the threads but sputtered out too quickly for him to keep track of anything significant. He shook his head in the hopes of beating his brain into submission. To his dismay, the shaking only caused a nasty headache rather than stopping the feeling of walking into an elaborate snare.

Deep breaths, Silversong. Deep breaths. He worked his lungs to such an extreme degree that he ended up dizzying himself, but at least now his anxiety had calmed somewhat. He breathed out again and focused, closing his eyes and peering at the many possibilities awaiting him. They came to him in fractured pieces like shards of broken ice, each one reflecting a different outcome depending on his choices.

From what he could glimpse, nothing *too* bad would come of the questioning at the Saltshore unless he somehow found a way to offend everyone. Luckily, he wasn't nearly as inflammatory as Palesquall could sometimes be, so at least the River-Stream wolves wouldn't unceremoniously toss him into a boiling geyser anytime soon. Still, the Warden was a problem—a thorn nestled deep in the very flesh of the Four Territories. Pulling it out would take a tremendous effort from all wolves who falsely believed the exiles were their only enemy.

But how to convince them otherwise? How to achieve peace without violence? Silversong released his grasp on the weapon before it could poke his brain. He studied the Warden at the front. Even now, he wasn't entirely certain she couldn't smell his blasphemous intentions. He needed to be very careful around her. If she suspected him of plotting against her…

His eyes found his sister striding beside Greyhail. The pair moved in a synchronized fashion, quick and nimble, Swiftstorm lending speed to her fellow sentinels by wrapping wind around their limbs. Silversong did the same for Frostpaw so he could keep up.

How loyal are you to the Warden, Swiftstorm? He feared to ponder the question further; the exiles should be everyone's top priority. Then, Silversong could see about amending the Wolven Code without bloodshed. All in all, he had two major challenges ahead of him, but which one would be harder to overcome? The piece of time, weakened as it was from its former use, couldn't reveal much about the far future aside from occasional glimpses. Though the immediate power it granted was more than enough to manipulate the currents of fate. He would make do.

The day brightened above the canopy of thick leaves, darkening the swaying shadows on the ground and reminding everyone of summer's ruthless heat. The diverse sounds of the vibrant Songwoods joined together to create a melodious tune that chased away negativity. The distant rushing of water added another layer to the music of River-Stream, a greater one that enveloped the croaking and the buzzing, the whooshing of the breeze and the chirping in the trees. A constant soothing roar. Silversong fought the growing temptation to remain here and forget the dangers he'd gotten himself into. He could see now why Frostpaw was so fond of this forest.

Near the front of the group, the lieutenant ran alone, downcast and silent, never once looking over his shoulder to acknowledge Silversong's existence. Whatever Frostpaw was going through, Silversong wanted to help. They were in this together, and no good would come of pretending they were strangers to each other.

Is this about your mother, Frostpaw? About you failing to avenge her? Maybe it was best to give the lieutenant some space to figure things out. The way he'd been acting recently spawned another theory. *Are you afraid you'll be punished for us working together without the approval of the Warden?* Silversong had never seen Frostpaw so afraid before. Not even when he'd faced the horrors of the Mountainmouth head-on.

There's got to be something I can do, Silversong thought, maintaining the currents around Frostpaw's limbs.

The Warden barked before Silversong could attempt to scout Frostpaw's future, her voice slicing through the melody of the Songwoods. "We're almost at the Saltshore. Keep up the quick pace. The sooner we get there, the sooner we can launch a proper counteroffensive against the Heretic."

Silversong's legs buzzed, and an excited tingle flashed from nose to tail. The wolves around him all perked up at the notion of bringing the fight directly to the exiles, but any victory now would be a hollow one. No matter how much Silversong believed the Heretic's days were numbered, he knew Ironwrath's influence would always taint the Four Territories. Things would never go back to normal. Wind's Rest would remain destroyed, and all the pain dealt to the Whistle-Wind Pack would forever haunt its history.

Still, the urge to deliver justice awakened a thrill in his bones. In the short darkness of every blink, Silversong saw himself leading the charge against the exiles, those under his command stamping them out like insects. The power of wolves united would defeat the Heretic. Ironwrath would achieve his ultimate goal, in a sense, but not in the way he expected.

Silversong lifted his gaze to the Warden again. Unity would be a difficult thing to achieve while she was in control, but by Motherwolf, Silversong would see it done. Division meant conceding everything to the enemy. He couldn't squander this opportunity to unify ancient rivals against a common foe.

The sky had dimmed by the time the forest dwindled around them, giving way to a stretch of pale boulders consumed by branching lichen. The only trees daring enough to sprout here were birches nestled deep in wide hollows in between the stones. The once thunderous sound of a distant river hushed itself until only the panting of weary wolves and swirling wind could be heard. They'd travelled very fast, and more than once Silversong had to strengthen the currents around Frostpaw's legs to keep him from falling behind.

Visions of oncoming events flashed in Silversong's head. He breathed out, readying himself mentally for all the questions to which he owed answers.

At the lip of the forest, the ground dipped into a wide channel of grey stones that bordered the den of this territory: a bone-white crest of geysers that was also the shoreline. It bathed in the pale rays of the sun and obscured a great body of water. From here, all he could see of the lake were fragments of deep blue in between the springs and the distant shapes of wolves standing guard around the heart of River-Stream. The sight awakened a feeling of longing within him, a longing for a future he'd denied.

Frostpaw took a deep breath, looking like he was about to faint. Silversong was prepared to tense the threads around the lieutenant just in case.

"We've arrived," announced the Warden, showing no signs of exhaustion. "My old home. The Saltshore. The pride of River-Stream Territory, and it has remained so since the end of the War of Change."

Guards patrolling the elevated shore spotted them. A howling broke out, urgent and loud enough to wake a hibernating bear. Voices young and old echoed the alarm, and a swarm of wolves poured out of the many holes in between the geysers. Silversong recognized dozens of his packmates from here. His tail beat the air, and his heart thumped wildly.

The Warden let loose her own voice. It resounded like calm thunder slowly breaking across the horizon, suppressing all in its wake. She turned to Silversong, her gaze sharper than her fangs. "Now, it's time we discussed the outcome of your little adventure, but first, I believe another reunion is in order."

The Warden directed her attention elsewhere, and Silversong thanked Motherwolf for the distraction. He'd been on the verge of backing away, of showing weakness—something he couldn't allow from here on. One day, he would have to stand up to everything she stood for. There could be no hesitation then. No fear.

Alongside his sister, he followed the Warden and her sentinels down into the ditch, stopping just before the rocky rise leading to the foot of the Saltshore. By now the crest was occupied on one side by the strong and proud wolves of River-Stream, and the other by the tired and defeated Whistle-Wind members. A line of sentinels separated the two packs, eager to carry out any command their leader gave them.

Silversong panted away the final remnants of his exhaustion, trying not to think about how thirsty he was. The salty aroma of the den worsened his discomfort, and the scent of wolves both foreign and familiar dizzied him.

Silversong could hear the gossip among the onlookers.

"Look! It's Frostpaw!"

"He came back."

"Looks like this Palesquall was telling the truth after all."

"Oh, Frostpaw. What's he gotten himself into?"

Rather than meet the faces of his packmates, the lieutenant peered at his own forepaws.

Silversong looked toward his family and fellow soldiers. Most of them uttered no sound, and those who did exchanged only unheard whispers. He caught the green eyes of Gorsescratch before the bully decided it was a better idea to stare at Hazel instead.

One day, Gorsescratch. One day. Silversong put aside his dislike for the corporal and found the face of his mother stuck between worry and anger. Cedargaze shifted restlessly, restraining herself from running up to him and causing a scene. Guilt riddled his heart and put an end to the thrill of seeing his packmates again. The heavy feeling multiplied tenfold upon sighting Chief Amberstorm standing away from everyone else.

The once proud Chief looked beaten and starved. His singed flesh outlined many of his bones, and his remaining fur was badly in need of grooming. His amber eyes gazed at nothing, devoid of the intensity every subordinate had feared in their younger days. Silversong wasn't even sure his Chief was aware of his surroundings. It was a terrible thing to behold and a stark reminder of the Heretic's cruelty.

Silversong bit his lip and suppressed a growl, wishing he could've done more to save Pinetrail and the others when the exiles had attacked Wind's Rest.

"So, the Warden has returned." A large male of black fur stepped forward, his yellow eyes singling out Frostpaw. "And it appears she's found the wayward wolves."

"Chief Riptide." The Warden gave him the slightest nod of acknowledgment. Nothing more or less than someone of his station merited from her. "I see you've been keeping my army on high alert."

A lithe she-wolf of deep grey fur joined her Chief. "We've been growing restless since morning, ma'am. Is there still a need to assault the Mountainmouth? The soldiers of River-Stream are itching for a taste of exile blood."

The wolves around her barked their approval and bared their fangs as if exiles would pop out of the Songwoods at any moment. Among the River-Stream members was someone who looked like an older, less handsome version of Frostpaw. He scowled at the young lieutenant who tried his hardest to ignore him. Silversong guessed this was Frostpaw's father. Wavy mud markings decorated his sides, marking him as a lieutenant too.

Come to think of it, where's my father? Where's Shadowgale?

The Warden's deep grunt silenced the din. "Assaulting the Mountainmouth is no longer necessary, Icetail. Don't take this as a victory, though. The Heretic and his lackeys are still out there, and we need to—"

A high-pitched cry startled everyone present. "SILVERSONG!"

"Oh, Motherwolf's mercy." Swiftstorm shrank in on herself, trying to appear as unworthy of attention as possible. "Here he comes."

"WHERE IS HE?! I NEED TO SEE HIM!" Shadowgale pushed Cedargaze aside, head darting in all directions until he found his son. His deep grey fur bristled. "There you are! I swear by my ancestors, I'll—"

Cedargaze bit Shadowgale on the tail and growled something into his ear. Shadowgale's expression was one of utter disbelief. His face fluctuated from displaying wrinkles of anger to wide-eyed glee, finally settling on something in between. He calmed himself and sat, much to Silversong's relief. Now was *definitely* not the time to make a scene.

Swiftstorm released a breath she'd probably been holding since hearing father's voice.

Greyhail chuckled in amusement.

"As I was saying..." whined the Warden in a dangerous tone as a few of her sentinels atop the den closed in around Shadowgale, fangs ready in case he interrupted her again, "... we need to discuss how to defeat the Heretic permanently. Banishment won't be enough this time. A moot is in order, and all parties present must participate. I'll have no objections."

Shocked murmurs resonated from the crowd gathered above, but Riptide growled to quiet the noisy mouths. "A moot between rival territories hasn't occurred since the Rise of the Fallen Titan."

"Indeed, my Chief," Icetail whistled, her voice whispery yet still somehow managing to sound sharp and clear. "But from all we've heard, the exiles are now a threat to every territory. I understand your reservations about hosting our *guests*, but remember, we can't give the enemy a chance to break River-Stream like they broke Whistle-Wind. A moot is in our best interest."

"Of course. You're right, my love," Riptide acknowledged Icetail. "All things considered, this is a fitting den for a moot. As I recall, this was also the gathering place of the resistance against the Fallen Titan." Riptide cut a dirty look toward Amberstorm and the Whistle-Wind Pack. "So be it. The sooner the Heretic is dead, the sooner things can go back to how they were. We'll have this moot within the Big Cave beneath the Saltshore. There's enough room there for everyone to hear things out."

Icetail fixed her golden gaze upon Frostpaw. "Yes. We all deserve answers." Her regard shifted to Silversong. The way her eyes narrowed turned his blood to ice. "Welcome to the Saltshore, stray subordinate of Whistle-Wind. You and your *partner* have much to explain."

Frostpaw tucked his tail so neatly under his belly it looked like he'd lost it.

Silversong's breathing quickened due to the added stress, the air suddenly thicker than honey. He lifted a trembling forepaw, barely able to string his thoughts together as the sentinels escorted him up to the Saltshore. He couldn't afford to make the wrong choices now, or he would lose all the advantages he'd gained so far and deliver the Four Territories straight into the maw of the Heretic.

CHAPTER 3

The Winds of Change

The Saltshore looked exactly like it had in the vision shown to Silversong inside the Mountainmouth.

In the dimming light, the shore shone as a white pearl between lake and forest. Geysers of all sizes jutted out from the rugged ground, exuding a salty aroma reminiscent of the ocean's spray. They exhaled fountains of steam that warmed old scars and invigorated the mind, granting Silversong a sense of peace and comfort when neither were warranted. It was like being seduced by the Empress all over again, except this time there was no obvious malice, no fangs poised to come crashing down on him.

Every now and then, round openings hollowed the ground, leading to caves and tunnel systems beneath the hot springs. It made the den seem more like a hive inhabited by wolves rather than bees. Silversong almost wished it were the other way around. Bees were far more hospitable than these River-Stream wolves. Every passing breath another one gave the Whistle-Wind refugees a distrustful look or a hateful scowl. Melting the frozen barriers of prejudice would prove a tougher endeavor than he'd thought.

He concentrated on the subtle aura he emitted, narrowing his gaze on the many threads rotating before him. *Think about everything you're going to say*, Silversong reminded himself. *Don't lie, but don't reveal the entire truth either.*

He found himself in the company of familiar faces as Chief Riptide led everyone across the den. The deeper colours of the River-Stream wolves surrounded them, mouths uttering all manner of gossip. Youngsters tried poking their heads into the moving crowd for a chance to glimpse the ones who'd braved the depths of the Mountainmouth. They also helped the spread of fanciful rumours, many of which caught the attention of the Whistle-Wind rookies who would no doubt make up their own embellished tales to the detriment of the truth. There was no end to the creativity of youth.

The Warden summoned Swiftstorm to the front, condemning Silversong to suffer the wrath of worried parents alone.

"We're not letting you out of our sight ever again, Silversong," his mother declared, her stern tone lessened by clear concern.

Shadowgale joined the scolding. "Do you have any idea how worried we were? Can you even imagine it? We had no idea whether your sister was alive or dead, and you just decide to leave us?!" He came very close to growling.

"I'm sorry," Silversong grunted, trying to keep his proud stance intact despite the weight of his guilt threatening to crumple him like a bundle of dried leaves. "I really am… but I don't regret a thing. I saved Palesquall from the exiles, and I figured out a way to beat the Heretic. You must understand."

"No, you must understand!" Cedargaze rounded on him, green eyes fierce as lightning. "I-I thought we failed as parents. I thought I failed as a mother. We were about to go after you, but the other lieutenants held us back."

One of those other lieutenants butted her head into the conversation. "We considered sitting on them until they saw reason. We would've done the same to you had we known your intentions. They came to their senses before then, thank Motherwolf. You really gave them quite the scare, Silversong."

Silversong couldn't look at his mother. He concentrated on the moving mass of wolves to keep from whimpering. Hazel watched from the side, clearly debating whether she should comfort Cedargaze or help her scold Silversong.

Shadowgale moved over to his mate and nuzzled her face. "It's all right, Cedargaze. He's alive, and so is Swiftstorm. We aren't failures. We'll look after them for as long as we live."

Again, the piece of time vibrated as if to challenge Shadowgale's claim, but Silversong couldn't foresee much with a head clouded by guilt. Near the front of the throng, Frostpaw walked in shame, head and tail hanging low as his father showed not two shreds of concern for his own son.

Silversong strained his ears to listen in on the conversation.

"I thought if I avenged mother, I could—"

Frostpaw's father bit him on his injured shoulder, making him cry out sharply. "But you failed! Perhaps if you'd killed that depraved murderer I would've thought better of you. But again you disappoint! Don't you dare mention Rippleshine in my presence again. You're the reason she's dead. You'll get only growls from me until you prove how sorry you are."

Silversong's heart lurched, the shock quickly swelling into white-hot anger. Heat bubbled up his limbs. He wanted to charge into Frostpaw's father and teach him a lesson!"

The young lieutenant quivered and whined something too low for Silversong to hear. Blood trickled from Frostpaw's reopened wound, the same wound Silversong had given him.

Other wolves around Frostpaw's age joined in on the needless cruelty.

"We don't care if you wanted to redeem yourself. You still failed!"

"She's dead because you woke her up, gullwit! She wouldn't have noticed that monster sneaking out of the den if it weren't for you."

"She got killed all because you were too afraid to sleep alone. You were always a coward, Frostpaw."

"You're not our brother anymore. We made that clear a long time ago. How often do we have to remind you to leave us be?"

Silversong turned his ears away before he did something he regretted. Why wasn't Frostpaw standing up for himself? He was a lieutenant! He outranked all of them except for his father. It took all Silversong had to not snarl at Frostpaw's ignorant family. Nothing good would come from Silversong's sudden aggression, but the impulse to comfort a friend was almost too strong for him to do the sensible thing.

I'll only make things worse if I come to Frostpaw's defense, he kept reminding himself.

While Shadowgale reassured Cedargaze, Gorsescratch padded up to Silversong, followed by a reluctant Tawnydrift.

"I'm not in the mood for your insults today, Gorsescratch." Silversong sighed, silently thankful he now had a scapegoat to receive the brunt of his boiling temper.

Gorsescratch stared straight at him without hesitation. The shame in his regard was almost as vexing as Tawnydrift's vacant expression. "Just thought I would brief you on how things have been going for us. Whistle-Wind, I mean."

Silversong relented, tail swishing impatiently. "Go ahead."

"It's not good," Gorsescratch admitted, taking care not to let anyone overhear. "If you haven't already guessed, we're not welcome here. Some of the scowls I've gotten from the River-Stream mongrels are worse than the ones Hazel keeps giving me."

"Oh, I wouldn't worry too much about that, Gorsescratch. You do have a tendency to attract a lot of scowls."

"Now's not the time for your wisecracks," Tawnydrift grumbled. "This is serious."

"I *was* being serious," Silversong grunted, gathering his nerves. "But fine. Keep talking, Gorsescratch."

Gorsescratch let the insult slide. "We're being treated worse than subordinates. We're not allowed to take anything from the River-Stream Prey Hollow. We're forced to forage for our own food and eat out of sight of the den. We can't go anywhere without spies watching us. We can't drink from the lake. We aren't allowed any medicine to heal our wounded, and worse yet, Chief Amberstorm does nothing about it. Besides checking in on his pups every now and then, it's like he's given up." The bully fixed a rueful glare on the gaunt Chief trudging along at the head of the Whistle-Wind Pack.

Silversong tried not to look at the deteriorated shell that once was the proud Whistle-Wind leader. "Have the lieutenants spoken to the Warden about this?"

"They have, and so did the Wise-Wolves." Gorsescratch craned his head toward Moonwhisper and Mistyfur. They watched over the Chief's growing offspring and looked like they hadn't slept in days. "But she said Chief Riptide can treat us however he likes so long as we remain at the Saltshore. His den. His rules."

"Your sister tried arguing on our behalf," Tawnydrift added through gritted teeth, "but the Warden convinced her to remain neutral. She's a sentinel now, and so she isn't allowed to pick sides. She's not the Swiftstorm we once knew."

You're wrong, Silversong thought, peering at his sister between the frames of dozens of wolves. He shook his head and released a heavy breath, feeling as though all his packmates were relying on him to secure for them a future free of hardship and despair. No matter how impossible it seemed to achieve such a goal, he had to try. "All right. We need to get this pack back on its paws."

"Agreed." A spark of hope lit up Gorsescratch's face.

"It'll be a tough climb, and we can't allow our differences to get the better of us." Silversong's bitterness toward the bully subsided. He couldn't let old grudges fester when his pack's survival was at stake.

"Of course." Gorsescratch lowered his head respectfully. "Anything for Whistle-Wind."

"Start by standing up for me whenever I challenge the Warden or Chief Riptide." A mixture of nervousness and excitement flowed through his body, stiffening his hackles. He would be playing a very dangerous game, but if the gamble paid off, he would be one step closer to getting the future he wanted. "Let it be known that Whistle-Wind wolves aren't pushovers, and we'll fight for our packmates until the end."

"Yes." Gorsescratch bristled and bared his fangs. "We fight until the end."

"Until the end," Tawnydrift repeated, edging closer to Gorsescratch as if seeking his attention, but the sandy-furred corporal hardly noticed her.

At the edge of sight, Hazel and Palesquall smiled in approval. They'd listened in on the entire conversation, and they hastened to pass on Silversong's declaration to every packmate. Gorsescratch did the same, but the message of hope failed to inspire Chief Amberstorm.

Hang in there, sir. We'll help you see the light again.

No sooner did most Whistle-Wind members stand proud behind Silversong than the ground dipped into a broad tunnel winding its way beneath the shore. There was enough space here for four grown wolves to stand shoulder-to-shoulder, but still the mere notion of being stuck underground reawakened awful memories of fleeing through the darkness as a swarm of spiders bit at his tail. He'd had enough of caves and tunnels for one lifetime.

A dozen or so sentinels remained at the surface in case of a surprise attack while Riptide led everyone else deep into the bowels of the Saltshore. Even though these tunnels were wide and airy, Silversong couldn't help but imagine them closing in to squish him. He focused on his surroundings to tame his anxious heartbeat. The moist floor here was rough, but not entirely unpleasant, and the glowing streaks of green erosion found all around the underpass brought relief to the eyes.

He noticed Frostpaw's father whispering to his Chief at the tip of the army. Something he said made Icetail look over her shoulder to study the young and depressed lieutenant. Frostpaw plodded behind, listening to the gentle whines of a she-wolf who sported a beautiful deep grey coat. Silversong squinted at her, intrigue tempting him to sneak an ear into their conversation.

Who in Motherwolf's milk are you?

Moonwhisper grunted.

Silversong jerked up in a start. He hadn't realized the Wise-Wolf was walking beside him. "Oh, Moonwhisper! Sorry, I-I was a little distracted."

"Hmph. Clearly," Moonwhisper snorted, sleeking her white coat. "Your return has made quite the impression on your packmates, Silversong. I haven't seen them this determined since…" She stopped herself short of mentioning the attack on Wind's Rest.

Silversong met her shrewd gaze without blinking. "Of course they're determined. They didn't come this far to give up now, and neither have I. The winds of defeat are finally blowing toward our enemies, and we'll be the ones in command of the tempest."

"And can we control this tempest without our Chief to guide us?" Moonwhisper shifted her focus to the one who was supposed to lead them through these difficult times. Amberstorm walked like an aimless loner, disconnected from the wolves he'd governed for so many seasons. "I tried everything to raise his spirits, but a sickness such as this has no easy cure."

Every moment Silversong spent looking at his Chief was like tearing open an old wound. "We should be there for him just as he has been there for us. It'll take time, but I believe he'll get through this despair and come out stronger than ever before."

"But do we have time to spare, Silversong?" Her question poked small holes into all his hopes. "Are our enemies foolish enough to wait until we return to our complete strength?" The way she asked her question made it seem as though she wasn't just referring to the exiles.

The piece of time shivered, and he peeked at the threads moving around his leader. He fought for a clear vision, but glimpsed nothing concrete about the Chief's potential fate. He sighed and put his attention toward more immediate matters. "The exiles are as bruised and bloodied as we were when I set out to save

Palesquall. Trust me, their wounds still need a good licking before they can even think to bare their fangs at us again."

Moonwhisper divided her attention between Silversong and her partner. Mistyfur was keeping the Chief's pups occupied… or more like his tail was keeping them occupied. He yelped as they tugged, yanked, and bit at it, all the while glowering at the amused wolves who refused to come to his aid. Moonwhisper banished the smile from her face. "Your certainty is reassuring. We're all eager to hear about your little mission. I hope for all our sakes that your actions are deemed necessary." Her gaze singled out the Warden near the front. "And I pray *she* above all others forgives the many infractions you've committed."

She'll have to if she's serious about defeating the Heretic. Silversong wouldn't concede ground to her… but he had to play it smart. He needed to remain on her side in the eyes of all wolves while supplanting her power in the long run, slowly wearing it away until her ability to command was severely blunted.

"I'll argue my case as best I can." Silversong tensed the threads of time, startling Moonwhisper.

"Did you feel something just then?" She frowned and sniffed around him.

"Don't worry about it." He gave her a slight smile, hoping it would ease her concern.

The tunnel connected itself to a small network of underground pathways like veins rooted to an unseen heart. Now would be as good a time as any to check in on Amberstorm. Silversong shuffled toward the Chief, offering apologies to the wolves he pushed aside.

Upon reaching him, Silversong struggled to find anything meaningful to say. He cringed at the singed patches tarnishing a once smooth grey coat. Before the massacre, he'd thought his leader handsome and strong, an ideal image to strive toward, but now all pride had been swept clean off his face. His muscles were withered, and his scent spoke of a neglect of basic hygiene.

"Sir…?" Silversong whined, ears lowered and tail tucked as a display of respect. To the River-Stream wolves, it must've looked like he was showing deference to a mangy rat.

The Chief twitched, and the only acknowledgment Silversong received was a vacant sideways regard.

"I—" Silversong swallowed, carefully going over all he was about to say. "I beat the Heretic at his own game, and now I'm here to help rebuild Whistle-Wind. You're not alone, my Chief. We're here for you."

Amberstorm pricked his ears, and Silversong liked to think the widening of those eyes was the spark heralding the start of a return to glory.

"But we'll need you to lead us again," Silversong whispered softly. "I have faith you'll overcome your despair. You were chosen as leader by Elder Shrillbreeze for a reason, and this is your ultimate test. Please don't let Pinetrail's death be in vain. Let her passing remind you of those you must still protect."

At the mention of Pinetrail, the Chief dropped his head and stared at the ground.

Silversong cursed in silence, wishing he could've relied on the golden circle to figure out the correct things to say. He wasn't good enough to use the weapon to such a precise degree. Not yet.

More practice. I need more practice.

He hoped the combined scents of numerous wolves was enough to conceal the acrid aroma of his stress. He couldn't display any weakness during the moot. The fate of Whistle-Wind—no—the fate of the Four Territories depended on it. The stuffy air loosened, and as the contours of the tunnel finally opened to reveal the vastness of the Big Cave, Silversong reminded himself of the Drowned Titan's warning.

Be wary of new threats rising from within. Be wary of yourself and who you trust.

"The Four Territories banded together once before," Silversong stated aloud, firming his resolve into an unbreakable bulwark, "and by Motherwolf, they'll do so again."

A moot such as this had only happened once in the entire history of the Four Territories. The winds of change were indeed blowing strong, and Silversong would make sure they blew in the right direction.

Here he would plant the seeds that would steer sworn rivals into a new era of peace, an era free of division. But he had to counter the Warden so she couldn't uproot those seeds before they had a chance to sprout.

Feeling the manifestation of time stirring inside him, he accepted the challenge.

CHAPTER 4

The Moot

Silversong had never seen so many wolves in one place before.

He stood at the foot of an enormous underground geyser centred within the aptly named Big Cave. The throng was mostly comprised of River-Stream members who harboured no love for an alleged code-breaker from a rival territory. They sneered and scowled and made no attempt to hide their hopes for a spontaneous execution. Silversong wouldn't put it past Chief Riptide to see to their desires personally.

While the River-Stream wolves eyed him like vultures about to swoop, his silent packmates watched like mice cornered by snakes, ready to confront the dripping fangs as a last resort. The sentinels formed a line between the rival packs, headed by the Warden who'd taken charge of the moot. Behind her stood the elite sentinels of the Great Chain, Swiftstorm and Greyhail among them, heads locked in conversation.

About me, perhaps?

The higher-ranking wolves formed the row closest to Silversong while the corporals, subordinates, and rookies were pushed further back. Riptide never took his eyes off him, his fiery yellow gaze exposing his disdain for any who didn't share the Blessing of Water.

Frostpaw stood in the front file, head drawn to the ground while his father frowned at him like he would a trespasser. Silversong couldn't ignore his pity for the crestfallen lieutenant, though he could do nothing about it. The same grey she-wolf from before stayed by Frostpaw's side and gave out encouraging nuzzles that were halfheartedly returned. Silversong creased his forehead, ignoring the sour sensation in his gut.

Among Silversong's own packmates, his parents and closest friends looked eager to fight for him no matter the outcome of the moot. Their fierceness awakened a tiny spark of comfort he hoped he could fan into a blazing inferno. Confidence was key, and right now, he had precious little of it, made worse by the acrid scent of stress emanating from those he meant to protect.

To liberate his eyes from the scrutiny of the crowd, he turned his attention toward the cavern itself. The constant stream of vapour blown out of the geyser's mouth moistened the rough contours and added a subtle glaze to the green streaks of erosion slithering around the expanse. Fiery sunbeams lanced through the open roof, allowing each minuscule droplet their moment to shine before they returned to a state unworthy of notice. Beyond the throng gaped a few openings leading to smaller caves beneath the Saltshore, and Silversong wondered about the purposes they served. This one was obviously reserved for gatherings and announcements of great importance, but he could easily imagine a smaller grotto being used to store medicinal plants and another for stowing away prey. The River-Stream den was a lot more intricate than Wind's Rest had been, and its wolves far outnumbered Whistle-Wind's even predating the massacre. Did Chief Riptide give mating rights to every pair during the final days of winter? The den was certainly large enough to contain several dozens more members.

Our den was much cozier than this one, though. Silversong dismissed a slight prick of jealousy. *Who needs so many tunnels and caves, anyway? We're wolves, not rodents!*

The Warden barked, her voice disproving the assumed frailty of her aged body. It resonated throughout the cavern and silenced everyone from lieutenant to rookie. Tails turned stiff, ears perked up, and heads snapped toward the one who owed answers to all their pressing questions.

Silversong gulped at the impact of so many eyes boring into him. He focused on the open roof above to alleviate the tenseness between his shoulders, but it still took all his willpower not to recoil and hide his tail. Not a trace of weakness. He drained his head of all but calming thoughts and collected himself, breathing in and out, in and out…

Time to plant the seeds of victory. Silversong firmed his muscles, refusing to let the situation widen the cracks in his confidence.

The Warden stepped forward, her stance radiating the certainty Silversong wished he had. She would let nothing compromise her faith; even her scent reeked of conviction. "Wolves of Whistle-Wind and River-Stream," she announced in a regal tone, "we are gathered at the core of the Saltshore to decide on a course of action regarding the Heretic and his vile followers, but also to receive answers about Silversong and Frostpaw's recent endeavors. The two of them shall be judged under the law of the Wolven Code, and I as its enforcer, shall have the final say on whatever verdict is delivered."

Silversong closed his eyes and focused on the constant spinning of the piece of time. He found no better alternative to counter the crushing pressure. All together, the River-Stream members barked their approval, drowning out the hesitant voices of the Whistle-Wind wolves.

Silversong purged all emotion from his face before opening his eyes. "Let's begin, Warden."

The Warden met his stare and matched the strength within it. No matter how much power Silversong had gained, he was still nothing more than an unruly pup to her, one she would have no trouble disciplining if he tested her. "Silversong. We've all heard of your unsanctioned *mission* to infiltrate the exiles and get close to the Heretic, but after you were separated from Palesquall in the Silverhaze Forest, details get blurry. Why don't you give us your account of events after the spiders offered you to the Empress."

As the threads making up his aura rotated around him, revealing an array of possible futures winking in and out of existence, Silversong worked on the truth—his truth, moulding it from mud to clay to stone until it was shatterproof. He recounted the tale of waking up in the lowest pit of the Whispering Hollow, powerless in the face of the Empress of Spiders and her seductive allure. Though no one would admit it, he could detect the unmistakable stink of fear scent wafting from the crowd as he narrated his ordeal. He briefly described the revelations of the Empress about a Titan named Stormstrider, a Titan who called upon a mysterious entity to grant him the powers of time itself—the catalyst for the War of Change.

A stray breath got caught in Silversong's throat. He swayed off balance. His vision whirled wildly, coming together only for him to find himself locked in Stormstrider's lengthy body at the moment of his death. A swarm of Forgotten Ones—in silvery shells of segmented metal—surrounded the gasping Titan in awe, and not even the shrill wails of a fleeing deer were enough to break their enthrallment.

The cruel brown eyes of a Forgotten One glared at Stormstrider. In his final breaths, the Titan coughed up a floating golden circle in which Silversong's consciousness now resided. The Forgotten One responsible for killing the Titan grasped the piece of time and lifted it high for all his subjects to behold. "Never forget that an immortal life can still be felled. Upon my name as Galdreth Zeken, King of Adania and all its vassals, I swear to forever remind our enemies of this day!"

Cheers filled the air under a blood-soaked sky, and Galdreth opened his mouth to swallow his prize whole.

"Silversong!" The Warden's growl yanked Silversong back to the present. "Focus on recounting your tale."

"Apologies, ma'am." Silversong cursed the golden circle for the untimely vision. He gathered his thoughts and continued his story, going over how Stormstrider was slain and how the piece of time was eventually taken all the way into the depths of the Mountainmouth, where it remained undisturbed until the Empress revealed its location to the Heretic. In return for this information, the Heretic unleashed his exiles upon Wind's Rest so the spiders could reclaim the Breezeway—originally their domain before Whistle-Wind and her wolves drove them out following the War of Change.

Silversong studied the faces of his packmates. Some displayed anger for the invaders while others expressed sadness for the home they thought they would never see again. Silversong had once considered the spiders to be nothing more than spiteful insects until he contemplated the injustices they suffered. There was no easy solution to the disdain shared between his packmates and the spiders. Given time, perhaps he could help resolve this dispute peacefully.

I'm getting ahead of myself.

Putting future problems aside, he detailed the remainder of his journey, careful to leave out his sympathies toward the exiles and the shared friendship between him and Frostpaw. He also took care not to mention the Fallen Titan at all. As far as the Warden was concerned, the tainted Forest Father existed only in the form of his corruption. Silversong talked about the death of Bonechew and the braving of the Mountainmouth, the plunge into the underground lake and his capture by the massive Titan lurking beneath its surface. He described the twisted hallways of the maze of madness and his one-eyed future, the finding of the piece of time and its wrathful protector, and finally… the destruction of the ruin itself and the subsequent escape of the exiles into the wilderness.

The stars had begun to outshine the rising moon by the time Silversong finished recounting his tale. A deep, uncomfortable silence was the only response he received. The wolves blinked vacantly and looked at each other to gauge reactions, the roots of doubt entangling all save those who'd witnessed the powers of time for themselves.

The Warden stopped the crowd before they could voice their disbelief. "So, my assumptions were correct. You now wield the powers of time." She took on a thoughtful expression as if already contemplating how to manipulate this situation to her advantage. "This is an interesting development indeed."

A quick signal of her tail caused every sentinel to tense up, heads swerving to Silversong. Only Swiftstorm expressed concern, but her eyes contained the same zealous light found in the Warden's gaze. Had it always been there? Had Silversong just now noticed it? Swiftstorm was a sentinel at heart, an extension of the Warden herself. Would she place duty above family? Silversong couldn't imagine it, but a chill ran down his spine nonetheless. His hackles stood erect, the pounding of his heart warning him of impending danger. His breaths shortened until a dizziness took over, obscuring all attempts at forming a coherent plan, and yet… in the vortex of confusion he saw tiny holes in his vision, each widening to reveal behind them a possible solution to prevent the oncoming chaos.

He compressed the threads of his aura, shrinking the golden circle's sphere of influence. Flies buzzed up his limbs as he drained more power from his weapon. When he could squeeze no more, he released the pressure. Faster than a lightning strike, the unseen threads sprang outward, and he froze their constant motion. Invisible spikes stabbed his brain. He winced, but refused to let go.

He'd caught everyone in time's grasp, sparing imprisonment to not a single body. He loosened the threads around their eyes, allowing them to move those without hindrance. The wolves in the front were completely frozen while those further behind managed only the most subtle of movements. He couldn't secure the threads furthest from him as efficiently as he could those closest to the weapon, but it hardly mattered.

While the Warden's face still divulged her hunger for the golden circle, her eyes revealed a fear of it, a fear of Silversong. If he wanted to, he could remove her from power right away, and none could raise so much as a paw to stop him. But such a drastic action would only lead to more violence, and he would prove himself no better than the Heretic. He had to distinguish himself from Ironwrath. Silversong had to do things the right way. Unity and change were possible without him becoming like the enemy.

The spikes impaling his brain dug deeper. He opened his mouth wide and growled, letting the sound vibrate through the threads and into every ear. "The piece of time is mine to wield! Deep in the Mountainmouth, it showed me a beautiful future free of the troubles we now face, and I can guide us there. Put your faith in me, and I swear by Motherwolf I won't lead us astray. The enemy is regrouping. Even now our victory dangles from the most brittle of branches. We don't have time to bicker and squabble, and we certainly don't have time to fight over my weapon. We must pursue a common goal. Please, listen to me. Listen—"

The spikes reached to agonizing depths. Silversong yelped and let go of the threads, stumbling and swaying as they snapped back to their natural state. An echo of the migraine lingered and applied pressure to his skull, but he ignored the pain.

The crowd broke into a panic, some fleeing to the corners of the cavern, others remaining in place, balled up or paralyzed by their own fright. Few had the nerve to stay put, and it took an effort from every sentinel to return some semblance of order to the gathering. It was efficient if not terrifying how quickly they managed to discipline such a large group of frantic wolves. He'd stopped the Warden before she could *convince* him to relinquish the piece of time. Giving her control over the weapon would be a detriment to the exiles, sure, but it would also elevate the Wolven Code to something far greater. The tiniest infraction would be punished as severely as the most heinous crime, and the sentinels wouldn't be satisfied until everyone was as virtuous as they. Silversong couldn't allow such extremism to flourish.

The panic subsided, and once everyone was herded back into place, the Warden took a couple paces forward, her emotions so neatly under control that Silversong found it increasingly difficult to believe she'd ever been afraid. "You gave us quite the display there, Silversong. I hope you weren't too frightened by the prospect of me forcing the piece of time out of you." Her anger had all but evaporated into unshakable confidence—the stark opposite of her sentinels, who were now more on edge than ever. "I'll admit, I am curious as to how efficiently I could wield these powers you've inherited, but I would never attack you so brazenly to get them. This is your earned victory, and its spoils are yours to enjoy so long as you remember where your loyalties lie."

Somehow her admission brought no comfort. Quite the contrary, in fact. Even so, he didn't give her the pleasure of sniffing out even a whiff of weakness. He flexed his muscles to keep from shaking and imagined himself as an unstoppable tornado whose sole mission was to reshape the Four Territories into a better home for all wolves.

"It's good we agree on this, Warden. Now, onto more pressing matters. The remaining exiles still pose a threat to us so long as the Heretic leads them. He must be hunted down. Every moment wasted on argument is another moment we allow our enemy to regain strength."

The Whistle-Wind wolves barked and yipped in agreement—only Amberstorm failed to join in.

"Hold your tail, pup." Riptide bristled and encouraged his lieutenants to follow his example. "You have no right to boss us around. I don't care if you swallowed time or earned Motherwolf's favour! River-Stream wolves NEVER take orders from one who doesn't share the Blessing of Water."

Silversong faced the Chief's yellow eyes without blinking and straightened out a tail that begged to be tucked. The instincts of an obedient subordinate fought against his display of defiance. His legs wanted to shake so badly, but he pressed against the ground to keep them in line. "I'm not asking you to obey me, Chief Riptide. I'm simply suggesting we take the quickest route to victory. Unless you have another idea on how to defeat the exiles, I *suggest* you refrain from interrupting me again."

His packmates yipped again, supporting him a little louder this time, but Amberstorm still kept his head lowered as if the floor were far more interesting than the fate of the Four Territories.

The leader of River-Stream looked like a geyser about to erupt. Silversong could practically see the steam whistling out of his nose and flattened ears. Before he could throw his tantrum, Icetail nudged his shoulder and whispered to him. Whatever she said soothed his temper. Several high-ranking wolves close to them grimaced and snarled at Silversong. He flexed the piece of time again, hoping he wouldn't have to drain more power from the weapon. His doubts got the better of him: he had to be strong, but not too strong. Had he messed this up already?

The Warden stepped in, stopping the snarls from evolving into threats. "Silversong *would* be right. Were it possible, hunting the Heretic would be the correct strategy, but knowing our enemy as intimately as I do, tracking him would be about as efficient as searching for a single minnow in a school of salmon. We simply won't find him unless he intends to be found. And by then he'll have us trapped and cornered. We're in a winning position. The exiles can't attack us in their weakened state. They can only spy and scheme, and so we have ample time to form a proper plan on how to exterminate them. Perhaps you have a better suggestion, Silversong?"

Silversong clawed at the ground and shook his coat.

The Warden was testing him, but his own anxiety clouded his foresight. He needed a clear head. He needed a credible plan. The Warden studied him like a predator studied its prey, wondering about the best ways to catch the elusive meal. He dulled his emotions and funneled his thoughts out of his brain until nothing but void remained—a trick every rookie learned when first trying to control the wind. He searched beyond the limits of his vision, stirring the weapon and tapping into its potency. Ripples disturbed his sight and reflected two possible futures. In one, his tireless pursuit of the Heretic led to the steady decline of the Four Territories. Every time Silversong was close to finding the enemy, Ironwrath managed to evade him. Wolves were spread far and wide, allowing the exiles to pick them off one by one until the Warden decided she was the better candidate to wield the piece of time.

In the other future, the combined might of the Four Territories stood defiantly atop a spire of obsidian stone, refusing to let the exiles break them. He recalled an old fable about a hungry fox who kept trying in vain to eat the turtle hiding in its shell. Eventually, the fox's teeth shattered upon the carapace.

The ripples dissipated, as did more of the weapon's strength. Thoughts streamed back into his head and formed a risky plan. "I do have a better suggestion. We unite the Four Territories as one, then we choose a location we're willing to defend." There. He'd done it. He'd suggested something so taboo in the Wolven Code that even thinking of it would've previously earned him a place in the Furtherlands. Not today, though, and certainly not in the future if he had his way. "The Heretic fears my potential. He fears I'll master the piece of time if he waits too long to strike. Let him come to us and blunder in his haste."

He found it impossible not to tremble as the crowd exploded into a fit of barking. Some demanded he be boiled alive in the hottest of geysers, others wanted to have his hide ripped from his spine, to have his name cursed and forgotten, and all the while Frostpaw stayed crouched and silent, eyes refusing to meet Silversong's. The young lieutenant looked so defeated, so alone. Only the Whistle-Wind wolves defended their own, matching the growls of their rivals despite inferior numbers. Silversong needed the Warden to agree to this alliance, or all would be lost.

"You Whistle-Wind wolves sicken me!" an elder of River-Stream barked. "Have you no shame in calling this one your packmate? If he were my son, I would drown him and feed his body to the crabs!"

Cedargaze bared her fangs at the outspoken elder. "Speak of my son again, and I'll feed you to the crabs."

"Of course it's River-Stream wolves who can't be bothered to see beyond their own muzzles," Hazel yapped. "Get your heads out of the water and breathe some good air for once!"

"Yeah!" Palesquall won the baying contest against a rival subordinate. "Maybe when you finally drain all the water out of your skulls, you'll quit being so narrow-minded."

One of Frostpaw's siblings showed his teeth to any Whistle-Wind member he could find behind the line of sentinels, all of which faced the riled crowd on either side. "You're lucky we even allowed you air-blowers to stay at our den. We took pity on your pathetic pack in its time of need. Clearly we made a mistake since you poor excuses for wolves have no problem housing code-breakers."

"You're no better than the exiles!" another River-Stream corporal hollered. "We should've chased you all away the moment you showed your stinking hides here!"

Frostpaw's father snarled at his sworn rivals. "You're all heretics in my eyes. May you rot in the Furtherlands alongside the Fallen Titan's bones."

"Go back to your territory!"

"Whistle-Wind deserved to have its den broken!" This time it was Riptide who spewed hateful venom. "How many code-breakers besides this one are you hiding in your numbers?! I'll have all of you expelled from my den!" He pointed his flaring nostrils at Silversong.

Silversong's heart banged against his chest. His limbs became shivering branches, and his blood boiled. Only his clenched jaws prevented him from hurling the insults he wanted so desperately to say.

Gorsescratch, however, held nothing back. "Say that again, scatfur, and you'll see who Motherwolf favours in battle." Tawnydrift crouched into an attack position at the bully's side, abandoning caution for him.

"How dare you?!" Icetail's eyes promised nothing but pain to Gorsescratch. "I'll rip your tail from your backside! I'll yank out your claws one by one!"

Silversong's parents crept closer to him, ready to protect their son should the threats evolve into violence. Amberstorm showed no such willingness to defend his soldiers; he remained where he was, hunched over and staring at his forepaws while the Wise-Wolves and elders sheltered his whimpering children. He'd lost all strength to lead.

The only one Silversong refused to look at was Swiftstorm. She was a sentinel, and he feared he might see her disappointment in him. He'd suggested breaking a fundamental law in the Wolven Code, a law enforced by her order. The mere idea of her shame frightened him more than the murderous wolves hungering for his blood.

This had to end, and fast, or the infighting would do the Heretic's job for him. Silversong braced himself for the headache he was about to receive and tensed the threads of time. Just before he could demonstrate the power of his weapon again, he caught a glimpse of the Warden signaling a command to Greyhail. The large Stone-Guard sentinel stiffened, and the ground below him rumbled, deep and precise, vibrating from one corner of the cavern to the other. The earthquake promptly shook the aggression out of everyone.

The uproar stopped long enough for the Warden to seize control of the moot. "All this commotion is unbecoming of good followers of the Wolven Code. As Warden, I demand you cease this embarrassment AT ONCE!"

The tremor stopped as if the Warden's voice had frightened it away. Silversong's heart pounded like it too wished to flee her presence. His head whirled, and he slowed his breaths until he successfully calmed his nerves. Not a soul dared break the cutting silence. From Chief to subordinate, all wolves faced the Warden and hid their tails as they would before Motherwolf herself.

The Warden's eyes lingered on Silversong, two pale whirlpools threatening to devour him. It took all his strength to stand his ground. "Yes, Silversong's suggestion is indeed blasphemous, and he would be tried and punished *severely* under different circumstances. But if a temporary alliance is required to defeat the Heretic, then it's a sacrifice we're obligated to make. For the good of the Four Territories."

Before anyone found the courage to voice their disagreements, Silversong cleared his throat and addressed the gathering. "Yes. I've seen it. Unity is the only way to truly defeat the Heretic. The piece of time never lies." He turned to Riptide and his disgruntled lieutenants. Silversong refused to let their hateful expressions get to him. "You don't have to approve of this plan, sir, but you're a Chief, and sometimes Chiefs must make decisions they don't like for the good of the pack."

Riptide looked on the verge of pouncing on him, but another slight nudge from Icetail diverted his attention. The two shared sharp whispers, and he at last gave a reluctant chuckle. "Lectured by a code-breaking pup. Never thought I would see the day. Have the end times finally arrived?" His hostility ended at a scowl, and Silversong quietly thanked Motherwolf for it. Better to be scowled at than growled at. "As long as there're conditions to this *unity*," he cringed, "and as long as the Warden sees it as a necessary evil, then I as Chief must agree to this strategy, though I take no joy in the participation."

There it was. Another steppingstone toward a future without division. It would take time—so much time—but in the end, all wolves would live as free souls without any law dictating who they should hate or love.

Mediated by the Warden, a discussion broke out over how the defense against the Heretic should be organized. There was much debate about the conditions of this alliance and how to make sure it violated as few rules as possible, but eventually a consensus was reached, a consensus Silversong argued against, but failed to counter. The wolves would defend the same location all while keeping to their own packs. A stupid decision for the sake of upholding the law. He wasn't about to say it aloud, though. Not when the Warden had just declared that the Wolven Code was to be respected at all times despite the circumstances.

The Warden chose Thornhollow as the main ground of defense, the den of Flame-Heart Territory. It was an impressive spire of obsidian stone, a material the Heretic would have great difficulty controlling. Since there were very few ways up the steep formation, it was a great deterrent against would-be infiltrators, and it would grant Silversong protection while he further studied the piece of time. The Heretic would no doubt attack before his strength fully recovered. He couldn't allow Silversong to master the weapon. In his desperation, Ironwrath would make mistakes, and these mistakes would ultimately lead to his defeat. Everyone was counting on it. Time wasn't on Ironwrath's side, and so hopefully haste would be his undoing.

You'll come for me wherever I am. Silversong tightened his grasp on the threads. *And you'll bring about your own ruin seeking the bait.*

Amberstorm added little to the discussion, only chiming in when someone pressed him for an answer. He let his lieutenants argue on Whistle-Wind's behalf, Cedargaze in particular. Silversong's mother was staunch and assertive; she acted as the voice of her pack, surprising the River-Stream lieutenants who thought their rivals weak and humbled. Silversong frowned at his Chief. Now wasn't the time for passivity, but there was nothing to be done other than participate in the creation of this mighty army. For the sake of simplicity, a name was given for the unlikely alliance: the Wolven Bulwark. To the exiles, it would inspire fear, but to Silversong, it was a reminder of how change was possible without bloodshed.

There're some who'll never accept change, Silversong thought grimly. *Do I dare hope for a peaceful resolution?*

As the moot neared conclusion, the fastest sentinels were dispatched to the lower territories to brief Chief Ashenfall and Chief Bronzeblood about the events following the breaking of the Great Chain. The two Chiefs would be informed of the temporary alliance and would be expected to aid the defense of Thornhollow. The Warden made her message very clear: refusal to join would be seen as treason. For all her fanaticism, Silversong was almost relieved the Warden carried the authority she did in this circumstance. Who would dare question the embodiment of the Wolven Code? Flame-Heart and Stone-Guard would join the alliance or be thrown to the Heretic.

Darkness had fallen by the time the planning was done and everyone knew their roles. The wrinkles of uncertainty still creased many faces, but Silversong couldn't deny the excitement bubbling up from his stomach. As the threads of his aura turned, he inwardly celebrated breaching the first barriers of the Wolven Code. Now all he had to do was keep up the pressure and argue for true unity. No more segregation. No more forced division. Apart they were weak. Together they were strong.

"And so our fate is sealed," the Warden announced, her low voice carrying across the cavern. "Under Motherwolf's gaze and by the virtue of the Wolven Code, may we be rid of the Heretic and all heretics to come!"

It took a few lone whoops to encourage an eruption of cheers. Whether eager rookie or grizzled elder, everyone participated in the thunderous howl. Silversong lifted his head high and joined the others, but for different reasons. Today marked the beginning of a new era for wolves, an era unbound by oppression. When they saw how powerful their kind could be united under a single purpose, they would abandon this ridiculous idea of keeping the packs separate. Then it would only be a matter of time until they saw the Wolven Code for the suffocating chain it was. For the body to become stronger, it first had to reject the disease infecting it. This was how he would defeat the Heretic: not by forcing change through domination, but by making the Four Territories see the value in working together to overcome great challenges.

The howling slowly dwindled until even the proudest of wolves turned quiet to await dismissal. Silversong wasn't done, though. He saw another way to cheapen the Warden's power before the night ended. "Ma'am, in the interest of maintaining morale and readiness among my packmates, I ask you to remove the restrictions placed upon us by Chief Riptide."

Riptide's forehead bulged over his eyes. Thankfully, the Warden interrupted whatever obscenities he was about to growl. "Has your newly acquired weapon given you a false sense of leverage?" She let the accusation soak into everyone's mind. "Whistle-Wind was in need of aid, and Chief Riptide gave it while respecting the boundaries of the Wolven Code. He could've let your pack wither into ruin if he'd wanted to, but he decided against it. His treatment of your pack is strict but permitted by law for as long as you're guests at his den. Whistle-Wind and River-Stream are rivals, and this alliance doesn't change that. If this is still difficult for you to accept, I encourage your elders to remind you of why the Four Territories must remain unfriendly toward one another even in times of crisis. If we erode the line that separates us from the exiles, we're doomed to become just like them."

Strict was nowhere near accurate enough to describe Whistle-Wind's treatment under Riptide. Silversong gritted his teeth in an attempt not to bristle. The Warden had all but stomped on him, and the smug look on Riptide's face was enough to make anyone growl.

"Now, if you're done making unreasonable demands, there's one matter we've yet to settle." The Warden's heavy gaze would've made a stone crumble, and yet Silversong met those piercing eyes despite the temptation to look away. "Silversong, while your decisions over the course of this calamity might've had noble intentions, they plainly violated the Wolven Code, and for that you should count yourself lucky I am a reasonable Warden." Her head snapped toward Frostpaw, who shrank in on himself at the front. "This goes for you too, Lieutenant Frostpaw. Neither I nor your Chiefs gave you permission to forsake your duties to pursue the Heretic. The two of you stand accused of desertion and forming bonds outside your respective territories."

All at once, Silversong's friends jumped to his defense, justifying his actions by blurting out any excuse they could think of. Gorsescratch eased closer to the front and whispered something to Amberstorm and the surrounding lieutenants. Cedargaze pricked her ears and gave a quick nod to Shadowgale as he joined the conversation, tail swishing idly. Silversong peered at the River-

Stream wolves, heart dropping upon the realization that no one was standing up for Frostpaw.

The Warden barked, her fierce voice quieting the Whistle-Wind wolves. “If any of you dare interrupt me again—regardless of your standing—you’ll each be given a penance you won’t soon forget, and I’ll allow Chief Riptide to decide the nature of your punishment. Am I understood?”

The Whistle-Wind Pack plunged into silence. Riptide grinned like he actually wanted his rivals to anger the Warden again.

“Good.” The Warden narrowed her focus on Silversong. “Since you and Frostpaw succeeded in thwarting the Heretic’s plans, I’ll allow your Chiefs to decide whether to punish you for your crimes or not. This is my final verdict.”

Relief washed over Silversong, the tightness around his shoulders loosening. “Thank you, Warden.” He bowed his head slightly, allowing her this one gesture of deference. He hadn’t expected such a merciful decree from her.

Frostpaw’s head darted from packmate to packmate, eyes swelled into panicked orbs, tail curled up against his belly. The Warden continued. “Don’t expect the same mercy if you decide to forego the law again. Should your leaders allow it, this is your one chance at leniency. I’ll give them a short moment to decide whether to forgive or convict.”

The moment was short indeed. Frostpaw’s father padded through the front row to speak softly into his Chief’s ear. On the Whistle-Wind side, everyone crowded around Amberstorm and gave their suggestions, but it was Gorsescratch’s who’d gained all the attention. Silversong gulped. Surely he wouldn’t be punished for beating the Heretic. The piece of time vibrated as his worries and fears covered the near future in a misty shroud.

The Warden cocked her head at Riptide, and the black-furred leader took a couple steps forward, ready to proclaim his judgment. “I’ve come to a decision on Frostpaw’s consequences.”

Oh, no! Silversong’s fur stood on edge. Frostpaw sat hunched over, eyes closed in anticipation of his punishment.

Riptide delivered his verdict in a neutral tone. “For aiding a rival rather than bringing him to my den, for abandoning his duties, for endangering himself and for sullying the name of River-Stream, Frostpaw is henceforth stripped of the title of lieutenant. He shall serve as a corporal until the end of his days. And until we depart to Thornhollow, no one is allowed to speak to him or offer him food from the Prey Hollow. He is to forage for his own meals in shame and remain alone to contemplate his errors."

The she-wolf beside Frostpaw barked at Riptide, her face contorted in outrage. "Father, you can't just—"

"I have spoken, daughter!" Riptide turned to her and growled, covering his fangs upon realizing he'd gone too far. "Perhaps he deserved to become a lieutenant after saving you from the snowcat attack, but he's no longer worthy of such a position. He chose to go against the Wolven Code despite his better judgment, and so this is his punishment to bear."

Icetail stood rigid behind her cruel mate. "I understand your desire to defend him, Snowleap, but this is for his own good. Guilt is the most effective way of ensuring one never repeats the same mistake again."

The Chief's daughter lowered her neck in reluctant compliance and spared Frostpaw one sympathetic look before parting his side. Soon, his surrounding packmates all distanced themselves from him as though he were carrying a plague.

Silversong's heart shattered into countless fragments, but he stayed put despite wishing he could run over to his friend and comfort him. Only now did Silversong understand how trapped he really was. He couldn't even show compassion for Frostpaw without drawing the ire of the River-Stream wolves. The balance he'd struck today was too fragile to test. He wanted to whimper, but doing so would display weakness to the Warden when he needed to be seen as an image of confidence and certainty. Right now, he was the opposite of that, but the illusion had to remain. He promised himself he would check in on Frostpaw later under the cover of darkness. He couldn't let his friend suffer alone.

Hang in there, Frostpaw. I'm still here for you.

Riptide returned to the front row as the Warden fixed her eyes on Amberstorm. Much to everyone's surprise, the Chief gave her a bow and moved forward, prepared to announce his verdict. Silversong couldn't care less whether he was punished or not. He'd already planted the seeds of victory. Amberstorm could demote him to rookie for all he cared.

"As Chief of the Whistle-Wind Pack…" Amberstorm began in a weak voice, "I hereby absolve Silversong of any wrongdoings and commend his bravery, for I believe his actions may have saved us all."

Shocked murmurs rose from the River-Stream bunch, and some of the sentinels tilted their heads in confusion. Hazel and Palesquall couldn't hide their smiles. Gorsescratch stared wide-eyed, a twitch of his tail following each anxious breath. There was no hatred on his face. Instead, there was… pride? Cedargaze watched Silversong much the same way, and Shadowgale could barely contain his excitement, panting and shaking like an overjoyed pup.

"For his heroic deeds, I officially promote Silversong to corporal." The hardening of the Chief's voice was almost as bewildering as the promotion. "May he bring honour to the name Whistle-Wind and may Motherwolf smile upon him."

"Silversong! Silversong! Silversong!" his packmates chanted. From the line of sentinels, he spotted Swiftstorm mouthing his name even though she wasn't supposed to bear any loyalties to her true family anymore. She stopped when the eyes of her fellow sentinels flickered to her. Gorsescratch joined in on the congratulations too, and it took some effort from the Warden to hush all the hollering.

Disdain showed in the shocked expressions of the River-Stream wolves, but none audibly objected to the sudden promotion. This was a Whistle-Wind affair, and no matter how much they disapproved of the decision, they had no right to interfere beyond judgmental glares.

There was a time when this promotion would've meant everything to Silversong. It was a day he'd dreamed of since he was a rookie fresh out of the nursing lairs. But as the Warden concluded the moot and wolves steadily trickled off into the tunnels of the Saltshore, all Silversong could do was stand there, the hollow feeling in his gut engulfing his entire body. The fog shrouding his foresight evaporated, revealing a simple truth: none of this mattered if the alliance formed today was broken by the Heretic or by the very wolves who'd agreed to join forces. Again, the Drowned Titan's warning washed over him—a tide foretelling larger waves to come.

Be wary of new threats rising from within.

The storm hadn't yet cleared. No. It was only beginning to pour, and the thunder was yet to roar.

CHAPTER 5

The Broken Chief

Steaming flesh and scorched bones littered the upturned earth, the land fissured by the passing of a furious tremor. Among the bodies were friends and enemies alike, united in death by a common end. All around them the battle raged on, wolves from all territories clashing against each other, the tenuous peace broken beyond hope of repair. The Heretic laughed at the predictable outcome as a great deer wreathed in shadow grinned crookedly from the corrupted heavens.

"Silversong?" a concerned voice called to him.

Silversong opened his eyes, and the light soaked up the vision like water on dry moss. He shook his head in frustration. Studying a potential future was difficult enough without being interrupted. At least he was getting better at controlling the piece of time. If not for the headaches that came after he wielded the weapon for too long, he would've figured everything out by now.

Through cracks in the creamy clouds, morning rays stabbed his eyes, and he squinted at the slight pain. Palesquall watched him curiously a tail-length away, head tilted and nose twitching.

"Hey, Palesquall. You caught me daydreaming," Silversong whined. The passing of time always eluded him whenever he studied possible futures. If he wasn't careful, he could lose himself in them for much longer than anticipated.

Palesquall's face returned to its playful state. "You know, just because you're a corporal now doesn't mean you get to doze off whenever you feel like it."

Silversong chuckled. "Look at you, scolding a corporal. The nerve. Shouldn't you be foraging for food right about now?"

From the smell of it, Palesquall had spent the morning marking medicinal plants instead.

In truth, it was difficult for Silversong to adapt to his new life as a corporal after he'd convinced himself he would remain a subordinate until he was old enough to become an elder, but slowly he adjusted. The other corporals had already accepted him into their little space just outside the Saltshore. By decree of Chief Riptide, no Whistle-Wind member was allowed to roam his den unless put under the strict supervision of a River-Stream lieutenant, and so Silversong's packmates were all but confined to the Suncap Woods, the mushroom-infested forest surrounding the lake they weren't allowed to drink from.

Finding food proved another challenge. The scaly deer native to this territory would sprint away the moment they thought they were being tracked, and the weird rodents were equally skittish, digging deep into their hollows under trees when wolves were out sniffing. Even finding a clean stream for fresh water meant a small journey into the mucky wilderness, but Whistle-Wind was nothing if not persistent.

"Eh, morning duty is almost over, anyway. And besides, I've already marked a ton of medicinal plants for you to harvest later. Shouldn't *you* be resting your lazy head right now? Or has the corporal urge to sleep all day not set in yet?" Palesquall joked. If he'd spoken like this to any other corporal, it would've earned him a nip on the ear or worse.

Silversong looked around instinctively. No corporals in sight, only mushrooms and mushroom-infested trees. If someone saw him acting too friendly around Palesquall or any other subordinate, it would tarnish his credibility as a corporal.

Silversong forced a frown on his face. "Be careful, Palesquall. You're my friend, but watch yourself. If anyone sees me letting you speak to me this way—"

"Right, right," Palesquall yipped, foregoing subtlety altogether. "Silversong is a mean and serious corporal now. Look at him frown. So heroic. So broody—"

Silversong knocked Palesquall over, the two rolling together on the muddy ground, laughing and pawing at each other's faces. Palesquall—and all the subordinates, come to think of it—had become much thinner as the days passed, the lack of food eating away at once strong muscles. The last to eat, the first to starve.

Although Silversong wasn't supposed to, he pitied the subordinates, his two best friends most of all. For them he risked offering regurgitated portions of his meals when no one was looking.

"Ahem," someone grouched.

Successfully pinning Palesquall, Silversong turned to the source of the voice and tensed, blood rushing to his head as he stumbled off his friend. "Gorsescratch! I was… uh… just teaching him a lesson." He faked a growl at Palesquall, who struggled not to break into giggles. Silversong thought about punishing him for real just so he would quit smirking like a rookie caught doing mischief.

Gorsescratch's unconvinced eyes watched them between two large trees. "Sure you were. Everyone else is already awake, and if you're hungry, you better get to the prey pile before the others finish it all. There isn't much. There's never much."

Silversong helped his friend up and shook off flecks of mud. The breeze changed direction, carrying Gorsescratch's scent to him through the earthy reek of the mushrooms. "Did you really come all this way just so I wouldn't miss a meal?"

Gorsescratch spared one dismissive glance for Palesquall before revealing why he was really here. "The Warden's messengers have returned unscathed. After long discussions, Chief Ashenfall and Chief Bronzeblood have agreed to join the Wolven Bulwark. We're leaving for Thornhollow tomorrow morning."

Silversong's heartbeat raced, his tail jerking up. "You could've mentioned that first!"

Palesquall panted loudly, eyes like plump berries in their sockets. "Yes! We're finally leaving this stupid territory!"

Silversong recalled glimpsing this exact moment days ago, but there was no way then to confirm when it would actually happen unless he spent all his focus analyzing the fleeting vision. It would've been a total waste of energy, and the safety of the messengers had been all but assured. They were two former Whistle-Wind wolves, renowned for their speed and agility before they even became sentinels. No exile could ever catch them. And besides, the distant future was far more important to study than the near one.

If I can peer into the bad futures, I can steer the Four Territories away from them.

"Also, Chief Amberstorm also wanted to see you," Gorsescratch added before turning around and padding in the direction of the makeshift Whistle-Wind den.

Silversong muttered a curse and followed his former bully through the damp woods, Palesquall trailing further behind, head bowed and tail low. Learning that Gorsescratch was the one who suggested Silversong's promotion was more surprising than the actual event. It seemed the bully really was trying to redeem himself. He'd even been present during the promotion ceremony when the wolves closest to Silversong had danced around him while weaving the wind into a complex pattern of leaves and grass. Despite those efforts, Gorsescratch still had a lot to make up for. Confessing his prior misdeeds to the whole pack would be another leap in the right direction.

"The sentinels are a problem, aren't they?" Gorsescratch whined in a careful tone as if the Warden herself might be nearby.

"Hm?" Silversong inclined his head toward the senior corporal.

"The Warden sees you as a threat." Gorsescratch tried to hide the worry in his voice. It made him sound confrontational if nothing else. "Only a gullwit would think otherwise."

"I guess you're not a gullwit then. Could've fooled me," Silversong grunted bluntly.

Gorsescratch grimaced but ignored the remark. "Is your plan to ruffle her fur until she decides the Wolven Bulwark is better off without us? My ancestors would frown upon me if I survived the massacre at Wind's Rest only to become an exile."

"She won't exile us." Silversong imagined himself confronting the Warden. Even in thought, her fanatical eyes drilled into his confidence. "As long as I have the piece of time, she can't do anything too drastic. She'll just keep preaching the Wolven Code until the other packs see how crippling her devotion really is. Then they'll reject her methods in favour of reason."

"And who'll they follow then? You?" Gorsescratch whispered softer than the breeze. "Did swallowing the piece of time scramble your brain? Our rivals won't rally behind you, Silversong. It's just not happening."

"Not in their current state." Silversong stared at the mystical threads, wondering where they would guide him. "I'm no leader, but I'll do all I can to unite the Four Territories. Do you think the packs shared this animosity toward one another during the Rise of the Fallen Titan? No. They understood that fighting together without prejudice was their only chance at victory. We're on the right trail, but there's still so much to be done before the cracks are truly mended."

"Back then the Wolven Code hadn't been solidified into law. It hadn't even been thought up yet." Gorsescratch caught a zephyr on his tail and lashed the bloodsuckers hovering around him.

Silversong did his best to ignore the insects. "The Wolven Code is supposed to be infallible, but the Warden already showed us how flexible its rules really are. It's a method of control, and once everyone sees the truth, they'll be more open to change. I'll guide them to this realization however I can."

"A blasphemous suggestion," Gorsescratch snorted and shook his head. "The Heretic's influence must've rubbed off on you."

Silversong stopped. *I'm not like the Heretic.* The mud sucked at his forepaws. *I'll never be like the Heretic. He would force the packs together through domination and violence.*

A troubling question lifted the fur on his back.

If it were between keeping the packs obedient to the Wolven Code or forcing them to submit to my reign, which would I choose?

The threads encompassing him reflected a future in which he became as much of a monster as Ironwrath. Whether sentinel or Chief, all wolves bowed to the awesome power Silversong unleashed, and as blood-soaked earth buried the bones of the vanquished, he demanded obedience from the broken, the bloodied, the beaten. He became a blinding light burning away all dissent.

No. That'll never be me. I'll never stoop to such levels.

Gorsescratch stopped to look over his shoulder at Silversong. "At this point, though, I'm trusting your judgment. Our pack is short on options as it is, and right now you're our best hope for a better future. So don't muck this up." He took off through the woods without so much as a backward glance.

"I won't." Silversong uttered to himself and hurried after the other corporal.

After a short sprint, they entered a small glade flanking the Saltshore. It served as a poor excuse for a den, and Palesquall grimaced as he padded into it. Weeds and pungent mushrooms choked the grass struggling to breathe, and bloodsuckers drawn to their helpless prey added to the irritable mood of

Silversong's packmates. The subordinates were all coming back from morning duty, but few had been lucky enough to catch a meal. The others were all up and about, the more optimistic wolves eagerly discussing the return of the Warden's messengers. It wouldn't be long now before the news spread among the returning subordinates.

The corporals stretched and greeted one another in their designated corner as the subordinates returned to theirs on the opposite side of the glade. They wetted their lips and waited for their superiors to finish picking from the prey pile at the centre. It was a measly mound of rodents and some thrushes, barely enough to feed a dozen wolves much less an entire pack. The lieutenants and elders, each flanking the mossy boulder on which the Chief sat, slowly got up and approached their breakfast alongside the young rookies. A pair of elders dropped two badger-looking things into the dug-out hollow occupied by the Wise-Wolves and the Chief's pups. Normally Amberstorm would be the one who ate first, but due to the scarcity of food, he'd permitted all ranks to feast before him for the sake of maintaining morale. Everyone knew the truth, though. As usual, someone would have to remind the Chief not to starve himself.

Tawnydrift neared Gorsescratch, the two licking each other in greeting. She offered no such welcome to Silversong and reserved an ugly scowl for Palesquall. "This is the second time you failed to bring food to the prey pile."

Palesquall looked to Silversong for aid. "I, uh…"

Silversong blew air out of his nose, drawing Tawnydrift's ire toward him. "He's far from the only subordinate who failed to add to the prey pile, and not for lack of trying."

Tawnydrift eyed him as if he were still a subordinate, but one look at his raised tail seemed to remind her of his new position. "Fine," she groaned, "but he better make up for his underperformance during the journey to Thornhollow." She signaled to Gorsescratch, and the two sauntered off toward their meals as the lieutenants finished theirs.

Silversong was about to go scavenge for his own morsel when Palesquall mumbled, "thanks."

"I can't keep defending you every day, Palesquall," Silversong reminded his friend, whose ears drooped. A thorn of guilt pricked Silversong's heart.

Before Palesquall could respond, Hazel walked up to him. "There you are. How'd morning duty go for you?"

Palesquall stared at her without making a single quip.

"Not good, eh?" She clawed at the ground and growled under her breath. "This isn't fair. The River-Stream wolves get to stuff their mouths every day while we're forced to eat nothing but fly-infested scraps!" She was a lot thinner than before, her bones showing beneath a brown summer coat.

"It isn't fair," Silversong agreed, "but we only have to endure these woods for one more day. If you haven't heard, the Warden's messengers returned, and we'll be off to Thornhollow tomorrow morning."

"Yeah, I heard." Hazel bared her teeth at the mud stuck between her claws. "And it doesn't change how I feel one bit. If Chief Ashenfall is as bug-brained as Riptide, we'll be no better off there than we are here."

At the mention of the Flame-Heart Chief, Silversong's thoughts coalesced into a vision of his packmates huddling together in a small cave of obsidian stone. "Look," he began, steering his eyes away from the other corporals gorging on their food at the centre of the glade, "I can't be certain of the future even after swallowing the piece of time, but I can promise that I'll do everything in my power to make sure Whistle-Wind endures. If we stay strong, we'll outlast those who abuse the Wolven Code for vain reasons."

"These River-Stream scatfurs can bite my tail!" Hazel barked and stormed off into the forest.

Palesquall leaped out of her way. "Whoa, she's *really* angry."

"For good reason." The smell of blood and fresh meat watered Silversong's mouth, but there was still something he had to do before eating. "The Chief summoned me. I better not keep him waiting."

"Right," Palesquall whined and walked to where the subordinates sat impatiently.

Silversong padded to the prey pile and picked out a semi-eaten rodent whose limbs were longer than its body. Fighting the temptation to dig in, he brought the corpse to the boulder on which the Chief perched and presented the meal while assuming the correct submissive posture. "I'm sorry for making you wait, sir. I was out testing the weapon."

“Hmm?” The Chief turned his distant and weary eyes to Silversong. “I’m not hungry.” But his body indicated otherwise. Beneath patches of flesh where grey fur had once grown the clear outline of bones revealed the cruel blows of starvation.

“Please, sir, you must eat.” Silversong used his nose to push the meat in the Chief’s direction, stomach groaning in protest at the act of sharing food. “I’ll keep bothering you until you do.”

The Chief scoffed. “You’re worse than the Wise-Wolves.” He finally relented and started munching on the rodent, spitting out the bones at Silversong’s forepaws. “There. Happy now?”

Silversong watched the subordinates ravage what little remained of the prey pile, his gut sinking. Marrow would have to satisfy his hunger for today, something his belly was more than unhappy about. “You called for me, sir?”

“Yes.” The Chief straightened his back in an attempt to seem grand. “I know you’ve answered many of our questions about the piece of time during our stay here.” His breaths trembled, and his head hung loosely. “And I know it’s impossible to go back, but if you could just…” he choked on whatever he was about to ask, “if-if you could lend me your weapon so I can relive my memories of her—”

“No, sir. I can’t.” Silversong could hardly bear to look at his once formidable leader now reduced to a grieving husk. “Pinetrail is dead, and so are the others. They’ve made their journey to Motherwolf’s den. It’s time to let them go.”

Amberstorm pulled his ears back and whimpered, perhaps for the first time realizing he was never going to see his mate again while he lived. “I-I’m not sure I can, Silversong. I thought I would be stronger than this. I don’t think I can be Chief anymore.”

“You must.” Silversong paced from side to side, the piece of time vibrating in his stomach. “Pinetrail sheltered you from the destruction of Wind’s Rest because she loved you, because she believed in you. Your soldiers are looking to you for hope, but right now you’re giving them nothing but doubts. Even in death, Pinetrail would expect you to fulfil your duty as Chief to the very end. You won’t save your pack by sinking deeper into your own sorrow, but by rising above it despite your loss. If you can’t do this, then give the title of Chief to someone more deserving. Because if you can’t present yourself as a strong leader at Thornhollow, we’ll be eaten alive by the other packs.”

The Chief froze and opened his eyes wide. Time's threads passed smoothly around him, hinting at his potential future. Some possibilities ended in death, but others showed a proud leader pulling his pack out of the darkness and into the light.

A bar of sunlight broke through the clouds to illuminate the Chief. He no longer whimpered. Instead, he surveyed the heavens as though hoping to find Pinetrail somewhere up there. "Your wisdom is commendable for someone so young. I should've promoted you long ago."

Silversong chuckled, amused at how little he cared about his promotion now. "Better late than never," he joked. "But really, don't beat yourself up over Pinetrail. You were a good leader then, and you still are now. We all believe in you, and we're all praying for your recovery. I see the spark in you, but it's up to you to ignite it."

The Chief lowered his head, amber eyes a touch brighter than before. "Thank you." He turned to the small lair the Wise-Wolves had dug out. "I should go see my pups."

As the Chief's tail swished slowly, Silversong smiled. "Is there anything else, sir?"

"No. Dismissed."

Silversong gave a slight bow and jumped off the boulder. Everything was slowly coming together. The Whistle-Wind Pack would become a fierce tempest indeed when its leader returned.

Striding into the surrounding woods, Silversong flexed the threads circling around him. For as long as the day was bright, he would study his greatest advantage over the Heretic and the Warden. The enemy never slept, so why should he? And when night came again, he would check in on a dear friend he hadn't had the chance to see since the moot ended.

"Oh, Frostpaw… I hope you're doing all right."

CHAPTER 6

The Price of Friendship

The Wolven Code wasn't meant to be questioned, only obeyed.

Silversong had once considered this strict set of rules flawless. Now he knew it for the poison it was, concocted by the First Warden to control wolfkind. Why couldn't others see this truth? Did they really think the law couldn't be abused to inflict injustices upon the underserving? If more wolves just opened their eyes, the fog of ignorance would start to clear, and the weight of the Warden's influence would diminish.

Then I can start amending this flawed order.

Silversong and Frostpaw's unsanctioned alliance had compromised the integrity of the Wolven Code, but the members of Whistle-Wind and River-Stream appeared to accept—however reluctantly—the benefits of the infraction. They couldn't deny that two wolves from rival territories managed to thwart and humble the Heretic himself. And then there was the creation of the Wolven Bulwark: a concept that contradicted everything the code stood for. Questions would arise in skeptical minds. Many would soon come to doubt the Warden, and those who'd punished Frostpaw for his heroic deeds would apologize for their treatment of him.

Those River-Stream wolves are scared of the change I bring. They're so captured by their own faith that they'll do anything to bolster their beliefs. Even if it means punishing someone who should instead be praised.

Silversong snuck out of the Whistle-Wind enclave as the stars lulled the sun to its slumber under a purpling sky. Tonight, Frostpaw wouldn't suffer alone.

Silversong wished he could've visited his friend sooner, but helping his pack and studying the piece of time had demanded his utmost attention. Already he'd made strides in his mastery over the weapon. The headaches had become more bearable, and he could peer into the future for far longer before his concentration broke. Still, most outcomes remained uncertain, and those he could see clearly were surrounded by twisted mires of complex decisions. Every choice sprouted different possibilities, and those too branched out until they grew into a tangled mess. He accepted that the future he wanted wouldn't be as perfect as he envisioned: he would make mistakes, he would stumble, he would topple under the pressure of responsibility, but he would always get back up to resume the fight.

He lifted his eyes from his thoughts. The Saltshore and the lake it crested were visible just beyond the forest. He shoved his ears forward and could faintly hear the sentinels barking orders as everyone settled down for the evening. Tomorrow was a big day, and a good night's sleep was a welcome prospect for those not on sentry duty. The Chiefs and lieutenants especially needed to conserve their energy.

Silversong squinted at the shadowy shapes disappearing into the tunnels of the den.

Frostpaw is somewhere in that cave system.

Silversong crouched upon arriving at the blanched stones leading up to the eroded home of the River-Stream wolves. Wiping off the mud on his pads, he climbed up, swift and silent, taking care not to get noticed by the patrolling sentries above. Getting caught would do no favours for him or his packmates. The Warden would leap at the chance to weaken him, and so he had to be extra careful not to give her an excuse to do so. Luckily, he had the piece of time to save him from any potential disasters.

He reached the top and compressed the threads of his aura. Even though most failed to notice when they were in proximity to the piece of time, some wolves—especially sentinels—proved perceptive enough to detect when the golden circle was near. He breathed deeply to soothe his jumpy nerves and crept through the dormant geysers, the briny tang stretching his nostrils wide.

He avoided the patrols and zigzagged his way across the shore, counting on the fresh scents of all the wolves who'd previously padded here to conceal his presence. All he had to worry about was not getting spotted; his silver coat would stand out like a hare in an open field here. He turned a corner and faced one of the entrances leading into the belly of the den. The hole was several tail-lengths away, and it promised safety from the scouring eyes above. Silversong prepared to sprint toward it.

Nearby paw steps alerted him to the presence of approaching wolves.

Shock jolted through his body and made his fur attempt to flee his flesh. He scurried behind one of the geysers just as two chatting sentinels rounded a corner and passed in front of the hole. From their voices alone, Silversong knew it was his sister and Greyhail.

Silversong peeked around the geyser, ready to use the unseen threads to his advantage.

Swiftstorm stopped and sniffed, nose shooting upward.

"Smell something?" Greyhail asked.

It took a little while for Swiftstorm to respond. "It almost smells like… forget it."

Greyhail chuckled. "Okay…?"

"It's nothing, really."

"You haven't been yourself lately. Is it because of your brother?"

"Of course it's because of him." Her whisper was sharp and loud. Silversong pulled his ears back, and his stomach sank. "He all but challenged the Warden's authority during the moot. I'm proud of all he's accomplished, but…"

"You feel his loyalties may be misplaced?"

Silversong hoped his thumping heartbeat wouldn't give his position away.

Swiftstorm paused again and shifted without making a sound. "I feel his heart is in the right place, but I fear he'll try to help the Four Territories in all the wrong ways."

"Hmm." Greyhail took in the salty air. "I believe he needs your counsel. You should speak to him tomorrow and ensure he follows the guidance of the Wolven Code from now on. Remind him the piece of time doesn't grant him authority over the Warden."

"He's not an enemy," Swiftstorm grunted firmly.

Greyhail looked confused. "I never said he was. But he does need to submit himself to the Warden and use his weapon for good. You haven't spoken to him since his promotion ceremony, and your old pack doesn't seem too willing to set him on the right track. His time spent among the exiles may have driven him to darkness. Only you can bring him back into the light now."

Silversong could almost feel the conflict stirring within his sister. "You're… you're right, Greyhail. I'll go see him tomorrow and harden his faith in the Wolven Code. It's my duty as a sentinel and as his sister."

"Good. I'm proud of you, Swiftstorm. We have a long shift ahead of us. Let's hope we're lucky enough to catch a spying exile." Greyhail grinned and licked his fangs.

Swiftstorm laughed at the idea. "If there's one thing the exiles are good at, it's skulking around in the shadows. I wouldn't get my hopes up."

"Who knows. Remember, the stink of the Furtherlands won't mask their scents here."

The pair strode away from the tunnel's entrance, and Silversong scuttled into it like a mouse fleeing a diving hawk. He tried shaking away his troubled thoughts to no avail. Was Swiftstorm really convinced he would make all the wrong choices? She couldn't be as brainwashed by the Wolven Code as the Warden.

Silversong let loose a drawn-out sigh, his forelimbs prickling. He would have to break his sister's loyalty to the Warden somehow. He put his worries behind him and pressed through the cave system, the streaks of green lighting the way ahead. The texture of the ground and the softness of the glow would've been calming if not for the nagging worry of getting caught. River-Stream subordinates patrolled the tunnels in shifts, though they were far fewer than those above. Sometimes they appeared without warning, and Silversong almost had to use the weapon to avoid their tired eyes. Thankfully, his caution prevailed.

Where are you, Frostpaw? He continued his search deep into the night, staving off the fatigue seeping into his body. The tunnels twisted and turned, and despite their soothing allure, they reminded him of the underground maze inside the Mountainmouth. He shuddered, trying to dig out the panic burrowing into his head.

Something flickered at the edge of sight: an image of different types of large prey, all hoofed and antlered. Silversong let the vision stream into his brain. The poor beasts were getting tortured by Rime, all of them fettered to the ground by festering roots that only tightened the more the victims squirmed.

Just as quickly as it came, the vision vanished. Silversong tried forcing it to return, feeling a chill up his spine. Why would Rime torture innocent prey? For sport? Disgust fouled Silversong's temper as he attempted to steer his thoughts toward more pleasant things. Justice would come for the exiles sooner or later.

Trying to locate Frostpaw in this labyrinth of snaking tunnels was pointless. Silversong resorted to using the piece of time to scry the near future and all its possibilities, letting it lure him to where the corporal slept by process of elimination. Going this way would lead him straight into the Wise-Wolves' lair while padding in the opposite direction would bring him before an astonished sentry. Striding into that passage over there would take him closer to Frostpaw. Silversong hated using the weapon for such a trivial thing, but at this rate he would be stuck wandering the tunnels until morning!

Maybe this is another way to beat the Heretic. Lure him into these tunnels and trap him down here forever.

His use of the weapon brought him to a grotto lit by streams of moonlight spilling in from dozens of smaller passageways. He released the threads of his aura, and they bounced back to their original state. Nostrils wide, he sniffed at each entrance until he detected Frostpaw's scent.

"There you are." Silversong crouched low and pushed through the small opening, the moonlight growing brighter the further up he padded.

He stepped into a round alcove hollowed out in the side of the den. It was large enough to contain several wolves, the smooth floor gradually descending to a steep drop-off overlooking the legendary River-Stream lake. Awe tugged at Silversong's lower jaw. The surface was clean enough to mirror the starry night in all its magnificence, and it reached to unknown ends like the sky itself. The inviting sight tempted him to plunge into the lake's embrace, to leap into the undisturbed reflection of the twinkling heavens above. The water dispersed the moon's radiance far and wide, illuminating the shore in a muted light.

It seemed like those passageways back there led to different alcoves each facing the wondrous lake, and the corporals had a choice of which to sleep in. Only a single wolf occupied this space, though, and he slept near the edge of the nook in utter solitude. He lay on his stomach, head facing the speckled water.

On silent paws, Silversong approached.

As he came closer to Frostpaw, Silversong noticed the corporal was twitching and mumbling about his slain mother between uneven breaths.

"No… don't go," Frostpaw made a few pup-like sounds, "he'll… he'll be there… he'll…"

Silversong settled beside the other wolf, fur brushing up against Frostpaw's. The sleeping corporal tucked his snout between his forepaws and shook as if the gales of winter were blowing early.

"I'm-I'm so sorry," he whimpered.

"Oh, Frostpaw." Silversong leaned against his friend, and Frostpaw shook no more. Silversong placed his tail atop the corporal's and licked him on his scarred shoulder. Needles of guilt pricked Silversong in the chest, but he continued comforting Frostpaw until those striking yellow eyes fluttered open.

"M-mother…?" Frostpaw whined in a slurred manner. He sniffed, then tensed, ears shooting up. He sprang to all fours and blinked rapidly. "Silversong?" The confusion on his face lasted mere moments before shock took over. "Silversong! What're you doing here?! You're going to get me exiled!"

"Shh!" Silversong got up too and tried to appear calmer than he was. "You'll get us both exiled if you keep yapping so loud!"

Frostpaw panted faster than he ever had. His eyes darted from side to side in search of an escape. "Why did you come here, Silversong?" He backed away.

"To see if you're all right?" Silversong couldn't keep his voice from cracking due to the lump in his throat. "I'm worried about you."

Frostpaw froze like a deer catching a whiff of danger, his fiery scowl slowly cooling off. He inhaled deeply and expelled a long breath, sauntering over to where he'd been sleeping and sitting at the edge. He peered at his own reflection in the still water. "We can't be friends, Silversong. Get that through your head."

Getting struck by lightning would've been less painful. Silversong pressed on the ground so his shaking limbs wouldn't collapse. He swallowed before the wedge in his gullet bloated to a choking size. Struggling not to whimper, he whined, "why not?"

"You know why," Frostpaw responded coldly.

Silversong released a trembling sigh and stepped toward Frostpaw, heartbeat quickening the closer he got. He dropped to his rump beside the dejected corporal, and to Silversong's relief, Frostpaw stayed put. Maybe isolation had made him desperate enough to accept any form of companionship, even from the one he claimed was no friend of his. "Because of the Wolven Code? Because it states we're supposed to be rivals rather than friends?"

"Exactly."

Silversong frowned and studied Frostpaw's face, hoping to find some doubt hidden in those creases, in that rueful look. "If we hadn't worked together as we did inside the Mountainmouth, we would've died, and the Heretic would've claimed the piece of time. We gave the Four Territories a chance to fight back. For that, I'm grateful we found each other." Frostpaw's lips quivered, ears flattening. "Without you by my side, I would've failed, and you know it. Our friendship—our code-breaking—saved the future, and there's not a single punishment the Warden could give me that would make me regret my choices."

Frostpaw scoffed and allowed his head to droop. "Easy for you to say, *corporal*." He glanced at Silversong once, twice, then peered into the lake again.

Something disturbed the surface and caused ripples to distort the reflected stars. Silversong squinted at his wavy double below. "It isn't fair. Your demotion. Your isolation. None of it is fair. You're a hero, Frostpaw. You risked your life many times in the underground ruin. I've never met anyone braver than you. Before this is over, we'll make your packmates see you for who you really are. We'll make everyone see the harm in blindly following the Wolven Code."

Frostpaw's hackles stood on end, and he gave Silversong a dire look. "I should haul your backside into a steaming geyser for saying that."

Silversong suppressed the queasy feeling worming through his gut and nudged Frostpaw on the side. "Maybe that'll get you promoted to lieutenant again."

Frostpaw snorted, his face softening. "It would certainly impress Chief Riptide, at least."

Chief Riptide can bite my tail! Silversong wanted to say, but restrained himself. Instead, he let the silence deepen. He thought he saw something huge slithering beneath the watery surface. It had to be a trick of the light. He tried leaning against Frostpaw again, but since the corporal was now wide awake, he shifted away. A bitter pang struck Silversong on the inside, but he endured the blow without reacting.

Frostpaw stole a few glances at Silversong, trying and failing to be subtle. "Hey." Silversong's ears perked up upon hearing the corporal's voice. "I'm… I'm sorry for being mean, it's just… there's a lot going on for me, and… and I'm happy for you and your promotion, it's just…"

"Shh. It's all right." Silversong succeeded in touching the corporal's shoulder, dragging his nose in circular motions along the stiff muscles beneath sleeked fur. He loosened some of the tension there. "I'm here for you."

Frostpaw stared at him in disbelief of the kindness he was being shown. The swelling happiness in those perfect eyes ignited tiny sparks all throughout Silversong's body.

"Why…?" was all Frostpaw could utter.

"You know why." Silversong risked moving his forepaw closer to Frostpaw's, stopping when they touched.

Frostpaw snapped his head forward, but his forepaw stayed beside Silversong's. "Okay." Frostpaw released a long and trembling breath. "Okay. We're friends." He chuckled nervously.

Silversong beamed, the sparks within bursting into little explosions of tingly warmth. He wanted to jump on his friend and lick him all over, but he doubted such affection would be appreciated. Thinking about it made his tail wag, though.

Frostpaw's gaze eventually returned to Silversong, and his mouth quirked into a smile. "You're silly."

"*You're* silly!"

"I'm not the one grinning like a little fox who successfully stole food from the Prey Hollow." Frostpaw bumped him on the shoulder.

"Take that back." Silversong tried his best to look serious, but Frostpaw's smile only widened.

"That pouty face you're making is adorable, little fox," Frostpaw teased.

"POUTY?!"

"Shh! Try not to wake the others, or you'll get us both exiled." Frostpaw's head darted around cautiously.

"I'll wake this whole den if you don't watch your muzzle," Silversong grunted in a playful tone.

“Please don’t.” Frostpaw gave a concerned laugh. “Snowleap would have your hide if she found out you were here.”

Silversong’s mood soured, the pleasant sensation tingling through his veins smothered in an instant. He dragged his forepaw away from his friend’s. “Snowleap, the Chief’s daughter who tried defending you during the moot. Is she…? Are you two…?”

Frostpaw caught on to what Silversong was implying and jerked up. “What? No! She’s the one I saved from the snowcat attack last winter. She’s pretty and all, but we’re nothing more than friends.”

“Ah.” A small sense of relief washed over Silversong, the warmth steadily returning. “I mean… you two looked very close. And who could resist a big strong male like you—”

Frostpaw sniffed loudly. “Enough of that.”

“Okay, okay. Just teasing.” Silversong giggled, the blood in his face near to steaming. He delayed his breaths in hopes of slowing the rapid drumming in his chest. His tail wagged uncontrollably. Why was he acting so… weird?

Frostpaw scrunched up his forehead and returned to observing his reflection in the water. “How’re you going to fix things, Silversong? The Wolven Code is as sacred as life itself to most wolves, and it was to me before I met you. Not everyone is lucky—or unlucky—enough to realize the value in seeing rivals as potential friends.”

The golden circle pulsed, sending vibrations to Silversong’s brain and causing his fur to act unruly. “I’ll have to convince the Four Territories that the only way to survive is if we favour true unity over the Wolven Code.” His eyes wandered across the lake and up to the pale slice of the moon reflected on the water. “It’ll take some effort, but I know I can get it done.”

Their eyes met once more, and the two shared a moment where neither could speak. Again, Silversong was hit by the feeling that all of this had already happened. He broke away, thoughts racing, trying his hardest not to think about the one-eyed version of himself from the maze of madness.

Frostpaw offered him a short nuzzle. If only it had lasted longer. “I trust you, Silversong.” He gritted his teeth and came close to a growl. “And I would like nothing more than another chance at killing Rime… but is undermining the Wolven Code a good thing? You’ll brand yourself an enemy of the Warden just like the Heretic.”

Silversong grimaced and straightened his back. "Leave her to me. She'll do nothing but keep us trapped in a bubble of ignorance until we suffocate. If we're to face the Heretic in battle, we must do it without her in command. I won't stoop to the Heretic's level to instill the change we need, but I also won't let the Warden drive us toward the other extreme."

Frostpaw's eyes swept across the blinking stars. "Then let me be the first from my pack to fully support you, Silversong."

"Really?" Silversong's tail lifted off the ground and swayed from side to side.

"Do I have a choice?" Frostpaw dropped his gaze, ears flattened. "My family has pretty much disowned me, and if my mother were alive, she would likely curse my name for bringing shame to River-Stream." Frostpaw's squeaking voice laid bare how deeply that pained him. "My packmates can't even stomach looking in my direction without sneering. I'm a stain on my territory. I'm the lieutenant who got demoted. It's all I'll ever be from now on. You're my only ally, Silversong. My only friend."

Silversong couldn't imagine how alone Frostpaw must truly be feeling. It was impossible to bear. "Frostpaw, look at me." Frostpaw turned to him, eyeballs trembling. "We'll show them how bad of a mistake they made. When this is over and the Heretic is dead, you'll be celebrated as a hero by your packmates, and when future generations look back on you, they'll remember you for your true qualities."

"You think so? You think they'll forgive me?" Frostpaw practically begged for reassurance.

"They'll have to." Silversong nuzzled him under the throat, burying himself in the paler fur there. It was cozier than any den could ever be.

Using his head, Frostpaw brought Silversong closer, returning the affection. Maybe Silversong should've listened to his instincts earlier. "Whatever happens, I'll always be your friend. Even though I'm not supposed to be."

"I know." Silversong couldn't have suppressed his ear-to-ear smile if he'd wanted to.

Nothing could break them apart.

Silversong wished he could use the piece of time to freeze them both in place for all eternity. He wished he could forget about the Heretic and the Warden and remain here in Frostpaw's embrace until old age took them. He wished he could forget his responsibilities to the Four Territories and all the troubles he had yet to face. But the night wouldn't last forever, and the days to come would always sink back into the same darkness they'd emerged from. A cycle continuing forever, a cycle none could escape.

From a shadowed corner of Silversong's mind, his own distorted voice seemed to laugh at him.

CHAPTER 7

The Departure

Silversong woke up next to a snoring Frostpaw, the details of a pleasant dream already leaking away into the bottomless pit reserved for forgotten memories.

A wide yawn squeezed moisture into Silversong's eyes, clearing his blurry vision. The air was cool, too cool for his liking… not like Frostpaw's fur… so cozy and…

Silversong would've settled back down near his friend if it weren't for the grey-blue sky heralding the sunrise. The stars still dotted the lake, poking tiny silver holes in the clean surface. Silversong stretched, battling the weariness in his muscles and the desire to snuggle up beside Frostpaw while the sun seared the clouds pink. Everyone would soon be awake and ready to leave for Flame-Heart Territory, and Silversong needed to return to his packmates before then.

Despite the snoring, the way Frostpaw slept was so endearing. His head rested on his forepaws, and the white tip of his tail twitched from whatever dream he was having. He hadn't mumbled anything about his mother since falling asleep. Silversong allowed himself a short pause to smile at the corporal before sneaking out the way he'd come, scuttling through the tunnels, time's threads ready to spring around any sentry still on patrol, but he was careful enough to avoid detection.

He emerged onto the Saltshore only to witness an orange globe of flame stretching its early rays over the horizon. There were still sentinels prowling about, and Silversong had to use the piece of time twice to evade their watchful eyes, only allowing himself to breathe properly once he padded on moist soil. The pungent scent of mushrooms and damp earth made him look forward to the departure. River-Stream Territory was beautiful, but its hospitality proved lacking.

He stepped on a cool, smooth surface, and the rainy fragrance shifted to a sharp metallic-tinged odour. Confused and disoriented, Silversong found himself in a dimly lit chamber facing a pair of pale blue eyes set in a furless face drained of blood. He'd seen this face before inside the Mountainmouth. It belonged to the Forgotten One known as Aelrion, the one who'd led the final remnants of his two-legged army deep into Stone-Guard Territory and into a bronze ruin, where they all disappeared at the climax of the War of Change. Why was Silversong seeing him now? Why was the piece of time showing him this ghost of the past?

A single blink brought him back to the present. He pressed his forepaws into the soil to reassure himself he was indeed in reality. Twice now the golden circle had caused these hallucinations—these visions—and twice now Silversong had no idea what to make of them. As much as the weapon was his tool to wield, it was still unpredictable. Hoping for no more random interferences, he continued through the woods all the way to the enclave. He got there in time to feign waking up alongside the other corporals. Today, history would be made, and he would set the packs on the right course.

The Warden howled not long after everyone was on their paws. The Chief barked and jumped off his boulder, head high and eyes lit by a renewed sense of purpose. Silversong smiled and joined the soldiers falling in behind Amberstorm, lieutenants at the front and subordinates at the rear. Together, they marched to the foot of the Saltshore where the Warden and her impressive retinue awaited them. There was no time for formalities. Half of the Wolven Bulwark was already assembled, and it needed to become whole.

The sun blazed above the horizon and lit the clouds aflame by the time the Warden took charge of the mighty formation. She moved out at the tip of the army, the sentinels following her in a straight line that divided Whistle-Wind and River-Stream. Silversong padded behind Gorsescratch as they marched away from the Saltshore and into the Songwoods, changing direction when the last pocket of defiant stars had conceded their light to the blooming day.

Eventually, they crossed the shallow region of a coursing river, the chill water rousing those not already fully awake. They paused for a while on the other side where the pines, oaks, and alders thinned out, boughs looming over a massive field of grass, the wind making waves across the rippling green expanse.

After burning so much energy, exhaustion now gripped the young and the old, and stomachs yearned for food due to the demanding pace the Warden had set. Hunting parties were organized, and the restrictions imposed on the Whistle-Wind members were officially lifted. As noon approached, watersnouts and an abundance of smaller prey were brought to the army, and not until every belly was satisfied did the soldiers push through the sea of grass, blades taller than the wolves were long. At least the field provided shelter from summer's ruthless heat.

Silversong relied on his nose to guide him through the dense stalks, the scent of his packmates tracing a clear line to follow through the sweet aroma permeating the air. Although the sheer number of travelling wolves hampered the army's speed, they still managed a good stride even as the sun crested the thick clouds as a brilliant white orb. When the field was at their tails, they took another break on a hillside. Beyond stretched a meadow of violet flowers, and in the distance lay a forest of blood-red leaves.

They'd finally reached the border of Flame-Heart Territory.

Silversong lounged among the other corporals, panting to cool himself off as Gorsescratch was going on about ancient battle tactics. He was surprisingly knowledgeable on the subject, especially when it came to how Motherwolf and her forces harassed the Forgotten Ones during the War of Change.

"Which elder taught you that nonsense?" a corporal named Nimbus snorted. "You're telling me the Forgotten Ones killed wolves from far away just by pointing weird sticks in their direction?"

"It's true!" Gorsescratch insisted, frowning at the doubtful corporal. "The weapons the Forgotten Ones created during the War of Change altered the field of battle in their favour for a while. You obviously never paid attention to your history lessons as a rookie."

"Hah!" Nimbus barked, grey fur sleek and green eyes glinting. "Some elders like to exaggerate tales they heard when they were younger which were already exaggerated by the previous generation. Your ears obviously aren't good enough to separate truth from fiction."

Gorsescratch sneered at that, but before he could scold Nimbus, Silversong came to his former bully's defense as much as he hated doing so. "He's right, Nimbus. The Forgotten Ones created many strange and powerful weapons after stealing the piece of time. They used up much of its power in the process, but it did give them an advantage, brief as it was."

Nimbus scoffed. He would believe nothing unless he saw it. As for the other corporals, they regarded Silversong as though he possessed the wisdom of an elder. It was all very awkward.

Tawnydrift's tongue cleaned the spaces between her claws. "I guess even the piece of time couldn't save the Forgotten Ones from the combined might of the Titans and their mortal children."

"Yes. They put an end to the war before the Forgotten Ones could create even deadlier weapons and dominate all lands. Despite the setback, the Titans ultimately achieved their goal." Silversong recalled the moment he'd swallowed the golden circle and travelled across time and space, witnessing history through those who'd also consumed the mystical shape.

"The Forgotten Ones would've needed a miracle to win," another corporal who'd remained quiet until now joined the conversation. "In the end they were all wiped out."

"Not quite." Silversong held off on blinking for as long as he could. He knew in the momentary darkness he would see Aelrion staring right back at him. "The last of them disappeared deep in Stone-Guard Territory… in a ruin of bronze." His eyes burned from the dry air, and he couldn't keep them open any longer. Sure enough, there he was, the pale Forgotten One whose gaze made ice seem hot. Even as Silversong tried blinking away the image, he couldn't banish the feeling of Aelrion watching him. The Forgotten One obscured glimpses of the not-so-distant future, and Silversong's attempts to peer through the spectral face rooted in his thoughts were of no avail. Like clouds engulfing the sun, the ghost of Aelrion severely dampened his access to the nearest possible outcomes.

He was thankful for hearing Gorsescratch's voice. It served as a good distraction from the confusion and the frustration. "Can you look into the past and figure out how and why the Forgotten Ones disappeared?"

Silversong sighed through his teeth. "No. I'm not strong enough to peer that far back for any significant period of time."

The corporals listening to Silversong all looked at something behind him. They got up and assumed respectful postures. "And besides, salvation lies in the future, not the past."

"That it does, brother."

His head whipped over his shoulder, ears pricked as a surge of excitement struck his heart. He stood on all fours and wagged his tail at Swiftstorm's approach, her athletic form visible beneath a shining silver coat. She was every bit the regal sentinel, strong and serene without a concern for how fate would treat her. She'd just finished talking to Cedargaze and Shadowgale by the looks of it.

"If it isn't any trouble, I would like to speak to my brother alone." She waited for her former packmates to honour the request. Quick departures demonstrated their respect.

A bowing of heads, a murmur of polite farewells, and the corporals dispersed in search of other pastimes. Silversong calmed his breathing and forced his tail to swish more slowly. He wasn't a pup anymore. "Hey, Swiftstorm."

"I know you were sneaking about the Saltshore last night," Swiftstorm admitted bluntly. Silversong froze. "Even if you were hidden among all the wolves of the Four Territories, I could still pick out your scent. You should've rolled in bleakthorn if you'd wished to hide from me, brother."

His smile vanished, his ears falling low, but he stood high despite the heavy shame pressing between his shoulders. "There wasn't any bleakthorn around."

"So, was it Chief Amberstorm who tasked you to spy on River-Stream? Or someone else?" Swiftstorm tried to imitate the Warden's drilling glare, but she found the effort wanting.

"I wasn't spying!" The accusation tore through him, but he kept his voice low so he wouldn't attract curious onlookers.

Actually, I was doing something far worse than spying.

"What were you doing there, then?!" She almost broke into a growl.

Checking in on Frostpaw… cozying up to him… sharing his lair. Last night's tender memories yielded to his fretting nerves.

"I…" Silversong sucked in a breath. He needed a level head to confront his sister. He couldn't let his emotions control him. "I can't say. But I promise I wasn't spying." He hated being so suspicious, but if Swiftstorm found out about him visiting Frostpaw…

If this gets out, Motherwolf herself won't be able to save us!

The conflict was clear as day on her face. Her loyalty to the Warden clashed against the love for her brother. Stuck between two difficult choices, she closed her eyes and snarled at the ground. "I won't force it out of you. Not today," she grunted to herself. "But Silversong, you heard me and Greyhail. This… disregard for the law can't go on no matter how powerful you think you've become. The Wolven Code is the line separating us from the exiles, and without it we're vulnerable to the same mistakes that led to the Rise of the Fallen Titan. You must trust in the Warden and in the rules that keep the Four Territories in check."

Far above, the clouds clawed across the sky to dim the sunlight. For some reason, it caused the piece of time to pulse within Silversong, begging to be used, but he maintained his focus on his sister. Besides, Aelrion's bloodless face still blocked his foresight. "Swiftstorm, blindly obeying the Wolven Code only serves to embolden the Heretic. He'll use the animosity between the Four Territories to break us from the inside, and when he finally strikes, we'll have no choice but to accept his reign or die. The sentinels must trust in me. You must trust in me. Enough of this needless separation. We must fight together, all packs as one, or we'll be at the mercy of not just the exiles, but also ourselves."

Swiftstorm stepped back as if just realizing she was talking to a total stranger. Her eyes were wide pools of green. "Greyhail was right. Your time spent among the exiles has changed you. Give the weapon to the Warden. She'll know how to use it properly."

"NO!" Silversong barked, the sting of his sister's distrust reaching deep into his bones. His fur stood upright, made worse by the sudden chill conquering the summer heat. The clouds devoured daylight and darkened into a brewing storm, but he couldn't look away from Swiftstorm's frightened face no matter how upsetting it was to see. "Your loyalty to the Wolven Code is so strong it blinds you to its flaws. I was like you once, but the things I've seen… the things I've done… they've changed me. I saw the truth, Swiftstorm. If I gave the piece of time to the Warden, she would win against the Heretic, but she would also force us into a life of utter devotion to the Wolven Code. Even that wouldn't erase the exiles for good. Oppression breeds defiance. It's the reason the Heretic exists and the reason we're now in this conflict. Nothing is truly resolved if the law doesn't change. If we don't change."

Swiftstorm appeared sickened by her own brother. She opened her trembling mouth. "You're… you're speaking like the exiles would. They're… they're…" Thunder announced the wrath of the storm yet to pour. A stray snowflake landed on Swiftstorm's nose and melted into a droplet. "They're here."

Silversong realized why the piece of time had begun pulsing madly. Wolves everywhere huddled together, eyes drawn to the black clouds forming the twisted face of the Fallen Titan, its jaws gaping wide over the meadow. Dreadful lightning crackled from within.

All around him, snow descended like tiny specks of death, shrouding a fractured army.

"Brace yourselves!" Silversong called as the first strikes of lightning wrought devastation on the Wolven Bulwark.

CHAPTER 8

A Meadow of Death

It all happened faster than Silversong could blink. Futures flashed and spiraled to equally violent ends, leaving behind a swarm of visions that consumed his focus. In them he saw wolves dying, blood flowing, chaos unraveling.

Silversong's sight whirled about like a maddened vortex, coming together long enough for him to push Swiftstorm out of the way as a narrow line of crooked lightning smote the ground where she'd been standing a breath ago.

An electrifying stream jolted through Silversong and singed some of his fur, the sour stench already invading his nostrils. A spray of earth pelted him and his sister, but the storm had much fury to spare. Out of the wretched mouth came more lightning strikes, one after the other, battering the assembled army and causing cries of panic between the thunder. How many wolves had already died? How many had yet to die?

Across the meadow, before the line of distant trees, stood a grinning Rime.

More glimpses of the near future shimmered in Silversong's head as he attempted to seek out the correct choices to make. His mind was liberated from Aelrion's glare, but the Warden took charge of the situation before Silversong could form a concrete plan. "Soldiers of the Wolven Bulwark!" Her voice put the thunder to shame, and all wolves froze upon hearing it despite the spewing lightning. Silversong barely dodged another strike aimed at him. "Space yourselves apart and charge forward! Those who cannot fight, make for the forest!"

A brief howling broke out among the army as everyone rushed into the meadow, the storm struggling to keep track of who to blast next. Silversong was thankful the Fallen Titan's true power was weaker here compared to the Furtherlands. The Wolven Bulwark surely would've been ravaged otherwise.

One look over his shoulder revealed the number of dead. About two dozen casualties littered the Flame-Heart border, comprised of Whistle-Wind and River-Stream members alike. Silversong uttered a silent prayer for their spirits and continued downhill. He cooled the boiling thoughts in his head and beckoned the wind to his command, making use of its vast reservoir.

Thorns from the violet flowers nicked his flesh and opened stinging lines across his entire body, but the pain was only an inconvenience. He dodged a few more bombardments from above, zigzagging to increase his chances of staying alive. He froze the outer threads of the golden circle, effectively stopping time within that section in case speed alone wasn't enough to save him. The exiles wanted him dead above all others except maybe the Warden.

At the front, the sentinels barked and snarled at Rime, their strides enhanced by the wind Swiftstorm wielded. Greyhail growled alongside her; they intended to avenge the Great Chain.

Rime laughed at their advance, jaws hanging wide open like the cruel face in the sky. He used his tail to signal something.

Silversong's heart lurched as exiles poured out of the forest behind Rime and trampled through the meadow, leaving trails of decay in their wake.

"LET BATTLE BE JOINED!" howled the Warden, the sentinels echoing her command.

"Shields of air! All of you!" Cedargaze's voice blared. "Corporals and subordinates of Whistle-Wind! Form a line for a frontal assault! Don't let the enemy break through! We'll support you from behind!"

Silversong joined the corporals and subordinates as they formed the vanguard. He could only hope for the safety of his friends now. Blood roared in his ears, the piece of time mimicking the pounding in his chest. Everything seemed to decelerate in the moments leading up to the clash. Swirling air gathered around his packmates, and the snowfall rioted in an icy flurry, pelting the life out of the meadow. This battle would either result in a temporary victory or a sound defeat. The two outcomes fought for dominance in his head, threatening his connection to the wind.

Chief Amberstorm barked something Silversong couldn't quite hear through the clamour of the nearing battle. Glancing behind him, he spotted Moonwhisper and Mistyfur guarding the young while the elders who could still fight defended those who couldn't as they ran for the forest.

Thankfully, Cedargaze repeated the Chief's orders from where the lieutenants charged, each of them presiding over a specific section of the van. "Wise-Wolves! While the enemy is distracted, go around them and flee into the forest! If the exiles win, run for the Flame-Heart den and don't let up until you reach it. Protect our youth! Protect Whistle-Wind's future!"

Silversong repeated the order for those who might not have heard. More lightning strikes forked out of the corrupted clouds, these ones aimed at the sentinels. He looked for Swiftstorm to confirm she hadn't been hit. A whirlwind whizzed around her, fangs ready to tear into an unlucky target. Greyhail rode the earth at her side, flinging condensed chunks of the ground at the exiles. Those who shared his Blessing did the same.

Chief Amberstorm barked again, and this time Silversong heard his voice clearly. "Flanking sections! Once the exiles break, close in around them! Funnel them toward the centre."

"YES, SIR!" Gorsescratch blared from one end, and the corporal on the opposite end repeated the acknowledgment.

Images of a combined force leading the exiles to the slaughter flashed behind Silversong's eyes. They could win this battle and destroy the exiles for good if Whistle-Wind and River-Stream worked together. "EVERYONE!" he barked at the top of his lungs. "WE MUST FIGHT AS ONE! RIVER-STREAM WOLVES, FUNNEL THE EXILES ON YOUR SIDE TOWARD US! LET'S CRUSH OUR ENEMIES TOGETHER!"

"BELAY THAT!" The Warden's voice resounded from the tip of the army. "I GIVE THE ORDERS HERE! FACE THEM HEAD-ON AND RUN THEM DOWN! REMEMBER THE WOLVEN CODE AND DON'T MERGE FORCES!"

Silversong wanted to conjure a lash of air and smack the Warden square on the muzzle, but she was too far away, and the enemy was fast approaching.

Motherwolf save us.

The piece of time surged like a damned river coiling in on itself. The exiles were a few tree lengths away. He blinked, and now he could smell their foul breaths. He could see the hatred in their eyes and the decay surrounding them. He blinked again, and chaos reigned.

The ground erupted at the frontlines, sending a hail of debris to shower the line of Whistle-Wind wolves. From newly formed craters slithered countless rotting roots strengthened by corruption, entangling those who failed to dodge or deflect. A breach opened on the Whistle-Wind side close to Silversong.

"STAND FAST! LIEUTENANTS, CLOSE THE GAP!" Amberstorm ordered, but more roots wormed up at blinding speeds to strike vulnerable throats. Lieutenants, corporals, and subordinates choked on bubbling blood and thrashed defiantly against death.

Silversong sheared several roots shooting toward him. Their defenses were broken. Blasts of air shook his eardrums. A barrage of fireballs conjured by Flame-Heart sentinels tore some exiles to flaming shreds, and the earth trembled as if a hungry beast were growling deep below.

Amid the cries of pain and the mad barking fueled by bloodlust, Silversong found himself facing three angry exiles. He'd already caught two of them in time's grasp, but the third stayed just out of range, the wariness on his face quickly morphing into fear. His name was Brokenjaw, Silversong recalled. He focused on nothing but the thought of a lonely breeze swirling into a massive vortex. He lifted his tail and snatched the wind, violent and unruly, and launched it at Brokenjaw in the form of a huge wave slicing through flowers and grasping roots. The exile jumped over it and ran seeking a fairer fight.

For a brief moment, Silversong considered talking some sense into the two wolves still bound by the threads. Logic quickly suppressed that thought. The bloodthirst in their eyes shielded them against reason, and only a fool would attempt to negotiate in an active warzone. Silversong tried to encase his heart in stone as he plunged his fangs through the threads and into their throats one after the other. It was the quickest death he could offer. He released them from time's grasp and watched them bleed out on the ground.

It's a soldier's duty, he repeated to himself, rejoining his packmates as they pushed through the savage horde. Thinned as they were, the exiles couldn't keep this assault up for much longer. If Silversong managed to unite Whistle-Wind and River-Stream, the Heretic's army could be stamped out here and now. On the other side, Riptide's forces picked off the stragglers and defended against the festering blows when they should've been on the offense. The sentinels were at an impasse. Every time one tried to break through the row of exiles, rotting tendrils yanked them back, and keen roots promptly burrowed into their vital arteries. The Warden boiled any exile she touched to steaming husks, but even she panted harshly as blood leaked from several holes in her coat.

Visions of pain flickered at the corners of Silversong's eyes—different types of large prey squirming and squealing as hatred oozed through their veins and soaked their hearts black.

Sharp points plunging into his shoulder cut off the distraction. Silversong yelped, tying unseen threads around the exile who'd ambushed him. Nimbus tore into the attacker. Silversong loosened the threads, and the mangy mongrel tipped over and lay lifeless on a heap of crushed flowers, her fangs still bared even in death.

"Thanks." Silversong clenched his teeth at the throbbing pain.

"Don't mention it—"

One moment Nimbus was there, the next he was everywhere, his limbs scattered all around, chunks of his sizzling flesh raining on Silversong. The string of lightning had been so narrow, so faint. The fading afterglow fractured his vision like a crack through a clear sheet of ice, and every strand of fur jumped up at the shocking wave passing through him.

Silversong's shoulders heaved, and no matter how much air he took in, it failed to calm his shaking bones. The ringing in his ears drowned out the yelping, the barking, the futile protests of the dying. He could almost be forgiven for forgetting his duty to Whistle-Wind. His duty to the Wolven Bulwark. Blood dripped from his fur—the blood of a packmate. Ruptured innards stuck to him—the innards of a packmate. It could've been him. It could've—

He shook his head and forced his body away from the smoking crater. There was nothing else to do but continue the fight. His hearing returned, and he joined Gorsescratch and Tawnydrift in their struggle. The pair dodged an array of whipping roots as the exiles moved to block the advance of the Whistle-Wind wolves.

Chief Amberstorm had taken charge of the lieutenants and had moved to the front, his former strength returned for the time being. Where the River-Stream wolves fought, Silversong picked out Frostpaw killing exile after exile on his way to Rime.

Sometime during the battle, the enemy had been pushed back, the majority of their numbers rallying behind Rime. The huge brute had commanded the meadow itself to save them from getting ripped apart by the sentinels. The flowers and roots fused together in a line, growing into a putrid fence hardened by corruption. It withstood anything thrown at it; from licking flames and bludgeoning stones to lashing air and slicing arcs of water, it endured relentless strike after relentless strike.

Rime couldn't contain his laughter. The face in the sky imitated his mad cackling. "It would've been a shame if you'd all died at the Great Chain. The sentinels deserve a much slower end."

Silversong saw disaster coming. He veered off from the corporals and hurried toward the sentinels.

"You'll rot alongside the Fallen Titan for all eternity!" the Warden snarled, her arcs of boiling water cutting at the fence but failing to breach it.

The barrier of thorns and decay widened, and Rime sighed behind it. "Please, Warden, think of something more original to say. I know your decrepit old brain may be addled by the Wolven Code, but that's no excuse for such lazy threats."

The Warden bristled, saliva dripping from her bared fangs. "When I get my fangs on you, I'll squeeze the blood in your veins until your insides pop out from either end."

Rime chuckled as if impressed. "Much better." Thunder rumbled across the sky, and from within the gaping mouth far above came a vicious crackling. "The Fallen Titan sends his regards."

The sentinels dispersed before the barrage of lightning turned them into bloody splatters. Silversong tried not to think about Nimbus. He halted right in front of one of the newly-formed craters, reeling as the ringing in his ears muffled Rime's laughter.

Upon the return of his hearing, Silversong realized he was now among the sentinels. There was a pause in the battle. The stray exiles had retreated to where Rime stood, pouring death into the earth and growing the rotting fence separating them from the Wolven Bulwark. The ugly amalgamation towered over them like a fetid wave, the spaces in its length too small to fit through. At least the elders and the youngsters had managed to flee during the chaos or they would've been confined to the meadow.

Silversong noticed the exiles were all staring at him. He couldn't help but shudder at the hatred in their eyes. Silversong growled. "Where's Ironwrath? Where's he hiding?"

Rime's twisted smile morphed into the beginning of a snarl. "He's been deeply wounded by your betrayal, *little lamb*." He licked his yellowed fangs. "Give him time. I'm sure he'll come around."

All the exiles laughed except for Ripper. "We should've killed you in the Silverhaze Forest. I would've delighted in feeding your body to the spiders."

"Don't forget about me!" Palesquall barked from where the subordinates were assembled. "Your master was too much of a gullwit to execute us, and now look at you! Bruised and humbled! Hah!"

Rime swerved his head in Palesquall's direction, missing him entirely and grinning at Hazel instead. "You're still alive, I see. Guess I'll just have to smash your skull in harder next time."

"Not on my watch," Gorsescratch growled at the same time Silversong barked, "I'll give you more than just a few scars if you go near her again."

Hazel refused to even bare her teeth at the Heretic's lieutenant. Instead, she lifted her head high and glared at him like she would a disgusting maggot unworthy of her insults.

The ground shivered to a continuous thudding sound coming from beyond the hillocks on the far side of the meadow.

"Ma'am?" Greyhail's worried eyes landed on the Warden, but her focus was spent elsewhere. "Ma'am, this quaking isn't us."

The thuds got louder and louder, and the exiles snickered to themselves. Something was wrong. Rime neared his own barricade of death. "I've laboured much these last few days, you see. Testing the limits of my new Blessing is an arduous endeavor, to say the least." All eyes shifted to the hidden source of the rumbling. "Behold! The versatility of the Fallen Titan's corruption!"

"Ma'am!" Greyhail barked more urgently, finally grabbing the Warden's attention. "Something is heading straight for us from up there."

One by one, wolves craned their heads to whatever was making those awful thudding sounds. Anxious as he was, the piece of time only showed Silversong flashes of the horrors to come.

Rime's low growl resonated through the stilled wave of oozing rot. "Never forget the mistake you made by throwing us to the corruption, Warden, for it has led to your undoing."

Over the rise, the monsters charged, hooves beating thunder into the earth as their shrill wails tore into everyone's ears. Silversong bit back a curse. There were dozens upon dozens of them! Deer, moose, and other antlered creatures Silversong hadn't seen before spilled into the meadow, their flesh decayed by the Fallen Titan's touch, their crazed eyes promising to inflict terrible pain on any who stood in their way.

"Stone-Guard sentinels! Barriers! Now!" ordered the Warden.

On command, all sentinels who shared the Blessing of Earth scurried to meet the stampede. If this failed, the Wolven Bulwark would be completely trampled. Silversong uttered a prayer under his breath, and Swiftstorm's bulging eyes locked themselves on Greyhail. Lightning stirred in the mouth of the shadowy fiend above, but before it could strike again, the ground itself thundered, drowning out the stomping of hooves. Out came high pillars of hardened earth. A great number of beasts broke upon them while others exploded through the makeshift barriers only to flatten the poor sentinels who'd erected those obstacles.

"NOW!" Rime barked.

The fence he'd constructed opened in several places to let the exiles through. The enemy tore into Riptide's forces, his lieutenants and corporals giving as good as they got while Amberstorm's soldiers supported them from afar. The subordinates attached condensed lines of wind to their tails and lashed the exiles. The corporals mauled those stunned by the strikes, and the lieutenants unleashed small twisters upon roots and flesh.

Yes! Keep fighting together! We might still have a chance!

Rime joined the fray, the wave of death splitting to let him through as his teeth ripped into his former packmates. Frostpaw released a battle cry and rushed toward him, but Rime jumped back before the young corporal could control his blood like he'd done inside the Mountainmouth.

"Almost had me there." Amusement entered Rime's growl. "Still eager to avenge your mother, I see."

"This is where you die, scatfur," Frostpaw returned the growl, but there was no amusement in his tone.

"An empty threat." The jaws of the Fallen Titan gaped wide, ready to rain vengeance on the descendants of the wolves who'd defeated him long ago. "This is where I killed her, pup. It's only fitting you should die here too."

A faceoff between an exile and a Flame-Heart sentinel blocked him from seeing the unfolding fight. Fire engulfed the air around the sentinel as her breath spewed an even greater spray of flame, leaving her opponent nothing more than a smouldering corpse.

Fear gripped Silversong's heart; he'd lost sight of Frostpaw and Rime. Silversong couldn't let his worries fester. He could only hope his friend would be able to hold his own.

Silversong twirled his tail and conjured a whirling vortex, waiting for the smoke to clear before he unleashed it upon the enemy. The Heretic interrupted Silversong's idea. The leader of the exiles had finally chosen to reveal himself by commanding a block of earth to launch him over the fence, his glowing green eyes fixed and unblinking. A deafening shockwave expanded from where he landed, staggering everyone in the meadow except for the rampaging beasts.

The formations were broken, and any hope for victory was quickly fading. Antlers gored the sentinels brave enough to try and buy the Wolven Bulwark more time. Black tendrils yanked exhausted soldiers to the ground, and the surviving exiles buried their fangs in the wolves still standing while the meadow itself worked against the Warden's army.

Throughout the mayhem, the Heretic only had eyes for Silversong. Ironwrath dodged the projectiles thrown his way, masterfully wielding his Blessing and overpowering the Stone-Guard sentinels who attempted to redirect his launched boulders and compressed missiles of earth. Spikes from the ground impaled the poor wolves who got too close to him. He ran in a straight line, strides swift and certain. The terrain itself erupted in several areas as though announcing his long-awaited arrival. Silversong flexed the piece of time, prepared to squeeze its threads around the Heretic, but the old exile stopped just short of entering the invisible aura.

"You have something of mine, little lamb," Ironwrath stated as if a battle weren't raging around him.

Silversong ducked as an enormous fang of earth zoomed over him, heading straight for the Heretic. It stopped a tail-length from Ironwrath's nose, and without even pausing to take a breath, he returned the chunk at a blinding speed from whence it came. Silversong knocked Greyhail over not a moment too soon. The projectile smashed into the flowers where he'd been standing, sending a shower of debris to blind exile and sentinel alike.

"As I was saying…"

"Come and take it!" Silversong snarled, the weapon within him spinning at an incredible speed. Futures flashed and died in the time it took him to blink. There was still hope for the Wolven Bulwark. All it needed was fuel to feed the fire.

"Look around you, little lamb." The Heretic nodded to the wolves struggling against the exiles and Rime's new twisted servants. "You're losing. You couldn't predict that I would snatch victory out from under you, and you also couldn't predict that Rime would corrupt the Forest Father's creations into mindless monstrosities. The piece of time betrays you. You can't wield it properly, and even if you could, you don't have the strength to assume control of the Four Territories by force. It's the only way to achieve true unity, and you know it. Give me the weapon, and I'll spare you and the lives of your comrades for now."

Silversong almost feared peeking into the future. Relinquishing the piece of time would inevitably lead to Ironwrath's triumph over the Warden and the Wolven Bulwark, but if the Heretic's *perfect future* was built on the bones of wolves Silversong cared about, he could never allow it to flourish.

I'll take the alternate way to peace, Ironwrath. The difficult way. The right way.

Silversong sprinted toward the Heretic. The old exile sighed and commanded the earth to slide him out of the weapon's reach.

Swiftstorm came to Silversong's side as a whistling whirlwind, casting wave after wave of slicing air at the Heretic. The barricades he summoned out of the ground could barely withstand her blows.

The Warden strode in the direction of her nemesis. An orb of water circled her, ready to spring into action. "My old enemy. A clever tactic: using the Fallen Titan's corruption to transform innocent creatures into your foul minions. Your depravity knows no bounds."

"It was Rime's idea," the Heretic grunted from behind his shield of reinforced earth. "You always underestimated his capabilities."

“Aye.” The Warden sighed, her shoulders trembling. “And I’ve paid a heavy price for my mistake, haven’t I?”

“Yes.” Ironwrath’s barrier shook violently. “But you haven’t finished paying yet.”

The thick block of earth hurled itself toward the Warden. Spinning gracefully, she narrowed her orb of water into a line thinner than a spider’s thread. It moved in slashing motions quick as a viper to parry the thrown barrier, reducing it to rubble. The Warden inhaled and brushed a forepaw to the side, the string of liquid death snaking through the air and whipping the Heretic’s forelegs.

Blood sprayed from the Heretic’s deep wounds. He winced at the unforeseen strike and fought to remain standing. The Warden prepared to attack again. Ironwrath growled and erected another earthen shield, this one far stronger than the last.

“Enough hiding!” Swiftstorm intensified the zipping wind around her and jumped high, pulling her forepaws inward to achieve the start of an impressive somersault. The currents of air accumulated at her tail, merging into one massive swirl. Just as she came down, she launched the roaring projectile at the Heretic.

Her attack reduced his shield to clouds of dust. Swiftstorm landed in an elegant fashion, intent on chasing after the leader of the exiles. The Warden stepped in front of her and faced Ironwrath, daring him to make the next move.

“If we are to die today, Heretic,” the Warden growled, her voice a frozen torrent of bitterness, “then we’ll at least make sure you won’t live to see another sunrise.”

Still convinced of his victory, the Heretic called on a small earthquake to further demoralize the Wolven Bulwark. “Unfortunately for you, I plan to enjoy many sunrises beyond this next one.”

A howling in the distant forest reached across the battlefield. Flames danced between the branches. A smell of smoke, a flash of fire, and out of the woods charged wolves of red and brown fur, the air around them igniting as they burned their way through the meadow. Flame-Heart had come to the rescue.

CHAPTER 9

Haunted

The Flame-Heart wolves burned their way ever closer to the fighting, the smoke rising behind them a warning of the destruction to come.

The Heretic sighed almost as though he expected these reinforcements. "I suppose the unnatural storm gave away our location," he muttered to himself.

A quick look at their numbers was enough for him to order a retreat. Silversong saw an opportunity to put an end to the old exile for good. He expanded the threads of time as far as they could reach. Ironwrath predicted the move, and the earth jerked him away at breakneck speed before the weapon's aura could so much as touch him.

Rime cursed and headbutted Frostpaw, pushing him aside. The Heretic's lieutenant silently commanded the tormented beasts to flee into the woods. As the putrid fence of flowers and roots withered away, the lesser exiles broke off from the frontlines and scurried after the abominations. Now only Ironwrath, Rime, and Ripper remained.

"Ripper! Enough!" Rime called out at the forest's edge. The Flame-Heart reinforcements were almost upon them.

Ripper tore out the throat of a River-Stream soldier and turned to run, but the earth itself caught him before he could break into a sprint. Greyhail trapped the exile in place. More Stone-Guard sentinels joined him in his struggle to subdue the thrashing mongrel. Ripper wasn't going anywhere now.

Rime sneered, spitting on the ground and taking off into the forest. Frostpaw got up and charged after the brute, but Snowleap caught her enraged packmate by the tail and yanked him back.

"Don't!" Snowleap hissed through clenched teeth. "We must stick together or they'll pick us off one by one."

Silversong faced Ironwrath again as the Whistle-Wind wolves surrounded the murderer, ready to avenge Wind's Rest. Swiftstorm and the Warden walked confidently in his direction—two hungry wolves closing in on cornered prey.

The threads of Silversong's aura retracted, and Ironwrath steered his focus to Chief Amberstorm and the air swirling chaotically around him. "You look terrible, sir. The breaking of your den and the loss of your mate has clearly taxed your spirit."

"Silence." Amberstorm wouldn't even waste a growl on the likes of the Heretic. "I couldn't save Pinetrail… but I can avenge her death."

"You'll have to wait a little longer, I'm afraid." The Heretic smacked a forepaw on the ground, and a huge block of earth propelled him upward.

"Coward!" the Whistle-Wind wolves cried. They launched sharp slices of air at the leader of the exiles. Some slashed into flesh, but most missed him as he descended in an arc toward the woods, escaping certain death.

"We can still catch him, ma'am." A keen breeze circled Swiftstorm's limbs.

"No," the Warden whined in a solemn tone. "He has the advantage unless we face him in the open. Besides, we have our own wounds to lick."

Silversong howled at the sunless sky, his voice announcing the end of the skirmish. His packmates joined him in declaring the battle won, and the River-Stream wolves also sang their victory even if only to prove they could be louder than their rivals. The face of the Fallen Titan blended into the greying clouds now pouring their sorrow on the ruined meadow. The members of Whistle-Wind who weren't in fighting condition emerged out of the forest away from where the exiles had entered, rejoining their loved ones and waiting for the Flame-Heart wolves to arrive.

It would take a while to count all the dead, and the cries of grief confirmed the casualties were abundant. The Heretic had almost succeeded in ending the Wolven Bulwark.

How?! Why am I so bad at controlling the piece of time? I should've predicted the ambush. I should've forced the Wolven Bulwark to fight together!

The faces of his friends, his parents, calmed him a little, but he couldn't shake off the disappointment in himself; it threatened to beat him into the ground.

He caught Frostpaw looking at him from where the River-Stream wolves gathered, his eyes carrying the weight of failing to bring a murderer to justice. Even now Silversong was powerless to comfort a dear friend. He wanted so badly to be at Frostpaw's side, to be close to the one who'd been there for him inside the Mountainmouth, but he couldn't. He wanted to scream his lungs out, but he couldn't. He could do nothing but wait for the Heretic to make his next move.

Rain trickled through Silversong's fur and dripped to the ground in bloody droplets. He shook off the remaining pieces of Nimbus still sticking to him and closed his eyes. Futures swirled in the threads, branching to different ends and sputtering out as quickly as they'd appeared. Nothing was ever certain. He opened his eyes to this truth.

"Sentinels! To me!" the Warden ordered, her soldiers falling in line to face the Flame-Heart wolves who slowed to a trotting pace, their coats sprouting fire. "Keep the prisoner still."

"Yes, ma'am." Greyhail growled at Ripper, who continued to thrash like a salmon out of water. "He's stronger than he looks. I can't maintain his shackles forever. Subdue him!"

One by one, River-Stream and Whistle-Wind wolves approached the exile and bit him all over until he could do nothing but wail in pain. Silversong cringed, looking away and shaking his head. He pointed his ears forward to lower the volume of Ripper's yowling.

The leader of the Flame-Heart contingent stepped forward, his carapace of fire dying to the rain. The protective flames of those under his command all snuffed themselves out in unison. "Warden. We came as soon as we saw the unnatural lightning. Chief Ashenfall has put me in charge of the patrol units here, and by Motherwolf, I'll incinerate the exiles wherever they choose to hide."

The wolves behind him barked the name *Flame-Heart*, the pride and passion in their burning eyes hotter than any fire. Although they were smaller in size, the sheer ferocity in their voices divulged their true strength.

"Who are you, soldier?" the Warden inquired.

Silversong leaned in to listen just as the patrol leader grunted, "my name is Lieutenant Blazefur, and I am at your service, ma'am." He sleeked his reddish coat, and the determined frown over his brown eyes deepened. The wolves he led dipped their heads to the Warden, tails hanging low.

"I thank you for your timely arrival, sir." The Warden briefly touched her nose to his. "We couldn't have held out for much longer despite our obvious advantage."

Shame glued Silversong to the mud, and he stared off to the side knowing the eyes of all sentinels were on him.

Blazefur's attention was instead drawn to the captured exile forced to the ground by the weight of several wolves pressing on him. "Ah, I see you've got yourselves a prisoner." He approached Ripper, eyes lighting up in recognition.

Everyone parted to let Blazefur through. He stood over the former Flame-Heart member. "I remember your scent and your face, exile. My, have you fallen low since you walked among us."

Ripper spat in Blazefur's face.

The wolves around the exile forced him down by sinking their teeth in whatever exposed flesh they could find. Ripper yowled and squirmed, but his torture had only just begun. Frostpaw's father rushed toward the exile and placed a forepaw on his face. Ripper convulsed and squealed as one of his eyes boiled in its socket. Silversong's mouth turned sour, and his insides twisted themselves into tight knots. His previous meal surged up his throat, but he forced it back into his stomach. The sounds Ripper made were sharp enough to shatter ice.

A bubbling line of melted gel leaked down Ripper's cheek, singeing his fur. The smell was almost as awful as the exile's shrieks. Frostpaw's father ignored the spasms of his victim. "Now, onto your other eye."

"STOP!" Silversong barked so loud it startled many of the wolves around him. "He's already beaten. There's no use torturing him."

The cruel lieutenant took his forepaw off the exile's face, but his angry expression remained. He made sure all the Whistle-Wind wolves could clearly see the wavy mud markings on his bluish fur. "I should've known you would express sympathy for the enemy. You are, after all, the code-breaker who corrupted my son."

"No one corrupted me," Frostpaw grunted harshly, though his constant trembling betrayed his confidence. "My choices were my own."

His siblings all rounded on him, hurling insults and other obscenities his way. Silversong growled under his breath and padded to Frostpaw's side. The corporal's eyes darted in all directions, searching for an escape.

"Don't," Silversong whined into his ear. "I'm here for you."

Frostpaw froze. His brothers and sisters stopped antagonizing him, their hatred instead drawn to Silversong.

"Get away from him." Frostpaw's father crouched and prepared to pounce on Silversong.

"Why?" Silversong challenged the lieutenant's glare. "You don't treat him like he's your son. Why do you care who stands beside him?"

"I've had enough of this!" Saliva dripped from the lieutenant's bared fangs. "Get away from him before I boil *your* eyes out instead!"

For the first time, Frostpaw stood up to his father without fear. He frowned and stepped between his kin and Silversong, breathing heavily.

"Don't even think about it." Amberstorm crept through the crowd to defend his corporal in case a fight broke out. Gorsescratch licked his teeth, and the other Whistle-Wind wolves rallied behind their leader.

Chief Riptide snarled at Amberstorm, encouraging his underlings to join his example.

"This has gone far enough," the Warden declared, her sentinels putting themselves between the Whistle-Wind and River-Stream members. "Darkwave, stand down."

Frostpaw's father bowed his head reluctantly and edged away from Ripper.

"Silversong," the Warden's low whine sparked an uneasy chill. "Rejoin your packmates. Now."

As Silversong distanced himself from Frostpaw, he heard Riptide whine, "you see, ma'am? He's untrustworthy. He thinks he can ignore the Wolven Code because of the weapon he wields."

"You must take the piece of time from him," Icetail added more fervently.

"Be silent," the Warden ordered, waiting for Silversong to return to the Whistle-Wind side.

Silversong shuddered once he stood among his packmates. He failed to remain steady as his parents licked his face, as his friends nuzzled him. He'd done all he could for Ripper. An exile he may be, but no one deserved such torment. Silversong took in the resentful looks of the River-Stream wolves. The Wolven Bulwark was fracturing after only one attack from the Heretic. How could a union between the Four Territories hope to stand strong when prejudice so easily threatened to knock it over?

We're united in name only for the moment. If the Warden had allowed us all to fight as one from the start, the skirmish might've resulted in a decisive victory for the Wolven Bulwark! Surely the others see this. Surely this is enough for them to at least start questioning the Warden's authority.

Blazefur watched the intrigue in silence and wetted his lips.

The Warden squinted at Ripper, the disgust on her face worsening the longer she stared. "We'll take the prisoner to Thornhollow and question him there. If he cooperates, I'll see about allowing him a quick death."

Ripper's whimpering turned into mad laughter.

Blazefur scoffed and padded to where his fighters stood. "Ma'am. Allow us to escort you to our den after the dead are given their proper rites."

The Warden's eyes scanned the fallen wolves ranging from River-Stream rookies who'd had their whole lives ahead of them to lieutenants who'd still been in their prime to exiles already luring in flies and other insects that feasted on death. "I'm afraid there's no time to commemorate those who gave their lives for the Four Territories today, but their sacrifices shall forever be remembered. Lead us to Thornhollow, sir."

"As you command." Blazefur signaled for his subordinates to aid the injured while the strong and capable formed a perimeter around the weak. Some needed their wounds cauterized, and their cries of pain echoed across the scarred meadow.

The stench of scorched fur and dried blood would've been bad enough without the reek of rot stinging Silversong's nostrils. He doubted he would ever forget the stink of this battlefield. The crows seemed unbothered by it as they shamelessly gorged on the dead.

"Can't they at least wait until we're gone?" Hazel glared at the scavengers pecking at fallen Whistle-Wind soldiers.

"Crows have no shame, Hazel." Palesquall reserved a look of disgust for those digging their beaks into the decayed flesh of one of Rime's slain abominations. "And no meal is too foul for them."

Cracks of daylight spidered through clouds relieved of rain. The strong aroma of damp earth brought a fleeting comfort to Silversong's nose, and when all wolves were accounted for, the Wolven Bulwark departed into the red forest, tails facing the dipping sun.

Silversong walked among the Whistle-Wind wolves under the white trees reaching feebly for the sky. None of them were particularly large, but their blooming crowns made up for their lack of height. He would've been impressed had their leaves not mimicked the deep crimson of blood—a reminder of the skirmish still fresh in his memory. His head slumped below his shoulders, and the weapon within him shuddered. The threads showed him the inevitability of the attack, but not how he could've overcome it: the Warden never would've allowed two rival territories to become one, even in the face of death. Some things, it seemed, were fated no matter the choices he made.

This is ridiculous. Why can't you be more useful?! He realized he was baring his teeth and controlled himself. He peered into the threads in hopes of catching a glimpse of events to come.

Palesquall squeezed through the corporals until he walked beside Silversong. "Hey."

Silversong licked his friend in greeting. "Hey. How're you holding up?"

"I'm surviving. It's all I can do, right? At least I wasn't kidnapped this time." Palesquall chuckled, but his raised fur gave away his anxiety. "I'm just happy I'm still alive. I'm happy you're alive too."

Silversong smiled. He was so lucky to have Palesquall as a friend. Hazel too. "Yeah. I guess it could've been much worse. Just don't go dying on me in the next battle, eh?"

"No promises." Palesquall looked straight ahead. "The Chief seems to be doing better."

Silversong studied Amberstorm from a distance. Although he still appeared gaunt and somewhat malnourished, he now strode like a leader again, tail up and head above shoulders. "I think he's finally realizing he still has a pack to protect." Silversong glanced at the subordinates behind him. "How's Hazel? I only saw her briefly after the skirmish."

"She's the one who asked me to check on you," Palesquall admitted. "She's more worried about you than anyone else, and I don't blame her. I saw how the sentinels were eyeing you after the Heretic escaped. It's like they're just waiting for the Warden's command to rip the piece of time out of your belly. You don't think she would actually give the order… do you?"

Silversong surveyed the Warden at the front of the formation, her white fur sleek as she spoke to Swiftstorm, no doubt trying to poison her against him. The golden circle confirmed the Warden was a temporary ally at best. If he wasn't careful, she could be the end of him. "I think it's unwise to assume she has any limits. For now, though, she needs Whistle-Wind on her side. She won't jeopardize the Wolven Bulwark by killing me for the piece of time unless I give her a lawful excuse to do so."

Palesquall frowned in consideration, but before he could say anything else, Gorsescratch bit him on the tail. "Get back to your position, subordinate!"

Palesquall grimaced, but obeyed his superior and returned to Hazel. She watched intently from where she walked, her green eyes a welcome sight amid all this deep red. Silversong offered her a short nod and a subtle smile. No matter the future he stumbled into, he would ensure she always had a place in it.

The day dimmed into an orange evening by the time the Warden decided her army needed a break. The huge formation broke off into separate groups depending on which territory they served, lounging and resting among square-shaped pillars poking out of the yellow bracken. Lieutenants organized hunting parties, and off they stalked to feed the assembly of wolves. Prey was abundant here judging by the fresh droppings and deep hoofprints impressed in the earth. Hungry bellies wouldn't have to wait much longer to be filled.

A troubling thought wormed into his brain. More prey meant more potential monsters for Rime.

Silversong dared to let his eyes close under the stretching shadow of a thick outcrop, his racing thoughts slowing to a more reasonable speed. A gruff voice chased away any notion of sleep.

"Greetings. The Warden says you're the one who swallowed the piece of time."

Silversong opened his eyes to Blazefur standing between Shadowgale and another Whistle-Wind lieutenant. Silversong rolled onto all fours just as his father grunted, "Lieutenant Blazefur wanted to meet you. Chief Amberstorm allowed him through."

A twitch in Blazefur's face indicated he noticed the aura of time encompassing him.

You're a perceptive one, aren't you? Silversong peered into the threads surrounding the Flame-Heart lieutenant, picking out two contrasting fates. In one, the Heretic ripped into Blazefur's throat while he guarded the entrance to his den. In the other, he stepped up as a leader revered by all who served him. Silversong allowed his body to be inspected by Blazefur's nose. Silversong expressed no such interest in the newcomer.

"I would like to speak to him alone," Blazefur chuffed in a casual tone.

"Out of the question," Shadowgale responded sharply.

"It's fine, father," Silversong insisted. "I'm not a pup anymore."

Shadowgale exhaled through his nose. "Sometimes I forget that, but if you're sure, I'll respect your choice." He gave Blazefur a suspicious stare. "Come find us when you're done talking to my son and we'll escort you back to your pack."

"As you wish." Blazefur flicked his tail up and invited Silversong to inspect him out of formality. Silversong stayed where he was, and when the Whistle-Wind lieutenants were out of earshot, Blazefur grunted, "he seems like a good father. It's more than I can say for mine."

"Why're you here?" Silversong tensed the threads around the reddish lieutenant who bristled upon feeling the unseen force. Silversong released him, satisfied at the damage done to Blazefur's confidence. "I'm a bit tired, so you'll have to explain yourself quickly."

"I'm here because you failed to predict the Heretic's attack today." He regained most of his composure, though his tail now twitched uncomfortably. "I think it's best if you—"

"Surrendered the piece of time to the Warden?" Silversong flexed the weapon, causing Blazefur to backpedal in shock. "You've come because the Warden convinced you I'm not worthy of this power. Don't deny it. I won't fault you for falling for her arguments, but if I give her the weapon, we'll become nothing more than mindless drones who think only of obeying the Wolven Code. Every waking thought, every dream, consumed by a desire to worship the Warden's doctrine. I promise you, I won't—"

"—stop using the weapon until the beasts rot in the ground alongside their masters!" Galdreth scolded the poor Forgotten One in front of him. "Is every Northerner a superstitious fool who refuses to seize an opportunity when it presents itself beneath his very nose? Where's Aelrion? Where's this *Crownless King* of yours? You must bring him to me."

The lesser Forgotten One covered in a thick but intricate fabric stepped away from Galdreth, away from the weapon inside him. In this unnatural room of carved stone and wood entirely too smooth to have belonged to any tree, every sound resonated louder than it should've. "He's… he's held up in the Grimfort. It's been under siege since almost the beginning of the war. He may not be a true Northerner, but mountains crush me if he isn't the leader we need in a time like this. After the Highlords were killed, the beasts have thirsted for King Aelrion's blood. The Mother of all Wolves especially."

"They've thirsted for mine too, but they've failed despite their advantage." Galdreth's brown eyes wandered above the one facing him. Even though Silversong's consciousness was confined to the golden circle, through a glassy opening in the room he saw familiar structures surrounded by great trees. "They wanted to slaughter the best of us at the start of their invasion. However, humanity's luck prevailed against fate."

"So it seems, Your Majesty." Beads of water formed on the smaller one's face despite the lack of moisture anywhere, and he brushed a forepaw through his neat black mane. "Still, luck is a fickle mistress. Any moment the tides may shift, and I feel as though they already have. The primitives from the Stormlands have taken up arms against us. Two of the three tribes have given themselves over to the *Great Deer* I keep hearing so much about. As we speak, our southern border is beset upon by those uncivilized savages. I'll wager you ran into some of them on your way here."

Wrinkles formed on Galdreth's forehead. "Your king, Aelrion, has Stormlander blood running through his veins, does he not? Strange of you to insult his people no matter how misguided you think they may be. Moreover, I hear the Chieftain of the Cloudfoots has joined humanity's resistance against the beasts."

More droplets of water appeared on the lesser Forgotten One's face. He lifted his forepaws to shake them from side to side. An odd gesture. "I meant no offense to the Crownless King. I just can't fathom why anyone would betray their own kind."

"Perhaps they see this war as retribution for how they were treated by the Northern Kingdom. This continent is small, but not so small that two different nations can't share it. Traitors to their own kind the Stormlanders may be, but so are we all in a sense. How many crimes have we committed against our own species in the name of greed or because one group thought themselves better than another? My line is notorious for its conquest of nations less powerful than it." Galdreth rubbed the curly hair sticking out around his mouth. "Perhaps this is the very nature of humanity. Perhaps it can't be helped."

He lifted his eyes to the roof of the unnatural chamber while the other Forgotten One stared on in confusion. Galdreth gave an empty chuckle. "But why should it matter if we're not the noblest of creatures? We claimed this planet, and it's ours to either cherish or tarnish. The beasts seek to upend the true order of things."

"Indeed." The lesser Forgotten One nodded, avoiding Galdreth's eyes. "As I was saying… the pressure on the southern border is relentless, and every time a wildgod leads an attack against one of our strongholds, our numbers suffer as does our faith. The Great Deer—"

"I've encountered this *Great Deer* of yours before, although he wasn't so *great* last I saw him." A satisfied smile stretched Galdreth's pink lips. "Leaped right into my trap and wailed like babe when I killed his galloping friend. These wildgods aren't invincible. Aelrion must be brought before me so we can form a proper counteroffensive. You Northerners have lasted long on your own, but you can't endure forever. It's time to change the strategy."

"Your Majesty," the nameless Forgotten One lowered his head and removed a strand of black hair from his eye, "I'm grateful for the aid you offer. We've put the foreigners who joined your caravan to good use, and your journey here must've been no less perilous than our defense against the beasts, but the only reason we Northerners have lasted this long is because of Aelrion—King

Aelrion—and you intend for him to desert his post so he can answer your summons? Where's the strategy in this request?"

"Listen carefully. I've travelled far from my kingdom to the south all because of a vision I had. A vision I induced through relentless study of the piece of time." Galdreth stepped toward the submissive Forgotten One, forepaws locked behind his back. "Go to the Grimfort and retrieve Aelrion. Convince him to meet me in the Underground City of Brëargathand. I've already ordered my subjects there. Together, we can vanquish our doom. You must trust me not because I'm some foreign king from a foreign land, but because I'm your fellow man, and I fight for humanity itself. Victory is possible if the correct circumstances are met, and I'm doing my best to meet them. Now, do you intend to keep fighting a losing battle? Or shall you become a vital instrument that brings this war closer to its end?"

The would-be messenger recovered from his shock, his steady blue eyes staring at Galdreth almost in awe. "There're many passageways out of the Grimfort… but I doubt he'll abandon his soldiers because of a mere vision you had. Especially one conjured by this… *piece of time*."

"That's why it has to be you." Galdreth's eyes seemed to glitter. "You've known him since he was an orphan on the streets. You watched as the Steelsworn Brotherhood trained him in the art of combat. He raised you to nobility upon the High Council's dissolvement. You helped him become the man he is today. The piece of time has shown me more than just the future, you see. Aelrion trusts your judgment. Bring him to me in the Underground City. It's the only way we can avoid our extinction. Leave now and suffer no rest until your task is done. Time is of the essence."

Silversong's vision blurred out of focus, and upon blinking again, he found himself staring into confused brown eyes. He looked every which way, pressing his forepaws into the earth to confirm he'd indeed returned to the present. The cool touch of the ground helped soothe his disorientation. Forcing in a deep breath, he tried to lower his thumping heartbeat.

"You were saying…?" Blazefur tilted his head, his wariness exposed by his crouched posture and quivering tail.

Silversong blinked again and bit back a growl. "We're done here. You can inform the Warden she can come see me herself next time rather than send a lackey to relay her wishes."

Blazefur's lips lifted to display his teeth. He looked around at the vigilant Whistle-Wind wolves and thought better of showing aggression. He sniffed in contempt and strode toward Shadowgale. Silversong rolled over and frowned at the now clear sky.

"Why is this happening to me?" he asked expecting no answer, and although fatigue tempted him to slide into a quick nap, he knew his dreams would bring him straight to Aelrion. The last leader of the Forgotten Ones haunted him from the past, and he wouldn't relent for as long as the golden circle turned.

Even when the hunting parties returned carrying an abundance of prey, Silversong remained where he was, fear crushing his hunger. Maybe he wasn't cut out for this after all. Maybe he should relinquish the piece of time to someone more deserving. But who could he give it to? Certainly not the Warden.

As evening light faded, so too did his resolve to stay awake, and when slumber finally claimed victory, his dreams delivered him directly to Aelrion.

CHAPTER 10

The Prisoner

Night had fallen when the Warden's orders reached everyone's ears. The Wolven Bulwark would journey to the Flame-Heart den under the moon and stars.

Silversong finished licking the blood off a thick bone and padded to where Ripper was being confined, the blue-grey moonbeams filtering through the forest roof. If the exile could be persuaded into renouncing the Heretic, he could disclose some valuable information regarding Ironwrath's movements. The piece of time was a good tool when it came to raw power, but the future was always a guessing game, and every choice added more possibilities to the already overflowing range of outcomes. When others had used the weapon, it had been in a much stronger state, its capabilities close to boundless, but now its threads were strained due to excessive use and the cruel touch of entropy. Still, Silversong saw himself amending these broken packs; he saw himself triumphant over two enemies who each had a different way of destroying the Four Territories.

He closed his eyes for a moment, and upon opening them again, he realized he'd stepped into a past reflection of this place. Pillars stretched their white lengths to rival the height of the moon, and the surrounding structures flaunted a glossy light stolen from the stars above. Everywhere he looked, constructions more impressive than the last demanded admiration, all of them promising to leave an imprint on history… all of them lost to time, forgotten like yesterday's sunrise.

Another pace took him back to the present. He stopped in front of Greyhail and Swiftstorm. The pair frowned at him like he had no business being here.

Silversong forced a neutral expression on his face. "I'm here to see Ripper. I may be able to extract some useful information from him."

Swiftstorm showed him nothing but doubt. "Since when are you an interrogator, Silversong?"

He maintained a stiff posture. "He's more likely to speak to me willingly. Ripper is one of the first exiles I encountered after leaving Wind's Rest. He even agreed to introduce me to the Heretic. We have somewhat of a history."

"Forgive me, but you've been worrying me very much lately." Swiftstorm shifted her weight to release some tension from her shoulders. Greyhail displayed no emotion at all. "Your time among the exiles has clouded your judgment. You don't respect the Wolven Code as you once did. The piece of time won't save you from the Warden's wrath if you stray too far from the light, brother. There's still time to repent."

"You don't trust me." A sour lump formed in Silversong's throat. "Did the Warden *convince* you not to trust me?"

Greyhail added his unwelcome voice to the discussion. "The Warden is known for her wisdom, and she too is worried about you. She sees the wolves of the Four Territories as her children. When a pup misbehaves, their behaviour must be corrected, no? You're no exception, Silversong."

"She can confront me herself if she thinks I'm *misbehaving*." Silversong hoped the restless flicking of his tail conveyed impatience. "Now, may I speak to the prisoner? You've nothing to lose and all to gain. If Ripper knows where the Heretic made his den, we can harass him and goad him into a fight he'll lose."

Greyhail and Swiftstorm shared a concerned look before letting Silversong pass into the bustle of sentinels preparing for the departure. He zigzagged his way across the enclave, taking care not to bump into anyone. The less attention he attracted, the better. Ripper was being guarded by two Stone-Guard sentinels at the far end of the encampment some distance away from the rival packs. The ground gripped the exile's paws tightly, and his legs trembled as if they'd been forced to stand for a long while. His wounds hadn't been licked at all. Dried blood crusted his fur, and the ugly trail caused by his melted eyeball still smelled foul.

Silversong couldn't help but feel pity for Ripper. The sentinels holding him certainly shared no love for the exile judging by the newer bite wounds puncturing the more sensitive spots of his mangled body. Silversong tried to mimic the untroubled expression of the jailors. "Swiftstorm and Greyhail allowed me through. I'm here to see the prisoner."

"You saw him," one of the guards grunted. "Now be on your way."

Silversong wasn't sure if this was Stone-Guard humour or if the sentinel was serious. "May I speak to him alone?"

"No," the other guard grunted without emotion.

"Not alone," her partner muttered in the same tone.

Ripper's good eye lifted itself to Silversong, then flicked between his captors.

"Fine. Stay here then." The unseen threads wrapped around the two sentinels faster than a viper's lunge, constricting their entire bodies and freezing them in place. From the minuscule particles of light to the very air Silversong breathed, all of it flowed around the guards like a river parting around a pair of boulders. The sentinels disappeared. Only their featureless, pure black shapes remained. He'd secured the threads too tightly. In a panic, Silversong loosened his grasp on the outer layers of their bodies, and thankfully they reappeared, but were still utterly incapable of moving or perceiving the passage of time. They wouldn't remember their confinement when Silversong released them.

Ripper gasped and squirmed in place. Silversong clasped the exile's limbs in the threads before he could free himself from the earth imprisoning him. "What trickery is this? What've you done?"

"The same thing I did to the other exiles who tried their luck with me during your failed ambush." Silversong barricaded his uncertainty behind a calm demeanor.

"It wasn't really a *failed ambush*, was it now?" Ripper's snarl morphed into a toothy smirk. "Looks like it had the effect we wanted."

"Which is?"

"Fear." The exile tried in vain to break the threads binding him, his upper body pushing uselessly against the immovable force. "Look around you, gullwit. You all thought you had us beaten. You thought we would just give up our righteous cause because of one little setback. No. You've only emboldened us. You're our prey, and we'll keep hunting you until the Four Territories surrender to Ironwrath. I can smell the tension in the air. None of you trust each other. Your so-called allies are losing faith in you, Silversong. They're all starting to see you for the confused pup you are."

"You're wrong." Silversong's hackles rose against his best efforts to keep them down. He buried his worries about the exile being right and feigned disinterest in Ripper's taunts. "You'll see. I'll unite the Four Territories my way, and when I do, Ironwrath won't survive long against our combined might. Day by day I get better at controlling the piece of time. Soon I'll be able to predict every move your master makes. You may think us afraid and distrustful of one another, but our spirits remain steadfast, and your attack today only fueled our desire to see the Heretic dead."

Ripper coughed up a raspy laugh. "You're hilarious. If you think the wolves of the Four Territories can be allies for more than a few days without ripping each other's throats out, then you're dumb enough to chase your own tail. The Wolven Code is nestled too deep in their heads, and it needs to be yanked out by force! Ironwrath could've done it swiftly, but you sabotaged him before he could deliver us to salvation. Now we all suffer because of you."

"And I would sabotage him again!" Silversong growled through gritted teeth. "Ironwrath would've brought death and destruction to all packs until we submitted to him. He would've used violence to force the change we need. I won't. I'll play the long game and unite the Four Territories by showing them how strong we can be as a single force. I won't destroy the Wolven Code. I'll amend it."

Ripper's empty eye socket twitched, and his snarl returned. "You're insufferable. Why the master spared you, I'll never understand."

"Where is he, Ripper?" Silversong gave his best growl, feeling it rumble out of his throat. "Which piece of Flame-Heart Territory does he infect?"

Ripper broke from Silversong's bulging eyes, tail slowly curling under his belly. "He doesn't stay in one place for too long. You'll never find him."

Useless information!

Silversong chose a different strategy, covering his fangs and lowering his quivering tail. "It's not too late for you to change, Ripper." Silversong squinted at the potential futures flashing above the exile. Some were difficult to make out, but others were clear as the stars. "You can help me secure a better future for us all."

Ripper scoffed. "I'll never help the Four Territories."

"I asked you to help me, not the Four Territories." Silversong held Ripper's questioning glare, their noses almost touching. "You must understand that I'm not on the Warden's side. To me she's as much of a menace as Ironwrath is, and she'll need to be removed from power before I can mend the animosity between the packs."

Ripper quirked his head to one side, his good eye widening. "And you think you can overthrow the Warden without violence?"

"There might be some violence." Regret stained Silversong's voice. There was no point being unrealistic. "But if I can get all the packs on my side… if I can convince them the Warden is no good for our cause, if I can remove her from power lawfully, then I'll have achieved my goal."

Ripper's face lit up for a moment, but his head quickly sagged below his shoulders. "You should go back to your packmates. We're leaving soon by the looks of it."

Silversong eyed the sentinels padding about the enclave and listened to the hubbub of whines and grunts. Disappointment heavy in his heart, he turned to the prisoner. "I wish you would see reason, Ripper. Ask yourself if the gruesome death awaiting you at Thornhollow is a worthy price to pay for staying loyal to a master who would discard you like a bone without a second thought."

Before Silversong could release the sentinels trapped in time, Ripper muttered, "what really happened to Bonechew?"

Silversong tilted his head sideways. It seemed an age ago when his unlikely saviour had rescued him from the Empress of Spiders and her seductive whispers. He cringed at the memory of frozen water spikes penetrating deep into Bonechew's flesh. "We fought in the Songwoods, and Frostpaw killed him. He died quickly."

Ripper frowned and released a hot wave of air from his nostrils. He spoke no more.

Silversong distanced himself from the exile and released the two Stone-Guard sentinels caught in time, finding it slightly amusing how they panicked upon realizing they'd lost control over the earth keeping the prisoner bound.

When Ripper was fettered to the ground again, Silversong untied the threads around the exile's limbs and blinked innocently at the two suspicious guards. "Actually, I have nothing to say to the prisoner. I'll be heading back now. Try not to tire yourselves out."

The jailors exchanged puzzled looks as Silversong strolled away from them.

I wonder if they'll ever figure it out.

The piece of time vibrated, sending an awful premonition: he was drowning, but there was no water around him, only air that wouldn't enter his lungs.

The trees closed in on him much like they had in the Silverhaze Forest, but when he looked around, they hadn't moved in the slightest. An overwhelming pressure squeezed his chest. He gasped for air, brain spinning, heart lurching. In the confusion, he spotted a pair of pale eyes piercing into his soul. He focused on them, vision narrowing on the Warden who studied him from a distance. The horrible sensation ended, and he sucked in a massive breath.

Silversong locked his gaze to the forest floor and distanced himself from the Warden. Paying no mind to the skeptical looks thrown his way, he moved toward his friends and family, where the eyes of the surrounding wolves mirrored the gentle light of the climbing moon. He noticed Frostpaw and Snowleap whining to one another where the River-Stream members gathered. They seemed to be getting rather close.

Silversong shook his head and hoped Snowleap would at least keep Frostpaw in good company during the journey to the Flame-Heart den.

They're nothing more than friends, Silversong reassured himself as he entered the Whistle-Wind enclave to be greeted by his Chief. Silversong lowered his tail and assumed a respectful stance.

"Corporal," Amberstorm acknowledged him, and for all those scars and unseen wounds, the Chief gave off the impression of a solid leader renewed by hope. "Are you ready?"

"As I'll ever be, sir." Silversong took in every packmate watching the Chief from the youngest rookie to the most revered lieutenant. They were waiting for something—anything—to animate their resolve.

Amberstorm finally caught on. "Whatever happens at Thornhollow, just know that I'm so proud of you all. We survived the Heretic's attack on our home. We survived the mistreatment from the River-Stream wolves, and we'll survive the fires of Flame-Heart all the same. The winds of change are blowing strong. Not just for us, but for all packs. If we're to overcome the challenges we've yet to face, we'll need to cast aside the differences keeping us apart from our allies. I believe in Silversong's vision. Only by working together can we save the Four Territories!"

There were some cheers, and there were some uncertain voices who joined them. The more fundamentalist types stayed silent. Going against the Wolven Code was still a new and frightening concept to most, even if it was for a good cause. They would come around eventually. Drastic times always gave rise to drastic changes.

"Riveting speech, eh?" Palesquall joked beside Hazel, coaxing a smile out of Silversong.

"Yeah." Hazel's tail swished from side to side, the pride in her eyes brighter than all the stars. "Looks like our Chief is officially back!"

"How'd you manage it, Silversong?" asked Palesquall.

The question caught Silversong off guard. "Huh?"

"Come on." Palesquall grinned. "We know you did something. Some time-magic-thingy, maybe?"

Silversong laughed. "If only it were that easy. No, it was all Chief Amberstorm. I just… reminded him that he still has a pack to run, is all."

"How simple." Palesquall faked a yawn. "And BORING! I'll stick to believing you did a time-magic-thingy to him."

"All right, you caught me," Silversong jested.

"Knew it!" Palesquall yipped.

Hazel shook her head and nudged them both playfully.

The moon reached its zenith, and the Wolven Bulwark marched through the woods again, noses pointed to where the sun would rise. Instead of being idle, Silversong used this time to pass on his concerns about the Warden to the other corporals, trying to influence the way their loyalties swung. If the piece of time had shown him the folly in blindly following the Warden, who were they to argue? Soon the entire pack heard whispers about the sentinels and how they would lead the Four Territories astray if their authority wasn't challenged.

Futures branched out like tangled vines, each one leading to a different end. He knew the choices he'd made today would affect all wolfkind for ages to come. Though Ripper's allegiance was still in question, Silversong seemed to have successfully wounded the Warden's grasp on Whistle-Wind.

Fatigue tugged at his bones by the time they came to the edge of the forest. A massive field of short grass leaned away from the breeze and pointed toward an obsidian spire silhouetted against the starry night. Its shape resembled a huge stalagmite, its edges stark and uneven. From here it looked like something sharp had clawed out an empty black space from the ground to the sky. How anyone could claim such an ugly thing for a den was beyond him. In the shadows of his thoughts, Silversong saw the hideous formation yielding to the hungry earth while wolves scrambled to flee from the collapse. Was this a potential danger he needed to counter?

Can the Heretic even cause an earthquake powerful enough to shatter this enormous structure? Would he dare? If he destroys the Flame-Heart den, he'll have so few wolves to dominate afterwards. No. The casualties would be too much even for him.

Silversong considered a troubling possibility. *Unless he's pushed to the absolute limit.*

Blazefur came up from behind the Warden and howled, "welcome to Thornhollow! Chief Ashenfall eagerly awaits your arrival."

The golden circle pulsed to the swift rhythm of Silversong's heartbeat. The Four Territories would either unite or succumb to their differences here. Silversong would have to steer them in the right direction. Away from the Warden. Away from the Wolven Code.

"Here's where the real battle begins," Silversong whispered to himself as he followed the others toward the giant spire splitting the night in two.

CHAPTER 11

Thornhollow

The closer Silversong came to the spire, the more it dominated everything around it—a great shadow glowering over a weed-ridden field. Wolves atop the height howled to announce the arrival of the Wolven Bulwark, and soon Silversong was walking on the smooth surface of the den as a narrow pathway funneled the army up and up and up.

He noticed Flame-Heart scouts surveying the new arrivals from atop platforms jutting out over the main road. Considering how cramped everyone was, it would be nothing short of suicide if the Heretic decided to attack the den in a conventional manner. Thornhollow indeed lived up to its expectations.

The sleek ground should've brought comfort to sore pads, but it only accentuated the pain, and the continuous clink of claws dizzied Silversong as much as the wafting miasma of mingled scents. Relief flooded through him when the narrow pathway opened into the first level of the den. The distorted reflection of the stars lit the flattened surface, and judging by the spots of dried blood and scattered heaps of ripped fur, this seemed to be some kind of training area. Sharp outgrowths of obsidian enclosed the space now hosting a dozen more Flame-Heart wolves, led by a male whose coat was black as soot. The brown fur marking his belly and throat reminded Silversong of a cattail.

An interesting contrast.

"Bleaksmoke." Blazefur greeted his packmate as an equal, tail raised. "I saw the Warden's army safely through the Fireleaf Forest. The exiles ambushed them in the Twilight Meadow, and they've suffered heavy losses. If we hadn't been there, I fear the Heretic might've won."

"That's no good," Bleaksmoke whined in a nonchalant manner as if he were discussing the weather. He tasted the air and licked his lips. "That's no good at all."

"Where's Chief Ashenfall?" the Warden grunted firmly, tail unwavering.

"Mother is waiting for you up at the top… ma'am." Bleaksmoke's smile showed a few teeth too many, and his orange eyes inspired no sense of hospitality. "I'll take you to her."

Silversong walked over to Gorsescratch and whispered in his ear, "I'm going to check on my friends for a bit."

Gorsescratch glared straight ahead before giving a reluctant nod. Silversong padded over to Hazel and Palesquall just as the Wolven Bulwark moved into a darkened tunnel barely wide enough to accommodate four wolves standing shoulder to shoulder. Little openings were sometimes hollowed out here and there, barely large enough for the slim and supple to squeeze through.

"I don't like this place," Palesquall murmured, his fur sticking up like quills.

"Me neither," Hazel admitted. "It's like we're walking on solid night. Something about this stone isn't right." She scratched the obsidian and grimaced. "It makes no sound."

At the front, Blazefur looked at the three of them over his shoulder. Surely he was too far away to hear their comments, though.

"I agree." Silversong inhaled, ash and withered smoke saturating the air. The pathway abruptly became a ledge overlooking a steep and spiky descent. The wolves closest to it shuffled fearfully away.

"Watch your step." Bleaksmoke giggled loud enough for Silversong to hear it.

"That one isn't right in the head," Palesquall remarked.

Hazel scoffed. "Look who's yapping."

"I'm more right in the head than either of you!" Palesquall lifted his tail and smacked the subordinate behind him in the face. "Sorry!" he blurted out.

"Oh, yeah?" Silversong shouldered his friend teasingly.

"Yeah! Don't act like you never dreamed up a whole scenario where Gorsescratch sabotaged your promotion." Palesquall nudged him a little harder. "And you have to be completely crazy to pretend you're loyal to the Heretic only to snatch his prize from right under his nose."

"You don't believe I was sabotaged?" Silversong's ears dropped, and it took more effort to keep up the pace.

"Silversong…" Hazel began, "Moonwhisper told us all about the medicine she and Mistyfur fed you. The concoction is likely to create false memories that seem real. Now, no one ruffles my fur worse than Gorsescratch, but don't you think it's a little unlikely he would go through so much trouble just to spite you? Besides, he's also the one who first suggested your promotion to corporal at the end of the moot. I think he's finally matured… somewhat."

One day, Gorsescratch. Silversong stomped on the ire bubbling within him before it stole his focus away from more important matters. Hazel and Palesquall lost themselves in another argument that endured until the army arrived at the entrance to the second level—a small gap in the spire wide enough to fit two wolves coming through, a perfect chokepoint if the exiles raided the den.

The second level was far more spacious than the last, the stark contours breaking off to reveal an open plateau supporting an array of curious Flame-Heart onlookers. Wide-eyed stares lingered on the visitors from every corner and tucked away place. The young sat behind older supervisors, tails still despite the arrival of so many newcomers. The Flame-Heart Pack clearly valued sheer discipline above all other virtues.

A few wolves jolted upon noticing Ripper being driven forward by his jailors. Did they recognize the prisoner? Brown hackles stood raised, and golden eyes bulged.

The ground was slightly elevated at the centre, and there waited a small group of important-looking wolves. Bleaksmoke's ears perked up at the sight of one of them, and as he halted, so too did the mass following him.

"Chief Ashenfall grows impatient, Bleaksmoke," a lithe she-wolf who couldn't have been older than Cedargaze whined matter-of-factly. Her reddish fur stood out for being a deeper shade, and her yellow gaze caught the shine of the dipping moon.

"And I too grow impatient, sweet Scorchfang. When are you going to realize we're meant for each other?" Bleaksmoke padded up to her and moved in for a nuzzle, but she yanked her head back quicker than a frog hopping away from danger.

"I'm sure you told your previous mates the exact same thing before they..." Scorchfang closed her eyes and breathed through clenched teeth, "suffered hunting accidents."

Silversong frowned at the troubling implication.

"Terrible hunting accidents." Bleaksmoke hung his head low, but his swishing tail revealed his true feelings or lack thereof on the matter. "But in all honesty, mother chose poorly. She'll pair us together one day or another, and then we'll have so many pups together, sweet Scorchfang."

Scorchfang tensed, halfway between a snarl and a grimace.

A queasy mole tunneled through Silversong's stomach.

"She *chose poorly...*?" Amberstorm aimed a questioning glare at Blazefur.

Blazefur answered before anyone else could elaborate, "Chief Ashenfall chooses who to pair together as mates. It's how things have been done since she was chosen as Chief. Natural love is an affront against duty, she claims."

Appalled murmurs emanated from both the River-Stream and Whistle-Wind side. Silversong couldn't imagine many things more sickening than having a mate chosen for you by someone else. And the way Blazefur had explained the new custom without even flinching...

Silversong's lips quivered, and it took all he had not to snarl.

Hazel wrinkled her face in disgust. "That's horrible!" She couldn't keep her voice down, and who could blame her?

Palesquall shared the same sentiment and openly frowned at Bleaksmoke.

The Warden's rumbling growl stifled the upset voices. "It's an unorthodox method of ruling, I'll admit, but nothing about it goes against the Wolven Code." She focused her attention on Bleaksmoke. "Now's not the time for pursuing your fancies. Take us to your Chief."

Scorchfang recoiled as Bleaksmoke passed by her, his tongue sagging. Bearing his pups clearly wasn't an attractive prospect at all. The wolves around her urged her forward, and she finally found the courage to join Blazefur's strides.

Silversong wished the threads of his aura reached as far as Bleaksmoke. Someone like him was bound to cause trouble. The golden circle vibrated, sending images of wolves wreathed in flames, their pleas for mercy breaking into incomprehensible cries.

Among the Flame-Heart spectators, Silversong caught the eyes of a shadowy mother standing in front of four subordinates. Three of them looked nothing out of the ordinary, but one of them sported fur far darker than any of the watching wolves, and his eyes… his eyes were a vicious yellow like…

Rime!

Silversong barely managed to contain his gasp. He sleeked his raised fur and tried in vain to control the pounding in his chest. Snapping his head forward, he stowed away the quick conclusion he'd come to, promising himself he would investigate the odd family later.

If you are who I think you are, maybe I can use you against the Heretic somehow.

Frostpaw scrutinized the yellow-eyed subordinate too, lips twitching as if tempted to reveal fangs.

The legion of wolves strode across the plateau and passed under an opening at the far end. The new pathway guided them all onto a broad ledge winding its way up the spire like a coiled serpent. Silversong gulped upon looking over the rim, his stomach plummeting. He could see across the entire field and much of the Fireleaf Forest, the trees looking like tiny shrubs from up here.

Just as Silversong's legs began to feel the labor of the climb, the throng passed into a cave situated beneath the top of the den, the slits in the stone allowing starlight to leak into the chamber. A pile of blackened bones gathered at the centre, and the piece of time delivered to Silversong quick flashes of wolves engulfed by flames, screaming as smoke filled their lungs. This was a place for execution, reserved for those who'd broken the Wolven Code but were undeserving of the cruel fate of an exile. The entire room reeked of ash and sour fumes. The invisible residue from previous executions stung the eyes.

Blazefur called for a pause, and the Warden allowed it. "Embertongue, Wildflame, take the prisoner to Lawbreaker's Hole and guard him until he's ready for interrogation."

"Yes, sir!" Blazefur's subordinates collected the exile from the watchful sentinels and ushered him into a tunnel leading downward.

"You have a prisoner?" Scorchfang peered at the darkened crevice leading into the bowels of the den. "He's one of ours, isn't he?"

"Not anymore," Blazefur remarked.

"Who cares who he is. We'll sear off his hide later. Come! We're almost at the top!" Bleaksmoke yipped.

"I hope Lawbreaker's Hole is secure." The Warden's tail twitched at a slight draft.

"It is," Blazefur and Scorchfang responded at the same time.

"Good. Let's keep moving."

Silversong ducked under the exit of the cave and continued up the broad slope leading to the crowning level of the den.

"I'm starting to hate Chief Ashenfall already," Hazel grumbled, her hackles stiff. "The forced pairings and this joke of a formal escort boils my blood. Does she think we have time for all this? She could've met us outside or even on the first level. Why make us climb the whole wretched spire?"

"Because she can. Because it's a way of flaunting her power." Silversong tasted the cleaner air here. Only a trace of smoke soured his tongue. "She wants everyone to know we'll get nowhere without groveling at her forepaws first."

"I'm very good at groveling, as it so happens," Palesquall joked.

"The only thing you're good at is being a thorn under my tail." Hazel gently nosed him.

Palesquall bumped her a little harder. "And like a thorn under your tail, we're almost inseparable."

Hazel licked him on the face—a rare display of affection coming from her. Palesquall looked shocked. "I guess I've gotten used to the itch."

Silversong smiled at the two of them, ignoring the good and bad futures alike winking in the threads. He would ensure the survival of his friends whatever happened.

The pathway straightened out and reached between a pair of obsidian teeth pointed skyward, marking the entrance to the final level. Silversong whispered goodbye to his friends and rejoined the corporals as they walked onto the summit. His packmates assumed their places in a corner away from the River-Stream wolves, separated by a line of sentinels much like during the moot under the Saltshore.

A she-wolf who could be none other than Chief Ashenfall observed them from atop a shelf extending below the spire's brittle tip. Standing proud as the sun yet to dawn, she was the perfect incarnation of regal confidence. A pale red line traced itself from her neck to her tail like a comet streaking through a sea of deep brown fur, and the darker shade around her eyes only served to highlight the heat in her constant glare. She was smaller than the other Chiefs, but to consider that a disadvantage would be the last mistake a fool ever made. Even without the piece of time hinting at her ruthless ways, Silversong knew she had no patience for those who questioned her authority.

Scorchfang cleared her throat and sat among her peers below the shelf supporting her leader. As much as Bleaksmoke obviously wanted to sit beside her, the other she-wolves forced him away. Scorchfang faced the gathered guests. "Wolves of Whistle-Wind and River-Stream, it is my pleasure to introduce to you our illustrious leader, Chief Ashenfall of Flame-Heart. She extends to you her hospitality until the threat of the exiles is over."

Chief Ashenfall's lips stretched into a mockery of a smile. "Welcome, my dear visitors." Her voice was smooth as ice and just as cold. She scanned the wolves before her, sizing up her rivals and tapping her claws on the obsidian shelf. "I must say I expected more of you."

The Warden took a few paces forward, tail high and neck craned up. She looked like a tsunami poised to douse the wildfire burning above. "We were beset upon by the exiles in the Twilight Meadow, and if not for Lieutenant Blazefur's speedy arrival, we would've suffered even greater losses."

Ashenfall looked down to where Blazefur sat. "I knew I'd chosen the leader of my patrol units wisely. You'll be the first among the lieutenants to feast from the Prey Hollow until summer comes again."

"Thank you, ma'am." Blazefur's tail swished, but he kept his pride to a minimum.

"It's no surprise the exiles fear us." The Flame-Heart Chief narrowed her eyes on the Wolven Bulwark, weighing the value of the assembled army and smirking at the concerned faces looking up at her. "There's a reason every beast dreads the flame. Oh yes, earthquakes, tornados, and floods often leave behind devastation, true, but fire… fire cannot be tamed once unleashed, and its hunger can never be sated." Her entire frame ignited into a whirling inferno. The wolves in the front row backed away on instinct while those further behind gaped in awe. Ashenfall's spectacle lit the entire platform ablaze as if daylight had arrived early, and Silversong had to squint to lessen the pain of the stabbing brightness. "Fire consumes and consumes until entire forests are reduced to ash and once green fields become black as the stone you now stand on. Make no mistake. My pack is destined to save you from the exiles. Not even the Heretic can withstand the heat of Flame-Heart's wrath."

She put out the burning cyclone around her. Now it was her lieutenants who ignited into howling cheers. Scorchfang, Silversong noticed, gave only a few lukewarm hoots. The golden circle buzzed, delivering to Silversong images of wolves praying for mercy as flames closed in from every corner; wolves from all territories forced to worship a blazing Chief who cared for nothing but the power she wielded.

Many of those who weren't under her leadership already stared at her in admiration.

A fire's hunger can never be sated.

Silversong would need to poison the Wolven Bulwark against Ashenfall before her ambitions got too hot, and he had to start now. "No pack alone can stand against the Heretic and win. It's why we must all fight as one. Only together can we defeat the exiles and ensure such a threat never rises again."

Silence. Futures flashed and sputtered out like dying embers, and as all heads turned to Silversong, he fought the temptation to hide among the corporals.

Ashenfall's unnerving smile widened, her sharpest fangs on display. "Ah, there he is. The famed *Silversong*," she whined his name as if tasting it. "The wolf who swallowed time."

"That's me. And you're making a terrible mistake, ma'am. Overconfidence is how the Heretic managed to escape the Furtherlands in the first place." Stressed voices rose within the gathering, and he could see Frostpaw cringing from the River-Stream side.

"Quiet, Silversong," the Warden growled—a deep rumble warning him of dire consequences should he continue. Confronting Swiftstorm's glare was like pressing his eyes against wasp stingers, and the crouched postures of the Flame-Heart lieutenants weren't much more comforting to look at either, but he had to go on for the sake of weakening Ashenfall's position.

Put the flame out before it spreads. Silversong forced his eyes in Ashenfall's direction. The way she scowled at him, it was a wonder she hadn't ordered his execution. No gruesome death awaited him tonight, though. The piece of time revealed as much.

Silversong's parents pleaded in silence for him to apologize for the interruption. The counsel came too late. All he wanted to say was already leaving his mouth. "You may think yourself safe atop your spire, but if I don't receive your trust and support, we'll be playing right into the Heretic's game. We've already rejected the true purpose of the Wolven Bulwark, and this error has caused many unnecessary deaths in the Twilight Meadow. It's time we stood united not as rivals, but as allies!"

A clamour erupted from the River-Stream side. Some called for Silversong's execution, but to his relief, a few lieutenants and corporals argued in his favour. They'd witnessed Ironwrath's capabilities for themselves, and they'd seen his forces tear through new and experienced fighters alike. If foregoing the Wolven Code was the only way to win against such a monstrous threat, maybe it should be done. Silversong's unspoken movement was gaining ground. He dared to let the tide of uncertain futures drown his brain, studying the fractured outcomes he'd just created. He pushed the visions aside to conserve his focus and waited for the Warden to soothe the uproar. She barked nothing despite the fury she expressed, and Ashenfall watched the unfolding chaos as though immensely entertained.

Against all odds, one of the more unlikely outcomes prevailed. Blazefur spoke up from below Ashenfall's platform. "Trust you? Support you? You have the piece of time and still you failed to predict the Heretic's attack. You failed to win us this war when you faced him on the battlefield. The Warden told me everything on our way here. You're too weak to control the piece of time. You should give it to someone better suited for the task."

"He's right, brother," Swiftstorm grunted from the line of sentinels, her solemn expression more frightening than the Warden eyeing him like a plotting raven. "You've been confused ever since you swallowed the weapon. It's time to let go of the burden."

"Listen to your sister, Silversong," Greyhail added.

"We can boil his blood until he's forced to give up the weapon, can't we?" Darkwave licked his front fangs and roused the meaner lieutenants. Few openly supported the idea, thankfully.

Frostpaw snarled at his father from behind, and his siblings snarled back at him in return.

"Indeed we can." Icetail squinted at Silversong. "If necessary."

"Mother, no!" Snowleap barked. "Whatever faults Silversong has, he tried to encourage us to fight together in the Twilight Meadow from the very start. Things would've gone differently if we'd listened to him."

Riptide appeared grieved by the losses they'd suffered. Wolves under his care had died. If indeed he'd fought alongside Whistle-Wind from the start, could needless death have been avoided? He stared at the stars in consideration while his mate glowered at their daughter in outrage. "Lower your voice at once! Don't speak these obscenities in the Warden's presence!"

Darkwave's anger began to overflow, "I'm sick of this code-breaker tempting us to go against the Wolven Code. Let's tear off his silver hide here and now!"

The Whistle-Wind wolves formed a blockade around Silversong. The little ones whimpered for the comfort of the Wise-Wolves. Moonwhisper and Mistyfur faced the riled mob without budging. Silversong closed his eyes and searched desperately for a way out of this mess.

"Let's tear out the piece of time from his belly!"

"Give it to the Warden!"

"No! We should give him another chance!"

"If we just start working together, we can avoid more death!"

"Why shouldn't we trust him? He can see the future, after all!"

"Blasphemy!"

"The Wolven Code is sacred! Execute him before he starts corrupting our young ones!"

"You'll have to get through us first!" Hazel snarled.

"If you insist," Blazefur grunted.

"No one is attacking any of my soldiers while I still breathe!" Amberstorm warned.

Howling from the lower levels culled the stiffening tension. Riled wolves huffed loudly instead of outright growling, and the more violent among them resorted to scowls and heated glares to convey their rage.

As the swell of possible futures hit Silversong from all angles, he opened his eyes and announced, "the Stone-Guard Pack is here!"

The whole assembly calmed itself even further until only the high-pitched voices of the scouts below could be heard. The Warden ordered her sentinels to reform in a straight line. The glance she gave Silversong exposed her true intentions. She would've let a riot ensue if it meant a chance at claiming the piece of time for herself. She was getting bolder.

He stared straight ahead to avoid looking at his sister and the others who'd convinced themselves he was no good for the Four Territories. They would see the truth soon enough.

Ashenfall lounged atop her shelf like her den hadn't almost been the location of a bloody brawl. "Bleaksmoke, Scorchfang, won't you go and greet our new guests. Don't waste any time bringing them to me."

"Happily, mother," Bleaksmoke yipped as Scorchfang grouched, "yes, ma'am."

Scorchfang's friends attempted to follow her.

"Ah, ah, ah." Ashenfall prevented them from tagging along. "Just the two of them is fine."

Scorchfang craned her head around and smiled reassuringly at her friends before suffering the unwanted affection of the Chief's son. Together, they parted the gathering and descended the spire, leaving Ashenfall to smirk in amusement at Scorchfang's clear discomfort. Hazel glared so intensely it was miracle her eyes hadn't combusted. Ashenfall noticed her and frowned.

"Ma'am," Blazefur called to his leader, "I must inform you of something."

The Flame-Heart Chief hopped off her platform and grinned at Silversong, eyes ignited by the heat of ambition. "While we wait for Chief Bronzeblood, do enjoy the beauty of Thornhollow. Long shall it stand as a bastion for those who would put their faith in me—and the Wolven Code, of course—and I hope all of you find solace upon its height. Take care not to stumble over the edge, though." She laughed and padded toward Blazefur so she could listen to his whispers.

Once more an image of the spire collapsing flashed through Silversong's mind, the roads leading to this specific fate buried under layers of uncertainty. If this doom did come to pass, he hoped Thornhollow's destruction would at least claim the life of Ashenfall in the process. She would light her entire territory on fire if it meant keeping her power. Danger was closing in all around him, and the arrival of the Stone-Guard Pack only added to the peril.

Blazefur and his Chief concluded their murmurings and turned to Silversong, snarls and bristling fur causing the Whistle-Wind wolves to stand on edge. Silversong peered at the threads and searched for the likeliest outcome of this unsettling display. The air escaped his lungs. "No! Don't!"

Ashenfall inhaled deeply and stretched her jaws wide. A tiny flame sparked to life at the tip of her tongue. A blink later, and the flame expanded into a white-hot orb blown swiftly out of her mouth.

"HAZEL, LOOK OUT!" Silversong extended the threads as far as they could go, but it was too late. The fireball streaked through the air, missing the other subordinates by a hair and exploding right in Hazel's face.

CHAPTER 12

A Bulwark Made Whole

The threads reached like a swell of water about to extinguish a fire that had already eaten its quarry.

The force of the explosion staggered Hazel and burned one side of her face to the flesh, but she only yelped and yowled after her mind registered the impact. Silversong caught her in time's aura just as he did the rest of his packmates. He blew a strong jet of air through the threads and onto her face before the flames could do more damage. The awful stench of scorched fur pained his nostrils and fueled the sweltering rage boiling through his veins. Ashenfall would die for this!

His emotions were reflected in the eyes of everyone around him: Gorsescratch and Palesquall looked ready to avenge Hazel's suffering without a care for their own lives; Amberstorm was about to pounce on Ashenfall; the Wise-Wolves had nearly summoned two rampaging vortexes prior to being caught in the threads; Hazel's family, alongside the lieutenants and corporals, were poised to charge headlong into the group of Flame-Heart wolves protecting their Chief. If Silversong hadn't frozen them all, it would've meant the end of the Wolven Bulwark, and he would've been forced to support the Whistle-Wind Pack by fighting any who opposed them. He needed to prevent this bloodshed, or the Heretic would win.

Ashenfall's predatory gaze drilled into Silversong. Her tail beat the air in anticipation. She wanted Whistle-Wind to attack her only for a chance at taking the weapon for herself. She couldn't fathom the thought of someone else wielding the powers of time.

Silversong tried not to give in to the crackling temptation urging him to tear her face off.

"Don't do it!" Silversong loosened the threads and allowed sound to vibrate into the ears of his packmates. "If you attack, all is lost."

Ashenfall's unblinking stare begged him to abandon logic and unleash his anger upon her. She licked her lips and wagged her tail. He would give her nothing but the silent promise of death delivered to her by his own eyes. She smiled upon receiving it. The start of a migraine made him wince, but in the threads he saw a road to her demise paved by her assault on Hazel. The Flame-Heart Chief had outed herself as a treacherous tyrant only a gullwit could trust. Silversong smiled back.

"WHAT IS THE MEANING OF THIS?! STAND DOWN NOW!" The Warden's fury poured over the gathering and forced tails to press against bellies. "Explain yourself."

"Oh, it's very simple, ma'am," Ashenfall whined like she'd done nothing wrong. "I've been informed that Silversong is quite the unruly pup. It seems the piece of time has convinced him he's above the Wolven Code and your authority. As devout a follower of the Wolven Code as I am, it was my duty to remind him of his place. Tonight, he learned a valuable lesson indeed: his poor choices affect not only himself, but also those closest to him. I'll have no code-breakers in my den."

Swiftstorm looked near to fainting. She leaned against Greyhail for support. Which side would she have chosen if it came to blows? Silversong ignored the piece of time's dreaded answer.

"All the same," the Warden made no effort to conceal her growl, "you won't punish anyone who's not a member of your pack unless I grant my express approval. Understood?"

Ashenfall killed her smile and narrowed her eyes on the Warden, showing only the mildest sign of submission. "Of course, ma'am. I just thought you may've needed some help in correcting insubordination. Flame-Heart discipline is legendary, after all."

"So I've heard." The Warden flicked her tail up and let her gaze drift to Silversong. "You may release them. I trust their emotions have calmed long enough for them to see reason. Though I wouldn't have gone so far, do take this whole ordeal as a lesson. However severe Chief Ashenfall's punishments are, her judgment is sound. Never forget your place again, Silversong, or others close to you may also feel the heat of justice."

The threads bounced back to their original state, and Silversong exhaled in relief as the spikes poking his brain retracted. All at once, wolves rushed to comfort Hazel, licking her where she'd been burned. Her whimpers stabbed Silversong in the chest. His legs trembled, his blood warming up to a furious temperature. It took all his willpower to keep still while Amberstorm approached him. A dire expression creased the Chief's face, his eyes sometimes hopping to his children huddled in a corner.

"Sir." Silversong bowed his head and lowered his tail despite his whole body wanting to be near Hazel. The Wise-Wolves inspected her wound, the two listing off concoctions they could use to soothe and heal her scorched face. Palesquall whined softly into her ear, stopping her whimpers for the moment. Gorsescratch stared thorns at Ashenfall, the minute possibility he would blindly attack growing into a more probable outcome every passing breath.

Please don't do anything stupid, Gorsescratch.

"Be honest, Silversong. Is there a way we can rid ourselves of Chief Ashenfall without compromising the integrity of the Wolven Bulwark?" Even as a whisper, Amberstorm's utterance hit Silversong like a landslide. "She's too dangerous. We mustn't let her conspire against us. She wanted Whistle-Wind to attack her so she could have a good excuse to try and take the piece of time from you. She's probably been planning this since she learned of your exploits."

"I know." Silversong focused on the road leading to the tyrant's demise. Many pitfalls lay in wait upon it. He would have to tread lightly. "She's a threat to us all now. Whistle-Wind, River-Stream, Stone-Guard. She'll do anything to get her fangs on the weapon. We'll make the others see that she's as much of a menace to them as she is to us. If the majority recognizes her for the monster she is, they'll pry her teeth from the power she grasps… then we'll have justice for Hazel."

Amberstorm nodded in acceptance. Under the gentle moon, he seemed every bit the leader he once was, scars or not. "And the Warden? It looks like she'll back Chief Ashenfall so long as she doesn't explicitly go against the Wolven Code. The Warden's authority can blind even the most rational wolves to the greatest of outrages. If the sentinels stand against us, we're finished."

Silversong looked at Swiftstorm, who'd managed to compose herself thanks to Greyhail's encouragement. Conflict still waged war deep inside her, Silversong could see it in her eyes. "The Warden is already losing some support among the River-Stream wolves. We're supposed to be united, but she divides. She prevents us from becoming our strongest selves. The wolves here are starting to open their eyes to this truth. We'll spread more discontent among our rivals until the Warden's authority is weakened to a point beyond recovery. Then I take control of the Wolven Bulwark."

Silversong's heart jumped into his throat, and he bristled from the icy chill sliding down his back. He hadn't meant to sound so ruthless. It wasn't like him. Darker thoughts brought to light similarities between himself and the Heretic. Maybe the piece of time was corrupting him, maybe… *NO! It's up to me to establish a new order based on unity and understanding. I won't achieve my goals through needless violence like Ironwrath would. I'm different. I'm better.*

Amberstorm turned to where his closest rivals were, not seeming to care too much about Silversong's troubling admission. "All right. I trust you. We should begin by luring the River-Stream wolves to your cause. If we can get someone on the inside to vouch for you, it'll be a good start. I heard some of them speak up in your favour before Hazel was…" He stopped short of mentioning Ashenfall's assault on Hazel.

Silversong had to compress his anger before its heat evaporated his senses. He turned to where Frostpaw sat, his eyes sometimes glancing at Hazel while his packmates and the Flame-Heart lieutenants murmured among themselves, the scent of agitation sour as ever. "Yeah. And I have just the one for the job."

The sound of wolves padding and panting below silenced the hushed voices. Everyone reassumed their positions. Palesquall stayed at Hazel's side, rubbing against her to reduce her bouts of shivering. Silversong wished he could be close to her too. From here it was difficult to see the damage done to the right side of her face, but he was sure it wasn't superficial. Ashenfall would pay a steep price for Hazel's pain.

Amberstorm's pups remained tucked under the Wise-Wolves, shaking as if winter's breath had invaded the tepid night. The little ones had already been through so much hardship, and it would only get worse until the time for healing began. All of them had been robbed of the innocent joys of youth, and it wasn't fair. One of them whimpered for Pinetrail, the tragic sound drifting across the den and extracting some pity even from the River-Stream wolves. Moonwhisper's milk would have to suffice for the pup, and she herself looked ready to howl her sorrow to the watching stars. Luckily, she had Mistyfur there to support her.

After an uncomfortably long pause, a mix of huffing and wheezing turned every head to the entrance framed by the two large fangs of obsidian. Scorchfang came hurrying through, the fur on her back lifted in distress thanks to Bleaksmoke trailing her from the rear.

"Oh, quit overreacting!" he yipped without a care for how many ears turned his way. "I was just fooling around!"

Scorchfang cringed and ground her teeth. In speedy strides, her peers cut her off from the unwanted pursuer, leaving Bleaksmoke to pout beside Blazefur, trying to get a sympathetic reaction out of him. The stoic lieutenant gave the Chief's son nothing but a disapproving frown. Ashenfall seemed to derive pleasure from Scorchfang's discomfort which almost prompted Silversong to snarl.

The source of all the huffing and wheezing wobbled onto the crowning platform and plopped onto the ground, limbs yielding to the considerable weight they supported. Had more cracks formed on the spire's peak?

Some of Silversong's packmates gasped, heads tilted in confusion while an array of light-coloured wolves crowded around the big one, sniffing and prodding and uttering whines of encouragement as if the climb to the top was an achievement to be celebrated. For such a large individual, perhaps it was. The Stone-Guard members were the opposite of their leader. Bones showed where muscles should've been rippling, and their taller statures only further exposed the issue of malnourishment.

"Anyone got… something to… eat?" the fattest of all wolves grunted over the shameless rumbling of his stomach.

Ashenfall leaped onto her high shelf and greeted the newcomers, but even she looked taken aback by the condition of the Stone-Guard Pack. "Chief Bronzeblood… welcome to Thornhollow."

“Hey. I figured out a better way to beat the Heretic,” Palesquall snickered, his voice barely discernible. “Why don’t we get this oaf here to eat all the exiles for us?”

The subordinates around him giggled, but the joke failed to cheer Hazel up.

Four wolves inspected their girthy Chief more carefully than the others, putting ears to his throat and listening to his labored breaths. Stone-Guard’s Wise-Wolves, Silversong guessed. They looked as though their Chief had stored away all the food meant for them inside his bulging belly.

Bronzeblood lifted his large head only a little. Any higher would’ve been a great undertaking. His copper-tinted fur was turning grey, and the sockets around his brown eyes begged for sleep. “Your ancestors should’ve chosen a better den. Something much lower to the ground, maybe.”

The Flame-Heart wolves present scowled at the comment, and Ashenfall’s lips quirked into a dangerous smile. “Shall I fetch my Wise-Wolves? Sounds like you need something to ease your breathing.” She made it sound a threat.

Bronzeblood’s eyes widened, and he closed his mouth until air filled his cheeks to the limit. Everyone surrounding him backed off, and Silversong turned his head to spare himself from witnessing the Chief spewing out all the contents of his considerable stomach. Instead, Bronzeblood belched so loud it shook Silversong’s ear fur—a thunderclap fit to wake all creatures no matter how deeply they slept. He wouldn’t have been surprised if even the Heretic heard the rumbling noise from wherever he hid.

Agonizing moments passed before the Stone-Guard Chief cleared his throat and sighed. “No need. I feel much better now.” He attempted to stand, but his legs wouldn’t have it. His weight smacked the ground again, and Silversong could’ve sworn another crack appeared on the spire’s peak. Many of the onlookers winced. “I’m fine! I’m fine!” He denied the Wise-Wolves who attempted to see to him. Only now did Silversong notice how few the Stone-Guard members were. Even Whistle-Wind in its current state outnumbered them.

The Warden let her voice carry across the plateau. “The time for introductions has passed. The Wolven Bulwark is now fully assembled, and we must focus our efforts on defending Thornhollow.”

Ashenfall scoffed and lowered herself to her stomach, placing one forepaw atop the other. "So, we just sit around in my home until the Heretic attacks us? I expected a better plan."

The Warden's regard was nearly a glare. "You'll refer to me as *ma'am* or *Warden* from now on."

Ashenfall managed to hide her irritation at being publicly scolded. "Yes, of course… ma'am."

The Warden's gaze landed on Silversong. "At the Saltshore, we decided this would be the correct strategy to follow according to Silversong's input. He can see the future, supposedly. And I believe my messengers were rather clear on the subject."

Clever. She was putting any potential blame on Silversong should the strategy fail.

Ashenfall pulled back her ears and licked her front teeth. "Actually, they failed to mention it was *his* idea. I don't trust him. How do we know the piece of time hasn't scrambled his brain. He's proven himself disobedient and petulant—two reasons he shouldn't wield this power."

"Maybe some time in Lawbreaker's Hole can fix his head. It has a way of making wolves see the error in their ways," Blazefur suggested, and the lieutenants loyal to him grunted in agreement. Scorchfang wasn't one of them.

The Warden searched among her sentinels until she found Swiftstorm. "Don't you worry about his poor conduct. I'll get it under control."

Silversong found it shockingly difficult to take in his next breath.

Snarls from the Whistle-Wind side answered Blazefur's veiled threat. Amberstorm outright stomped on the idea of Silversong's imprisonment. "I assure you, Silversong is neither a gullwit nor is he an ill-meaning delinquent. Day by day, he becomes stronger at wielding the piece of time, and day by day the Heretic grows more desperate to seize it. He knows his cause is living on borrowed time; he knows once Silversong masters the weapon, he'll discover a clear way of defeating the exiles for good. The Heretic can't wait this out. In his desperation, he'll use all he has to strike at us, and we'll be ready for him when he does."

"The Heretic seems far more cunning than even the Warden gives him credit for." Ashenfall observed the Warden's lack of a reaction, trying to measure her character. "Somehow I doubt he'll play into our expectations."

Again, an image of Thornhollow collapsing snuck into Silversong's thoughts. He tried grasping the omen and the roads leading to it, but they slipped out of reach.

"You underestimate his tenacity." Bronzeblood released a guttural sound from his throat. "He'll attack us. It's in his nature. Make sure there're no metals of any kind on this spire, for he can control them just like Stone-Guard himself. Motherwolf is testing the Four Territories by allowing the Heretic to master this exceedingly rare ability. We should prepare for his assault."

"And you should've had him executed when he still belonged to your pack." Amberstorm confronted Bronzeblood, eyes narrowed to slits. "How many guards did it take to safely escort him to the Furtherlands? More than a unit, I heard. A dozen corporals and two lieutenants! He was too dangerous to be kept alive. You could've prevented so much destruction by putting him to death, Bronzeblood!"

"NO!" Bronzeblood barked, the fat on his face jiggling. "A would-be usurper deserves banishment!"

"No one disputes your right to judge code-breakers, sir." The Warden stepped in before the argument evolved into a barking contest. "Indeed, I've known the Heretic longer than anyone. No matter how cunning and patient he is, he'll be forced to attack us eventually. Rime's power is far less effective here than in the Furtherlands, so his ranged options are limited to flinging earth and stone at the spire and maybe ordering a few lightning strikes. He'll use Rime to corrupt more prey to his side, but I doubt they'll have much of an effect unless we meet him on the field, which I have no intention of doing. The advantage of a good defense is ours to exploit. The piece of time is also in our possession which goads the Heretic into attacking us prematurely."

Silversong flinched at another vision of Thornhollow's collapse. He managed to freeze the omen in his head this time. The raging earth shook the spire to its foundations, and the wolves lucky enough to survive the falling blocks of obsidian faced the Heretic's wrath.

The image slipped out of focus, replaced by a remedy to Thornhollow's doom—the Stone-Guard Pack, all of them working together to counter the violent earthquake. Silversong eyed the wolves under Bronzeblood's leadership.

As discussion regressed into debate, he looked inward and put pressure on the golden circle. It was time for him to unlock the weapon's true potential as Stormstrider and Galdreth had done before him. Regardless of how blunted its power was, he would force the piece of time to guide him to victory.

He closed his eyes only to find a long-forgotten ghost staring at him in the darkness.

CHAPTER 13

A Sentinel's Duty

A spiderweb of choices stretched out before Silversong, as many leading to his downfall as to his triumph, each weaving a different line to a different end. He grasped at the certainties and likely possibilities, using them to shine light on the next moves he should make. There wasn't much time before the Wolven Bulwark turned on itself thanks to Chief Ashenfall's hunger for power.

If the weapon hadn't lost so much of its potency, all his problems would be unfortunate memories by now, but a drained weapon was still better than none. He would simply have to make do.

He put all his attention on the roads leading to Ashenfall's death. He needed her gone, or she would all but invite the Heretic to attack a weakened Wolven Bulwark. Spreading discontent among the other packs was the way to go. However, an obvious problem poked holes in that endeavor: the Warden's sentinels were nothing if not observant. They would report any disloyalty if they saw it, and then Silversong would be one leap away from execution. The timestreams hinted that speaking to Ashenfall directly might reveal something he could use against her.

He opened his eyes and sniffed the stuffy air of the grotto Whistle-Wind had been designated. Only a day had passed since the conclusion of the gathering up top, and still Silversong knew he would never get used to this cramped space near the bottom of the den. Trickles of daylight leaked through tiny slits in the low roof, and the lopsided ground promised many nights of rough sleep. Even so, Silversong was thankful Ashenfall had chosen this room for them out of spite. If the spire ever was on the verge of collapse, at least Silversong and his packmates had access to the quickest route to safety.

River-Stream had been granted a larger cavern on the second level, and Stone-Guard an even bigger one near the top. It hardly seemed fair, but Chief Bronzeblood had practically begged to be nowhere near the field below—for fear of the Heretic—though he would never admit it.

Hazel bit off a whimper in the corner claimed by the Wise-Wolves. They chewed on succulent plants the corporals had found in the field and licked the burned side of her face. Palesquall nuzzled her on the neck while Gorsescratch watched intently from the other side of the grotto. Silversong padded toward her.

Hazel's ears perked up upon his arrival, and her tail swished against the smooth floor. She offered a shaky smile. "Hey, Silversong. How do I look?"

A lump swelled in Silversong's throat as he took in the damage done to the right side of her face. From cheek to eye, her fur was completely gone, revealing nasty blisters on leathery flesh and patches of bright red where the fireball had concentrated its heat. It was as much an ugly sight as it was a painful one. Her fur would never sprout back, and this blemish on her face would forever remind onlookers of Ashenfall's cruelty. Silversong wanted to whimper, but he allowed only anger to break through his shell of confidence. Ashenfall would pay for this.

Somehow, Hazel peered through his rage and found his hidden sorrow. "That bad, huh?" she winced as Mistyfur licked one of the sensitive spots. "I'm surprised Gorsescratch hasn't stopped staring at me considering how ugly I must be now."

"You're not ugly," Palesquall whined before Silversong could comfort her. "A scratch on a gemstone doesn't make it less beautiful."

Hazel's green eyes opened wide. Her tail ceased swaying. "Oh? Am I a beautiful gemstone now?"

Silversong promptly turned his head to Palesquall, who gulped and puffed up upon realizing how romantic he'd sounded. "I... uh..." He looked like a flustered snowball. "Don't make it weird, Hazel! Ugh, I guess this serves me right for trying to cheer you up."

Hazel chuckled and nudged him on the cheek. "I'm just teasing. Feel free to give me more colourful compliments, Palesquall. I think your last one was very sweet."

Palesquall snorted. "You'll have to earn them from now on."

"Challenge accepted." Hazel nosed him gently.

Silversong tilted his head and sniffed for any signs of mutual attraction between the two subordinates. He'd never thought of Hazel and Palesquall as a potential couple, and the piece of time certainly hadn't hinted at such a thing, but it dawned on Silversong how much sense it made. His best friends were practically inseparable, and it would come as no surprise if their petty bickering was but a prelude to a more passionate bond. Gorsescratch might find it tempting to bully Palesquall now, but the mongrel could go chase his own tail if he thought he had a say in Hazel's choice of a mate.

There he was, whining something to Chief Amberstorm who seemed too preoccupied by the yipping and yapping of his pups to listen to anything the corporal had to say.

"I'm sorry, Hazel." Silversong licked the good side of her face. "I should've predicted this. I should've mastered the piece of time before we even set off to Flame-Heart Territory." Everything inside him seemed to increase in weight, his legs close to buckling under the pressure.

"Don't go falling on your belly like Chief Bronzeblood, now." Palesquall bumped him on the side. "Heh, I'm still surprised the spire survived the impact of his gut TWICE! He could've killed us all!"

"Quit exaggerating. The joke might've been funny the first time, but now you're just dragging it out." Hazel tried to remain still for the working Wise-Wolves.

"Always the critic, Hazel," Palesquall dismissed her feedback.

Hazel ignored the comment and placed a forepaw atop Silversong's. "Listen. None of us think this is your fault, Silversong. I can't even imagine how confusing and disorienting it must be to carry the piece of time, but you managed to get us here all the same. The Heretic would've won by now if not for you, so take pride in your accomplishments for once."

"Yeah," Palesquall added. "It's a miracle you're still sane after all you've been through."

Silversong couldn't deny himself a chuckle. "Sometimes I think I *am* going insane, actually. More often than not."

"Well, before you completely lose your head, just promise me you'll let me know when there's a chance to tear off Chief

Ashenfall's face, okay?" Hazel's whine was uttered in a humorous manner, but her intense eyes were the opposite of playful.

Silversong gave her a partial smile. "Deal. I'll give you a heads-up if I see an opportunity for some payback."

"Who goes there?!" a corporal named Quickhop barked in front of the tunnel leading to the outside den, alerting everyone to the presence of an intruder.

"Stand down," the Warden's whine echoed from inside the tunnel. "I'm here for Silversong."

The whole pack froze and turned to Silversong. He tensed as though a massive flood were heading straight for him. Would the Warden try convincing him once again to relinquish the piece of time? He frowned and faced the exit of the grotto, steadying his breaths. He'd glimpsed this possibility in the threads. If he displayed no weakness, the Warden would take nothing from him.

"Go to the Wise-Wolves." Amberstorm pawed his pups away, much to their disappointment. "Run along now."

Still on edge, Quickhop backed off to let the Warden stride through. Silversong gasped, heart seized by frigid claws. Trailing her like a dutiful servant was Swiftstorm, her silver fur lit by the light squeezing through the slits above. He hadn't seen *this* in the threads!

They halted at the centre of the small cave, scanning the wary wolves all around. Few could withstand the strength of the Warden's gaze without flinching. Silversong was among them. He stared at those pale eyes livened by a zealous spark, refusing to feel intimidated. She sniffed and kept her white fur sleeked. At her side, Swiftstorm calmly shook her head.

The Warden ceased moving and addressed the entire pack. "I sense a certain tension in the air. A tension created by wolves who fear they may have done something to anger me. Be assured, there is no reason to fear my sentinels. To disrespect the Wolven Code is to disrespect yourself. We are simply here to uproot rebellious thoughts before they sprout. If any of you wish to confess your wrongdoings, now is the time. I offer you penance, and through punishment, you'll be reborn a virtuous soul without corruption."

Silence was the answer to her offer, and the tension only worsened. Swiftstorm's face showed no emotion at all, but sometimes a twitch of her tail or a lifting of hackles indicated her unease. Had the Warden forced her to come here?

The leader of the sentinels released a regretful sigh. "I smell the corruption spreading within your souls like weeds invading a once healthy field. I don't enjoy doling out collective punishment, but how else am I to encourage code-breakers to reveal themselves to me?"

Amberstorm barked for the Warden's attention, startling some of the more nervous wolves. "There aren't any code-breakers here, Warden. You waste your time, I'm afraid."

"Oh, but you're wrong, aren't you, sir?" The Warden came within a tail-length of the Chief's face, but he stood his ground without tucking tail. The lieutenants edged closer to Amberstorm as Swiftstorm's calculating eyes searched for ways to neutralize them should they attack her leader.

"Is your posturing necessary, ma'am?" Silversong lured the Warden's ire away from the Chief and directed it straight onto himself instead. He straightened his tail and refused to break eye contact. "You said you were here for me, so I don't see why you're harassing my packmates. They've done nothing wrong."

Cedargaze and Shadowgale appeared ready to pounce in front of the Warden to keep her far from Silversong, but they found the restraint to not commit such a foolish act. The living embodiment of the Wolven Code stood over him now. He bowed his head only a little to appease her temper.

"And you, Silversong?" The Warden's untroubled voice carried strength enough to make him shiver. "Have you done nothing wrong? Have you not gone against the Wolven Code? Have you not disappointed your sister? Yourself, even?"

"Perhaps." Silversong closed his eyes and opened them on Swiftstorm, on her face betraying not a lick of concern for him. He allowed the piece of time to guide his choices and selected the future where he avoided conflict, but remained unshakable. Though nothing was ever certain, he took the gamble. "I don't deny your accusations, ma'am, but I don't disobey your authority without reason. I've seen futures where blind loyalty to the Wolven Code leads to our downfall, and so I choose defiance as a way of hardening the Wolven Bulwark. If the law encourages hatred between the packs, and this hatred leads to infighting and distrust, is it not my duty to heal these gaping wounds before the Heretic can exploit them? We have the numbers, but we don't have the strength, separated as we are. Think of how strong we can be as a united force. The exiles wouldn't stand a chance!"

Fear entered Swiftstorm's green eyes, and she exhaled loudly, but it was the Warden who spoke for her. "The Wolven Bulwark must not forget the code that binds it. You would have me removed from power, Silversong. This I know. If your actions don't speak for themselves, your eyes certainly do. I cannot allow your plotting to continue. The Wolven Code is sacred. By obeying it, our victory is assured. *You're* the one who threatens stability, Silversong. Good always triumphs over evil, and the Wolven Code is good. Your disregard for it has angered Motherwolf. Slowly you wear away the shield separating us from the Heretic. You would have the line blurred between us and the exiles! No longer can I abide your blasphemy!"

Silversong flexed the threads of his aura. If the Warden tried anything, she would be in for an awful surprise. "The line has always been blurred, ma'am. To think otherwise is to remain blinded by faith."

The Warden pulled her head back, sucking in air through clenched teeth. Dread overcame Silversong's packmates. They quivered and uttered silent prayers, waiting for the Warden to exercise her judgment. Swiftstorm bared her fangs at any who tried approaching Silversong. Shadowgale and Cedargaze whispered her name, hoping to get her attention, but she turned her tail on her parents.

The piece of time pulsed like a heart about to explode. Silversong's own fears clouded the near future. Just when he tensed the threads to freeze the Warden in time, she covered her fangs and assumed a less aggressive posture. "It's clear you can't be trusted, and so you leave me no choice but to tether you to someone I know is virtuous at heart. Your sister."

Silversong swerved his head to look at Swiftstorm, shock and confusion rolling over his anxiety. The flesh beneath his raised fur prickled as realization set in. "I'm to be her prisoner?"

"I'm to be your guardian, brother." Hearing Swiftstorm's voice caused an involuntary pang in his gut. "It's clear you need one, and who better to watch over you than me?"

"Until the Heretic is dead and your rebellious nature has been quenched, Swiftstorm is to watch over you for as long as the sun shines in the sky." The Warden beckoned her loyal servant over, and

Swiftstorm stood at her side like an eagle perched on a high branch. "I've given her permission to punish you for any infraction you commit. As a sentinel and as your sister, it's her duty to guide you into the light of virtue which your parents have failed to do."

His mother's sneer lasted until the Warden turned to look at her. Shadowgale's frown dissolved, and he stared at the ground.

Silversong wanted to bite down on the Warden's muzzle! He clenched his jaws to keep from growling, the boiling heat within him begging to be released. How dare the Warden use his sister against him like this?! He thought about killing the leader of the sentinels, but such a drastic action would bring only disaster upon the Wolven Bulwark. The packs would revolt against him, and Ashenfall would assert dominance afterwards. No. He needed to be smart about removing the Warden from power. He needed to concede to her for now.

"Is that all?" Silversong managed to ask without snarling.

"Yes." The Warden nodded to Swiftstorm and turned to leave the grotto. She stopped in front of the exit. "I pray you escape your own corruption before I'm forced to stamp it out myself, Silversong. And believe me, my methods of discipline are limited only by how much pain your body can take." She crouched and disappeared into the darkness of the tunnel.

Silversong gritted his teeth and dragged his claws against the ground, the scratch-resistant surface leaving him entirely dissatisfied. Swiftstorm eyed him warily. "This is for your own good, brother."

Silversong couldn't take it anymore. Quick as lightning, he willed the threads to remove his sister from the currents of time. Disgust clashed against the storm of anger within. His packmates stared in astonishment at Swiftstorm's black outline, some tucking their tails on instinct as Silversong addressed the Chief. "I need the support of the other packs now more than ever. I'm confined to Swiftstorm only by day, so I'll have to move during the night."

"We'll bring River-Stream into the fold first," Amberstorm grunted. "You said you know someone on the inside who can vouch for you. It's Frostpaw, isn't it?"

"Yes." Just hearing Frostpaw's name calmed Silversong's flaring emotions. "I'll speak to him when I have a chance. For now, though, I must go to Chief Ashenfall. She needs to know we won't ever tuck our tails to her. She can try to intimidate us, but we won't succumb to her bullying. She's reckless, but the piece of time has all but confirmed she'll reveal a weakness if I confront her today."

"Be careful, Silversong," the Chief warned. "We can't lose you now."

"May the wind guide your steps, son," Cedargaze whispered as if fearing Swiftstorm still had the ability to hear.

"Good luck," Shadowgale grunted under his breath.

Silversong released Swiftstorm and assumed the position he'd been in upon freezing her. Breaking away from her gaze, he walked toward the exit.

"Where are you going, brother?" Swiftstorm followed him without realizing she'd been tied in time's threads a moment ago.

"To Chief Ashenfall," Silversong admitted, ducking his head and pushing through the tunnel. Sometimes one had to put a paw over the flame to truly test its heat. "I would like to give her a piece of my mind."

As Swiftstorm trailed him in silence, he wondered how to weaken her loyalty to the Warden. His tangled emotions still shrouded his access to future events, but he knew there must be a way to disconnect her from the Wolven Code.

Oh, Swiftstorm... don't you trust me? Don't you trust your brother?

All he could do was hope and pray she would see reason in the end.

CHAPTER 14

The Flames of Tyranny

"If you seek out Chief Ashenfall, others might see it as intermingling," Swiftstorm argued. "Don't give me a reason to punish you, brother, please."

Silversong passed a few wolves on his way to the top, all the while trying to pretend his sister's threat affected him much less than it actually did. He frowned and continued forward, striding onto the first level of the den. Young Flame-Heart wolves dueled one another there, ripping into each other's coats under the instruction of older corporals. One trainee barely old enough to be a subordinate yelped as her opponent forced her onto her back. She tried rolling over, but her larger adversary moved in for her exposed belly, nipping at the most sensitive areas. She yowled for one of the instructors to save her, but they laughed at her failure to defend herself. Silversong scowled at the cruel lesson.

"I'm not intending to cozy up to her, Swiftstorm," Silversong grunted, still fuming at the Warden for using his sister against him. "I'm confronting her because she's from a rival pack, and I'm merely acting as the Wolven Code expects me to act."

Swiftstorm stopped in front of him, her eyes meeting his. She showed more emotion now than she had in the grotto, at least. "You can't run about insulting Chiefs for no good reason."

"No good reason?!" Silversong's hackles rose, his heart burning. "She attacked Hazel! My friend! Or do you think her assault was justified?"

A few curious corporals lifted their ears and observed Silversong without making it too obvious. The metallic scent of blood hung thick in the air, and the growls and yelps of the fighting wolves worsened Silversong's bitter mood.

Swiftstorm had no answer, and Silversong took this as a sign of conflict within her. She could still open her eyes to the flaws of the order she followed. "Hazel was your packmate too, Swiftstorm. Remember when we all played together in the Breezeway? When you pretended to be the Fallen Titan?"

Swiftstorm's lips quirked into a subtle smile. "I remember her refusing to partake in those little games. She scolded us about how disrespectful it was to the wolves killed by the Fallen Titan. I suppose she was right, but I think she was just scared of my convincing performance."

"She definitely was," Silversong grunted, trying to tug his sister's loyalty back where it belonged. "She respects you, Swiftstorm. We all do. But when you don't stand up for us, it makes us think you don't care about our pack anymore."

Swiftstorm bristled and fixed her eyes to the ground. She lowered her ears and forced a scowl on her face. "I do care… but my loyalty is to the Warden and the Wolven Code. You must understand this, brother."

Silversong's head slumped, his hopes crushed for the moment. "I understand."

The poor subordinate who'd been beaten by her older packmate lay bleeding on the obsidian, her whimpers spent, her eyes frozen in terror. The corporals who'd encouraged her abuse congratulated the victor, licking the blood off his muzzle while whining praises. Silversong padded away from the dueling grounds before he found the nerve to give those instructors a demonstration of their own cruelty. Antagonizing Flame-Heart would do little to mend the divide, and so he suffered the laughter of those brutes without interfering.

When Ashenfall dies, I'll make sure things change around here.

"You're really serious about confronting her, then?" Swiftstorm hurried to keep up.

"Unless you're planning on stopping me, yes." Silversong entered the darkened tunnel leading to the second level.

Swiftstorm studied the tiny holes hollowed out in the side of the spire. "I'm not. As long as your actions don't threaten the stability of the Wolven Bulwark, you may speak to Chief Ashenfall as you please."

Stability of the Wolven Bulwark? Silversong almost chuckled at the absurdity of the statement. The Wolven Bulwark was far from stable, but he kept his muzzle sealed so as not to start another argument. He drew on the power of the piece of time, willing it to reveal the correct things to say when confronting Ashenfall.

The tunnel abruptly became a ledge, and he scuttled away from the steep descent. The wind howled strong today, buffeting his fur and reminding him of home. He wondered if he would ever return there, and if an understanding could be reached between Whistle-Wind and the spiders. The golden circle showed him glimpses of this potential future, but not the choices required to make it a reality. He still wasn't good enough.

The ledge curved and ushered him onto the second level where wolves lounged in the sun or feasted from the large Prey Hollow located within an obsidian outgrowth jutting out at the far end. Flame-Heart only had one place to store food, and of course, Ashenfall's pack dictated who ate first. It was Flame-Heart, then Stone-Guard, then River-Stream, and finally Whistle-Wind. Luckily, the field below had an abundance of prey just waiting to be caught. So long as no overhunting occurred, the Wolven Bulwark had enough resources to last until winter.

I pray we crush the exiles long before then.

The wolves not on patrol froze upon sighting him, and an uncomfortable silence ensued. A few sentinels were there, but their eyes were instead drawn to Swiftstorm. Greyhail stiffened in his corner, and Swiftstorm gave him a brief nod before directing her attention back to her brother. In no time at all, many scowls were aimed his way, and a pompous lieutenant halted him in his tracks. At her side was the shadowy mother Silversong had spotted upon first arriving here, tail tucked and ears flattened.

"State you business," the lieutenant grunted. "Outsiders aren't allowed to roam this level of the den by decree of Chief Ashenfall."

Chief Ashenfall can bite my tail.

Silversong met her deep yellow eyes and took in her thick scent. "I'm here for your Chief. I'm sure she'll wag her tail at the prospect of speaking to the one who swallowed the piece of time."

The lieutenant took one look at Swiftstorm, hesitated, then motioned the timid mother away. Silversong watched wide-eyed as she scuttled onto the pathway leading up the spire. Where were her children? Where was the subordinate who looked so much like Rime? Silversong wanted to ask her a few questions. Maybe he could corner her when she was alone.

Ashenfall's pretentious crony flicked her reddish tail. "She's in the lair so graciously offered to the Stone-Guard wolves. The entrance lies just before the Cave of Punishment. It's an unassuming little opening. Sniff for the scents of the occupants. I'm sure you'll find it."

Cave of Punishment… Lawbreaker's Hole… this whole den could use some cheer, Silversong thought to himself as Chief Riptide emerged from a tunnel in the obsidian floor. Silversong hadn't noticed it before now. The entrance was shadowed by a thick black tooth shooting out of the plateau.

The lieutenant who'd stopped Silversong now did the same to the River-Stream Chief. "Hey! You're not allowed up here. The second level is for Flame-Heart wolves only. Stay in your grotto unless you're sending wolves out to do their daily duties."

Riptide squinted his yellow eyes as if adjusting to the light, his black fur dishevelled. From inside the tunnel behind him, a pup-like squeaking could be heard. "We're getting thirsty, and our young ones need a real source of water to drink from! They're falling ill."

The lieutenant scoffed, pressing her nose against Riptide's. "There's plenty of pools to drink from in your grotto. Our illustrious Chief saw to your needs personally."

Riptide snarled, startling the lieutenant. "Is this a joke?! It doesn't take the wisdom of a Wise-Wolf to know that drinking from those stale pools is as unsavory as drinking our own waste! Out of respect for the Wolven Code, I'm willing to suffer being confined underground, but this is unacceptable. I won't have members of my pack dying of thirst! Not while I'm Chief!"

Flame-Heart soldiers clustered around the disgruntled Chief, fangs bared, but he stood fearless before the angry crowd like a deer who'd found the courage to point its antlers at the relentless hunters. A newfound respect for Riptide blossomed in Silversong despite the Chief's treatment of the Whistle-Wind Pack. Now he understood the discomfort he'd put his rivals through, and hopefully he regretted his decision of having them restricted to the Suncap Woods.

It's never too late to overcome your flaws, Silversong remembered one of the main lessons his elders had taught him.

Considering the soldiers all around her, the lieutenant had the nerve to snarl back. "I don't care if you River-Stream mongrels do drink your own waste. Chief Ashenfall's conditions were clear. The Wolven Code compels you to obey them. However, if you were to beg my Chief to reconsider, perhaps she'll oblige. Give me a demonstration right now of how you'll beg. Go on! Tuck your tail and show me your belly, *sir*," she mocked to the laughter of her packmates.

Silversong found himself snarling at the lieutenant. A nudge from Swiftstorm urged him to hide his fangs. This was wrong. No one deserved to humiliate themselves for a simple drink of good water. Quickly, Silversong searched the threads for a way to grant Riptide his request.

Scorchfang intervened before he found a good choice to make. "Peace, Sunpelt. There's no need to antagonize our allies even if they are from a rival territory. All they need is some clean water."

"Stay out of this, Scorchfang," Sunpelt showed her teeth to the other lieutenant. "Or should I inform the Chief of your desire to aid a rival pack? I wonder if it's finally time for Bleaksmoke to become your mate."

Scorchfang flinched at the insinuation, and the wolves closest to her openly frowned at Sunpelt. "I've done nothing to deserve such a punishment. You know this. I'm simply saying it wouldn't be right to weaken the Wolven Bulwark by allowing its soldiers to die of thirst. Or do you disagree?"

Silversong wanted Scorchfang to bite that ugly grimace off Sunpelt's face. Greyhail put himself between the two lieutenants before a scuffle broke out. "All right, enough. Chief Riptide, by my right as a sentinel, I allow you to find a better source of water for your pack. Scorchfang does raise a good point. The Wolven Bulwark needs all its members in good shape to defend against the Heretic. Now, get going."

"Thank you," Riptide grunted, pushing Sunpelt aside and leading a sorry-looking file of pups and rookies across the plateau. His eyes met Silversong's, and surprisingly there was no hatred or contempt in them.

Icetail emerged last out of the tunnel and stopped beside her mate, halting the disorganized file. They all looked bothered by the sunlight. "My Chief?"

Riptide counted the young wolves whose tongues were utterly parched. "Let the others know I'll be back soon to lead the second group to a clean source of water. Until the young satisfy their thirst, the lair must be guarded. Understood?"

Icetail looked over her shoulder at the Flame-Heart wolves dispersing around the tunnel. "Yes, my Chief." She returned underground to relay Riptide's orders.

I hope you're doing all right, Frostpaw. Just thinking about his friend alone and thirsty in the dark put thorns in Silversong's heart.

One problem at a time, he reminded himself, walking to the opening at the far end of the second level. Scorchfang studied Silversong from afar, but he pretended not to notice her. Swiftstorm followed him onto the winding ledge coiling up the spire. While he could, he savoured the strong breeze as it washed away the scent of noxious smoke.

Silversong looked down at the patrol units padding through the grass, his stomach recoiling. From this high up, the wolves looked like tiny ants crawling through a patch of featureless green. He dulled the uncomfortable sensation in his gut by talking to Swiftstorm.

"Don't you see how the Wolven Code can be used for evil?" His heart thumped louder, encouraging him to be wary of the things he said. "It's unfair to confine the River-Stream wolves underground, and if not for Greyhail, some of them might've died of thirst! And don't get me started on Chief Ashenfall choosing who to pair together as mates." He shivered in disgust.

"Quiet, brother," Swiftstorm warned, her tail going stiff. "I'll not hear these blasphemous complaints out of you. The Wolven Code may sometimes seem unfair, but it must be obeyed all the same. Every disobedient thought blurs the line between you and the exiles."

The exiles have a point, though. They're just too extreme. Silversong dared not whine the truth aloud. There had to be a way to get Swiftstorm on his side! Calming his breaths, he used the piece of time to confirm his fears. His sister was tangled deep in the Warden's web, and it would take great effort to slice through the threads binding her to the Wolven Code. At least she could still be saved.

They came to the discreet entrance Sunpelt had mentioned. Just before the Cave of Punishment was a gap in the obsidian height, and sure enough, the scent of Stone-Guard wolves was strong in there. The smell of dry earth and dead grass overpowered the bitter aroma wafting from the nearby cave, and Silversong pushed into the sizeable lair.

Stone-Guard wasn't a large pack, and its lack of members made the grotto seem even bigger than it was. It expanded to the side away from the Cave of Punishment and curved halfway around the central spire. Light filtered through cracks in the black stone, bouncing off the reflective floor to illuminate the malnourished wolves lounging about the space—corporals and subordinates relieved of duty by the looks of it, and they all lifted their heads upon detecting Silversong's foreign scent. One look at Swiftstorm kept them from alerting the pack to an intruder which allowed Silversong to roam the lair without interruption.

Around the corner, he heard the voices of Ashenfall and Bronzeblood.

"… expect me to starve? No, it won't do. The only way I'll help you is if—"

"Silence!" Ashenfall hissed. "He could be here any moment."

"Who? Me?" Silversong rounded the corner, eyes locked on Ashenfall.

Her lips parted to form a smirk. She lay on the floor facing Bronzeblood, his Wise-Wolves, and his lieutenants. Sunpelt's submissive servant was there too, head tucked under her leader's lower jaw. She was quivering, and her eyes remained fixed on her children huddling around Bleaksmoke. Why were they here? Silversong glanced at the subordinate who had the familiar yellow glare, stifling a shiver. Something was off about all of them.

The rotating threads encompassed the suspicious group. Bronzeblood tensed, eyeing Silversong warily as the Wise-Wolves and lieutenants edged away. Ashenfall had no reaction, but her fearful subject stopped all motion, her gaze now resting on Silversong. Had her quivering been an act? Some of her children openly scowled, but the others merely bristled and hid behind the Chief's son. Bleaksmoke tilted his head, and strangely enough, panted. All at once, futures bloomed across Silversong's vision—a mother and her children sneaking out of the den at night to meet a figure wreathed in shadow; Ashenfall and her son plotting in private; Bronzeblood sending his starving wolves to scour the field of all resources; fangs squeezing the life out of Amberstorm…

Silversong shook out the disorienting omens. Those futures weren't certain, but they were vivid enough to not ignore. He would have to tread very carefully here. "Don't bite your tongue on my account, ma'am," Silversong whined to Ashenfall in a controlled tone. "Feel free to continue plotting."

A direct accusation was the best choice here. Let Ashenfall know he was on to her game.

The Flame-Heart Chief snorted in an attempt to cover up the nervous twitch of her eye. "Ah, Silversong. I've been waiting for you. Come, sit."

Silversong remained standing.

Ashenfall banished the first creases of a frown. "Fine. Suit yourself. Bronzeblood and I were simply discussing ways in which his pack can contribute to the hunting efforts, seeing as how they're… quite out of shape, in case you haven't noticed." She smiled warmly at Swiftstorm. "No intermingling here, sentinel. Just business."

"Right." Silversong restrained himself from calling out her lie. Poke her too much, and she would lash out, and he needed her tamed for now. "I won't keep you long, then."

Ashenfall forced the submissive mother to lower her head so it almost touched the floor. She yelped at the uncomfortable position, which earned her a bite on the neck from Ashenfall. "Don't move. Keep your head low. Be a good little plaything, now."

The four subordinates yelped and ran to comfort their mother, but Bleaksmoke put himself in front of them, smoke trailing out of his nostrils. They cowered in front of the Chief's son. "Uh, uh, uh. Behave now, or we'll singe your mommy's whiskers and force you to remain tail-tuckers for life."

Ashenfall nodded approvingly, then used a forepaw to push her victim's head against the ground. "We talked about this, Cindersky. You're nothing more than a tool to be moved how I wish, and tools don't complain."

"I…" a defiant glare burned strong on her face, but she smothered it quickly before Ashenfall noticed, "I apologize, ma'am," Cindersky squeaked, groveling under her Chief's forepaw. "I live to please you. I'll be a good tool from now on. I beg you to punish me dearly for yelping. It's the only way I'll learn."

“Maybe later once I’m bored.” Ashenfall dragged her claws through Cindersky’s fur, looking up at Silversong and grinning at his discomfort. “You were saying?”

Cindersky…?

He’d heard the name before. He sucked in a breath, remembering when he and Frostpaw had fought Rime in the underground pit. “I knew it,” he uttered, his assumptions confirmed.

“Excuse me?” Ashenfall pressed her claws into Cindersky’s flesh, causing her to wince.

“Nothing.” Silversong pushed aside the questions he had and faced the tyrant. “I have a message for you on behalf of my pack: you won’t intimidate Whistle-Wind, and should you attack one of our members again, we’ll repay the insult in kind. You already owe us a debt for harming Hazel, and if it’s within the bounds of the law, we’ll force you to make up for that.”

Ashenfall threw her head back and laughed like the lunatic she was. “How dramatic! I barely even touched her! And besides, she was already terribly ugly, so I doubt I ruined her chances of finding a mate. If anything, her new makeover should render her a more exotic choice, wouldn’t you agree?”

For the briefest moment Silversong flashed his fangs and considered ripping the smirk off Ashenfall’s face. It took all his restraint not to pounce on the scatfur. His legs shook, and his tail tip quivered, but he forced his lips to cover his teeth and breathed in and out, in and out…

“Struck a nerve, did I?” Ashenfall licked the sides of her mouth, and Silversong feared to even think about the depraved thoughts going on behind those flaming eyes. “Oh, cheer up. I would pair the two of you together if it was within my power. You obviously care for her like only a mate would. Or maybe I would scorch the other side of her hideous face and tie her to the most beautiful Whistle-Wind male I could find. Imagine the irony!”

“Enough!” The heat within Silversong boiled his senses to vapour. “Your tradition of forcefully pairing wolves together as mates is disgusting. I don’t care if it’s not against the Wolven Code. It’s unacceptable! You can’t just threaten to unleash your son on wolves you don’t like!”

Bleaksmoke growled at Silversong, and Cindersky's eyes swelled into trembling orbs, but Ashenfall only stiffened. "Whatever do you mean?"

"Scorchfang." Upon saying her name, the piece of time vibrated, and Ashenfall breathed heavily. "I know you at least threatened to make Bleaksmoke her mate."

"Do you now?" Ashenfall came close to a snarl, her frown bulging over her eyes. "A would-be usurper like her should feel privileged I would even consider bonding her to my son."

There it was. The revelation Silversong had come for. The golden circle mimicked the rhythm of his heartbeat. He would bring Scorchfang to his side and use her against Ashenfall, but he needed to gather more information first.

Swiftstorm finally broke her silence. "All this yapping about mates has me thinking," she addressed Ashenfall and Bronzeblood like they were rookies caught doing something they shouldn't. "A Chief needs a consort to support them, and neither of you seem to have one."

"A temporary setback, sentinel," Ashenfall explained, her fury subsided. "My last mate died after being bitten by a viper at the end of spring, and I'm not done mourning him," she whined without a trace of sorrow.

Bronzeblood burped, flaps of fat wriggling at the slight motion. "I have a mate. She's over there." He lifted his muzzle and pointed his nose at an unassuming subordinate lying in the shade. "My third one since winter."

Swiftstorm shook her head disapprovingly. "The Wolven Code does allow you time to mourn, so I suppose it's not a pressing matter."

Ashenfall gave a satisfied flick of her tail and chuckled. "You're Silversong's sister, are you not? He could learn a thing or two about manners from you sentinel types. Be sure to teach him how to behave. Only a good follower of the Wolven Code is worthy of wielding the piece of time, and right now, he's straying far from the Warden's good graces."

"I think we're done here." Silversong spared one final glance at Cindersky's children before turning around and sauntering off. His limbs still shook, and his nerves still burned. He was very much looking forward to seeing Ashenfall dead.

"Have Scorchfang brought to me, plaything," Ashenfall ordered Cindersky. "Run along now. You stay here, Bleaksmoke. You'll be wanting to see her, I bet."

"Oh, yes, mother! Very much!" Bleaksmoke panted.

"Bronzeblood, pay attention. This is how you discipline your most unruly subjects."

Disgust oozed through Silversong as Cindersky hurried past him, her tail tightly tucked. He refused to seem pressed, showing his back to Ashenfall and taking his time to head out. Then on the way down the spire, he ran into Cindersky and Scorchfang coming up the ledge. The opportunity was too great to pass up, and he caught all but Scorchfang in the threads of his aura.

He stared at her defiant yellow glare and found her boldness inspiring. "Listen to me very carefully. I think there's a way we can help each other."

CHAPTER 15

A Hope for Flame-Heart

The stars fought a losing battle against a relentless swarm of clouds, yet even in the throes of defeat they shone defiantly bright.

Silversong stood between Chief Amberstorm and Hazel on a stretch of field hidden from view of the spire, the night breeze carrying the scent of grass and sweet flowers. According to the piece of time, this was the best place for a secret meeting.

Crickets chirped from the nearby hillside which shielded the location from the watchful eyes of the patrol units beyond. They circled the den in shifts some distance away—four groups representing each territory. Sneaking out of Thornhollow hadn't proven too difficult since Silversong was free of Swiftstorm until the sun dawned, and the weapon was good at shining light on the correct routes to take to avoid detection.

Blinking, Silversong glimpsed details about the meeting yet to occur. "They're almost here."

Amberstorm curled his tail up, and Hazel made an effort to loosen her tensed shoulders. Under the murky clouds, the burned side of her face wasn't so obvious unless Silversong looked closely. His heartbeat became more intense as he thought about bringing Ashenfall to justice. Motherwolf willing, retribution would be just one leap away after tonight.

"I trust you to speak wisely, Silversong," Amberstorm grunted, eyes locked on the stalemate between the stars and clouds. "Most of my lieutenants think I should be the one to represent Whistle-Wind, but your mother brought up a good point. I don't have the piece of time hinting at the right things to say."

"I won't disappoint, sir," Silversong grunted firmly, stilling his swaying tail. "Chief Ashenfall's days are numbered thanks to this opportunity."

"Good." Hazel planted her claws in the ground.

She'd volunteered to come along, wanting desperately to play a role in Ashenfall's demise. After using the piece of time to confirm Hazel's safety if she participated in the meeting, Silversong couldn't deny her request.

Other scents entered the cool breeze drifting downhill: wolves, one of them Scorchfang. The crickets ceased chirping. Turning his head to the height, he spotted three silhouettes sneaking their way to lower ground.

Good. They respected the condition of the meeting.

Neither party could bring more than two wolves to partake in the conspiracy. The small number ensured the chances of getting discovered remained low, and the extras could serve as advisors or protection if negotiations turned sour.

He calmed his breathing and raised his head. He needed to project confidence and authority, there was no room for hesitation. Hazel flicked her tail and lowered her ears slightly, but she didn't smell of acrid nervousness, instead, her scent suggested excitement. Amberstorm imitated Silversong's stance, and even though the Chief's body hadn't fully recovered from previous neglect, he still looked like a proud leader through and through.

As the newcomers approached, Silversong got a better look at their faces. Scorchfang strode in the middle like a Chief leading her soldiers to victory, a determined frown set above glowing yellow eyes. He recognized one of her companions. She was one of those who'd shown distaste at Sunpelt's threat earlier in the day. Her black tail brushed the grass, and her orange gaze scrutinized Silversong. Scorchfang's other companion was a pretty male whose russet fur was neatly groomed. His regard was fair, and his deep amber eyes bounced between Silversong and his packmates.

Frostpaw is far more handsome, though. Silversong scowled at the unwelcome thought. Maybe not unwelcome… but inappropriate at a time such as this.

The rival group stopped a couple tail-lengths from Silversong, none of them indicating whether they'd sensed his aura or not. Some of the stars pierced through the veil of darkness above, and Scorchfang began the meeting. "I see no reason to exchange formalities, so if it pleases, let's get started."

Futures flashed in the threads above Scorchfang, some contradicting one another, many confirming she was indeed a worthy asset to use against Ashenfall. Silversong cleared his throat and addressed her respectfully. "As you wish."

Scorchfang stared questioningly at Amberstorm, probably wondering why he was allowing Silversong to speak in his place. "You claim there's a way to depose Chief Ashenfall lawfully. I tried doing so once, but I failed. How can you assure me the outcome won't be the same now? Why should I agree to join your conspiracy when I stand to lose not only my dignity, but so much more?"

Silversong focused on the air slowly leaving his lungs, draining his head of all but the things he needed to say. "Chief Ashenfall called you a would-be usurper. Can you enlighten me on the context of this title?"

The pretty male in Scorchfang's group sniffed. "Why must you hear this tale? It shouldn't be of any import."

"It is of every import." Amberstorm's deep voice lured all eyes to him. "How else can we avoid the same errors Scorchfang made when striking against the tyrant?"

The second Flame-Heart member nodded in agreement, and the would-be usurper released a long sigh. "Chief Ashenfall's rise to power was illegitimate. Her lust for total control was always insatiable, and as a lieutenant, she orchestrated the death of the former Chief by manipulating him into choosing her as his mate, then poisoning him when he ate his favourite snack from the Prey Hollow. She stole a deadly plant from the Wise-Wolves' lair, caught a hare, then rubbed the subtle poison all over it. As the Chief suffered and slowly perished, he named her as his successor. For a time, her reign was tame and ordinary, but as the days passed, she couldn't resist the desire for more power. She wanted to govern every aspect of our lives! So I called a gathering to expose her as a code-breaker. It was the only lawful way to remove her from power… but I lacked sufficient proof of her wrongdoings."

It all clicked together in Silversong's head. "And since then, she threatens to have Bleaksmoke bonded to you as a mate. A way to keep you in line."

Scorchfang glowered at the mention of the Chief's son, lips curling to reveal sharp fangs. Hazel almost had the same reaction.

"And because she enjoys watching me squirm." Scorchfang gritted her teeth. "Bleaksmoke has always been… strange. Even as a pup. But if he'd been raised better, he wouldn't be the callous lout he is now. Chief Ashenfall singled him out among her litter and made sure he was completely dependent on her from a young age. The older he got, the more she moulded him into her personal tool to terrorize those critical of her reign. He's killed many of his *mates* already. The moment he loses interest in them, he complains to his mother, and she plots to have them disposed of."

Somehow, Silversong managed not to bristle, unlike Hazel and Amberstorm. "I'm surprised Ashenfall hasn't paired you and Bleaksmoke yet, considering your attempt at removing her from power. She doesn't strike me as the forgiving type."

Hazel dug her claws into the earth. "How do you endure it? If I were in your place, I would've killed Ashenfall even if it meant my painful execution afterwards."

"Because I still have hope." Scorchfang firmed her muscles, her tail tip quivering in the air. "After failing to expose Chief Ashenfall's crimes, I quietly gathered those I knew would support a coup against her. Her loyalists outnumber us, but over the seasons I've assembled a formidable resistance. We're just waiting for the right opportunity to strike."

Amberstorm sniffed incredulously. "This is a clear violation of the Wolven Code. You would start a civil war in your own pack if you openly rebelled against your Chief."

Scorchfang gave him a challenging glare. "Yes… but it's better than letting a sadistic tyrant slowly destroy Flame-Heart! And standing aside while she abuses everyone around her is also against the Wolven Code, even more so than plotting a coup, as I see it."

Silversong agreed, but his arrival here had created a better option. "There's something you're not telling us. How do you know of Chief Ashenfall's crimes? I doubt she spoke openly about her ambitions."

Scorchfang lowered her eyes in shame, forepaws trembling. "Because… because I once admired her greatly when we were corporals, to the point of infatuation even. But the feeling was one-sided. She saw how blinded I was by admiration, and she used me like she uses everyone else. She returned my affections only to keep me dependent, to keep me obedient. She confided in me her plots and schemes because she knew I would never betray her. Only after she became Chief was the veil lifted from my eyes, and I saw her for the monster she truly is. I… I know it's pathetic, but deep down, I find myself hoping she still feels a certain fondness for the time we spent together. And I like to think it's the only reason she hasn't yet killed me."

Silversong pondered how someone could be so evil as to exploit a packmate's vulnerability like that. Ashenfall was worse than the Heretic in every way imaginable!

Hazel shook her head and attempted to approach Scorchfang, but the Flame-Heart lieutenant backed away. Pity sparkled in Hazel's eyes. "You deserve so much better than her, Scorchfang."

Scorchfang looked at Hazel's scarred face and bowed her head. "On behalf of Flame-Heart, I ask your forgiveness. My Chief's assault on you brings great shame to me and my pack."

"There's nothing to forgive." Of all the responses Hazel could've given, she grinned. "And don't worry. I'll get back at your Chief one way or another."

Amberstorm cleared his throat. "I apologize in advance for asking, but Silversong mentioned you were summoned by Ashenfall earlier today. Was it simply to torment you further?"

Scorchfang scrunched up her forehead, studying Silversong and sleeking her fur. "Yes and no. She enjoyed humiliating me in front of the Stone-Guard wolves, but afterwards she commanded me to request a formal gathering from the Warden. At the top of Thornhollow, before the Wolven Bulwark, I'm to accuse Silversong of being a code-breaker and request he be put to death."

Amberstorm and Hazel bristled in outrage. Silversong maintained a steady gaze despite the pounding in his chest. "And upon executing me, she'll move to claim the piece of time for herself, right?"

Scorchfang nodded. "She convinced Chief Bronzeblood to speak out against you, and she'll probably try to get Chief Riptide on her side next. It'll be a sham trial based on testimony alone, but my *Chief* is convinced the Warden's dislike of you makes her more open to having you executed. I'm to request this gathering in a day's time."

The golden circle pulsed in Silversong's stomach, sending him visions of his trial and subsequent execution should he let events play out. He shivered, almost impressed at how quickly Ashenfall had devised a solid plan to capture the piece of time for herself.

Amberstorm growled, hackles hardened. “We must stop Ashenfall before this gathering is called!”

“NO!” Hazel barked, tucking her tail upon noticing Amberstorm’s shock. “Pardon me, sir, but I think the best course of action is turning this trial on Chief Ashenfall.” Silversong smiled at Hazel. He knew she would figure it out. Hazel turned to Scorchfang. “When everyone is gathered, instead of accusing Silversong, why not accuse your Chief of being the code-breaker who deserves death?”

Scorchfang recoiled, and Silversong could almost see the memory of her previous failure enter her head.

“She already tried this before!” the pretty male protested. “Chief Ashenfall won’t allow her to live if she makes the same accusations again.”

Scorchfang’s other companion grunted. “This can only end badly for the resistance. We need Scorchfang to lead us!”

“If we have solid evidence of Chief Ashenfall’s many crimes, would you be more inclined to accuse her once more?” Silversong asked, flexing the piece of time so the others could feel its aura if they hadn’t already.

Scorchfang froze, her fear scent quickly fading. “Can the piece of time prove her crimes somehow?” Hope flickered in her gaze, her tail going stiff.

“It can,” Silversong confirmed, holding on to the vision of his success. In it, he saw himself conjuring a clear reflection of the past. “But I need to practice something first, and we need River-Stream on our side during the trial. Even if Ashenfall is lawfully deposed, her loyalists and the Warden won’t take kindly to our victory. We need River-Stream to defend us should chaos erupt.”

“And how’ll you accomplish that?” Scorchfang asked, head tilted. “I doubt Chief Riptide is eager to take orders from a Whistle-Wind member.”

“There’s a corporal named Frostpaw among the River-Stream wolves. He’ll vouch for me. I’m sure of it. Together, we can convince Chief Riptide to cast aside his prejudices.” A tender warmth soaked through Silversong at the thought of his blue-furred friend.

“You’re certain of this, then?” Scorchfang’s tail twitched, and she started breathing faster.

Silversong took a pace toward her without blinking. “Nothing’s ever certain, Scorchfang, but this may be your only chance at seeing

Chief Ashenfall dead and your pack freed from tyranny without provoking a greater conflict. What say you?"

Scorchfang neared Silversong on delicate steps. He couldn't detect any trace of fear or hesitation within her now. The passion in those yellow eyes outshone the stars, and in a stable voice, she answered, "I accept."

Tonight, a hope for Flame-Heart had been rekindled.

CHAPTER 16

Portal

"I'll ensure the entirety of Whistle-Wind stands behind you, Silversong," Amberstorm grunted at Silversong's tail, careful to mimic his steps so it looked like only one set of paws had walked here. They couldn't be too careful when patrol units were about.

Hazel whined behind the Chief. "I'm worried about getting River-Stream on our side. How far can we trust Frostpaw since he's been disgraced and demoted? We're betting a lot on him not trying to redeem himself in the eyes of his Chief by standing against you."

The hurtful comment tugged Silversong's attention away from the sinuous path they needed to take so as not to get noticed. He looked over his shoulder to frown at Hazel. "You don't know him like I do. He's a good wolf, and he has a good heart. He'll stand up for me like I would for him. I would bet my life on it."

Hazel stared in surprise. "Sheesh. It almost sounds like you're defending a mate the way you speak of him. I'm just wondering how he'll manage to convince the more hostile members of River-Stream to support you."

Silversong snapped his head forward, tail stiffening and heart burning in a shockingly comfortable fire. The heat spread through him like a creeping tide, and he shook his head to rid his thoughts of Frostpaw.

Focus, Silversong, focus! He willed the piece of time to show him the correct route to follow, silently praying neither of the wolves behind him smelled the anxious scent he was surely emitting. "I'll-I'll sneak into the River-Stream lair later tonight and lay out the plan. I'll have Frostpaw's backing, and together, we'll convince the more devout members of his pack that they must either support me or accept a future where they'll be forced to tuck their tails and grovel at the mere mention of Chief Ashenfall. Because if she consumes the piece of time, she'll use it to dominate everything. The Four Territories, the sentinels, the exiles, EVERYTHING."

"Yeah, that argument would convince me, all right," Amberstorm muttered.

Thankfully, Frostpaw wasn't mentioned again as the three wolves snaked around the spire far from the patrol units. It would take a while to sneak back into the den this way, but it was the safest option according to the golden circle. Scorchfang and her wolves would be spotted, but since they were returning at irregular intervals, they had the excuse of simply being out to relieve themselves. The night deepened, and the weeds and plants slowly gave way to patches of short grass.

A glint caught Silversong's eye. Atop a flattened hillock a short distance away, something seemed to absorb the streams of starlight leaking through the somber clouds. The shine lured him to the source, Amberstorm and Hazel following close behind. Silversong failed to stifle a gasp when he reached the top of the rise, his eyes going wide in recognition. Centered on the mound was a smooth object poking out of the ground. It was as clear as newly formed ice coating a pond, but within its depths whirled a multitude of dim colours like a rainbow behind a sheet of fog. An otherworldly sensation crept throughout him the longer he stared. As if the thing might be trying to lure the spirit out of his flesh! The piece of time shuddered, and so did he.

"Motherwolf's milk," Hazel's breaths sounded panicked, "what is that thing?"

"Whatever it is, leave it alone." Amberstorm's fur stood on end. He crouched, ready to flee at a moment's notice. Silversong wouldn't have blamed him if he did. "It's making me feel uneasy. I don't like it."

"It's a portal." Silversong's voice wasn't his own despite coming from his mouth.

Amberstorm and Hazel turned to face him, and he teetered on the brink of fainting. His vision stretched until it bounced back to how it should be, but he wasn't looking at his packmates anymore. The setting sun and the orange-tinted sky lit the surrounding field, but there was no Thornhollow in sight. Beyond the wide expanse of grass was a forest of red trees, some still spewing smoke from where fire had licked life clean.

He was inside Stormstrider's body again, peering through the aura of time at the Forest Father and Motherwolf. A new Titan was also present: a huge raven whose feathers made shadows seem bright. Together, they faced the object as it had been during the War of Change—a circular platform crowning the grassy mound, its ever-shifting colours now vibrant and alive.

"I'm surprised the humans haven't demolished this one yet," Motherwolf grunted, her voice a rushing river, her eyes a swirling cluster of fiery stars. Everything about her was celestial, from her smooth black fur deep as the night to the way her stance suggested unyielding permanence.

"They do have a habit of destroying all natural beauty." The Forest Father quivered, the spiraling markings on his brown fur shining bright and green. "And yet, humanity is capable of far worse. I've never been more certain our invasion of their homeworld is justified."

"Yet their homeworld it is," the shadow-touched raven croaked, his eyes like orbs of oblivion. "It is their right to cherish or destroy anything under their sun. It is we who commit a cardinal sin by invading a realm not our own."

"Is it also their *right* to destroy our creations?" The Forest Father's starlit antlers glowed more intensely. "You heard from Stormstrider the fate our children would've suffered if we hadn't intervened. I care not how many fundamental rules we're breaking by involving ourselves in mortal affairs. I care only for the survival and prosperity of all prey!"

"Then we better remedy the shortcomings of our initial attack." Motherwolf flicked her hefty tail, the motion forming a wave of air that swept across the field below. "Aelrion still lives, as does Galdreth far to the south. Those two above all others concern me dearly. And a few lesser rulers who've managed to persevere against all odds still pose a threat to us if we don't snuff them out soon."

Stormstrider shivered at the pulsing of the piece of time. A trick of the eye made the coiling white patterns on his flesh move slightly. "A quick victory was always unlikely. The probability was too low, the humans too spread out. We're still in a good position. Aelrion must die. Galdreth must die. Humanity is breaking, but they can unite it. THEY MUST DIE!" His neigh rolled like thunder out of his mouth.

"How does our army fare, Trickster?" the Forest Father asked the huge raven. "My forces have encountered little worthy opposition across this realm. Two of the Stormlander tribes have even pledged themselves to me in the hopes I'll spare them from extermination."

"The traitors among our creations have mostly been wiped out, and a few more Titans have fallen to humanity's resistance." The giant raven pecked at the ground in frustration. "But my shadows retrieved their corpses before the enemy could be granted an opportunity to consume their hearts."

Each of the Titans immersed themselves in the uncomfortable silence spreading like a sickness all around them. Among other things, the idea of having their strengths devoured by mortals was beyond unthinkable.

The raven's beady eyes focused on Stormstrider. "I grieve for our losses. As an immortal being, I shudder to think of the potential nonexistence awaiting me should I be felled in this war. At least these mortals may live a second life in spirit form should they meet an untimely end, but for us… for us there's no second chance, is there, Stormstrider?"

Stormstrider began hyperventilating. "We can't escape the circle… we can't escape the circle…" he repeated. "Time and space… so frail to his touch. Why did they look for him?! Why did they reach too far?! The answer to everything. The dreaded remedy. Nothingness would've been better than this alternative! The eye swallows. Again and again, it swallows!"

"Stormstrider?" The Forest Father nudged him on the shoulder. "Look at me. You're here. I'm here. We're going to be all right, my friend."

"I've been searching for him in my dreams…" the raven uttered, his feathers fluffed out, "the Traveller." All heads swerved to him. "I-I need answers, you see. Lately I've been feeling as though we're all pawns trapped in a game we don't understand. Who is the Traveller, really? And why does he grant the impossible to those who find him? Does he always ask for something in return? Where does he take those who accept the bargain? I must know the truth. I must find the Traveller. Even if I'm to have my wings clipped and my talons rooted to this mortal realm for all eternity, I must find him. How did you do it, Stormstrider? If you can help me on this journey, I'll be in your debt forever."

"You'll be in his debt forever." Stormstrider leaned back as if the mysterious entity stood directly in front of him. Something odd happened to his blue eyes. The insanity within them vanished, and he took on a more stoic expression. "The Traveller found me. I allowed myself to be found, dragged into a maze of madness where the senselessness itself began to make sense. I surrendered myself—body and soul—to him, and in return he granted me the power to change the course of the future. You'll meet him only if your pursuit of knowledge is desperate enough to warrant his attention." Just as swiftly as it had gone, the madness returned to his gaze, and he began muttering nonsense about eyeballs on worming tendrils.

"Enough of your babbling, Trickster!" the Forest Father bellowed. "Can't you see Stormstrider's mind is fractured from all the futures he's glimpsed? Don't make him relive whatever happened between him and the Traveller."

"Forget the Traveller!" Motherwolf's growl shook the earth. "Focus your attention on the problem facing us. Humanity's most dangerous leaders still live, and we must slay them at once."

The raven gave Motherwolf a blank stare. "Yes… you're right. Perhaps my search for answers can wait until this war is concluded. Remind us how we should proceed, Stormstrider."

The Great Stallion squinted at the threads visible only to him. "Motherwolf stays here and leads the assault against Aelrion. Let fly your trickster ways, Ravenlord. Spread confusion among his forces." He lowered his eyes to the Forest Father. "You and I reinforce the far south before Galdreth reclaims too much ground. We push him back to his city. We surround him there. We make him seek his own death! Only we can bring about this fate now. Swear to me you'll not let your emotions control you. Galdreth is ruthless. He'll employ any tactics to slay a Titan. He'll test your restraint to its breaking point! Play into his game, and all may be lost!"

"I swear I'll control myself as I always do, my friend. I'll see you there." The Forest Father smiled and stepped toward the colourful circle rising from the ground. "Let all prey become the hunters for as long as this war rages on!"

As the shrill battle cry echoed across the field, the Forest Father dove for the circular object. In the span of a single blink, strings of every colour blossomed out of the surface to enfold the Titan, turning his flesh to glass. The tendrils then pulled him into the portal in a whistling *swoosh*.

"Once more into the sun I leap." The stallion compressed his body above his hind hooves before thrusting upward and diving for the portal. The multicoloured strings bloomed across his entire vision and entangled him too, soaking his essence into every strand.

The strings yanked Stormstrider into the portal, and the vibrant colours became utterly transparent, revealing two bewildered wolves blinking at Silversong under a cloudy night.

"A *portal*...?" Hazel tasted the name of the foreign object, wrinkling her nose as she moved in for a tentative sniff. "You looked out of it for a moment there, Silversong. Did this... *portal* do something to you?"

"No. It can't." He studied the muted colours in the strange surface. "This one's broken, and I doubt I would have the means to use it even if it wasn't." His memories zoomed in on the time when he'd spoken to his alternate future, when he'd seen a peculiar design on a closed entrance of stone—a circle dented in seven equally distanced places and gapped at the bottom, a circle bearing eight stars all connected to the shape itself.

Amberstorm avoided looking at the inactive portal. "We should return to Thornhollow. The others must be eager to hear all about our secret meeting."

"Yes," Silversong agreed, drawing once more on the power of the piece of time, using it to guide their steps toward the Flame-Heart den without getting spotted.

They arrived at the entrance to the spire, crouched and almost perfectly hidden by the grass and gloom of the night. Silversong stopped, pricking his ears at a sudden vision. A line in the threads alerted him to another secretive meeting between wolves of different allegiances.

"Silversong?" Amberstorm called out to him atop the slanted pathway of obsidian. "You coming?"

Hazel paused to give Silversong a concerned look over her shoulder.

"You two go on." Silversong turned away from his co-conspirators, curiosity getting the better of him. "There's something I must do first."

"All right." Amberstorm made a quiet whistling sound. "But be careful."

"Don't worry." Silversong looked back at Amberstorm and Hazel, offering them a reassuring smile. "I'll be quick as a breeze."

He connected himself to his Blessing as tightly as a bough to a tree, then darted around the Flame-Heart den when the patrol units weren't looking, paws lightened by swirls of air as he followed the guidance of the golden circle. He halted near the backside of the spire and hid behind a black outgrowth poking out of the central structure.

He waited there until moonbeams punctured tiny holes in the heavy clouds, until a wolfish figure silhouetted against the glint of obsidian carefully dropped down from a subtle opening in the height. He couldn't help but feel a tingle of satisfaction. Smaller four-legged shapes trailed the main one, each of them struggling not to lose balance as they hopped from ledge to ledge all the way down to even ground.

The largest silhouette checked on the lesser ones before padding off into the field, urging the others to follow in a straight line. They crouched and kept low to the grass. Silversong let the breeze pass around him so he wouldn't alert the sneaking group to his scent, then stalked his targets into the night.

CHAPTER 17

A Beautiful Crime

Silversong pursued the five wolves until they were a good distance away from the den.

When the wind calmed into a soothing whisper barely strong enough to sway the grass, he relinquished his influence over the current and followed the scent trail in front of him. The field was thicker here, the thistles and other prickly plants now sprouting in abundance. All around, the scuttling of small prey interrupted the high-pitched tunes of the singing insects, tickling the fur in his ears.

The five prowling shapes disappeared over an elevated bump in the field. Silversong hurried after them but stayed put at the top, concealed by the black-berried bushes there. Through the leaves, he had a clear view of the four subordinates and their mother. Three looked nervous, but the largest one remained at Cindersky's side, head raised as if trying to match her stature—as if trying to prove his bravery. He was the one whose eyes reminded Silversong of a certain exile responsible for shattering the Great Chain. The piece of time shuddered in response to his shiver.

"Is he coming…?" one of the subordinates squeaked, staring into the wide opening of a tunnel hollowed out in the ground a few leaps away.

"Shh!" A cowering sibling nudged her on the shoulder. "Be quiet."

The third frightened subordinate uttered not a sound, but the fourth and bravest let his thoughts fly from his mouth without care. "Why is he late? I have battle training tomorrow morning. I can't be sleepy or I'll get thrashed!"

Cindersky rounded on them. "Behave, all of you. Remember your manners. Be respectful and speak only when spoken to."

"Yes, mother," the four whined more or less in synchrony.

"I miss Charredstep," the most nervous of the four squeaked. "He was always so nice to me."

Cindersky flinched as if struck.

"He wasn't even our real father, gullwit," the outspoken one grunted. "Besides… he never liked me very much."

"No one likes you very much," the louder of the two sisters remarked.

"It's sad he got killed by a bear." The other male scratched at the ground. "When I finally learn how to weave fire, I'll scorch the beast's bones black!"

Cindersky let out a low growl to silence her children, and they quieted their muzzles. All four of them should've learned how to control their Blessing by now, but it all made sense why they couldn't. The reason was almost too tragic to contemplate.

Rime emerged out of the tunnel, fur darker than the night and eyes a bright shade of yellow. The scars on his face gave him a dangerous look, and the smile reaching near to his ears chilled Silversong to the marrow. Instinct begged him to intervene and save the Flame-Heart wolves from the Heretic's lieutenant. He managed to stay put, observing from the bushes while the piece of time pulsed and vibrated. A testament to his restraint.

The four siblings curled their tails to their bellies and waited for the exchange of formalities. None of them so much as looked at the huge exile while he studied each of them in turn.

Rime's gaze eventually rested on their mother. "Hey, Cindersky."

"Hey, Tiderunner." Her voice was so light Silversong had to strain his ears to listen. Her shadowy fur flowed to the breath of a breeze, her tail hanging loosely as she looked over her shoulder. "Everyone. This is your father. Your real father."

The subordinates glanced at Rime, then pretended to look elsewhere. Rime chuckled and moved in to inspect each of his children. He started by sniffing those who quivered behind Cindersky all while reassuring them he meant no harm. He gave particular attention to the fourth one before memorizing his scent last. "You're a brave one, aren't you? Bold and unafraid, just like me when I was your age. Take care of your siblings. Even though they may tease and annoy you, they'll always rely on you for protection."

Pride seemed to infect the yellow-eyed one. He lifted his tail and straightened his ears, giving Rime a slight nod. Cindersky introduced them all by name. "The Wise-Wolves named him Brightflare. This one is Flickerfur. He's Dawnshade, and she's Smokepelt."

"Not the names I would've approved, but all things considered, they're decent enough. It's good to finally meet you all." Rime's swishing tail slapped the grass, and his excited scent travelled all the way into Silversong's nose. "Cindersky has been telling me so much about each of you."

So this isn't the first time you two are meeting here. Silversong wondered how Cindersky had managed to keep her secrets from Ashenfall. Surely she would've suspected Cindersky's litter of being halfbloods by now since none of them could weave fire. Normally wolves their age would've taken any excuse to wield their Blessing.

Maybe Ashenfall already knows? She could be using this knowledge against Cindersky, forcing her to act as a plaything to be humiliated on a whim lest her children be exposed as halfbloods.

"Did she say how strong I am?" Brightflare yipped. "Yesterday, I wrestled a bone out of an older corporal's mouth!"

"He let you win, gullwit," the one called Flickerfur whined.

"Did not!"

"Did so!"

Cindersky showed her teeth to express her displeasure, but Rime's chuckle prevented her from reprimanding her children—his children. "I'm sure you're all very strong in your own ways."

"Is it true you're an exile?" Smokepelt squeaked.

"I heard you shattered the Great Chain." Dawnshade whispered behind his mother, probably hoping her frame would hide him from his father's gaze.

"Manners!" Cindersky barked, startling all four of the subordinates. "Tiderunner, I'm sorry. Maybe it wasn't a good idea to bring them here."

"It's all right, Cindersky," Rime reassured her, his tail straight and stiff. "Yes… it's all true. I was banished for the crime of loving your mother… and for killing the one who found out about our love. Your mother and I convinced everyone I was at fault for it all. We conjured up a lie where I was the villain, where I maliciously seduced Cindersky and threatened violence if she refused to meet me in the Twilight Meadow. We did it to protect you, our unborn children. None of you would've been allowed to breathe your first breaths if your packmates found out who your real father was. And so Cindersky persuaded Ashenfall to choose for her a new mate right after my banishment. She fooled all of Flame-Heart Territory into thinking you were truebloods. I was ready to give up in the Furtherlands, but then I met Ironwrath, and he showed me how the Fallen Titan's corruption can be my strength instead of my curse if only I allowed it to seep into my soul without a struggle. Yes. I became Ironwrath's lieutenant and shattered the Great Chain because he promised me a future without the Wolven Code, a future where my—our—beautiful crime would never be punished." His gentle smile made Cindersky stare at her forepaws in contemplation.

"Whoa," was all Brightflare could say.

Flickerfur pawed at the ground. "Why not run away together after you were found out?"

Cindersky turned to Flickerfur and sighed. "River-Stream and Flame-Heart would've wanted our blood. No matter where we ran, we never would've been safe. Our packmates would've reported our escape to the Warden, and once her sentinels caught a whiff of our scent, it would've been over for us. She could never allow such a blatant mockery of the Wolven Code to go unpunished. Her role as Warden would've been brought into question if she failed to bring us to justice. Rime taking the blame was the only way to keep the four of you safe."

Rime grunted approvingly. "You did a good job making sure none of them were infected by the Wolven Code, else they would be far more frightened at this revelation."

"How could I have raised them to hate their real father?" Cindersky looked at Rime and faced him as an equal. "To hate the love which once bound us?"

A frown formed on Rime's forehead. "It still binds us. You must join me, Cindersky. Ironwrath carved out this tunnel for us. It leads deep into the Fireleaf Forest. You and our children can escape from the maw of this wretched territory. You won't have to live in fear of other wolves suspecting the truth anymore. You won't have to grovel at the forepaws of a tyrant. You won't have to keep lying about Charredstep's death. You'll be free and safe… and once Thornhollow is destroyed and the Wolven Code is broken, we'll finally be able to live as a true family."

“*Destroyed…?*” Flickerfur squeaked. “Mother, he can’t mean it.”

“I’ll miss Ashleap if we go…”

“Yeah… we have friends back at Thornhollow.”

“Friends who would gladly tear off your hides if they found out you were halfbloods,” Rime stated bluntly, earning him a dire look from Cindersky. “It’s only a matter of time before Ashenfall reveals the truth to everyone. None of you can weave fire or water. You’re all abominations according to the Wolven Code. It’s not fair, but it’s the truth. Until Ironwrath is victorious, you’re all much safer far away from Thornhollow.”

The subordinates succumbed to uncontrolled whimpers, hiding their faces in their mother’s fur.

Cindersky bristled, and smoke drifted out of her nostrils. “I’ve heard about the things you and the other exiles did after your escape from the Furtherlands… all the pain and suffering you inflicted on the Whistle-Wind Pack, all so the Heretic could empower himself. And don’t get me started on torturing prey into obedience. I was shocked to learn of this from the Warden’s debriefing. No, Tiderunner. We’ll be no safer among your new *packmates* than we are here.”

“Rime. My name is Rime, Cindersky. And I would’ve thought you of all wolves would see the good of Ironwrath’s cause. Anything is justified if done in the name of freedom! But maybe you’re just like the others. Maybe you need further convincing.”

“Your master abandons dignity and honour in the pursuit of his goals.” Cindersky revealed fangs without snarling. “He wouldn’t hesitate to sacrifice you or us if it meant victory for him.”

“You’re wrong!” Rime snapped, making his children flinch. “I’m loyal to him, and he’s loyal to me. The only reason he hasn’t attacked Thornhollow yet is because you’re still here. I made him promise not to launch his assault until after you’re all safe in the Fireleaf Forest. He wouldn’t dare betray me.”

The opportunity to steer the future the correct way was right in front of Silversong. He jumped out of the bushes, the blood in his veins prickling. “She’s right, Rime. He’ll sacrifice anything to win. Even you and those you care about.”

Rime crouched and pushed his corruption into the ground, hackles hardened. The grass withered into brown blades where he stood. Cindersky bounded away from him, barking for her children to stay behind her as she put herself far from whatever fight was about to ensue. The subordinates all hid at her tail.

Foul-smelling roots erupted out of the soil, sharp ends aimed at Silversong. He sprang out of their reach and expanded the aura of time to its limit, catching Rime in its grasp. He wrapped the threads around the exile and froze all but Rime's head. His eyes swelled into outraged orbs. The blackened roots flopped to the ground as if they too were shocked at the unexpected move.

Before Rime could do more than snarl, Silversong approached him. "I'm not here to fight you."

"You brought him here?!" the exile growled at Cindersky. Drool dripped from his long fangs.

"I brought myself here," Silversong let loose a growl of his own. "At a moment's notice I can end you in various ways, so I suggest you control your temper." The headache hadn't yet come, and until it did, he intended to keep Rime tightly secured.

Cindersky gasped, realizing who'd interfered in the meeting. "It's you! You've caught Chief Ashenfall's interest, young one."

Young one? You're older than me, but not old enough to speak to me like you're an elder. Silversong ignored the odd comment. "I imagine I've caught the interest of many wolves… for better or worse."

"If it's Chief Ashenfall, it's definitely for worse. She intends to have you tried and executed for being a code-breaker," Cindersky grunted, calming her rapid breaths. "You can release Tiderunner. He won't attack you."

"I won't?!" Rime barked as if the mere thought of not sinking his teeth into Silversong's throat was preposterous.

"Yes. You won't." Cindersky's flame-touched glare warned Rime against arguing. "Listen to reason for once and quit snarling like a pup throwing a tantrum."

Rime's eyes bounced between Cindersky and Silversong before he finally covered his fangs. "All right. But this better be good."

Glimpsing no immediate danger if he released Rime, Silversong loosened the threads around the exile and retracted the aura of time until it returned to normal size. No headache had come. He was getting better at wielding the weapon. "Everything I said about the Heretic is true. You're his tool, Rime, much like Cindersky is Ashenfall's tool. It's just not obvious to you because he treats you better, but he'll sacrifice you without a second thought if it means victory for him. He's more like the Empress than he would care to admit."

"Even if your claims are true—and they're not—it just means the master is ruthless enough to win by any means necessary whereas you're too weak-willed to even contemplate the use of violence as a solution." Rime's nostrils flared, claws puncturing the ground. "You could've wrestled control of the Four Territories out of the Warden's mouth if you weren't so determined to end this conflict without bloodshed. Instead you gave her control of an army infected by the Wolven Code. An army we'll crush because any hope of true unity is dashed so long as she leads the charge. You saw it in the Twilight Meadow, and yet still you insist on changing a flawed system without baring your fangs. Revolutions may be started peacefully, but they're always ended violently."

Silversong allowed the exile's arguments to sweep his thoughts under a heavy tide of truth. For all Rime's faults, he was right about many things, but he was also wrong about so much more. "I have bared my fangs more times than you can imagine. Wolves are finally starting to see tyrants and fanatics for who they really are, and they're finally starting to trust in my vision. I haven't wrestled control out of the Warden's mouth because the more she tightens her jaws, the more control slips through her teeth. There's no better way of dismantling her power than by letting her do it for me. When the packs finally come around, I'll have a much easier time fixing the Four Territories. Yes, there might be some who'll never abandon the old ways, and yes, some violence may be necessary to quell those who're truly blinded by the Wolven Code, but the piece of time has shown me a thriving future born of my actions, a future where wolves aren't forbidden from loving who they wish. Your master would bring about this future through dominance and bloodshed whereas I seek to achieve it through more peaceful means."

Rime scoffed, his gaze falling to the rotting grass beneath him. One of the blades stood green as ever in defiance of the surrounding corruption. The exile squinted at it in consideration.

Cindersky neared her mate, paying no heed to the subordinates begging her to stay away. "He's right, Tiderunner. Silversong's influence is spreading even among my packmates. A Whistle-Wind subordinate who defied the law and stole the piece of time from under the Heretic's nose. If this subordinate had stayed true to the

Wolven Code, the Four Territories would've fallen to the exiles by now. A Whistle-Wind corporal who challenges the Warden's authority. If this corporal really can see the future, maybe he ought to be trusted. Maybe there's hope for a more benevolent Chief to rule over Flame-Heart. Silversong's very existence is a symbol of defiance. He's a shining beacon unafraid to expose the shadow of oppression. A shadow we're all living under."

"And how many are still blind to this shadow?" Rime lifted a forepaw to stroke the blade of grass defying his corruption.

"Too many," Silversong cut in, flicking his tail and keeping it raised. "But that number is poised to dwindle after my play against Chief Ashenfall. You can count on it."

Cindersky cocked her head to the side, clearly wondering how Silversong was going to outmaneuver her tormenter.

"You may have the piece of time, Silversong, but you don't have much of it." Rime glanced at his children and shook his head upon seeing the fear in their eyes. "Ironwrath won't wait around for wolves to start thinking for themselves."

"You said yourself he won't attack us so long as Cindersky and your offspring are still at Thornhollow." Silversong challenged Rime's doubtful glare. "Convince him to chase his tail a little while longer, and I may yet deliver the future he's always wanted. But he'll have no place in it. And you… you'll have to face justice sooner or later. The massacre at Wind's Rest hasn't been forgotten."

"Hmph." Rime lifted his head and grimaced. "It was an ugly den, anyway. And I seem to recall Ironwrath offering you all a way out if you simply joined us."

Silversong wanted to bite off Rime's face and remind him of the pain he caused that day. An enticing fantasy, and it would have to remain just that. "You should go. Deliver my proposal to your master and reflect on how loyal he really is to you."

Turning to his forbidden mate, Rime's expression softened. "If you reveal Cindersky's secret, you're dead… as is your sister and the blue scatfur you've taken a liking to."

"Your threats don't scare me." Silversong applied pressure to his limbs so they wouldn't tremble.

"They should." Rime's face was harder than stone, and his tail stiffer than an oak branch. "There's one thing I would like you to admit before I leave. Cindersky has already made me aware of Ripper's condition. Besides being short an eye, he's alive and pricklier than a boar's backside. Ashenfall is looking after him until the Warden is ready to begin the interrogation. If he can endure long enough, we'll get him out eventually. However, we never got closure on Bonechew's fate. You and Palesquall murdered him, did you not?"

Silversong cringed at the memory of the stray exile landing on frozen spikes of water. "A fight broke out, and he got impaled on blades of ice. You might know the move, being a former River Stream member and all."

"So it was Frostpaw, then?" Rime clenched his teeth as if imagining them crushing Frostpaw's throat. "Figures. You abused Ironwrath's trust and got so many of us killed. A reckoning is coming, Silversong, and you better be ready to suffer its bite."

"Likewise." An aching tenseness overcame Silversong. Rime backed off and joined Cindersky in a private conversation of whispers and low whines. Despite Silversong's pricked ears, he could only make out a few things.

"... we've been found out again. We're really terrible at this."

"... bound to happen."

"... least no one had to die this time. Know where to meet me next?"

"... won't be able to until tomorrow night... it's a bit far."

"... they safe?"

"... too busy plotting to care much."

"... sorry for snapping."

"... don't you worry about us."

"... if he tries anything—"

"We'll be safe. I trust him."

"... love you."

"... love you too."

After a brief nuzzle, Rime broke away from Cindersky and addressed his children. "Whatever happens, you'll all be in my thoughts. Take care of each other while I continue the fight for freedom." He refused to look at Silversong and crouched into the tunnel dug out for him by the Heretic, disappearing into darkness.

In an isolated area such as this, the golden circle seemed a presence of its own. Had Silversong made the correct choices? Had he averted the destruction of Thornhollow? Yes and no. Tonight he'd divided fate into two paths—one leading to the collapse of the spire and the deaths of many, and the other leading to a time of unrest followed by an era of peace.

Silversong studied Cindersky's uncertainty. She thought him trustworthy, but not enough to abandon her wariness completely. "I guessed there was more to Rime's story than seduction and murder. I won't speak of your secret to anyone, but Rime was right about one thing. You aren't safe at Thornhollow so long as Chief Ashenfall reigns."

"She already knows about my crimes against the Wolven Code. It's how she keeps me obedient," Cindersky admitted, pausing to growl at the heavens. "I pray she meets an untimely death every night, but Motherwolf hasn't seen fit to grant me such a mercy."

"Maybe I can." Silversong motioned for Cindersky and her children to follow him back to Thornhollow. "Come, I'll explain everything along the way."

CHAPTER 18

Pieces of the Chain

"You should get some sleep before you head to the River-Stream lair," Chief Amberstorm suggested in the darkness of the grotto. "A fatigued mind is as sluggish as a fatigued body."

All around him, Silversong heard voices locked in quiet conversation, discussing the risky plan set in motion by Hazel. He'd quelled many fears already, but the more the wolves whispered, the more those fears sprouted back up, harder to suppress than before.

"There's no time to spare, sir," Silversong addressed the Chief in a respectful but blunt tone. "Every passing moment brings the sun closer to dawning, which means I'll be tied to Swiftstorm all day. No. We must gain River-Stream's support now."

In truth, Silversong couldn't have fallen asleep even if he wanted to. Not when Ashenfall was actively plotting against him. Not when her downfall was just around the corner.

"All right, Silversong," Amberstorm grunted. "One more thing before you go."

"Yes?"

Amberstorm lowered his voice. "You like Frostpaw, don't you?"

A spark jolted through Silversong, lifting his fur and startling him wide awake. His heart thumped louder, chest warmed by a gentle heat. Fear followed, squashing the pleasant sensation and warning him of potential rejection. He could barely see the threads turning before his eyes, and as if caught in their choking grasp, he froze.

"So, that's a *yes*," Amberstorm chuckled in amusement. He looked… not angry, but concerned. "Your reaction wasn't very subtle when Hazel mentioned him back in the field, just like it isn't subtle now. You're not fooling anyone, Silversong."

"I… I…" Silversong couldn't speak. His heart had taken control of his brain and was preventing him from denying the truth.

"I'm not mad at you," Amberstorm admitted, instilling some relief in Silversong.

"Y-you're not?" Silversong's limbs shook like frail branches.

Amberstorm sighed. "Who am I to deny your heart its desire? I would've much preferred it if you'd chosen someone from our pack, but times are changing, and so must we."

The small bit of relief trickling through Silversong became a flood. "Most Whistle-Wind males prefer she-wolves, and the few who don't are already taken. But even if that wasn't the case, none of them interest me as much as Frostpaw does."

Motherwolf's milk, does it feel good to say it out loud!

"Fair enough," Amberstorm softened his voice to a whisper. "Do your parents know?"

An uncomfortable pressure squeezed Silversong's gut. "No. And I would rather keep it that way for now." He thought about why this was his response, unable to get a clear answer. "It's not that I think they wouldn't support me, it's just… it isn't time."

"I understand," Amberstorm whined gently. "I hope you succeed in bringing about an ideal future for all wolfkind, Silversong."

"Thank you, sir." Pride shone bright within Silversong, brighter than the piece of time itself. "I won't let you down."

"If you're not keen on resting, best you be off, corporal," Amberstorm grunted.

"Yes, sir." Silversong turned to leave, feeling giddy and excited. *Finally, I get to see Frostpaw again!* His thoughts lingered on the memory of snuggling in the alcove overlooking the great lake of River-Stream. Happy bees buzzed in his stomach. *Together, we'll erode the barriers between our packs.*

The piece of time dashed his hopes, the threads closest to his eyes showing him the consequences of leaving the grotto tonight. Chief Amberstorm would die. Smoke enveloped him in a black shroud, and in the confusion, sharp fangs tore into his throat, severing vital arteries and rendering Whistle-Wind leaderless.

Silversong found the Chief's scent and padded up to him. "Sir!"

"Yes, Silversong?"

"I can't leave. You'll die if I go to the River-Stream lair tonight." Silversong relayed his vision to the gasps of the surrounding lieutenants.

Amberstorm silenced the worried wolves. "If you don't go, can our plan still succeed?"

No. Silversong already knew the answer before clearing his head and drawing on the strength of the golden circle. He would be put on trial, and it would be Whistle-Wind and Scorchfang's rebels versus Flame-Heart, Stone-Guard, and the sentinels. Nowhere near enough. River-Stream would stand aside, a skirmish would ensue atop the spire, and blood and death would be the only victors. The Wolven Bulwark, broken and ununified, would collapse under the Heretic's inevitable assault.

"No," Silversong admitted reluctantly.

Amberstorm thought for a long moment. "Then why are you still here, corporal?"

The cold response surprised Silversong, and he hesitated. "Because… because you'll die if I go, and I don't know if there's a way to prevent your death."

"And is a Chief's duty not to lay down their life for the good of the pack should it be required of them?" Amberstorm recited one of the tenets of the Wolven Code, ironic as that was.

The lieutenants present protested, but the Chief wouldn't budge. "Go, Silversong. That's an order. I'll remain here and choose who next deserves the mantle of Chief should your vision come to pass." He sniffed until he detected the scent he was seeking out. "And I'll see that my children remember me as a good and loving father."

A void expanded in the pit of Silversong's stomach, and he couldn't feel his own legs as they led him through the tunnel and out into the cool night. He forced the weapon to reveal ways in which he could avoid Amberstorm's death, but the answer was the same every time: return to the Whistle-Wind lair and watch over your packmates. Of course, doing so would mean forsaking River-Stream as a potential ally—something he couldn't afford.

The piece of time doesn't know everything. I can still save Amberstorm. I won't let him die! He held firmly onto those thoughts as he snuck his way up the den, freezing stray Flame-Heart sentries before they could smell him. He released them when he was far enough away, the process repeating itself a few times until he reached the second level.

He concentrated on his surroundings to soothe his fears. The low temperature was a welcome change from the blistering days of summer, and the billowing clouds covering the moon foretold a greater change to come. A change everyone would have to accept

The heat of summer, the rains of spring, the snows of winter… everything changes, and so must the Wolven Code.

Flame-Heart wolves slept in corners, their gentle snores countering the silence of the night. Silversong glimpsed no immediate threat in the threads, meaning they were all fast asleep. He eased his focus away from the troubling vision of Amberstorm's death, and another warning promptly filled the space in his head. He saw himself gasping under the dawning sun, drowning in a waterless sea, failing to suck in the tiniest amount of air. This future was thankfully avoidable. All he had to do was not waste too much time in the River-Stream lair.

Crouched and feeling adequately stealthy, Silversong snuck toward the thick tooth poking out of the smooth floor. In the gloom, the hole under the outgrowth was almost invisible. The River-Stream soldier guarding the entrance started, and just as alarm entered her eyes, Silversong caught her in his aura.

"When I release you, don't growl or snarl, and certainly don't wake everyone up by barking like a confused gullwit." He allowed the sound of his voice to enter her ears. "I'm here to offer a proposal to your Chief."

He released the soldier. She tensed, assuming a defensive posture. "I know who you are."

"Did my silver coat give it away?" Silversong joked to put her mind at ease. "Or maybe it was my blue eyes."

The sentry found no humour in his quips, and it took a little more convincing for her to let him enter. As he padded through the narrow passage, he returned his focus to the piece of time and all the necessary behaviours required for diplomacy. River-Stream's support was as paramount as Scorchfang's role in the upcoming trial.

The River-Stream grotto was indeed larger than Whistle-Wind's. It contained a few pools of stale-smelling water and supported a greater number of wolves. However, the mood here was as downcast as the makeshift lair below, and a sense of desperation hung over the darkened cave lit only by green-glowing grubs crawling about the roof. Wolves slept or padded to-and-fro without purpose. Elders congregated in their corners, lieutenants huddled around Chief Riptide and Icetail, and Frostpaw sat alone while peering at his own reflection in one of the ponds. Silversong released his grasp on the piece of time just as Snowleap noticed him.

Any moment now...

Heads swerved in his direction, followed by many snarls. He gulped and forced his body to display no signs of anxiety. He would represent the Whistle-Wind Pack as strongly as its founder had in a bygone era.

"You!" Riptide's yellow eyes pinned Silversong where he stood. "What is the meaning of this?!"

Silversong repeated to himself the things he was about to say, making sure his explanation would suffice. "The time has come to choose the fate of your pack, Chief Riptide." The River-Stream wolves stopped snarling and pricked their ears to listen. "Before the coming day ends, Scorchfang will request a formal gathering from the Warden under the pretense of accusing me of being a code-breaker deserving of death, but when everyone is gathered at the spire's peak, she'll betray Chief Ashenfall and accuse her of being the real code-breaker instead."

As he spoke, suspicious glares made him think twice about whether coming here had been a good idea or not. "I'll expose her by using the piece of time to prove her many crimes, but I'll need your support throughout the trial. Once Ashenfall is cornered, she'll lash out at me, and we must all be ready to thwart her while remaining in the good graces of the law."

The sour tang of nervousness worsened, and some of the senior members of River-Stream whispered among themselves in consideration.

For all his posturing about River-Stream's devotion to the Wolven Code, Riptide appeared conflicted if his frown was anything to go by.

It seems Flame-Heart's treatment of your pack has made you more open-minded.

Noting her mate's indecision, Icetail took the initiative to respond first. "Why should we trust anything you say, Silversong? Everyone knows you're a code-breaker even if you haven't yet been formally accused. Your very presence here threatens the integrity of the Wolven Bulwark."

Darkwave and a few more lieutenants grunted in agreement, but Snowleap and several others refused to openly support Icetail's claims. In his lonely corner, Frostpaw stiffened. Silversong gave him a sharp look, warning him not to interfere yet.

Silversong managed not to quiver upon feeling the heat of Icetail's fury. The strong scent of her anxiousness contrasted her scowl. "Icetail, you know I'm not the one threatening the integrity of the Wolven Bulwark, and I think you know who the real culprit is. You're just too afraid to say it."

The snarls returned, nastier than ever, but Silversong faced them without flinching.

"I'll not hear your insults, cur!" Spittle flew from Darkwave's mouth. "Go back to your lair and do whatever you filthy Whistle-Wind wolves do far away from us. Go! Or do we have to chase you out?!"

Icetail's golden eyes narrowed on Silversong, her grey fur bristling. "You think the Warden is driving us toward ruin?"

There you go.

Silversong feigned a surprised reaction, ignoring Darkwave's ugly snarl. "I suppose I misjudged your lack of courage. Forgive me."

"Hold your tail!" Icetail protested. "I-I never said the Warden is responsible for our army's shortcomings."

"Shall I punish him for such blasphemy, ma'am?" Darkwave crouched, ready to pounce on Silversong.

Icetail chose silence as a response. Silversong couldn't look away from her trembling regard. "Who else but she is responsible, Icetail? I tried to minimize our casualties during the Heretic's ambush. If the Warden had allowed us to fight together from the very start, we could've won a decisive victory over the exiles. How many wolves did we lose in the Twilight Meadow? How many could've been saved if the Warden hadn't ordered us to fight separately?"

"So many," one of the River-Stream elders whined. A father of one of the dead, perhaps?

Silversong continued. "A more insidious threat now looms over us all, and the Warden does nothing about it because she believes this threat doesn't explicitly go against the Wolven Code.

You already know who I'm referring to. It's Chief Ashenfall! A tyrant who assaulted my packmate! A tyrant who bullies you into skulking around in the darkness! A tyrant who tried preventing you from accessing a clean source of water! And where was the Warden during all this? Absent! Believe me, she wouldn't have lifted a single paw until some of you started dying of thirst!"

"He's right," one of the River-Stream Wise-Wolves whined to a group of parents whose children had most likely suffered from dehydration.

Silversong took a deep breath, composing himself for the truths he needed to present. "The Wolven Code was created to divide. To remind us of the reckless greed that caused the Rise of the Fallen Titan. The lawlessness of our ancestors must never be repeated, but in accepting this set of rules, we've chained our own freedoms to an extreme solution. Must we really look at other packs in disdain? Must we punish those who only follow their hearts? Must we tuck our tails and show our bellies to a tyrant Chief? Look around you. Are these hardships a worthy price to pay to uphold tradition? Look at all the evil allowed to thrive so long as it's deemed *lawful*. Look at the exiles and all they've accomplished. The Wolven Code creates more problems than it fixes. Our enemies were pushed to one extreme by another extreme, and now the Heretic is poised to destroy us all because we refuse to stand united. The Wolven Code is flawed, and it must be amended!"

The growls came first, then the insults, then the threats. The pools of stale water stirred and bulged, reaching for Silversong. He tensed the threads of his aura, feeling as though the whole cave were closing in on him. The near future winked away, drowned under the rising dread. His fur stood on end from the passing of a chill, and it took all his strength not to tuck his tail at the approaching fangs. Despite his failure to convince the entire River-Stream Pack of the Wolven Code's flaws, there were some who refused to join the devoted—Frostpaw, Snowleap, Icetail, some elders and one of the Wise-Wolves, a few lieutenants, several corporals, and a dozen subordinates, and most surprisingly, Chief Riptide himself.

Silversong cast a pleading look Frostpaw's way.

Now would be a good time to speak up.

Darkwave charged toward Silversong, fangs dripping saliva. Just as Silversong prepared to remove Darkwave from the stream of time, Frostpaw jumped to Silversong's side. "FATHER! STOP!" he barked.

Darkwave skidded on the smooth floor, stopping a tail-length from Silversong's muzzle. His blue fur bristled, and hatred lit his yellow eyes aflame. "How dare you stand beside him? You're no son of mine!"

Frostpaw flinched, his tail lowering and his posture deflating, but upon turning to Silversong, he found the courage to stand strong and face his father's wrath. "So you've said countless times already." Though his voice quavered, he managed to make it sound powerful. "I can't allow any of you to attack Silversong. Not after all we've been through together. Cover your fangs, curse you! He saved us all inside the Mountainmouth. He gave us a chance to fight back against the Heretic, and you DARE threaten his life? You insult our honour! Is this how River-Stream repays courage and valour? You should be ashamed of yourselves!"

Jaws dropped in shock, and Frostpaw's father took a couple paces back. Those snarling now gaped at the disgraced corporal… the brave corporal, the corporal who'd helped Silversong do the impossible. One of their own had stood up for a rival. Silversong looked at Frostpaw's resolute face and smiled, a familiar heat soothing riled nerves.

"But… but he insulted the Wolven Code," came a voice from a cluster of corporals. "Insulted it in front of us!"

Frostpaw took a deep, trembling breath. "The more I think on it, the more I come to realize that maybe Silversong is right about the Wolven Code."

That earned more than a few gasps.

One of Frostpaw's siblings growled at him. "Mother would be ashamed of you, Frostpaw!"

Frostpaw choked on a whimper, eyes closed and forepaws shaking. Silversong nuzzled him and licked the healed wound on his shoulder, feeling the tensed muscles underneath. Frostpaw leaned on Silversong, and the wolves around them either stood still in disbelief or openly scowled at the public display of affection. Snowleap tilted her head.

Frostpaw opened his eyes and held Silversong's gaze. The briefest of smiles cut the corporal's shame to pieces. "Yes… she would be. But I choose not to live in memory of her. I choose to live for myself and who I wish to be."

"A code-breaker," Darkwave hissed in disgust, refusing to spare his son from unjust anger. "By Motherwolf, I'll not see you corrupted by a Whistle-Wind scamp! The dishonour it would bring to me would haunt my kin for generations to come! No. I'll give you one chance to redeem yourself, Frostpaw. Bring me Rime's hide, and I'll think about forgiving you."

Frostpaw nearly jumped, his hopes for gaining his father's approval revived. Silversong could feel it in the corporal's quickening heartbeat. He could see it in Frostpaw's pricked ears, in the widening of his eyes. He wanted his father's love more than anything.

Don't listen to him, Frostpaw. You're better off without him.

"You must also stay away from this… this blue-eyed freak!" Darkwave ran his tongue along his teeth. "Don't let him so much as sniff you!"

Frostpaw glanced at Silversong, then at Darkwave.

Please don't, Frostpaw. Stay beside me, please! Silversong's frantic heartbeat begged Frostpaw to remain where he stood. Icy claws gripped Silversong's stomach and squeezed.

Before a decision could be made, Riptide finally spoke up. "I don't like Silversong, and I certainly don't like his criticisms of the Wolven Code… but I don't like Chief Ashenfall even more. She's dangerous and unpredictable. She must be stopped. Frostpaw also has a point. Silversong's actions inside the Mountainmouth were… commendable. It wouldn't be right to treat him like an exile. I see this now."

Relief loosened the tension in Silversong's muscles. "You'll stand for me, then?"

Riptide peered into Silversong's eyes and gave a slow nod. "I've no other choice. For the good of my pack, I must join your conspiracy. May Motherwolf watch over us all."

Uncertain murmurs filled the cave.

Darkwave couldn't hide his disapproval. "Motherwolf doesn't watch over code-breakers nor those who would let themselves be tricked by one!"

Riptide's growl echoed through the expanse, grinding every whisper into pure silence. "Do you question my judgment, Darkwave? Am I simply a fool being played by Silversong? Am I not capable of making my own decisions? Your counsel is appreciated when appropriately given, but your insults are not. Do not speak out of line again, understood?"

For only a breath, Darkwave exuded defiance, his eyes burning, his frown deepening. A blink later, and he became the perfect example of sincere deference. "My apologies, sir. It won't happen again."

Riptide shook his head. "It better not. I understand your reservations more than anyone. The Wolven Code is sacred, and we're working to undermine it. But if we don't get rid of Chief Ashenfall, she'll doom us all in her lust for power. She doesn't care a lick for the Wolven Code! She'll use it as a weapon to get her foul mouth on the piece of time. I've seen the way she looks at Silversong. The Warden is too preoccupied by the exiles to see her as a genuine threat, and so we must act in the Warden's stead."

Or maybe the Warden knows exactly how dangerous Ashenfall is. Maybe the Warden is counting on Ashenfall making a move against me. The Warden isn't a gullwit. A zealot, maybe, but not a fool. Maybe she's just waiting for the right moment to steal the piece of time from me.

"You made the right choice," Silversong found himself whining. "I know you doubt me, but before this is over, you'll see the value in working together against a common foe. A true alliance must function without hate. Only then can we achieve great things."

Riptide swiped his tail and ordered his wolves to relinquish control over the bulging pools. The stale water returned to the cavities, and Riptide sighed. "You're turning everything upside down, Silversong, but your arguments are sound despite how much they frighten me."

"Take heart, Chief Riptide." Silversong maintained eye contact. "We can't remain stuck in our old ways forever. Life is all about change, and to deny it means fading into obscurity as time passes us by." The golden circle pulsed, and he quickly added, "Ashenfall or one of her cronies might come by later seeking your support against me. Play along, and say nothing of this meeting."

After giving Frostpaw a reassuring smile, Silversong turned to the exit, leaving the River-Stream wolves to contemplate the future of the Four Territories. His tangled emotions and throbbing anxiety calmed into a steady flow of satisfaction as he emerged onto the second level of Thornhollow, mind open once more to glimpses of possible events. The sentry posted outside eyed him suspiciously, and he snuck away until she was out of sight.

He stopped, hackles rising at another vision of himself thrashing in silent pain, lungs desperate for a breath, just a single breath!

His head zipped over his shoulder, heart dropping into a frozen pit. Swiftstorm and Greyhail stared at him from the opening at the far end, eyes bulging out of their sockets and mouths agape.

I took too long in there!

Silversong wasn't close enough to catch them in the threads, and even if he was, they would remember spotting him sneaking about the second level. The piece of time couldn't erase memories. There was nothing to do but wait for them to arrest him.

The fog of his fears clouded the terrible vision of him gasping for air, and as the sentinels approached, he wondered how the Warden would punish him. It was almost troubling how quickly his brain had conjured up various methods of torture. Which one would be administered to him?

Swiftstorm's face frightened him most of all. She was no longer simply his sister, but a sentinel, and sentinels had no mercy for code-breakers.

CHAPTER 19

Again

"Can't I just—"

Greyhail bit the air a whisker-length from Silversong's face. "I forbid you from speaking until we reach the Warden."

Heart racing, Silversong followed him up the winding ledge, his steps bringing him closer to the leader of the sentinels. Swiftstorm trailed the two of them some distance behind, taking care not to stray into Silversong's aura.

If I freeze Greyhail, she'll have plenty of opportunities to attack me. I'll never reach her in time to catch her in the threads. The notion of fighting his sister brought him more pain than her distrust in him. *Even if I somehow manage to escape, it'll just bring the ire of the sentinels down on my packmates. No, I have to face whatever consequences lie ahead. The future depends on it.*

The piece of time showed him glimpses of how he could alleviate his punishment. If he answered the Warden honestly, he would avoid her more creative methods of interrogation.

Silversong imagined himself answering the Warden's questions, chuckling at the absurdity of it all.

Why were you sneaking about the second level?

Oh, you know. I was just trying to get River-Stream to join my conspiracy against Chief Ashenfall. Scorchfang is in on it too, by the way. Oh, I almost forgot. I'm also slowly turning everyone against the Wolven Code. Surprise!

A blue-grey light put an end to the long night. Today, Chief Ashenfall would make her move against Silversong. He had no time to waste. He passed the entrance to the Stone-Guard lair and strode through the Cave of Punishment, the blackened bones at the centre reminding him of his potential fate should the trial not go his way. Bleaksmoke stood in front of the tunnel leading into Lawbreaker's Hole, Ripper's prison. Ashenfall's son panted upon seeing Silversong, a frenzied glint livening those disturbed eyes.

On the other side, the road straightened between two large fangs of obsidian reaching for the clouds. Greyhail drove him onto the plateau where the off-duty sentinels rested. Swiftstorm halted at the exit. The spire's peak loomed over the sleeping Warden, its brittle tip bearing a few more cracks. Greyhail padded to wake her.

She opened her eyes and listened to Greyhail's report, shooting a glance at Silversong. He firmed his muscles before the urge to recoil got too strong. He wouldn't submit to her. He wouldn't let her frighten him. If he showed weakness now, how could he strive to wrestle the Wolven Bulwark out of her grasp?

I must be strong as an unwavering vortex. I'll give her nothing!

The Warden stood and stretched, sleeking her white coat. As if sensing their leader waking up, the slumbering sentinels opened their eyes and got on all fours. One by one, they surrounded Silversong. Ashenfall twitched atop her shelf extending beneath the spire's peak. She lay on her stomach, her sleep disturbed by the movements below. She opened tentative eyes, and they widened upon noticing Silversong. Her lips parted into a smirk.

Silversong banished the scowl from his face before it became too obvious. He couldn't flaunt his power. Not when there were so many wolves to account for, many of which were out of the aura's reach.

The Warden neared him, the grace of her movements matched only by the intensity of her gaze. Silversong breathed deeply, trying in vain to quiet the pounding in his chest. She stopped and stared thorns at him, determined to see him flinch, to see him break. He resisted and swished his tail slowly, pointing his ears skyward.

The Warden sniffed, unimpressed. "Explain yourself."

Silversong frowned and imagined himself as the unwavering vortex facing off against a violent tsunami. Which would survive the clash?

There's only one way to find out.

"You'll have to be a little more specific, ma'am," Silversong whined casually.

Some of the sentinels snarled at his response. Greyhail bared his fangs, and Swiftstorm froze at the exit. The Warden merely shook her head. "Oh, Silversong. Don't do this to yourself. Your sister spoke so highly of you back at the Great Chain. From her tales, I'd hoped to one day make you a sentinel. But now I see how wrong she was to vouch for you. You're insolent, insubordinate, and downright blasphemous at times. It's a wonder I haven't executed you yet—a testament to my patience and mercy."

Silversong's blood turned hot in his veins, but he limited his aggression to a defiant glare. "Sorry to disappoint, Warden. Whatever you may think of me, I have nothing but the Wolven Bulwark's best interests at heart."

"So you say." The Warden returned the glare without blinking. "Greyhail has informed me he caught you sneaking about the second level of the den. Care to explain why you weren't sleeping in your lair like a good member of Whistle-Wind?"

From her shelf, Ashenfall glowered at Silversong. "So, you disobey the conditions of your stay here. I demand punishment!"

The Warden craned her head to Ashenfall, and the Flame-Heart Chief looked away, feigning submission. "In due course, ma'am. First, I would like to hear Silversong's defense, if he has any."

Silversong scoffed. "I just wanted to get some fresh air before the sun dawned, and the view from the second level is quite spectacular, I must say."

"To die for, really," Ashenfall added drily.

The Warden growled, the sound rumbling out of her mouth like thunder. It shook Silversong to the core, and he failed to suppress the tiniest of whimpers. "All right, Silversong. I've had it." She turned to his sister. "Swiftstorm! To me!"

Swiftstorm obeyed like a disciplined pup, scurrying over to her master and awaiting further orders. Though her face was blank as a sun-bleached stone, her scent smelled strong, sour, frantic.

The Warden studied her in consideration. "Swiftstorm, since it's your charge to watch over your brother, it should be you who doles out his punishments whenever they're needed. We can make an obedient soldier out of him yet."

Swiftstorm hesitated for only a breath before nodding. "Yes, ma'am. How should I punish him?"

Silversong couldn't believe his sister wasn't resisting. How could she choose the Warden over him? Over family? His thoughts whirled about in a dizzying circle. She had to be tricking the Warden somehow, there was no way Swiftstorm would—

"Your brother has wasted his breaths by refusing to speak the truth when interrogated," the Warden explained, eyeing him like a trapped deer she intended to slay. "Teach him not to be so wasteful next time."

"Oh, this should be good." Ashenfall grinned eagerly from above, tail brushing her shelf as she panted.

Swiftstorm stepped toward Silversong, lifting a trembling forepaw to his throat. Her nose touched his. Silversong managed a pleading whine. "Swiftstorm, please! I'm your brother, your family—"

She touched him, and the air rushed out of his lungs until there was nothing there but aching pain. He collapsed to the ground and thrashed like a drowning pup, fighting for a breath to no avail. He never could have fathomed such agony, such pure panic. He opened his mouth wide, spasming as he tried sucking in the air around him. Black spots flecked his vision. How long had he been convulsing? How long had Ashenfall been laughing? His lungs were about to rupture. He could feel it.

Just before he lost consciousness, air filled his lungs, dulling the pulsing pain in his chest. He savoured every breath, welcoming them, worshipping them. How could something so basic taste so sweet? He inhaled more and more, bringing himself back from the brink of death.

"Again." The Warden's voice was ice to his ears.

Swiftstorm lifted her forepaw as he lay on his back, trying to grasp at unseen threads, trying to make them freeze her in place, but he was too panicked to use the piece of time. "NO! PLEASE! I'LL—"

She touched his throat again, this time pressing harder. The pain returned tenfold like a boulder ramming into his chest. He opened his mouth, but nothing came in or out. He writhed and kicked, but no movement could lessen the primal dread gripping every nerve. The helplessness crushed him, his body begging for a breath, just a single breath!

It finally came—the reward for reaching the surface right before drowning. He lurched to the side, trying desperately to swallow all the air he could. The relief was slower on arrival this time, and when it hit, it was promptly snatched away once more.

"Again," repeated the Warden.

He closed his mouth to keep the precious air in, but as Swiftstorm pressed on him again, the contents of his lungs exploded out of his nostrils and through his clenched teeth, sending sprays of mucus and saliva everywhere.

Again.

The Warden's voice echoed in his head.

Again.

And again the torture continued, Silversong flailing like a fish out of water, Ashenfall laughing her insides out, the sentinels cheering Swiftstorm on, the Warden refusing to exercise her supposed mercy.

MOTHERWOLF, SAVE ME! PLEASE! MAKE IT STOP! JUST MAKE IT STOP! Silversong prayed, his vision going black again, his chest heaving uselessly. The clouds above darkened, or was he simply losing consciousness? No... there was a face in the clouds now—a twisted deer wreathed in shadow.

The Fallen Titan snarled in the direction of the Fireleaf Forest, and within his gaping maw crackled furious lightning.

Swiftstorm released Silversong.

Instinct took over. He gulped down as much air as he could take, but he dared not feel relief. Not yet. He squirmed away from his sister. She was too close. He couldn't get far enough! She would do it again, and again, and again!

"GET AWAY!" he yowled.

His vision cleared, the black spots fading. He rolled to the side and watched the sentinels peer over the edge of the plateau. His panic subsided, as did the aching cramp in his chest. He regained control over the piece of time just as the sentinels sounded the alarm.

Their howling voices resonated throughout the den. "The exiles are attacking! Bare your fangs! The exiles are attacking!"

CHAPTER 20

A Death Foretold

Like a woodpecker boring into a tree, the piece of time drove into Silversong's skull a dire warning: Chief Amberstorm was going to die today.

The Warden assumed control of the situation, ordering her sentinels down to the second level. Howls sounded from below, summoning all wolves to defend the chosen chokepoint. The entrance to the second level was the most defensible position. While Flame-Heart wolves harassed the ascending exiles, the remainder of the Wolven Bulwark would reinforce the largest platform, preparing for the inevitable clash.

Swiftstorm sprinted toward Silversong.

NOT AGAIN!

He flinched, scrambling away from her, the pain in his chest growing more unbearable the closer she came. Instead of resuming the torture, she spared him a pitiful look and continued through the exit and down the spire. Greyhail hurried to keep up. Silversong puffed loudly, the threads escaping his control. Soon he was alone and facing Chief Ashenfall, her eyes weighing his strength or lack thereof. When had she dropped from her shelf? Why was she looking at him like he was cornered prey? Why was he still lying here, helpless and afraid?

His senses returned, sharp enough to pierce through the confusion and the panic. As Ashenfall moved his way, he forced himself onto all fours and flexed the unseen threads, daring her to come closer despite his shivering body. She stopped to lick her lips, almost as if savouring the thought of murdering him right here, right now. She decided against it and turned to follow the sentinels.

Silversong clenched his teeth and swallowed his terror. He would never see Swiftstorm the same way again. She'd changed, and she'd chosen the Wolven Code over family. There was no time to feel anything but profound sorrow at the betrayal. Regaining his focus, he let the threads guide him into the Cave of Punishment where he saw Ashenfall disappearing into Lawbreaker's Hole alongside Bleaksmoke.

Those two are up to something. Why aren't they heading to the second level?

The vision of Amberstorm's death returned. Smoke consumed him. Fangs tore into his throat. He lay in a pool of his own blood, eyes closing for the final time. Silversong had to get to him quickly. Amberstorm could still be saved.

He ran out of the cave, using the currents created by his movements to increase his speed. As he descended the winding ledge, he saw why the Fallen Titan's mouth was aimed toward the Fireleaf Forest. Upon the field, tiny shapes approached the spire—Blazefur's patrol units. Roots grasped at several of his soldiers, yanking them to the ground so the exiles at the forest's rim could finish them off. The wolves stationed around Thornhollow returned to the safety of the den, hearing the orders howled from above.

Lightning crackled within the Fallen Titan's mouth, and out came his electrifying wrath, smiting wolves under Blazefur's command and sending bursts of blood, earth and severed limbs high into the air. The resulting thunder shook Silversong's eardrums as the clouds spewed frozen droplets. Stinging hail smacked Silversong, but the sharp pellets were nothing compared to having his breath stolen from him by his own sister. He trembled. The primal urge to breathe had been taken away so suddenly, so painfully. He could almost feel it happening again.

STOP! I'm stronger than this! He ignored the phantom ache in his lungs. He wouldn't let this setback defeat him!

He caught up to the Stone-Guard wolves. They padded in three ranks, blocking him from pushing through. He had no time for this!

"He's coming for me!" Bronzeblood bellowed from the front. "I'll beat you again, Heretic! And this time I'll finish the job!"

From the corner of his eye, a dozen or so leaps above him, Silversong caught Bleaksmoke chasing Ripper. The exile had escaped! No… how could Ripper have escaped when Ashenfall and her son had gone into his prison? As far as Silversong knew, the only way in or out of Lawbreaker's Hole was through the tunnel in the Cave of Punishment.

Again, Amberstorm's death entered Silversong's thoughts. He gasped.

Bleaksmoke forced Ripper to jump down onto one of the uneven ledges extending out of the main structure. Bleaksmoke pursued the exile, encouraging Ripper's dangerous descent. Silversong urged the golden circle to reveal a faster way to Amberstorm. In the threads, he saw the road he needed to take. Turning tail on the Stone-Guard mass, he leaped for a narrow shelf jutting from the spire, weaving the air into an upward jet pushing against him. The move softened his landing. He did this again and again until he reached a secluded platform overlooking the field.

At the lip of the Fireleaf Forest, something strange occurred. Instead of charging toward the den, the exiles turned to face the Heretic and his lieutenant. The two of them seemed to be arguing. Teeth flashed, and hostile postures hinted at the start of a fight. Some of the exiles surrounded Rime, but as the mouth of the Fallen Titan shifted its aim toward them, they backed off. Large prey tortured into servitude by Rime emerged out of the woods and closed in on the Heretic, antlers eager to skewer and hooves ready to trample.

Realization struck Silversong like lightning. Rime wouldn't allow the exiles to assault Thornhollow so long as Cindersky and his children were still inside. Harassing the patrol units was one thing, but this… this was breaking a promise.

Silversong jumped to lower ground while keeping an eye on the developments below. It looked like Ironwrath had conceded to Rime. The corrupted beasts withdrew, and the exiles followed them into the forest. Rime spared one last look at Thornhollow as if searching for his family, then sprang beneath the crimson leaves. The hail became a light drizzle. The face of the Fallen Titan faded into the black clouds, and after an agonizingly long moment, Ironwrath too melded into the woods. And so concluded another one of the Heretic's blunders.

Silversong had no time to appreciate this outcome. Fear entangled his heart as the golden circle reminded him of Amberstorm's imminent demise. Silversong jumped onto an outgrowth just below the second level, the commotion above failing to capture his attention. An old tunnel was hollowed out in the spire's main body, leading to the first level of the den. He squeezed through, paying no mind to the lack of space. Getting stuck was the least of his worries. He emerged on the other side and ran in the direction of his packmates.

Blazefur and his surviving soldiers bolted in the opposite direction, running for the second level. Silversong's packmates followed several leaps behind the patrol units. Amberstorm's eyes widened upon seeing Silversong. The golden circle pulsed, his vision consumed by a flash of light. In the blinding sheet, he glimpsed fangs lunging through smoke into an exposed throat.

"CHIEF AMBERSTORM!" Silversong cried at the top of his lungs.

The Chief stopped at the front of the moving file, and Silversong prepared to stretch the threads of time to save him, but it all happened so fast.

"The prisoner has escaped! Defend yourselves!" Bleaksmoke announced atop a stark ledge overlooking the Whistle-Wind Chief.

Directly beneath Bleaksmoke, on a narrower platform, Ripper pressed on his haunches and leaped high into the air. He'd wanted to wait until the Whistle-Wind soldiers had passed him before he continued his escape, but upon being sighted by the wolves below, he'd panicked.

Ripper unwittingly crashed into Amberstorm.

Silversong lunged forward, pushing the threads outward, but the fire had already been blown out of Bleaksmoke's mouth, and he'd already jumped into the black veil trailing the flames, and the fireball had already swallowed the exile and the Chief in its suffocating layers. Bleaksmoke landed in the shadowy cloud. The sounds of a scuffle ensued, and within the darkness Chief Amberstorm yelped, his last choking breath finally drawn. The threads hadn't reached far enough. Silversong hadn't been quick enough.

NO! The sting of defeat punctured Silversong's heart, and he froze like the two wolves he'd just caught in time's grasp.

He allowed the smoke to clear.

Anguished cries and bays of rage replaced the coughing of the Whistle-Wind wolves. In no time at all the entirety of the pack was clustered around Amberstorm's corpse, the Wise-Wolves applying pressure to the gushing wound in his throat. Ripper and Bleaksmoke stood facing one another, frozen in time and surrounded by angry wolves. The Warden had abandoned her position on the second level to inspect the commotion. A few wary sentinels accompanied her.

Fresh blood stained the exile's mouth—Bleaksmoke's blood—and thick crimson lines streamed from the wound in his neck, the bite no doubt given to him by Ashenfall's son. Only a little deeper, and it would've been a killing blow. The exile had managed to strike Bleaksmoke on the shoulder before being caught in the threads. Teeth bared, the treacherous Flame-Heart fiend had even more blood dripping from his fangs. A mixture between Amberstorm's and Ripper's.

An aching growth expanded at the pit of Silversong's throat, and he couldn't blink no matter how dry his eyes became. The incredible weight of his failure pressed harder and harder on him until he could stand no more. He collapsed, heart turning into a block of ice, rapid breaths slowing. His ears blocked out the whimpering, the barking, the howling. He tried reversing the course of time, banging against an invisible barrier on every attempt, pain ricocheting all throughout the inside of his skull. Exhausted, he freed the exile and the culprit.

Enraged members of Whistle-Wind bit and tore at Ripper's flesh. The exile yowled wordlessly in his torment.

"He killed him!" Bleaksmoke licked the blood off his teeth. "He killed your Chief!"

A pause in Ripper's torture lasted long enough for him to screech out, "NO! IT WASN'T ME—"

The Warden charged into the exile and dug her claws into his hindquarters. Ripper convulsed as she turned his own blood against him. "Silence, wretch! For the murder of Chief Amberstorm, I sentence you to die!"

It seemed there would be no interrogation on the Warden's behalf.

Tendrils of smoke drifted out of Bleaksmoke's flaring nostrils. "If you would, ma'am, open his mouth. Allow me to give him a taste of Flame-Heart justice."

A slight frown creased the Warden's forehead, but she nodded and forced the exile's mouth wide open.

"Wait." Silversong's voice came out too weak for anyone but himself to hear.

The sweltering anger in the prisoner's eye turned to horror as Bleaksmoke breathed fire down his throat, melting him from the inside out. Everyone except the Warden and Bleaksmoke backed away, cringing and gagging at the revolting execution. The sheer agony displayed on Ripper's face was something Silversong never wanted to see again, and he pressed his ears back in a futile attempt to block out the disturbing sounds the exile emitted in his final moments. Ripper could only voice a rasping gurgle, jaws forced open as they were. The heat liquefied his insides into a tar-like substance, and slowly it began to ooze out of his belly as a single mass of sizzling black flesh. The Warden released her control over the exile, and he collapsed atop his scorched entrails, body limp from the stroke of death, his remaining eye vacant. Bleaksmoke sniffed in satisfaction, and he looked on the verge of giggling, tail swishing side to side.

Silversong avoided looking at the disgusting sight and dared to wade through his whimpering packmates. Some still howled in either rage or sorrow, but most sought comfort in one another. Palesquall leaned against Hazel, and she nuzzled him while trying to remain strong for his sake. Cedargaze and Shadowgale huddled together while Gorsescratch let loose a song of vengeance strengthened by Tawnydrift's voice. Where the sentinels gathered, Swiftstorm bowed her head beneath Greyhail, who sheltered her from the odd looks she was getting. Even though she'd once served under Chief Amberstorm, it was still considered inappropriate for her to mourn her former leader.

More of the Wolven Bulwark descended to witness Whistle-Wind's loss, the sentinels stopping them from coming too close. Frostpaw made a move to run toward Silversong, but upon catching Darkwave's glare, Frostpaw decided to stay where he was, ears flattened and tail drooping.

A wide smile splitting his face in two, Bleaksmoke padded to join his mother among the Flame-Heart wolves, his mission a success. How had Silversong not foreseen this?! Scorchfang's eyes shifted between Silversong and her Chief, obviously putting it all together. Silversong, still in disbelief, returned to where Amberstorm's body lay.

There he was, lying in a pool of his own blood, his pups pulled back by the nape of their necks while crying out for their father to wake up. Twice now they'd suffered through the death of a parent, and twice now they would have their innocence ripped to shreds. But they would endure. Whistle-Wind would endure.

The rain lessened into a weaker spray, still feeding the steady stream of water and blood as it flowed down the den. The Warden gave out orders to take up defensive positions, but Silversong couldn't move. He thought about his one-eyed image haunting the Mountainmouth. He'd been warned of this fate, of this outcome, and yet he'd been arrogant enough to assume he could divert the course of the future. Was his destiny already set in motion? Was he just feeding an endless cycle? Did his choices really matter? Would he end up a one-eyed shell of who he was now? Would he try and fail to sway his past toward a better future? A good future?

He closed his eyes, and in the void a ghostly face stared back at him, challenging him to see his purpose through to the bitter end.

CHAPTER 21

The Last Farewells

The day was all too similar to the final hour of Wind's Rest.

The clouds, now mountainous swells of grey, poured their sorrow upon a field of muddied earth and swaying grass. The Whistle-Wind Pack trudged onward without voicing a whine or whimper, the deep silence broken only by the constant pattering of rainfall. In the distance a rising knoll beckoned the wolves, its height stretching out of the ground like a bump on otherwise smooth flesh. There, Chief Amberstorm would receive his last farewells, and the winds would cleanse his body before carrying his spirit to Motherwolf's den.

A circle had formed around the Wise-Wolves dragging the Chief's body toward his ultimate resting place. The formation was as much to display the respect they all had for him as it was to shield him from the eyes of the onlookers pretending to be on patrol. This was a Whistle-Wind matter, and it was a loss for Whistle-Wind alone to suffer.

Together, they climbed the knoll on leaden legs. On this day, they were one single group unseparated by rank, and they would mourn as equals under the unrelenting rain. The Warden had been kind enough to allow them this *courtesy*, as she called it. To think she'd hesitated on allowing the Chief his proper rites for reasons of safety.

If Swiftstorm hadn't been there to convince her...

Silversong's blood turned hot. He forced the beginning of a snarl away. Now wasn't the time for anger to surface.

Swiftstorm should be here. I don't care if she's a sentinel. She deserves to mourn too.

He fought the instinct to gasp for air as the Warden's voice echoed in his head.

Again. Again. AGAIN.

Silversong inhaled deeply, surprised at how easy it was to draw breath. He shook, trying to free himself from the panic, the fear, the pain. He would have to confront his sister about this, otherwise he would forever dread the mere thought of her.

At the top of the knoll, the rain poured harder. The Wise-Wolves carefully laid Amberstorm's body at the centre and joined the others, heads bowed and tails hanging low. Silversong couldn't remember who'd started the howling, but he found himself lending his voice to the melancholic tune, and for as long as it lasted, time itself seemed to pause its course. The golden circle continued spinning, denying the oddly comforting illusion.

One by one, the wolves closest to Amberstorm approached his body and licked the bloody stains off his fur. They offered him prayers and reminisced about joyful moments imbedded in memory.

"We were so happy for you and Pinetrail," Chief Cedargaze whined while leaning against Shadowgale. "You two really were the perfect wolves to lead this pack. Now the burden of leadership weighs on my shoulders. As your successor, I swear to uphold your ideals and honour your memory. Whistle-Wind shall know peace under my reign. This I promise you, sir."

Pride flickered against the icy void in Silversong's heart, enough to keep hope alive just barely. Amberstorm had made a fine choice selecting Cedargaze as the new leader. Dedicated to her duty as she was, Whistle-Wind had brighter days ahead. There would be no formal ceremony for her ascension today, however, not until the pack returned to its former strength.

"Elder Shrillbreeze was wise to choose you as Chief, sir." Shadowgale could hardly control his shaking voice. "The land is a far more bitter place without you."

"You were such a feisty little rascal." A motherly elder smiled over Amberstorm's body. His eyes were closed as if he were locked in the deepest of dreams. "Always begging me for milk when it was time to study the Wolven Code. Always eager to learn battle tactics when it was time to nap. Oh, I'm going to miss you. Be sure to give Pinetrail my regards when you see her. I'm sure she's very eager for you to reach Motherwolf's den."

“I never thought I would be the one saying these last farewells to you,” Amberstorm’s father grunted into his ear. “Everything has turned upside down in my old age. To think I would live to see such turmoil plague the Four Territories.” He grimaced. “Madness. Utter madness. You were taken from us too soon, my son. We need your guidance now more than ever.”

“You cared for us more than you cared for yourself, and your rule was one of honour and integrity.” Moonwhisper comforted her whimpering partner, nuzzling him as he tried and failed to voice his last farewells. “You may not have been a Wise-Wolf, but you had the heart of one.”

The now orphaned pups crawled up to their father’s body and licked him on the face, pawing and nudging him in the hopes that he would wake up and remind them that everything was going to be okay. The swelling pain in Silversong’s throat worsened the more desperate their efforts grew. They yelped and yowled when Moonwhisper and the elders finally dragged them away.

Washed of blood, Amberstorm looked like he could open his eyes at any moment and order them all back to their duties. His scars had been healing fine, the seen and unseen alike, and he’d been determined to deliver his pack from the clutches of despair. He’d trusted in Silversong, trusted in his vision of a better future, and Amberstorm had given his life to see it done.

If Silversong had reacted faster to Ashenfall’s treachery, if he’d seen the signs more clearly, could Amberstorm have been saved? Guilt pressed in on Silversong from all sides regardless of the answer. Drawing an unsteady breath, he approached Amberstorm and whined his last farewells. “I’m sorry it had to end like this, sir. I wish there’d been another way to bring River-Stream to our side while also saving your life. Maybe… maybe I could’ve—” He choked on a whimper, swallowing quickly before it escaped his mouth.

“It’s not your fault, Silversong,” Hazel whispered from behind, her statement echoed by Palesquall, Cedargaze, Shadowgale, and many more.

For some reason, hearing those comforting whines broke him. Like a beaver’s dam ruptured by the river’s wrath, the whimpers exploded out of his mouth. His friends clustered around him, leaning against his body and sharing the sting of this terrible loss.

The warmth they offered brought little solace, but without it he surely would've remained a frozen husk incapable of even thinking.

When he could finally whine again without whimpering, he focused all his energy on a pledge. "Your deeds in life speak for themselves, sir, and so I have nothing more to say other than this: your sacrifice wasn't in vain. I won't let Chief Ashenfall escape the fangs of justice. I won't let the Warden divide us further, and I won't let the Heretic terrorize us anymore. The Wolven Bulwark stands, and we'll fight for a better future together."

He broke from his friends and returned to where the corporals were, waiting for another to come forward. Gorsescratch stepped up next, limbs shaking as he neared his fallen leader. He hesitated, turning to look at Silversong and Hazel before steering his eyes back to Amberstorm's body.

Gorsescratch sighed. "Sir… you were a good and honourable leader as others have already said, but there's one grave mistake you made that taints your legacy even now." Concerned whines and outraged looks sparked a sudden tension within the crowd of mourners, and all wolves leaned forward, the lieutenants prepared to haul Gorsescratch away should he cross the line. "Your mistake was promoting me to corporal, for my actions have proven me unworthy of the rank."

Silversong's ears perked up just as Tawnydrift yelped, "Gorsescratch, no!"

Gorsescratch ignored her and elaborated on his statement. "How do I begin? Hazel." He met her eyes, breaths short, and flinched at her growing frown. "I've… I've always fancied you. Ever since I was a subordinate. And my feelings only worsened when I got promoted to corporal. You became a close friend of Silversong's, and more and more I resented him for it. In my jealousy, I sabotaged his promotion. One deer was all the Chief asked him to claim, and he had his fangs locked around the throat of one before I knocked him off his prize. By all rights he should've succeeded. If not for me, he would've been a corporal that very evening."

Legs feeling weightless, Silversong stared in amazed silence. It wasn't because of Gorsescratch's confession. Rather, it was because Silversong thought Gorsescratch would never find the courage to confess. All around, snarls stretched the faces of wolves who'd once held Gorsescratch in high esteem, and Tawnydrift tucked her tail while letting her head droop in defeat. She should've been thankful since Gorsescratch had omitted her involvement in the sabotage.

Moonwhisper gasped. "So those weren't false memories after all."

"How dare you?!" Hazel's growl contained enough venom to instantly paralyze Gorsescratch, and the burned side of her face only served to sharpen the strength of her scowl. "You're a disgusting scatfur, Gorsescratch! Even the thought of you fancying me sickens my stomach!"

Gorsescratch winced and stifled a yelp, head hunched, ears pulled back, tail quivering against his belly. This couldn't have been easy for him to hear.

"I wanted to believe Silversong's accusations were faulty memories created by the plants the Wise-Wolves fed him." Palesquall cursed himself for ever having doubted a friend. "I wanted to believe even a bully like you wouldn't go so far as to sabotage your own packmate. I'm surprised you refused the Heretic's offer to join him back at Wind's Rest. You would fit in better among the exiles."

"It's not too late to send him to them." A lieutenant bared her fangs at the shunned corporal. "This crime is grave enough to perhaps warrant banishment."

Cedargaze creased her forehead as though considering it.

"NO!" Tawnydrift released a high-pitched cry. "He regrets his crime! He's sorry for everything! He's working to undo all the wrong he did! Please, ma'am, have mercy!"

"Tawnydrift…" Gorsescratch lifted his head so he could look at his only friend, "don't."

"You should be ashamed of yourself, Gorsescratch!" Shadowgale barked.

"Code-breaker!"

"Foul mongrel!"

"Send him to the exiles!"

"You disappoint us, son."

"ENOUGH!" Silversong's voice silenced the barking and the growling. Nerves aflame, he rounded on his packmates for focusing on something so unimportant compared to the real threat. "Gorsescratch has made many mistakes. Some worse than others, but I can confidently say they're mistakes he regrets. Even though many of you can't yet find it in your hearts to forgive him, I think he's earned a second chance. Since the massacre at Wind's Rest, he's proven himself a loyal corporal to this pack, and he deserves to stand as one of us against the exiles and those who would see Whistle-Wind subdued. His crimes are a thing of the past, and to dwell on them more than necessary means blinding ourselves to the future Chief Amberstorm died for. It takes great courage for Gorsescratch to admit his wrongdoings, and we'll need that courage in the battles to come."

Some stared at the ground in contemplation while others shared unheard whispers or simply looked around to see how much their packmates had been swayed by Silversong's arguments. Hazel's teeth were still bared, and Palesquall's frown hadn't loosened in the slightest, but their restraint confirmed their willingness to forsake useless grudges.

"Thank you." Gorsescratch bowed his head to Silversong. The built-up tension within him slackened upon facing Hazel's fury. "I know now you can never be mine. You deserve far better, but if I'm to die before this is all over, I would rather die without lies weighing on my conscience."

Gorsescratch broke from Hazel's scowl and walked over to Tawnydrift, wincing as all corporals but her recoiled away from him. His one and only friend stayed by his side, her worried expression taking on an edge of pity. Gorsescratch accepted her nuzzles, burying himself in her fur and whimpering in her embrace.

Silversong urged himself not to feel sorry for his former bully, but as the whimpers continued, he couldn't ignore the instinct to reassure Gorsescratch somehow. He wasn't the sum of his mistakes. He'd shown remorse and a willingness to take accountability for his actions. He deserved a second chance as far as Silversong was concerned. Whether the others would forgive him or not was another matter entirely.

"Silversong is right," Cedargaze whined, green eyes surveying her pack. "Condemning Gorsescratch now is a waste of time. If the one he wronged urges forgiveness, then I'm inclined to let him remain among us."

A few murmurs and a couple sighs were the only reactions to the Chief's verdict.

Cedargaze sleeked her snowy fur. "If anyone has anything else to say to our late Chief, now is the time."

When the ceremony concluded, the Whistle-Wind Pack joined together for a final howl. The song echoed far and wide, announcing to all the sorrow brought by Amberstorm's passing. The wind answered the mournful voices and swept across the field to carry Amberstorm's spirit to Motherwolf's den beyond the stars. One by one wolves trickled away from the knoll until only Silversong and his friends remained. Cedargaze would prepare the pack for Silversong's inevitable trial. He'd already told her the truth about Amberstorm's murder and who the real culprit was. She would inform her subjects about Ashenfall's treachery, but before he joined them, there was something important he had to test first.

Palesquall sat beside him. "I can't believe he's gone." His voice was gentle and on the verge of cracking.

Hazel stood firmly at Silversong's other side. "None of us blame you for this, Silversong. It happened too fast for even the piece of time to predict."

"And of course, Gorsescratch has to make this all about himself," Palesquall added. "I'm sorry I doubted you."

Hazel shook her head and licked Silversong on the shoulder. "I'm sorry too. I should've listened to you from the start. At least now everyone sees Gorsescratch for the scatfur he is."

Silversong pressed his claws into the earth and exhaled through gritted teeth. He turned around and padded further away from the Flame-Heart den.

"Silversong?" Hazel called out. "Where are you going?"

Silversong scowled so intensely his face began to ache. A swarm of visions whirled about in his head, and the golden circle trembled as if sensing his pounding anger. The time to mourn was over. "If we're going to thwart Chief Ashenfall and the Warden, it's time I used my weapon to its fullest extent."

Again, the golden circle shook.

Justice is coming for you, Ashenfall.

CHAPTER 22

The Precipice

"Silversong! Wait!" Hazel barked.

"Has he gone crazy or something?" Palesquall yapped from behind. "We have to get back to Thornhollow and prepare for the trial! Ashenfall won't close her eyes until she sees you dead, Silversong!"

The near future flickered across Silversong's eyes, and he stopped to let his friends catch up to him.

"Hey." Hazel nosed him on the cheek. "You don't have to do everything alone. Whatever it is you're planning, let us help."

"Yeah—wait, huh?!" Palesquall cocked his head sideways. "Does nobody listen to me anymore? Our whole pack is probably waiting for us at Thornhollow, and if the sentinels notice we haven't returned yet, they'll think we're up to something. We don't have time to waste."

"You're right. We don't have time to waste, Palesquall." Silversong gave him a sharp glance. "Which is why I'll force time to be on our side for once."

"Sure. Whatever that means," Palesquall whined in a confused tone. "But can you at least do it in a safer place?"

"No place is safe, gullwit." Hazel pointed her tail at the spire. "Least of all Thornhollow."

Silversong's whiskers twitched. "They're coming."

"Who's coming?" Palesquall and Hazel uttered simultaneously.

"They're almost here."

"WHO'S ALMOST HERE?!" Once again, their voices came out as one.

Off to the side, a River-Stream patrol headed their way, led by Snowleap and comprised of four other wolves, one of them

Frostpaw. A spark of relief ignited within Silversong as the breeze carried his scent and those of his friends toward the approaching group. The two subordinates tensed and remained cautious, but a grunt of reassurance from Silversong was enough to make his friends assume a more neutral stance.

In the shadows cast by the light of the near future, Silversong glimpsed the River-Stream wolves dying by a silvery blade slashing through the air, cutting head and limb from body and leaving the ground a thick mixture of blood and mud. Though these deaths were avoidable, the very thought of them dragged Silversong's heart low. To deny this fate, all the soldiers had to do was remain alert. Silversong would make certain their eyes and ears were wide open. Especially Frostpaw's. The closer he got, the more his presence shredded Silversong's fears like a swift current slicing through leaves on a branch.

"Uh… Silversong?" Palesquall eyed Silversong's flicking tail.

Silversong immediately stopped all movements, embarrassment heating his face.

Hazel's gaze flickered between Silversong and Frostpaw, but she said nothing.

Snowleap halted a tail-length from Silversong and bowed her head respectfully. "Let me be the first from my pack to express my condolences for Whistle-Wind's loss. Though the Wolven Code forbids us from officially mourning the death of a rival Chief, I still feel this needs to be said. When you and Frostpaw were in the Mountainmouth, Chief Amberstorm fought for the safety of your pack, and his stubbornness convinced my father to let them stay at the Saltshore to recuperate. I doubt anyone else could've persuaded him in such a way. Take comfort in knowing Chief Amberstorm's courage won't be forgotten by the River-Stream wolves."

"Thank you," was all Silversong could whine.

Frostpaw moved up to stand beside Snowleap. He lifted a forepaw as if to come closer to Silversong, but restrained himself. His bluish fur clung to him thanks to the rain. "Are you all right, Silversong?" Worry widened those bright yellow jewels he had for eyes.

"Yes, Frostpaw. I'm fine." Silversong hoped he hadn't sounded too distant. It was the only way to hide his grief. "Thanks for asking."

Frostpaw opened his mouth to say more only for a smaller corporal to interrupt him. "At least your Chief's murderer met a fitting end."

"I heard the scatfur melted from the inside out." The youngest in the patrol grinned approvingly. "It's a good alternative to being boiled alive. I only wish I'd been there to see it."

"It wasn't the exile," Silversong revealed the truth to the perplexed wolves. "It was Bleaksmoke. Under the order of his mother, he killed Amberstorm and blamed it on Ripper."

Shock replaced confusion in the faces of the surrounding wolves, and eyes bulged like plump berries in surprise at the revelation.

Snowleap inhaled sharply. "Would Ashenfall go that far in her quest for more power?"

"A weakened Whistle-Wind Pack means a stronger position for Flame-Heart." Hazel gritted her teeth.

"And a dead Amberstorm is one less obstacle for Ashenfall to jump over." Palesquall growled at the ground.

Snowleap clamped her jaws tightly to imprison another gasp, her deep grey fur going stiff. "A grave accusation. I don't suppose you can use the piece of time to prove Chief Ashenfall's treachery during the trial?"

"You read my mind. Yes, it should be possible." Silversong exhaled, feeling as though the slightest misstep would mean disaster. "And if anything, Chief Ashenfall's actions prove how easy it is to abuse the Wolven Code. It's high time others see how oppressive this system really is."

Sparks of excitement made his muscles twitch. He would never get tired of admitting his aversion to the Wolven Code. There was a heretic within him, but a heretic of a different kind. He was beyond fearing repercussions from the Warden. She'd already administered the greatest of punishments. There was nothing else for her to do, and so she could bite his tail if she thought she could keep him from improving the lives of all wolves!

Frostpaw was the only one in the River-Stream patrol who appeared willing to follow Silversong to whatever end. The others still had their doubts, but they would come around.

"I can't say you don't worry me, Silversong," Snowleap admitted, studying Frostpaw's determined expression. "But if there's a future where wolves like Chief Ashenfall can never rise to power, then I must fight for it. For River-Stream's sake."

"Good." Silversong met her golden gaze. "To properly expose Chief Ashenfall, there's something I need to practice first."

Frostpaw broke from the patrol and came within a whisker-length of Silversong's face, warm breath providing some comfort against the dampness. Silversong sniffed it in.

"If there's anything I can do to help," Frostpaw panted, "just say so."

Silversong couldn't resist a tender smile. He stared into Frostpaw's eyes without fear of judgment, heartbeat quickening. "Thank you, Frostpaw." Back in the River-Stream lair, he'd worried about Frostpaw taking the side of his father. Now those fears were effectively squished.

Frostpaw smiled back, his beauty unmarred by the rain. "You've taught me so much, Silversong. I'll always be here for you."

Silversong thought he accidentally stopped time only to realize he was just staring without saying anything. He opened his mouth to whine a response, but Frostpaw's gaze had him completely stunned.

Silversong shook his head until he could focus again, ignoring the tingly sensation in his veins.

He caught Hazel and Palesquall glancing at each other, but their questioning looks were nothing compared to Snowleap's bewildered face. "Uhm… count us in too, I guess. Whatever you need, we'll provide within reason." Was there jealousy in her regard? Or just puzzlement?

No. It must be my imagination.

"I need your protection." Silversong's field of view folded in on itself, revealing in the darkness an angular face of sickly white flesh. "I-I feel as though—"

"—we're on the precipice. We can either continue the climb to glory or accept the deep plunge into oblivion." Galdreth's long shadow stretched before him, shading Aelrion and a portion of the main road cutting through the underground den.

Behind Galdreth stood a familiar behemoth of black crystal—the future guardian of the piece of time. Its construction was finished, the Heart of the Mountains glowing steadily within its chest like a newborn sun yet to swell.

The orange shine illuminated the sparsely populated lanes and structures. The workers were so few now, but they continued their tasks despite wearied eyes and somber expressions. They were indeed on the precipice; the precipice of defeat. It hung in the air like an invisible haze, dampening any hope of outlasting extinction. These Forgotten Ones knew their end was near, but they pressed on without pause.

Moths without a light to guide them. Bees without a meadow in sight.

If Aelrion had been covered in fur, he would've bristled. "Enlighten me, Galdreth, how do we *climb to glory* after these recent defeats? Our defenses are broken. The beasts have won. Your visions were false. I can't save humanity even if I do consume your foul weapon, and now you say this… monstrosity you've constructed won't be enough to take back our strongholds." He gestured to the crystalline giant. "I've neither been a king nor a commander for very long, but it hardly takes a strategic mind to recognize when a fight is hopeless."

Galdreth smoothed some of the creases in the deep green fabric covering his forelimbs. "You discredit yourself, Aelrion. You're a commander worthy of the history books, and though you bear no royal blood, you're a king who needs no crown to inspire reverence."

Aelrion frowned at the praise, his metallic shell scratched and dented in many places. "Your flattery is an insidious poison. One you've already used on your own people, not to mention the thousands who joined your northbound caravan. Do you think me deaf? I hear whispers of an *ashen-haired* saviour even among my own soldiers now."

Galdreth scrutinized Aelrion from head to hind paws. "Is it not a soldier's right to have someone to look up to? To have something to hope for?"

"I'm not a saviour!" Aelrion snapped, baring his little fangs. No wonder Galdreth remained unphased. "I know your cursed weapon somehow convinced you I'm meant to lead humanity to an unlikely victory, but by now I would've expected you to see how utterly duped you were! I'm no one special. Just a man who was too blind to notice he was climbing a mountain too steep even for him."

Galdreth's face suddenly became very somber. "You're so much more than that."

Aelrion gave an exasperated, joyless chuckle. “Oh, am I?”

“Unconvinced?” Galdreth studied Aelrion like a Chief might study a rival leader. “Your mother was a tribeswoman from the Stormlands, and your father was a peasant indebted to his betters. In your youth, you contracted a strange sickness that drained the colour from your skin and the years from your life. Those factors alone should’ve been enough to condemn you to a pitiful existence, yet still you strived to achieve the noble goal of uniting two peoples who are as different from one another as fire is to frost. You worked your way from a man of lesser blood to a respected knight, and from there you upended the corrupt aristocrats dividing your continent. And if the beasts and their makers hadn’t declared war on us, you would’ve succeeded in tying the Stormlands to the Northern Kingdom. Even if we ignore your prowess on the battlefield, your previous accomplishments speak for themselves.”

Aelrion sighed at the reminder of his deeds, though Silversong understood little of them. “It’s funny. When I was declared king by the High Council, there were riots and revolts, but come this war those who opposed me for my heritage instead begged for my protection.”

“And you so graciously gave it to them.” Galdreth brought his forepaws together.

“Of course I did. We’re all human in the end.” Aelrion looked at the workers and the builders going about their tasks. In a way, he seemed to envy them. “We judge each other for the littlest things and scoff at our slightest differences. But when calamity strikes, all prejudice is forgotten in favour of perseverance. The instinct to survive shatters all barriers drawn by different nations and cultures.”

“There’s more to humanity than just surviving. And those who joined the beasts disprove your sentiment. However you wish to put it, they betrayed their species.” Galdreth grimaced.

“It was they who were betrayed.” Aelrion’s frown drew downward. “They were tricked into servitude by the cursed Great Deer. They believed he would spare them if they worked against us. If I’d been among them, I might also have been deceived. They were just trying to survive. Blame not their misjudgment. They had families to protect and loved ones to care for, and they were all fooled by a cruel lie.”

"Perhaps you're right." Galdreth stared at his own shadow before turning to the blocky colossus standing perfectly still behind him. "I've been meaning to ask." He shielded his eyes from the light. "Before she died, I heard your mother called you by another name. A name from the Stormlands. I would have you reveal it to me."

Aelrion appeared taken aback by the strange request. "It would mean nothing to you. My Stormlander name is mine to cherish and mine alone. Besides, I doubt you summoned me here to dwell on my past. If there's nothing else, I would rather return to my army above and die under the sun while it still shines."

Galdreth stroked the growth of brown hair around his mouth. From the distant look in his eyes, Silversong guessed the Forgotten One was peering into the future. He faced Aelrion once more. "Perhaps you don't need to die at all." He used a forepaw to beckon someone over.

From a shadowed corner, a group of darker-skinned Forgotten Ones emerged, and their apparent leader came forward. Everything from her easy stride to the deadly look in her brown eyes reminded Silversong of a snake prowling the high grass for prey. The smooth hide of an unknown beast covered her body, and her hair was strange compared to the other Forgotten Ones. It was woven into thick black strands and to Silversong's surprise, the many beads decorating her mane made not a clink as she halted in front of Galdreth.

She brought one forepaw to her chest while the other rested on the pointed metallic stick strapped to her waist. A sign of mutual respect? "King Galdreth." Her voice was deep, and she spoke in a drawn-out manner.

"Aelrion, this is Spearsage Angara-kal, one of the last survivors of the Jeweled Desert." Galdreth gave a slight bow of his head to her. "Her homeland, Harzima, was ravaged by insects and the plagues they brought, but her warband escaped the region before it was too late. She intercepted my army on our way here. She's a fierce warrior, and she also possesses great wisdom. In many different matters, she's proven to be a worthy advisor."

Aelrion squinted at her, sizing her up. She was a tail-length shorter than the others, though no less intimidating for it. "You abandoned your people?"

Her eyes became sharp as brambles, and her scowl would've made a stone quiver. "The swarms descended on us like a sandstorm. No warning. No pity. Our incendiary arrows and explosives were not enough to keep them at bay. I fought until my body started failing and there was no more sweat to cool me off. We all did until we realized victory would have to be won another day. There is no shame in retreat so long as the cause is not lost."

"A wise lesson, Angara-kal, and one Aelrion should take to heart." He put a forepaw on her shoulder, and the gesture calmed her somewhat. "Indeed, perhaps it's time to conserve the numbers we still have and fight another day."

"The desert mouse hides when the prowlers stalk," Angara-kal agreed.

Now it was Aelrion who scowled. "Are you suggesting we flee from the last bastion of humanity? To where? Civilization itself has fallen to the beasts. Nowhere is safe. Not even the endless seas."

A new light glinted in Galdreth's eyes. "Oh, I agree. Direct confrontation is suicide, but perhaps we can outlast them."

"Outlast them? How?" Aelrion clenched his forepaws tightly, his eyes reddened by lack of sleep. "They have spies lurking everywhere, some as small as flies. They'll find us no matter where we choose to go."

"Perhaps the answer is not *where* we choose to go, but *when*," Galdreth whispered to himself before drawing on the power of the piece of time. He made it swirl faster than it ever had, luring it from the confines of his stomach all the way up to his mouth. He released the golden circle, and it drifted away from its master, eddying as it increased in size and only stopping once it was many spans wider than normal. Moving images came to life within the shape from behind a veil of fog—wolfish shapes, barking and yelping in between flashes of orange light. Galdreth moved to touch them, an invisible force stopping his forepaw from pushing through. "The future is a whirlpool shifting endlessly within a river of change, but the past… the past is a frozen pond. The past cannot change. The past is always certain."

Aelrion and Angara-kal gaped at the imposing shape and the obscured images inside it. The fog shifted, revealing numerous two-legged silhouettes fighting on ruined lands. *BANG! BANG! BANG!* They aimed loud sticks at each other, killing without pause. Metallic *eagles* soared high at speeds so incredible they sliced white cones through the air, spewing destruction below. A distant light brighter than the sun blinded most of the fighters, and those facing the other way turned in time to witness the herald of their doom. The light bloated to a colossal size, engulfing everything and everyone. A crushing *BOOM* followed. A breath later, there was nothing but fire all around, and presiding over the devastation was a gigantic black cloud in the shape of a mushroom. No more Forgotten Ones. No more fighting. Only death. The fog shifted again, this time showing unarmed silhouettes fleeing from crystalline behemoths. They chased their prey around unnatural pillars of glass in various states of disrepair, all taller than the tallest trees Silversong had ever seen. Searing orange beams vaporized any who found themselves cornered by the monsters, and even through the fog, Silversong noticed the snowflakes drifting from a shrouded sky.

No, not snowflakes, Silversong realized. *Ash.*

"We destroy ourselves?" Aelrion uttered in disbelief. Something odd happened to his eyes. Droplets of water leaked from them. He looked sad. "This is our future if we win against the beasts?"

The uncertain futures evaporated. Galdreth willed the piece of time back to its former size and promptly swallowed it. "Rivers dry up, mountains wear away, the tides come and go, the seasons shift, and the lands change, but human nature does not."

Aelrion gripped the base of the blade attached to his waist, more droplets falling down his cheeks.

Shock and despair overcame Angara-kal by the looks of it, and she whispered something akin to a prayer under her breath. Yet beyond those deep eyes worked a mind that searched for the secrets behind such awful destruction.

"My friends," Galdreth clasped his forepaws together, "the piece of time hasn't shown you anything new. We've been fighting amongst ourselves since the dawn of humanity, and we'll continue to do so for as long as the sun chases the moon. We'll just have more spectacular weapons at our disposal."

Aelrion gave Galdreth a solemn stare. "Why do we fight if this is to be our end? Can we not become more than this?"

"Ever the optimist." Galdreth considered the question. "The future is never certain, Aelrion. But even if it was, it changes nothing. The beasts seek to upend our rightful dominion over this realm, and in doing so, they threaten the balance of all. I seek only to put humanity back in the equation. Whether our future is one of prosperity or destruction, we must fight for it… because we're human. And so long as a single human yet breathes, our defeat is not a conclusion."

He unfastened a strange contraption tied to his side. It was a curved object made entirely of black metal, hollow yet solid, and it fit perfectly in Galdreth's forepaw. He offered it to Aelrion. "Take this. You'll need it. It's a revolving pistol—lighter than a rifle and able to fire six shots before needing to be reloaded. Dare I say, it's accurate enough to blind even a wildgod's eye. It's made of darksteel, so the metal-manipulating cripple won't be able to control it. I only wish we could've constructed more advanced weapons, but circumstances demanded mass-production at the cost of quality."

Metal-manipulating cripple? Does he mean Stone-Guard?

Aelrion hesitated, then took the weird weapon and a small container accompanying it. "I fail to see how this can make a difference. If your monstrosity can't—"

"You're missing the point. You'll understand soon enough, though." Galdreth took off the ornament circling his head and peered at his reflection in the gemstones. "You must lead the last remnants of humanity far to the south, to my old city of shining white marble. Many blueprints and innovations granted by the piece of time are immortalized on parchment there, stowed away deep in the palace vaults so neither the beasts nor the passing of the ages can spoil their value. The knowledge they offer can rekindle the spark of humanity into the chaotic inferno it was always meant to be."

"Your plan makes no sense," Aelrion pointed out. "Every city save this one is likely still infested by the enemy, and why not bring your blueprints here in the first place? Why leave them behind?"

Angara-kal opened her mouth to speak, but Galdreth raised a forepaw to cut her off. "Ever since I swallowed this illusive weapon, the majority of my focus has been spent paving the road to victory. The choices I made won't make sense to you now, but in the end, you'll see the pieces of the puzzle coming together. Return to your army, absorb into your forces those who followed me, accept Angara-kal as your advisor, then head south. It's the only way. I won't allow humanity's legacy to be forgotten, and neither should you. I understand your doubts, but every choice I made has led to this. We're on the precipice, and we must continue the climb."

"Do you have to be so cryptic?" Aelrion used the back of his forepaw to rub his glistening forehead.

"Believe it or not, if I elaborate, I'll be risking the future I fought so tirelessly to make possible," Galdreth explained.

Angara-kal gripped her metallic stick and brought it before her. She pressed something on its length, and it extended to twice its size. She smacked the blunt end of it on the ground, causing a slight ringing sound. The pointed tip glinted in the light of the towering behemoth. "I trust in his vision, Crownless One. So should you. King Galdreth has accounted for every possibility. Every outcome. He has worked himself to exhaustion trying to carve out this pathway for us, and now it is time we marched upon it."

Doubt still lingered in Aelrion's eyes, but no more water leaked from them. "It's a dangerous road to the south. The enemy is preparing for a final assault on humanity. They'll intercept us. There's no telling how many soldiers I'll lose."

"If you can make it to the Bronze Temple at the southern end of this continent, you'll find your way to safety." Galdreth peered at the unseen threads circling around Aelrion.

"I'll… I'll seek the counsel of my advisors. We'll take everything into consideration. Then we'll see." Aelrion's forepaws trembled despite him speaking confidently. Galdreth and Angara-kal glanced knowingly at each other, and the darker Forgotten One nodded. "And you? I've granted you free reign over the Underground City and its inhabitants. You'll no doubt wish to join me on my southbound quest should I heed your advice."

Galdreth smiled. "I've fulfilled my role as best I could. Alas, I've reached my journey's end. Gather my men and make use of them. They answer to Caelina Mezrek, my general. I believe you two have already met."

"Yes." Aelrion stiffened in his metallic shell. "I would sooner leap into an active volcano than be the target of her flaming temper."

Galdreth's smile stretched wider. "You don't climb the chain of command so quickly without a certain attitude as you should know." He put the circular ornament back on his head and closed his eyes, sighing as his troubles passed onto the shoulders of another. "The future is yours, Aelrion. Humanity's future is now yours."

Just as Aelrion turned to leave, Galdreth called out, "one more thing."

Aelrion's frost-touched eyes landed on Galdreth.

"Don't lose your sword."

The transition back to the present was as seamless as Silversong's voyage to the past. He blinked at Frostpaw and the other wolves.

"You blacked out for a moment there, Silversong." Frostpaw whined in a worried tone. "Did something happen?"

"Nothing you would understand, and nothing I can properly explain." Silversong nosed Frostpaw gently. "As I was saying before, there's something I need to practice, and if it all goes smoothly, Chief Ashenfall is as good as dead."

Without waiting for a response, Silversong moved forward, the piece of time pulsing like a second heartbeat. The sudden vision had been confusing and disorienting, but it had at least shown him another way to wield the weapon, a way to expose Ashenfall's crimes.

If Galdreth can produce a reflection of the uncertain future, the opposite should be possible.

If the past was a frozen pond, and under the surface Ashenfall's treachery was preserved, Silversong could shine a clear light on it. He almost laughed at the convoluted chain of events leading up to this moment. If Galdreth hadn't killed Stormstrider, if he hadn't taken the piece of time, if he hadn't travelled all the way into the Mountainmouth, none of this would've been possible.

I guess I have you to thank, Galdreth. Silversong wondered how the Forgotten One leader would feel knowing his sworn enemy now wielded the piece of time. *I'm on the precipice, and I must continue the climb.*

CHAPTER 23

From Past to Present

The evening sun burned through the dissipating clouds to illuminate a swath of open field gradually descending to a distant ruin battered by the ages. Silversong stopped and panted as the others halted behind him.

This is as good a place as any.

All at once, images of death flashed in his head and coalesced into the face of the Heretic scowling at him, green eyes piercing deeper than flesh. "Stand around me facing outward. The Heretic is near. He'll attack when he thinks I'm distracted. If we're vigilant, we can end the threat of the exiles for good."

"But Rime is still out there," Frostpaw growled out the name of his mother's murderer. "As long as he lives, the exiles have another leader in line to take charge."

"We'll bring him to justice soon, Frostpaw," Silversong whined knowing the answer wouldn't satisfy the blue-furred corporal. "Take your positions and keep your eyes peeled. The Heretic is tunneling his way toward us as we speak. He'll strike quick as a thunderbolt."

Frostpaw obeyed, and Snowleap whined to comfort her packmate. "Don't worry, Frostpaw. Rime can't escape the fangs of justice forever."

The fangs of justice…

Old memories brought Silversong back to the Mountainmouth, within the maze of madness where he'd spoken to his alternate future. Loud as a bellowing moose, the warnings of his one-eyed image echoed between his ears, chastising him for not letting Ironwrath consume the piece of time.

Hazel padded up to him and offered a gentle lick. "Maybe this isn't a good idea, Silversong. Maybe we should head back and gather reinforcements."

"There's no time, Hazel. He's already on the move, and the Warden is probably out there searching for us too. She knows we're missing by now," Silversong explained, focusing on the many errors he could still make. "She'll haul my rump back to Thornhollow and place me under Swiftstorm's guard, and my sister won't let me practice anything until the trial starts. It's now or never."

A pressure squeezed his lungs upon thinking of Swiftstorm. He imagined sharp fangs crushing his terror like brittle bones. It worked.

"All right, Silversong," Hazel exhaled. "I trust you."

"Don't worry," Palesquall yipped without the slightest concern. "We'll make the Heretic eat his own tail when he shows his ugly face here!"

Silversong smiled. "Good. I know I can count on all of you." He caught Snowleap's golden eyes. "Thank you for helping me. May our alliance strike a decisive blow against those who would rather see us as enemies instead of friends."

The two corporals he didn't know within the River-Stream group shivered, but neither expressed any desire to leave. Snowleap merely inclined her head and turned to the surrounding field, scanning it for any abnormalities. The others followed her example.

Silversong breathed in and out until his anxiety subsided.

Now, how do I practice something I've never tried before? How did you do it, Galdreth?

Unnumbered possibilities danced across his vision, many of them showing his demise as clearly as the blazing sun. He removed all doubts from his head and began drawing on the power of the piece of time, influencing the speed of its rotation. He turned toward the obsidian spire fronting the Fireleaf Forest and worked on coaxing the golden circle up his stomach and into his throat. It turned faster and faster, spinning without slowing—a whirlpool of light within his mouth. He remembered Galdreth using the weapon in a similar manner. Only, instead of aiming for the uncertain future, Silversong concentrated on the certainty of the past.

This is how I'll expose Ashenfall.

The weapon pulsed. Then like a thread pulled to its snapping point, it tensed under the immense pressure Silversong was exerting on it, and even as he released the golden light from his jaws, he could feel its power draining steadily. There it floated before him, separated from its master yet still tied to his command by an invisible string. Silversong fed his orders through the connection, and the circle expanded to twice, thrice, then to dozens of times the size it had been, large enough to contain within it several wolves at least.

Thoughts still narrowed on the unchangeable past, the land and spire framed by the golden circle projected mirror images of how they had been moments, days, seasons ago, all blurring alongside one another until Silversong couldn't distinguish how recently or how far back he was looking. Thornhollow was there in all its ugly glory, then it wasn't, the cycle repeating itself countless times before Silversong let the Forgotten Ones intrude on his mind. Their presence caused a disturbance in the whirling shape. Like waves crashing into each other, the echoing projections collided, and the ripples caused by the impact settled into a detailed battle unfolding during the War of Change.

Their backs to Silversong, the Forgotten Ones shouted incomprehensibly as their troops moved into formation, aiming stick-like weapons at the approaching tide of howling beasts. A bleeding sun tinged the clouds red as loud bangs resonated in unison from blasts of white smoke. Orders were given, and soon after came another series of deafening booms. The assailants at the front collapsed in droves, but those behind trampled the corpses of their comrades. Again and again the awful booms sounded, and more and more beasts became lifeless obstacles for those in the back to tread over. The leaders among the Forgotten Ones bellowed out more commands, and the kneeling soldiers closest to the charging horde raised metal-tipped shafts of wood. The opposing forces collided, and any semblance of order was gone. Though the beasts far outnumbered the Forgotten Ones, their zeal on the battlefield was more than matched.

The vision within the golden circle was so vivid, so lifelike. Silversong reached out a forepaw and…

… an invisible force stopped him from pushing through. He promptly put his forepaw back on the ground, feeling slightly foolish. It seemed bringing something from the present into the past violated a fundamental law governing the piece of time.

A terrible wind ripped out the blades of grass and shook the focus of the Forgotten Ones. The distraction caused the deaths of many, and just as they recovered from the gale to rejoin the fray, a deep and piercing howl cut newfound courage to fragments. The leaves of the forest trembled to the countless beating wings of a flock of ravens—black specks taking to the clouds. They croaked to announce the arrival of their Titan.

A shadow springing to life, the Ravenlord exploded out of the woods, maneuvering gracefully through the air and spawning behind him darkened echoes of himself, talons outstretched and aimed at the enemy. The Forgotten Ones hit the ground as the winged Titan and his echoes swooped up dozens upon dozens of two-legged shapes, bringing them high into the sky before dropping them like discarded scraps. Some managed to shoot down the Ravenlord's echoes, but the sly trickster only spawned more.

Once more the bone-chilling howl resonated, loud as thunder and equally dire. Out of the forest charged Motherwolf herself, eyes like blazing clusters of flickering stars, her four generals trailing her on either side. Whistle-Wind was a vortex of rage and speed, River-Stream an unstoppable wave of destruction, Flame-Heart a tempest of blistering fire, and Stone-Guard—whose hind legs were paralyzed—surged forward as a landslide breaking through whatever dared stand in his way. Beams of searing light radiated out of Motherwolf's gaze to incinerate a mass of Forgotten Ones, leaving behind nothing but blackened metal and scorched bones. The wind gathered in separate places and swirled into mighty twisters, all rampaging through the chaos and flinging scores of enemies across the battlefield. Severed limbs rained on those unfortunate enough not to have been granted a quick death, but still the Forgotten Ones fought through the ever-worsening odds.

At the frontlines, Motherwolf barked and stomped her forepaws on the ground. An earthquake strong enough to make a mountain shake forced the remaining Forgotten Ones to huddle low. Out from under them sprung a fountain of magma shooting for the sky. It swallowed all who couldn't get out of the way in time, its ravenous hunger only ending once molten stone solidified into obsidian. Black against the bloody sky, the stark spire signaled victory for the beasts and defeat for the vanquished. They turned to flee, but the wolves, bears, and antlered prey gave no quarter, picking off the retreating forces one by one without mercy. The resistance was broken, and now the extermination had begun. The routed army ran in Silversong's direction.

One of the terrified two-legged creatures stopped in front of him, still clutching the stick-like weapon so many others had wielded. Silversong squinted at the small figure and nearly gasped upon realizing how young she—he thought it was a *she*—looked.

This is a child! A Forgotten One pup!

Those bulging eyes shouldn't have carried such terror and fury. She raised her weapon and aimed it at Silversong.

Does she see me?!

The stick made a clicking noise, but no loud bang came afterwards. The child growled and threw the weapon on the ground, choosing instead to take out a silvery fang of metal strapped to her side. It was way too big for her, but she lifted it over her head regardless. She screamed at the top of her lungs and hurled the blade at her target.

The metallic fang spun through the air. Silversong instinctively dodged sideways. Concentration broken, the golden circle shrank back to normal size in less time than it took to blink. Shock turned his blood to ice, and he leaped to the rapidly whirling shape, closing his mouth around it and swallowing quickly, only allowing himself to breathe once the piece of time rotated calmly in his stomach again.

He'd done it! He'd successfully conjured a reflection of the past. Now Ashenfall was truly done for!

"Uhm… Silversong…?" Palesquall's worried voice dampened the triumphant spark.

Silversong took in his defenders, and all except Palesquall growled at the Heretic who stared wide-eyed a dozen leaps away. Earth dirtied Ironwrath's coat, but his green gaze was sharp and fervent as ever. Silversong would've shivered if those eyes were aimed at him. Instead, the Heretic's interest was drawn to the same thing Palesquall was gaping at—a long shaft of greyish metal poking out of the grass right where Silversong had previously stood.

"What in Motherwolf—"

The weapon the Forgotten One child had thrown pulled itself out of the ground and in one cutting motion came down on Silversong's neck.

Thwack!

The blade bounced away from Silversong. Quicker than a grasshopper, Palesquall had conjured a lash of wind and had used it to parry the deadly blow.

The Heretic grunted in annoyance, willing the metallic tooth to zip toward Silversong, its flashing tip ready to skewer. Silversong dodged the obvious attack and connected himself to the breeze, head drained of all but the desire to see Ironwrath soundly defeated. Wind circling around him, Silversong charged his nemesis.

"Wolves of River-Stream, attack!" barked Snowleap.

Hazel released a battle cry and sprinted for the Heretic. Palesquall joined her swift strides. Whirlwinds raged around them, and they quickly caught up to Snowleap and the others, lending them some speed. The Heretic growled, feeding his anger into the slashes and thrusts of the metallic weapon. Gashes appeared all over Silversong, but he ignored the stinging pain. The swirling currents of air lessened the severity of the blows, and he flexed the threads of time, prepared to capture the leader of the exiles.

As if seeing defeat approaching, the earth shifted beneath Ironwrath and yanked him out of danger's grasp. He stomped a forepaw on the grass, sending a rocky hail flying toward Silversong. He avoided every projectile, his allies getting closer to the target. The ground softened beneath them. Every time a paw landed, the soil itself tried sucking it under. Silversong urged the unseen threads into the ground, locking its contents in time and countering the Heretic's attempt at trapping everyone in place.

The clean blade from a forgotten era struck for the heart. This time Silversong tied the threads around the shaft, removing it from the constant forward motion. Ironwrath's eyes bulged in fear, and he brought another forepaw down. The earth swelled where he was, and a brown pillar sprouted beneath him, lifting him to the heights of safety. Silversong's allies surrounded the Heretic, saliva dripping from bared fangs. Silversong stopped under the enemy's shadow, the reach of his extended aura barely scraping the small platform the old exile stood on. He retracted the threads to prevent the beginning of a headache.

"A smart move, Ironwrath, but pointless. You're trapped and have nowhere to go," Silversong lied, the piece of time hinting at a few ways in which the Heretic could escape. "Surrender, and I'll give you a quick death. Something the Warden would never allow."

"Look at you, little lamb. You've really grown into a strong and capable soldier." The Heretic's gravelly voice was unshakable. On a small surface he stood, completely surrounded, and somehow he still managed to appear in control of the situation. "I'll take some credit for this change."

"I was always capable, Ironwrath. And I was always aiming for your defeat." Silversong grunted at Palesquall and Hazel. "Get him down, you two."

"Gladly," Hazel growled and motioned her tail from side to side until a thick vine of pure air appeared at the tip. She whipped at the Heretic's paws while Palesquall launched a barrage of condensed wind at the earthen platform.

Bringing his forepaws inward, the Heretic beckoned two blocks of stone to his aid. They erupted out of the ground and moved up to deflect the blows threatening his balance. The stones rotated around him, nullifying the attacks.

"Hold!" Silversong ordered, and his friends obeyed.

Caution prevented the Heretic from lowering his defenses. "Oh, little lamb. I see the struggle in your restless eyes, and I smell the anxiety in your scent. The conflict. Uniting the Four Territories through peaceful means has been a failed endeavor, hasn't it?"

Silversong tightened his frown so it crushed any potential doubt lingering on his face. "You're mistaken. The Four Territories are closer than ever to being truly united. Soon, we'll be a single force free of the Warden's tethers."

The Heretic considered Silversong's statements and shook his head. "You're still unsure of yourself. You think you're willing to make the necessary sacrifices to achieve this vision of yours, but when it comes to your sister? I think not. Blind faith has dragged her deep into the pit of zealotry like all other sentinels. Not even family is strong enough to break her from the Warden's influence now. Can you sacrifice Swiftstorm, Silversong? Can you?!"

Again.

The air escaped Silversong's lungs.

Again.

He couldn't breathe. He tried to inhale, but nothing came in.

Again.

He couldn't breathe! He couldn't—

I'm stronger than this! He envisioned himself as an immovable stone, refusing to budge to the slicing winds and the coursing waters. Not even the hottest flames could singe him. He was stone. Unyielding. He was stone. Unbreakable.

Something far beneath him seemed to quake against the contours of his paws—a rumbling language, complex like the countless minerals forming a rocky canyon, solid yet malleable like the different states of the earth. He opened his eyes, and the fear was gone.

The Heretic stared at him in disbelief. "H-how did you—"

Ironwrath quickly recovered from the unintended reaction, trying to distract Silversong. "You've lost, little lamb. You tried and failed. There's no shame in admitting it. Now give me the piece of time so I can start fixing this whole mess you've created."

"Quiet, scatfur!" Frostpaw snapped. "Silversong has fought tirelessly for the Four Territories, and he'll continue the fight long after we throw your bones in the Furtherlands where they belong. You're the one who's failed! You discarded so many lives in your search for the piece of time! Now look at you! A rat on the run."

The Heretic spared a glance at Frostpaw and scoffed. "It still makes me better than you, a pup who can't escape his need for meaningless revenge. Back in the Mountainmouth, you almost threw your life away for a chance at killing Rime. Come to think of it, your selfish choice could've killed Silversong also. I heard he risked his life to save you from the collapsing expanse. He obviously cares for you, and in the name of vengeance you were willing to toss him aside. Having no regard for your own life is one thing, but the life of a friend? Quite another thing entirely."

Guilt flashed across Frostpaw's face, and he stared at his own claws in disgust. Silversong wanted badly to reassure his friend, but Snowleap got to him first.

The glint of opportunity lit a flame in the Heretic's eyes, and the golden circle pulsed madly. Something bad was coming, and to Silversong's dismay, he couldn't seem to predict it. "You know, I expected you to be the first one to catch on to the little meetings between Rime and Cindersky. Despite their subtlety on quiet nights, your mother still caught them together, and I thought you would've been just as observant, being her son and all."

The phantom pulsing stopped, and Silversong tried puzzling out what had just happened.

Frostpaw lifted his head to glare at Ironwrath, limbs shaking and ears falling back. "Cindersky? The victim of Rime's seduction? The mother of that subordinate who looks like…" His mouth twitched, and his frown deepened.

"It's obvious to anyone who looks closely that her children are halfbloods." Ironwrath turned to Silversong, smirking. "Isn't it, little lamb?"

None of the wolves present had time to process the revelation as shrill howls broke out near the spire. The Warden had spotted the Heretic.

Ironwrath looked over his shoulder and huffed. "And here she comes. You think you have everything figured out, Silversong, but you don't even know the limits of the weapon you stole from me. Just now you unwittingly brought an object from the past into the present, and in your ignorance you released said object from the grasp of time."

Silversong rolled sideways just as the sharp shaft of metal missed him by a whisker. The Heretic stomped a forepaw on his platform, and the entire pillar disintegrated into a blinding cloud of dust. Silversong tightened the threads, but they caught nothing. When the particles cleared, Ironwrath was gone, the stones he'd used as shields abandoned. The only sign that he'd ever been there was an inconspicuous opening in the ground from where he'd first emerged.

While the others coughed and blinked to clear their eyes, the piece of time showed Silversong the breaking of the obsidian spire in painful detail. The collapse now seemed more imminent than ever.

The Warden and her sentinels were getting closer, all of them continuing the charge as if the enemy were still here.

I suppose they consider me their enemy too, now.

Silversong hardened his heart and forced his eyes wide open. He hadn't failed yet. Hope remained. From here he would move forward as an unstoppable force for change, a remedy against tyranny and oppression. The time was near to cast Ashenfall and the Warden into the shadows of history.

There's still hope for you too, Swiftstorm. I know you're not completely lost.

Under the surge of triumphant thoughts, the Heretic's voice lingered, taunting him, contradicting him, testing his resolve. Could Silversong really make the necessary sacrifices?

Blurry visions, good and bad, streamed into his head, and throughout them all the laughter of the exiles echoed like mad thunder.

CHAPTER 24

The Trial

"You knew about Rime and Cindersky?" Frostpaw asked Silversong while they waited for the Warden's approach. The others already had their tails tucked and their postures lowered. Snowleap gestured for Frostpaw to join her, the worry on her face unmasked.

Silversong whispered so only Frostpaw could hear him. "I followed Cindersky during the night and caught her and Rime together. She isn't his victim, Frostpaw. She's his lover, his mate. They tricked everyone into thinking Rime was a monster."

"He is a monster," Frostpaw stated firmly.

"Frostpaw…"

"He is!" Frostpaw snapped before storming off to join his packmates. The Warden wouldn't appreciate the two of them being so close to one another.

The piece of time shuddered, and Silversong allowed a chill to slide across his spine. He put Frostpaw out of his thoughts and contemplated a more pressing matter. He hadn't opened a mirror to the past just now. He'd somehow opened a gateway to it, and the gateway only allowed objects to pass through one way. The move had weakened the golden circle considerably, its strength now thoroughly dulled.

I can only open these gateways sparingly.

A constant blurriness obscured the near future. Sometimes clarity struck, but as soon as it came, a veil of fog shrouded even the likeliest of outcomes. If the Heretic had consumed the weapon in this state, he couldn't have done much to make the winds of victory blow in his favour. If events played out like Silversong hoped they would, the threat of the exiles would be short-lived. Nothing would stand against a united Wolven Bulwark. A free Wolven Bulwark.

The Warden slowed to a graceful stride, the sentinels behind her spreading to surround Silversong. He returned to Hazel and Palesquall, refusing to adopt the proper posture, and even as the Warden closed the distance, his tail remained lifted for all to see. Swiftstorm's presence shortened his breaths and increased the beating of his heart. His eyes flicked toward her like she was a predator ready to pounce. He wanted her far away, and it pained him to admit it.

I'll confront you after the trial, Swiftstorm. I refuse to be afraid of my own sister forever.

Greyhail and another Stone-Guard sentinel inspected the Heretic's tunnel. They sniffed cautiously around it, then commanded the earth to bury the entrance.

Like an avalanche stopping before it could lay waste to the forest, the Warden halted a whisker-length from Silversong's face, her breaths controlled and her expression blank. Her pale eyes dug into Silversong like bloodsuckers, and he found himself wanting to flee her piercing stare. He stood his ground, and she sniffed.

"Care to explain why you're in the presence of rival wolves, Silversong?" The question was more of an accusation than a mere inquiry.

"I figured I could use their help against the Heretic." Silversong pointed his nose toward the collapsed tunnel. "You just missed him, I'm afraid. You no doubt would've wanted to say hello."

"This is no time for jokes." The Warden's glower would've frightened a thundercloud.

"This is no time for accusations either." Silversong's response caused his friends to flinch. In truth, he wanted to cower, to tuck his tail and grovel at the Warden's forepaws. He was tempted to go onto his back even now. Then he remembered the purpose he'd given himself, and it was enough to counter his fearful instincts. No matter how sharp the Warden's glare became, Silversong wouldn't allow anything to pierce his shell of confidence.

She turned to Swiftstorm and beckoned her over. "It seems I failed to teach you proper discipline earlier. Shall we continue your lesson without interruption this time?"

Frostpaw tilted his head, and by the looks Palesquall and Hazel gave Silversong, they were questioning the nature of his *lesson*. Swiftstorm approached, and Silversong's lungs immediately expelled the air he'd just inhaled. He tried the trick of envisioning himself as a stone, but Swiftstorm was right there, and she was getting closer.

No, no, no, no!

His heart pounded to the point of bursting, and his tail slowly moved to press itself against his stomach. He forced it back up, swaying side to side, a nauseating dizziness scrambling his thoughts. His vision narrowed on his sister. He couldn't look away. Those green eyes bore no love for him. Not anymore. She would torture him until he broke. Again and again and again. His lips curled. His legs shook. His bladder emptied itself. He could hear his friends asking why he was so afraid, their voices twisting together like choking vines.

Instead of resuming the torture, Swiftstorm looked at the Warden and whined something about a trial. An important trial to expose a dangerous code-breaker. Yes. His sister was explaining how it would be wise to return to Thornhollow and continue the punishment afterwards. The packs were already gathering at the peak. They were waiting. Swiftstorm glanced at him. He flinched, fearing her touch more than death itself. If she lifted a forepaw in his direction…

He stared at her forepaws, eyes popping out of his skull. She was going to do it. She was going to touch him and steal all the air from his lungs again. She would—

"Silversong!" the Warden barked, halting the group of wolves following her. "Did you not hear me? Your lesson can wait. Swiftstorm is right. The trial comes first."

"T-trial…?" Silversong shivered alone, bladder completely emptied on his tucked tail. When had he assumed such a pathetic posture? When had the other wolves started padding toward the spire? Why were they all staring at him like he'd gone mad?

He picked out Frostpaw's worried face. Those yellow eyes, wide and bright, burned the weeds of terror growing all over Silversong. He saw how deeply Frostpaw cared about him. His expression said it all. Silversong's senses returned, and he gasped.

I froze like a cornered deer.

He shook himself, forcing his tail up despite the shame trying to push it low. He couldn't let his fear of Swiftstorm affect him like this ever again. It seemed Scorchfang had been ordered to request the trial earlier than anticipated, and all wolves had been called to Thornhollow's peak to witness the Warden's judgment. Silversong breathed in and out before joining the silent run back to the spire. Hazel and Palesquall enclosed him on either side, sheltering him from the sentinels. The two licked his fur and asked him why he'd panicked so inexplicably. He refused to elaborate. How could he?

The clouds resumed their battle against the sun in a final effort to see its light smothered before nightfall. The patrol units had all been pulled away, and only Blazefur guarded the entrance to Thornhollow, brown eyes vigilant and aimed at the Fireleaf Forest. He lowered his tail and bowed to the Warden.

The leader of the sentinels paused in front of Blazefur. "It would be an embarrassing affair should you be the one Scorchfang wishes to expose. Imagine the awkward silence as we all wait for you at the peak."

Blazefur stiffened at the comment. "My loyalty to the Wolven Code is greater than my love for Flame-Heart. I'm not the code-breaker in question."

The Warden nodded in approval. "I know. This is why I chose you to keep watch for the Heretic. He'll be tempted to strike while we're distracted. If you see so much as one exile place a forepaw on the field, you howl for backup, and I'll postpone the trial."

"Yes, ma'am," Blazefur grunted, giving Silversong a wary look. "May your judgment be swift and sound."

"It shall be." The Warden turned to face Silversong. "It shall be."

The climb up the spire took forever, and the closer Silversong got to the top, the more the weight of responsibility tried tugging him back down. On this night, he would either bring ruin or change to the Four Territories. One by one, his senses escaped him until he closed his eyes and floated in a perfect void. He'd come too far to fail. It wasn't a thought, just a simple fact. In the emptiness, a familiar pair of pale blue eyes watched him, the blackness around them resolving into Aelrion's determined face. Silversong mirrored the Forgotten One's expression.

We judge each other for the littlest things and scoff at our slightest differences. But when calamity strikes, all prejudice is forgotten in favour of perseverance. Perhaps the same could be applied to the wolves of the Four Territories.

Silversong released himself from the empty space, letting Ashenfall come into view. The tyrant was framed by two obsidian teeth marking the entrance to the topmost level. Regal as ever, she lounged upon the shelf protruding under the spire's cracked tip.

Ashenfall's lips settled into a smirk upon seeing her prize being escorted toward her. Inside Silversong was a power she intended to abuse the same way she abused everyone else. As he strode through the obsidian teeth, his packmates all turned to watch him from one end of the gathering, fringed by a string of sentinels cutting them off from River-Stream. In the middle, another line of sentinels barred River-Stream from Flame-Heart, and another separated Flame-Heart from Stone-Guard. These were the barriers Silversong intended to break before the night was done.

Scorchfang stood still as a stone beneath Ashenfall's shelf, ready to announce who the real code-breaker was, ready to expose the true menace who deserved to die. She met Silversong's eyes and nodded. He returned the gesture, noticing her loyalists moving through the Flame-Heart mass to stand closer to her. They would interfere should the trial go awry. Bleaksmoke wagged his tail in the front row in complete awe of Scorchfang, drool dripping from his lolling tongue. Cindersky found her children among the subordinates and whispered to them. Frostpaw glared at her like *she* was the one responsible for his mother's death.

The Stone-Guard side was quiet as expected, Bronzeblood eager to discredit Silversong at Ashenfall's behest. How would the incompetent Chief react to the complete reversal of the trial? He would wait to see how it all played out, of course, and he would begrudgingly accept the winner's authority to preserve his hide. Briefly, Silversong considered forcefully removing this poor excuse of a Chief from power.

Hesitation formed cracks in Silversong's conniving thoughts. He was beginning to think like Ashenfall, and the realization made his blood run cold.

No. I'm not like her. I'll try all the other ways first.

Darkwave scrutinized Frostpaw from the cluster of lieutenants near Riptide. Frostpaw hadn't stopped staring at Cindersky. A sudden pulse within Silversong's stomach warned him of all his careful plotting falling apart. Beyond his sight, he glimpsed a blurry vision of the blue corporal pursuing someone into the Fireleaf Forest… toward vengeance and death.

"Take your places," the Warden ordered, moving to the front to stand near Scorchfang.

As Snowleap and her patrol merged into the River-Stream army, Silversong silently begged Frostpaw not to do anything stupid. Not risking the Warden's ire by stalling the trial, Silversong walked to the Whistle-Wind quarter alongside Palesquall and Hazel. His packmates welcomed the three of them, and Silversong took his place among the corporals. A space had formed around Gorsescratch, a space breached only by Tawnydrift. Drawing out more than a few gasps, Silversong moved to sit beside his former bully. The two shared a look of understanding, and Gorsescratch smiled his thanks.

"We'll fight for you, Silversong. Always," Cedargaze whined to him from the front row.

"We love you, son," Shadowgale grunted beside his mate, his Chief.

Silversong smiled at his parents, but it faded when they turned to Swiftstorm, who entered the line of sentinels separating Whistle-Wind from River-Stream. They worried about her, about her allegiances. He did too.

His heartbeat pounded faster and faster, his breaths shortening.

NO! I'm done being afraid of her.

Stone—no, wind. I'm a gale whose force cannot be contained. I ride the waves wherever they crash and silence the flames wherever they spread, and not even the mountains in all their strength can withstand my constant bite.

A pocket of air swirled around him, buffeting his fur. He was ready.

A silence unlike any other befell the gathering. Not a soul dared move except the Warden who assumed the role of judge at Scorchfang's side. Anticipation swelled, and all the while Ashenfall grinned as if the prize she sought already rotated deep inside her gut.

Without delay, the Warden commenced the trial. "Soldiers of the Wolven Bulwark, it is through regretful circumstances that I have summoned you here, especially when the threat of the exiles is not yet over, but such a matter can wait no longer. Among yourselves breathes a code-breaker whose crimes against the Wolven Code stretch wide like an unfurled frond. So wicked is this code-breaker's soul that judgment must be dispensed tonight, for if we allow this vile fiend to continue drawing breath a day longer, there's no telling how far their corruption may spread. Scorchfang! Expose this wretch to the Four Territories so that I may mete out righteous justice."

I've got to give it to her. She knows how to make a dramatic announcement.

"Sounds like she's already decided you're guilty, Silversong," Tawnydrift muttered.

"We've got your back," Gorsescratch whispered.

"Yes, ma'am." Scorchfang straightened herself and whispered under her breath—a prayer, Silversong guessed. "The circumstances are regretful indeed, but justice can wait no longer. Chief Ashenfall." She turned to her leader whose orange eyes nearly exploded out of her skull in shock. She hadn't yet faced the main accusations, but just seeing her vexing smirk disappear like a wisp of smoke lifted Silversong's mood to ecstatic heights. "Too long have you ruled our pack through fear. Too long have you tormented those who question your cruelty. Too long have you held a position you do not deserve. Tonight, I flay the false coat you choose to wear and expose the monster underneath. Tonight, I bring closure to all those you wronged. Tonight, you face the fury of Flame-Heart."

The astonishment from the Stone-Guard and Flame-Heart wolves could probably be heard from the bottom of the den, but the accused cut all commotion to utter silence. "HOW DARE YOU?!"

"Scorchfang!" The Warden bristled like a porcupine. "Have you lost your senses?! Your Chief has been nothing but an honourable host to the Wolven Bulwark. You hinted at accusing someone else!"

I wonder who. Silversong shifted his weight from paw to paw, the duel between fright and excitement raging within him. He struggled not to speak up for Scorchfang. There could be no suspicion of a conspiracy. Not yet.

"Don't mind her, ma'am." Trails of smoke curled out of Ashenfall's nostrils. Though she sounded confident, there was an unmistakable twitch of her eyes and a nervous flick of her tail. "She tried something similar before in the hopes of usurping my reign. I thought she'd learned her lesson."

"Should I teach her some discipline?" One of Ashenfall's cronies asked.

"Ooh, can I, mother?" Bleaksmoke yipped from the crowd of riled Flame-Heart wolves. "She needs to be obedient before you pair us together!"

Scorchfang cringed and glanced at Silversong. He couldn't intervene no matter how much he wanted to. She had to stand up for herself and present the charges. Only then could he come to her aid.

"This is spiraling out of control, Silversong," his mother warned.

"Son, you have to do something," his father pleaded.

"Not now," Silversong grunted, the pressure building up. "Let this play out."

"You won't intimidate me anymore, ma'am." Scorchfang challenged her leader dead in the eye. "Last time I had no sufficient proof of your wrongdoings, and the Warden wasn't here to oversee a formal trial. Now I have everything I need to expose you for the code-breaker you are!"

Ashenfall swerved her head to face the Warden. "Ma'am, you can't seriously consider entertaining these obvious lies! I've always been faithful to the Wolven Code. You know this! You all know this!" She searched among her subjects for supporters. Some nodded in agreement, some muttered to themselves, others stayed silent, and all wolves loyal to Scorchfang glared at Ashenfall. The tyrant bristled, shifting her gaze to Stone-Guard in a silent plea for aid. None of them spoke up for her. Nostrils flaring, she gave Bronzeblood a death stare. He looked at her and hunched his shoulders.

The Warden considered the situation carefully. She beheld the stars poking through the clouds, then squinted at Silversong. Did she suspect him of flipping this trial on Ashenfall? The Warden's eyes found the Flame-Heart wolves. Surely she saw the faces of those wronged by their own Chief, saw the desire for justice, the hope for change and an end to the constant torment.

After a pause that seemed an eternity, the Warden relented. "The accused has been named, but I lack sufficient evidence to convict Chief Ashenfall of Flame-Heart. I have not witnessed any wrongdoings on her behalf. Have you, Scorchfang?"

Scorchfang exhaled a quavering breath. "I have, ma'am."

Ashenfall's furious gaze now descended upon the Warden, but the old sentinel faced the accused as a calm and collected arbiter. "Then name her crimes and let justice be served. But know this. Should you fail to provide credible evidence for your claims, I'll allow the accused to decide your punishment for wasting our time."

"So be it." Scorchfang closed her eyes, gathered her thoughts, then confronted her leader. "Chief Ashenfall, you stand accused of poisoning your former mate and Chief at the time, of conspiring to murder your own subjects for displeasing you, of…"

She gulped, meeting Silversong's gaze. There was a question in her eyes, a question Silversong answered by nodding.

Scorchfang continued the accusations. "You also stand accused of having the former Chief of Whistle-Wind murdered by your own son, Bleaksmoke. How do you answer these charges?"

Ashenfall scoffed. "Obviously I'm not guilty." She craned her head up to address the stunned gathering. "Honoured members of the Wolven Bulwark, the reason why Scorchfang is bringing up these frivolous charges is because she's a heartbroken wretch who refuses to get over my rejection of her. You see, when we were corporals, Scorchfang took a liking to me. She followed me around and practically worshipped the ground I walked on. I pitied her for how pathetic she was, so I humoured her affections and let her think we were closer than we actually were. But the mantle of Chief required me to break this illusion, and since then Scorchfang has become a bitter, spiteful mongrel who can't seem to understand a simple truth: she was never special to me." Ashenfall scowled mercilessly at Scorchfang, and the admission seemed to crush the young lieutenant. "I'll choose a proper mate for her one day. Maybe then she'll overcome her heartbreak."

Bleaksmoke hopped in place. "Me! Pick me! I can be her mate! I'll teach her to love me so she forgets all about you, mother!"

Scorchfang's legs wobbled, her hackles stiff. She composed herself and released a heavy breath, glaring defiantly at Ashenfall.

The tyrant's ears drew back, her dominant posture faltering. "Yes, maybe you're right, Bleaksmoke. I think you'll be a perfect match for poor Scorchfang. We'll teach her a thing or two about proper obedience."

Bleaksmoke yipped like he'd just found the perfect prey after a long day of hunting.

Scorchfang pushed through her obvious fear. "You see?" She turned to the troubled wolves who whispered about Ashenfall's complete abuse of power. "This is but one of many ways our Chief keeps us in line. She violates our freedoms and threatens us when she thinks we're acting against her interests."

The Warden's voice washed over the disturbed assembly. "While I don't condone the manner in which Chief Ashenfall enforces discipline, none of her actions go against the Wolven

Code. As her subjects, Scorchfang, you all are obligated to obey her just commands."

"But these aren't *just commands*, are they, ma'am?" Scorchfang singled out those loyal to her. "All who have suffered from Chief Ashenfall's abuse of power, speak up now lest your pain be forgotten!"

"Ma'am, this is absurd," Ashenfall protested, claws scraping against her obsidian shelf. "I implore you, don't entertain this charade any longer."

The Warden waited to see if any would dare speak out against their own Chief. If more than a few condemned Ashenfall, it would greatly improve the odds of Scorchfang's triumph. Ashenfall wouldn't abide traitors, and she would only end up digging for herself a deeper hole upon giving voice to her outrage.

"Come on," Silversong whispered under his breath. "Come on."

An elder loyal to Scorchfang grunted at the front. "When Chief Ashenfall paired Bleaksmoke and my daughter as mates, I tried teaching her to stand up to Bleaksmoke's bullying. She did, and for this she was lured into the woods where Bleaksmoke killed her. I have no doubt Chief Ashenfall helped cover up my daughter's murder!"

"Lies!" Ashenfall couldn't contain her fury. "She died in a hunting accident!"

"Did my daughter also die in a hunting accident?!" One of the Flame-Heart corporals barked. "All she did was refuse to become your personal spy, and as punishment you tethered her to your witless brute of a son. She died within a season. Killed by a bear?! Don't make me laugh! Bleaksmoke murdered her! Everyone knows it!"

"It's not true!" Bleaksmoke protested. "I never killed anyone! Darkfume's death was a tragic accident, and I loved her very much!"

The enraged corporal growled. "Her name was Shadowfume!"

"Whatever. Same thing!" Bleaksmoke gave his mother a pleading look. "Mother, say it isn't true. They'll believe you. You're Chief, after all."

"We won't believe anything from her," another one of Scorchfang's loyalists grunted. "Lying comes to her as naturally as breathing."

"Scorchfang put you up to this, did she not?" Ashenfall's stare promised retribution to all who'd spoken against her. "Warden, you can't possibly entertain these lies. None of my accusers have proof of their claims. Allow me to perform a few quick executions, then we can move on to the real menace threatening the sanctity of the Wolven Code." Her eyes descended on Silversong like flaring comets.

Ashenfall's cronies barked to defend her while others were reluctant to join either side.

Chief Riptide's voice rumbled out of his throat and demanded attention. "Though I can't comment on all these accusations, I can speak truth about Chief Ashenfall's character. Without the intervention of the sentinels, she would've had us dying of thirst, and she would've laughed as we perished one by one due to dehydration. She doesn't care about the Wolven Bulwark. She only cares about power. Killing the former leader of Whistle-Wind makes sense for someone like her. She would see it as a strategic move to get rid of a potential threat. If she's behind Chief Amberstorm's murder, you can bet your tails she's planning the same for me."

The River-Stream wolves backed Riptide's statements. The smoke drifting out of Ashenfall's nostrils thickened into black tendrils.

Chief Cedargaze raised her voice after the River-Stream wolves had their say. "You wish for proof of Chief Ashenfall's wrongdoings? Look no further than Hazel's face. Ashenfall's unsanctioned attack on one of MY soldiers reveals her true nature. Her soul is a rotten husk not even the Fallen Titan would savour."

Pride entered the tempest within Silversong, and he barked loud in support of his mother's claim. Others joined him: Palesquall, Gorsescratch, Tawnydrift, Shadowgale. Among the subordinates, Hazel bared her fangs at Ashenfall, not a touch of fear to be seen or smelled.

Ashenfall ejected tiny sprouts of flame from her mouth. She was too angry to even vocalize her rage.

The Warden tensed beside Scorchfang. "Chief Ashenfall and her son are innocent so long as no definitive proof is presented to the contrary. In truth, I'm beginning to feel like this is all some ploy to remove Chief Ashenfall from power, and I have some idea who could be behind such a conspiracy." Without mentioning

Silversong's name, she looked at him, zealous eyes searching for the truth.

It's time.

Loud as he could manage, Silversong announced, "I have proof of Chief Ashenfall's crimes."

"LIES!" Ashenfall growled, the flames she exhaled threatening to incinerate Silversong. If the Warden weren't here, he had no doubt Ashenfall would've already tried turning him into a sizzling pile of scorched meat. "How can you possibly prove these outrageous accusations against me?"

Silversong stood his ground as her tendrils of fire lit the entire platform in a dangerous, flickering glow. "By using the piece of time, I can open a mirror to the past and expose your crimes for all to see."

Ashenfall winced, the sides of her mouth twitching. "You can't do that. It isn't possible," she confidently whined, and though her voice was certain, the way she shifted on her shelf revealed how shaken she really was.

"He can," Snowleap claimed from the River-Stream side. "Out in the field, I saw him conjure the reflection of a battle that took place during the War of Change. It was so vivid, so real. I could almost reach out and touch the ancient event. If anyone can prove Chief Ashenfall's treachery, it's Silversong."

The corporals who'd been in Snowleap's patrol echoed her testimony. Frostpaw was the only one who kept silent. He never once looked away from Cindersky.

The Warden squinted at Snowleap for a long moment before eyeing Silversong again. "All right. No tricks, Silversong. Show us your *proof*."

Ashenfall clawed at her shelf as if trying to dig a hole she could hide in. "Ma'am, you can't let him trick you—"

"I have spoken," the Warden snapped, beckoning Swiftstorm to the front. "If Chief Ashenfall speaks out of line again, show her how precious the air she wastes truly is."

Silversong fought the memories of his torture. Flustered and outraged, Ashenfall could do little else but glower.

"Now, let's bring this madness to a close." The Warden swiped her tail to the side. "Silversong! Come forward so the whole gathering can see you."

Silversong obeyed without acknowledging her. He wouldn't tuck his tail to a sentinel ever again. He deliberately ignored Swiftstorm and stopped between Scorchfang and the Warden, staring at all the wolves he had yet to sway to his side. Many distrusted him still, but many more appeared willing to give him a chance, for he'd given them a chance to beat the Heretic.

"Open your *mirror*, Silversong," the Warden ordered.

Silversong stepped forward. Smiling at his friends and family, he willed the piece of time to rotate faster and faster. Up his body he pushed it until the golden circle whirled like a vortex within his mouth. He closed his eyes and released the shining shape. All at once the blurry visions of the future ceased. Wolves gasped and gaped in awe. Still connected to the weapon by an invisible link, Silversong let Ashenfall and her son dominate his thoughts. He blinked once, and the glowing weapon expanded wider and wider until none could look away from the imposing circle. Within the shape flickered foggy images of Ashenfall, Bleaksmoke, and all the wolves who'd been privy to the constant conniving.

Silversong realized something about the weapon. While he could conjure shadowy reflections of the past and peer into them from anywhere, he could only open a true gateway if the past he looked upon was directly linked to the circle's location in the present. A fool's hope ignited in his head. If he travelled all the way back to Wind's Rest and opened a true gateway there, could he save Pinetrail, Shrillbreeze, and all the others who'd fallen to the exiles?

Voices emerged out of the shape, some clear enough to discern.

"… I'll make sure no one knows your secret, Cindersky, if you swear to worship me whenever I demand it. If you swear to always lower yourself in my presence like I'm Motherwolf herself. From here on, you're my plaything. My entertainment. My cure for boredom."

"… Scorchfang's ambitions have been tamed for now. Bleaksmoke is a far more useful tool than I realized."

"… Rip her claws out. A fitting punishment for failing to bring me adequate prey."

"… Don't worry. They'll never discover the truth about my beloved mate's death. As far as the Wise-Wolves are concerned, a terrible sickness claimed him. I took care of the one who had her doubts."

"… The Warden is a fool for gathering all the packs here. It's only a matter of time before we tear each other's throats out. We must be ready. We must weaken our rivals and subjugate them before they can do the same to us. MY pack must remain the strongest of them all."

"… I must get my mouth on the piece of time whatever the cost! The naïve pup thinks he's on some kind of moral pedestal! Wolves like him need to be taught a dire lesson about power and who deserves to wield it."

Silversong braced himself.

"LIES! TRICKERY AND LIES!" Ashenfall bayed.

The Flame-Heart Chief dove toward him, fangs aimed at his throat. Out of her mouth spewed a torrent of fire, engulfing the shadowy images within the golden circle and swallowing Silversong whole. A massive wave of condensed air banished the flames before he could even feel the heat. Silversong's parents had saved him. He dodged Ashenfall's lunge, the brisk motion severing his connection to the piece of time. The weapon shrank back to normal size and hovered steadily in front of Ashenfall.

She gawked at her prize—the weapon she would use to elevate her power to greater heights. She ran for the golden circle, mouth wide open.

"STOP HER!" Silversong twirled his tail and formed a lash of air.

Seeing the opportunity presented at her forepaws, the Warden also leaped for the piece of time. Silversong whipped her legs, causing her to stumble. Scorchfang breathed in and exhaled a flickering orb of fire upon her leader.

It missed.

Hazel jumped in front of the projectile, inhaled, then released a sharp jet of air at the wayward fireball, causing it to explode and blowing the heat directly in Ashenfall's face.

Fur aflame and yowling, Ashenfall rolled on the ground, the stink of her burning flesh creeping up Silversong's nostrils. Before she could gain control over the fire and smother it, Scorchfang sprinted toward her and pounced, tearing into her chest and extracting desperate cries of agony. Ashenfall convulsed as piercing fangs ripped her rotten heart to shreds. She let out one last gurgling wail, one last defiant twitch, then she lay limp, all her power extinguished.

"MOTHER!" Tongues of dancing fire shielded Bleaksmoke as he charged in Ashenfall's direction. Scorchfang's loyalists caught him by the tail and yanked him the opposite way. Shocked and dazed, Bleaksmoke could do nothing but squeal as Scorchfang's allies turned his own Blessing against him. The flames surrounding him curled inward and burned him to a foul-smelling crisp.

Ashenfall's lackeys clashed against Scorchfang's supporters. At the corner of his eye, Silversong spotted two wolves sneaking away from the skirmish. He couldn't get a good look at them due to the smoky haze consuming the summit. The scent of burning flesh and blood overwhelmed his nose.

Silversong lashed the Warden again. He couldn't let her get to the piece of time.

"ARGH!"

Fangs dug into his shoulders, the pain reaching deep. The sentinels had joined the fray. He yelped and let go of his connection to the wind, trying to shake off his attacker. Greyhail banged into Silversong from the side, launching him off the ground.

"We must help him!" Hazel barked.

"To Silversong!" cried Cedargaze.

Silversong landed on his spine and struggled to get back up. Small twisters and arcs of air sliced at his assailants as the River-Stream wolves came to Scorchfang's aid. Chief Bronzeblood ordered his soldiers not to interfere, his eyes scanning the chaos for potential winners. Silvery forepaws pinned Silversong in place, pressing on his chest. His heart lurched, and his stomach plummeted. Swiftstorm had attacked him!

He could already feel the air fleeing his lungs. The frozen panic, the helplessness, the betrayal of family, it all hit him like a tumbling boulder.

Now nothing stood in the Warden's way. Quick as a tidal wave, she moved to swallow the piece of time.

CHAPTER 25

As the Threads Foretold

Silversong blocked out the clamour of battle and bared his fangs at Swiftstorm. "GET OFF ME!" He pressed his hind paws against her stomach and shoved her upward.

Rolling over and pushing himself back up, he could feel nothing but an electrifying terror jolting through his body as the Warden approached the golden circle, mouth eager to swallow it in one bite. It had all come to this. Forcing all thoughts out of his head, he called to the wind and tethered his very being to its vast potential, inhaling deep and preparing a blast powerful enough to shake the Warden's bones.

Something struck him in on the neck, forcing his lungs to expel the blast in a weakened state. It crashed against the Warden and knocked her over. She gave a frustrated grunt and recovered quickly. Zipping his head around gave him enough reaction time to dodge Swiftstorm's next assault. Wave after wave she flung his way, these ones so thick and condensed he thought they might be able to shatter stone. Sure enough, they broke against the obsidian and formed tiny cracks in the slick floor.

Silversong recalled one of the visions he'd once hoped to avoid, and everything clicked together.

Placing himself directly beneath the spire's tip, he used his tail to conjure an arc of his own. The air churned wildly around Swiftstorm's tail. She twirled once and launched a final attack. The slicing crescent zoomed toward Silversong at an incredible speed. He turned his tail so it faced the threat, then hurled his arc up just in time to redirect the deadly projectile. His deflection propelled the wave skyward, and just as the Warden pounced on the piece of time, her jaws shutting around the glowing weapon, Swiftstorm's diverted wind smashed against the brittle peak above, shattering it like an icicle.

"NO!" Swiftstorm yelped all too late, throwing herself out of danger. Silversong jumped sideways to avoid the falling debris.

An avalanche of black shards crushed the Warden before she could swallow the weapon. The crash of the impact demanded a pause in the skirmish. The scent of blood still thick in the air, all wolves turned to the fractured mound where the Warden's corpse lay buried. A mix of fear, confusion, and rage corroded any rationality still rooted within the gathering. Silversong released a trembling breath and ran toward the piece of time rotating calmly above the fallen rubble. Somehow, the golden circle had phased through the broken stone and now awaited a vessel to wield its remaining power. The sentinels looked on in sheer horror. Many uttered prayers to Motherwolf, begging her to resurrect their venerated leader. Their pleas would go unanswered. It was as the threads foretold.

Greyhail released Shadowgale's throat and hurried to Swiftstorm's side, but only silence answered his desperate inquiries. Swiftstorm couldn't take her eyes off the consequence of her misguided aggression. In a way, Silversong pitied her; pitied how deep she'd fallen into zealotry.

Silversong entered the aura projected by the piece of time and saw in the threads the divided packs he had to bring together, the bitter wounds he had to heal, the broken faith he had to repair. Beyond it all, he saw the future he wanted. He saw the Four Territories united as a massive pack ruled not by oppressive doctrine, but by respect and understanding. Holding on to his ultimate goal, he opened his mouth and swallowed the weapon once more.

All the events leading up to this moment flashed in his head and threatened to knock him off balance. He firmed his muscles and weathered the storm until his vision cleared. He blinked, realizing he'd caught the entire assembly of wolves in the expanded threads. Even in its weakened state, the piece of time commanded the respect of its wielder, and he found he had more control over it than ever before.

He studied the wolves around him, taking in their doubts, their fears, their anger. Greyhail had been about to attack Silversong while Swiftstorm was still in shock. Hazel, Palesquall, Cedargaze, Shadowgale, and all his other packmates had been fighting the sentinels, keeping them at bay, locked in an intense battle. Scorchfang loomed over Ashenfall's corpse, a look of relief on her bloody face. Something else twinkled in her eyes—the embers of ambition. Though Silversong would've preferred a fair trial for the treacherous Chief, he was relieved she was finally dead. Her son too. Amberstorm and all the others she'd murdered—directly or indirectly—had been avenged, and justice, however flawed the outcome, had ultimately been served.

To Silversong's shock, two wolves were missing from the summit. Cindersky was nowhere to be found. There her children were, guarded by several elders who kept the subordinates away from the fighting, but no Cindersky. His eyes swerved to the River-Stream side to make sure he hadn't just missed him the first time. The wolves there had worked through Ashenfall's loyalists and had been about to join Whistle-Wind in its defense of Silversong, but sure enough, Frostpaw wasn't there.

Frigid dread washed over Silversong. Cracks formed on the road to his perfect future, and visions of impending doom flooded his thoughts. The exiles were coming. The Heretic would strike in a final attempt to break the Four Territories and subjugate whatever remained of the survivors. To prevent this fate, all Silversong had to do was remain here and lead this fractured army into battle. By taking control of the Wolven Bulwark, he could crush the Heretic once and for all.

Silversong's victory cast a long and somber shadow. If he chose to lead in this desperate hour, Frostpaw and Cindersky would die. His heart grew numb, and he almost let a whimper escape his throat. He knew the right choice required a heavy sacrifice, but he also knew he wasn't strong enough to make it.

Feeling the approach of a headache, Silversong let his voice pass into every ear. There wasn't much time to prepare. "The Warden is dead! Ashenfall is dead! And their demise was their own doing. The Warden allowed the lure of the piece of time to cloud her judgment, and Ashenfall's attempt on my life finally exposed her for the treacherous tyrant she was. They were victims of their own actions, nothing more! On this night, the law clearly favours me, and all who cling to the Wolven Code must see it! I understand your confusion and your fears better than anyone, but I beg you, cast them aside now! For as I speak, the Heretic is about to launch a final assault on the Wolven Bulwark, and we must stand as one or be destroyed." Blurry flashes of the near future blinded him to the present—Frostpaw prowling the forest, tracking Cindersky as she neared a ruined meadow where Rime waited. "Frostpaw and Cindersky are gone, and they're in danger. I'm going to rescue them. You don't have much time. You must defend the spire and fight for your lives!"

He let everyone go, the threads snapping back into place. His warning would have to do. The longer he waited, the more his chances of saving Frostpaw and Cindersky decreased.

Bronzeblood avoided looking at Silversong. His eyes landed on Ashenfall's corpse, and he gulped. "This was an eventful trial. Not nearly as boring as I thought it would be."

Silversong frowned at the Stone-Guard Chief, anger sizzling in every paw. A foggy image dominated his thoughts: Thornhollow breaking, yielding to the hungry earth. "The Heretic might try to bring down the entire spire. You Stone-Guard wolves must counter his command over the earth. Make it your top priority."

Bronzeblood cocked his head up and sniffed contemptuously. "I appreciate your warning, but you're not in charge—"

"ENOUGH!" Silversong bellowed at the top of his lungs, his anger surging beyond the boiling point. He addressed the four packs in their entirety. "I've had enough of your petty desires to uphold tradition. If you wish to live through the night, you'll fight as one or be crushed by the Heretic!"

Silversong pushed the threads outward and tensed them around all who still looked at him like he was the villain. Bronzeblood actually bowed, tail neatly tucked. He got the message. Silversong retracted his aura, and Greyhail snarled. "You have no right to command the Wolven Bulwark, code-breaker!"

For the briefest of moments, Silversong considered making an example out of Greyhail, but upon glancing at Swiftstorm, he decided on restraint. "Set aside your fury, sentinel. Your leader is dead, and your order is broken. All you have now is your oath to the Four Territories. Tonight, they're under attack by someone far worse than me, and duty compels you to protect them even at the cost of your life." He dared to meet Swiftstorm's eyes, and it nearly shattered his confidence. She was shaking like a pup lost in a snowstorm. "I'm sorry it had to come to this, Swiftstorm. I can only imagine the turmoil you're going through. Despite how distant we've become, despite your treatment of me, I'll always be your brother."

Swiftstorm stopped shivering, all emotion drained from her eyes. Her vacant expression was even more upsetting than Greyhail's anger. "Get… get out of my sight. You're no brother of mine."

No bite could've pained him so deeply. Blood trickled down his neck from previous wounds, and a ruthless pressure compressed his whole body. He couldn't blink. He couldn't breathe. He could only stand still and lower his gaze. He'd lost a sister tonight. Whimpers tried to flee up his throat, but an aching lump barred the way out.

"How can we stand as one if you're leaving?" Riptide's voice gave Silversong something else to focus on.

"Let me go in your place. I'll bring Frostpaw back!" The worry in Snowleap's whine tempted Silversong to let her join him, but the Wolven Bulwark needed all its soldiers here.

"Why did Frostpaw abandon us?" Darkwave demanded. "Did he not learn his lesson last time?"

"Where's Cindersky? Did anyone see her leave?"

"Where could they have gone?"

Cedargaze padded up to Silversong. "Whatever you choose, I trust you."

Shadowgale joined his mate. "Follow your heart, son."

Hazel and Palesquall voiced encouraging whines. Without friends like them, Silversong would've perished long ago.

"I'm going alone. It's too dangerous for anyone else to come along. The Wolven Bulwark needs Cindersky and Frostpaw, and I intend to bring them back here in one piece." He quickly thought up an excuse as to why they weren't here. "Cindersky seeks to lure Rime out of hiding, and Frostpaw intends to slay him. The two have been planning this in secret since the restrictions on River-Stream were lifted."

Motherwolf, please let them believe me.

There were a few skeptical whines, but most seemed to accept the lie. Darkwave even grunted approvingly. "Heh. Guess I underestimated the little mongrel. Maybe I'll forgive him if he succeeds."

Silversong scowled at Frostpaw's father, the desire to reprimand him almost irresistible. "Tonight, you must all defend Thornhollow without allowing prejudice to affect your cooperation. I'll join you as soon as I retrieve the missing soldiers. But until then, find a safe place for those too young and weak to fight, and good luck." He padded to the exit, the wolves parting to allow him through.

"Flame-Heart is without a Chief!" Sunpelt, one of Ashenfall's cronies, cried out. "And you share some blame for this disaster! How can we defend ourselves in this state, code-breaker? How can we trust you aren't leaving us to our deaths?"

There was no venom in the lieutenant's growls, only blind agitation. Silversong would have a lot of explaining to do once this was all over. "My former Chief was also killed, but Whistle-Wind survives. Choose a new leader among yourselves once the Heretic is dead, but for now you must see your rivals as your allies. Until the battle is over, the Wolven Bulwark is a single unit unbound by the Wolven Code, and I won't abide any hindrance to it. Should we stand divided in this desperate hour, it'll mean our destruction. The piece of time has shown me this."

Ashenfall's loyalists would cause problems. They would be the first ones to desert or join the Heretic should he gain the advantage.

Scorchfang must keep them in check.

Bronzeblood and the Stone-Guard wolves also worried Silversong. The majority of them wouldn't submit to Ironwrath, but many were in poor fighting condition, and the exiles would quell them without much effort. Nothing could be done about it now, though.

"Chief Cedargaze, Chief Riptide, Chief Bronzeblood." Silversong stopped between the obisidian teeth. "While I'm gone, you're in charge of your own respective packs, but please, listen to one another's advice. It's the only way to win."

In hurried steps, Silversong descended the spire before anyone else could stall his rescue attempt. Strangely, he trusted the sentinels to heed his advice. They would assist the remaining Chiefs in preparing the defense of Thornhollow. They couldn't break their oaths. Even without a leader, they were fanatics to the core, and they would fight the exiles to the death. Details of the imminent attack swept across Silversong's brain—blood, slaughter, the earth shaking, pieces of the spire breaking.

Frostpaw must've followed Cindersky down one of the shortcuts. Blazefur would've stopped them from leaving otherwise.

He gasped at the bottom of the den. Blazefur was gone. A scent trail smelling of fresh blood led to the side of the spire where his body had been dragged. His life-essence still gushed from the deep puncture wounds in his throat, his eyes wide open in shock. The Heretic had done this, and he was waiting for Silversong's departure to begin the siege. It was all so perfect. The seed Ironwrath had planted by revealing Cindersky's secret in Frostpaw's presence now bloomed its deadly petals.

Silversong took one last look at the obsidian height and dashed for the woods, allowing the piece of time to guide him toward the runaway wolves. Even as the forest welcomed him into its grasp, he believed the Wolven Bulwark could repel the exiles until he returned, and when he did, Frostpaw and Cindersky would be right behind him. He would accept nothing less.

The wind latched onto his body, pushing him forward. He needed to act swiftly, or all would be lost.

CHAPTER 26

The Fangs of Justice

Frostpaw had made no effort to conceal his tracks, and Silversong found them easily. Darkness overhead turned the branches into shadowy fractures in the forest canopy.

Frostpaw, you gullwit! You're going to get yourself killed!

The piece of time pulsed irregularly, sending hazy images of a black spire surrounded by exiles. Silversong couldn't go back now, he'd come too far already. The Wolven Bulwark would have to fend for itself until he returned. He clenched his teeth and charged forward, the low branches smacking him in the face and leaving behind burning stings. The potential loss of Frostpaw pushed Silversong to a dangerous speed.

A vision of his own death caught him by surprise. Before the sharp antlers could skewer him, he stopped and skidded on the forest floor. He jerked his head up right as a massive deer exploded past him, missing his neck by a hair. It released an awful high-pitched cry. Silversong crouched, ears pulled back. He urged the swirling wind around him to gather at his tail and wasted no time striking the corrupted beast.

Condensed lashes of air tore into rotting flesh. Splashes of fetid blood sprayed the cooled earth, but the wailing deer was unbothered by the blows. It stomped its hooves, and the roots below came alive, bursting out of the depths and reaching for Silversong. He extended the threads of time and caught the decaying tendrils before they stabbed him, bracing himself for the antlered monster charging in his direction. He allowed the deer to pass into the threads, and when it was but a tail-length from his face, he jumped backward and released the sharp roots. Rather than piercing him to the bone, they gored the one who'd beckoned them instead.

Caught in a torturous prison of its own making, the corrupted prey cried and thrashed until Silversong put it out of its misery. He conjured an arc of air strong enough to sever the deer's head from its body.

Thwack!

Limp as a blade of grass his attacker slumped to the ground, and like stinking black snakes the roots returned to the deep earth.

Silversong continued his sprint through the woods before fatigue could set in, attracting the attention of more beasts tortured into servitude by Rime and the Fallen Titan. It all made sense why the monsters lingered here while the Heretic assaulted the spire.

Rime doesn't know about the siege on Thornhollow. Rime would never allow an attack on the Flame-Heart den while his children were still atop it, but his master had done it anyway. A desperate gamble.

The piece of time vibrated. Rime might betray the Heretic if Silversong presented the facts correctly. A burning hope fueled his tired legs. If the corrupted beasts turned on the exiles, victory would be assured.

The night reached its darkest hour by the time Silversong arrived at the edge of the Twilight Meadow. The sounds and grunts of the pursuing monsters lifted his hackles and hastened his racing heartbeat, but the sight in front of him unnerved him to the very core.

Cindersky faced Rime at the centre, and several leaps away prowled Frostpaw, who himself was being watched by corrupted beasts standing on ruined patches of ground where old blood had been spilled. Rime was waiting for the River-Stream corporal to make his move, and Cindersky was none the wiser.

Claws of panic seized Silversong's chest, and without heeding the piece of time, he rushed into the meadow as Frostpaw came ever closer to the one who'd killed his mother many seasons ago.

The smell of rot soured Silversong's nostrils and made him breathe through his mouth, but the taste was equally bad. Dead wolves lay strewn about the meadow, and whether they'd been allies or enemies in life, death had united them in the end.

Silversong's pursuers became an afterthought, as did the noise he was surely making. Fixated on saving Frostpaw, Silversong allowed the thorny flowers to take as much blood from him as they wanted. His vision narrowed into a tunnel, and when the stray exile noticed him, he let the threads of time fly. Shock slipped into rage on Rime's face as Silversong caught him and Cindersky in time's grasp. Off to the side, high in the air, Frostpaw was frozen too, teeth bared and mouth contorted into a hateful snarl. All around him were dozens of stilled monsters ready to slaughter in the name of their cruel master. If Silversong had delayed even a moment longer, Frostpaw would be dead, and Cindersky would've been mortally wounded by one of the charging beasts.

Of all things Silversong could've done to dampen the disaster about to unfold, he chose to scold the wolves who'd turned their tails on duty. Whether because of love or hatred, Cindersky and Frostpaw had risked more than their lives by coming here. Silversong was also far from blameless. The irony wasn't lost on him.

"Are you mad, Cindersky? Did you really have to see him tonight? Your leader is dead, your pack is in turmoil, and you think now is a good time for a romp in the meadow?!" Silversong shifted his glare to Frostpaw. "And you… you would've gotten yourself killed had I not intervened. Are you really so eager to throw your life away for vengeance? For a father who would only love you conditionally?"

Silversong allowed his voice to pass smoothly into all their ears. More corrupted prey surrounded him just outside the reach of his aura. He could still lose his advantage. He had to tread very carefully.

Even while frozen, Rime's expression hinted at a vicious desire to make Silversong suffer, and it proved a challenge not to flinch when confronting the huge exile. "Listen, Rime. You've been tricked. Your faith in your master betrays you. As I speak, Ironwrath is attacking Thornhollow. He put your children in danger knowing you would be too distracted tonight to notice his treachery. He played you for a fool."

Silversong loosened the threads around Rime, releasing him from the clutches of time. The black exile bristled and growled, yellow teeth dripping saliva. "You're lying! Ironwrath would never attack Thornhollow while my children are still there. I made him swear it!" Some of the larger monsters dragged their hooves on the ground, wanting to trample Silversong.

He calmed his hackles and refused to let fear ruin his confident demeanor. "Then your master is a liar AND an oath-breaker. Either way, he's forsaken you."

Rime lowered his gaze and paced from side to side, claws puncturing the earth. "No. He wouldn't. We were to wait until you all inevitably turned on each other before striking. I'm supposed to convince Cindersky to get our children to safety before then."

"Use your head!" Silversong barked, stopping Rime in his tracks. "It would've been a solid plan if I hadn't already eroded the boundaries between the Four Territories. The piece of time has helped a lot, and your master saw for himself how powerful I'm becoming. I managed to prevent the packs from turning on each other. The Heretic knew it was only a matter of time before the might of the Wolven Bulwark descended on him, so he decided to attack while I'm gone. It's his one chance at victory, and he took it. He knew about the meetings between you and Cindersky, and he made a calculated move by mentioning them where Frostpaw could hear. Ironwrath knew Cindersky would lure Frostpaw away from Thornhollow, and he knew I would try to save my gullwit of a friend! Look around you. Why do you think there aren't any exiles in sight? Where do you think they all are?"

Rime's forepaws quivered, and his breathing got heavier and heavier. As if hoping to disprove Silversong, he threw his head back and released a thunderous howl. The sound echoed across the meadow and dissipated in the woods beyond. A lonely voice unanswered. Rime shook his head. "No, no… NO!" The flowers around him withered into brown clumps, and the monsters under his command turned in the direction of Thornhollow.

Silversong took a careful pace forward, his tail straight and stiff. "I'm sorry, Rime, but you should've seen this coming. The Heretic is willing to sacrifice anyone and anything to dominate the Four Territories, your children included. This is how he repays his most loyal follower. You've always been little more than a tool he could use."

A deep rumble escaped Rime's throat. He breathed faster and faster, ignoring Frostpaw entirely now, his eyes drawn fearfully to Thornhollow's location. "He'll… he'll pay for this! I'll rip his heart out!"

Silversong untied the threads around Cindersky, and she gasped upon being released. "We must return to Thornhollow at once!" She looked to Silversong for guidance. "The Warden—"

"The Warden is dead," Silversong revealed.

Cindersky froze, unable to process the information. She shook her head as though Silversong had made a bad joke.

"The Warden… dead?" Rime whispered incredulously, eyes bulging.

"There's no time to explain!" A flood of warped visions drowned Silversong's brain, showing him a confusing swell of possibilities. Rime had no place in any of them. His presence in the upcoming battle would be a detriment to Cindersky's safety and the safety of his children.

Rime barked orders to the monsters he'd made, drool dripping from the sides of his mouth. In the clouds, the twisted face of the Fallen Titan began to form. Silversong let go of the corrupted prey still caught in time's aura and watched them join the others on their way to Thornhollow.

"You're right. We can't waste any more time here!" Rime declared, eyes meeting Cindersky's. "Let's go save our children."

"WAIT!" Silversong barked as loud as he could, hurting his throat in the process. He put himself between Rime and Cindersky. Before the exile could even think to thrash him, Silversong explained the potential consequences of Rime's presence on the battlefield. "You'll put your family in even greater danger if you join the fighting. And if the others see you helping Cindersky, you'll be risking her life too. You'll put the real father of your children into question. The time isn't right to reveal such a dire truth. The Four Territories aren't ready for it."

Rime stared in outrage. "I can't just stand back and—"

"We'll make sure your children are safe. These monsters you've created are more than enough to crush the Heretic for good." Silversong moved to stand near Cindersky, who glanced at him, eyes uncertain. "Leave Ironwrath to us."

The rough creases on Rime's face loosened as he looked to his mate. "Save our children. Then bring them here. It's time to leave the Four Territories behind us, Cindersky. We'll go to a place where we'll never be judged for our love."

Cindersky's head drooped, and she refused to meet Rime's gaze. "Where would we go, Tiderunner? The Freelands? You would leave our children without a pack? Without a sense of belonging?"

"They DON'T belong, Cindersky!" The harshness of Rime's growl startled her. "They're halfbloods! They'll always be shunned for something they can't help! Please!" he pleaded. It almost sounded like a whimper. "Please… let's just leave all this pain and secrecy at our tails for once. Let's head somewhere far away where we can be together in peace… let's… oh, Cindersky." The more he tried to contain his sorrow, the more it fought to be released. Silversong understood the feeling perfectly.

Cindersky approached the one she loved and nuzzled him on the cheek as he shivered. "Tiderunner, I know it's difficult, but our children deserve so much more than to live in isolation for the rest of their lives, and so do we. One day, they'll be accepted despite their true heritage, and then we won't have to hide our love any longer. Chief Ashenfall is dead, and the Wolven Code is changing thanks to Silversong. Because of him, we'll live to see a brighter future. I know it."

Silversong clenched his jaws at a stabbing migraine. He couldn't keep Frostpaw in stasis for much longer.

"I'll…" Rime swallowed, "I'll never be accepted. Not after all I've done. Even if Silversong himself vindicates me before the Four Territories, I'll be dead before the next season starts. Murdered by someone like him." He cocked his head at Frostpaw. "I'm done living a lie. I'm done pretending to be the monster the Four Territories think I am. Please, I'm begging you, bring our children here, and let's run far away. They don't need to live among wolves who'll hate them for being halfbloods."

"No, Tiderunner. I won't allow them to become loners." The wind blew strong and battered the meadow, sending grass and petals aflutter. "We can keep this lie going until the Wolven Code is amended. I promise to come visit you every night until then."

Rime's claws raked the soil. "No, you're not listening! I'll never be forgiven for shattering the Great Chain, for destroying Wind's Rest, for forcibly corrupting so much prey. If Ironwrath had claimed the piece of time, if he'd slaughtered all who cling to the Wolven Code, he would've established a more enlightened pack by force. The weapon would've made his reign unquestionable, and I would've been his top lieutenant. No one would've given any thought to my crimes then! Silversong ruined our chances of living peacefully in the Four Territories, Cindersky. Now quit arguing and bring our children here!"

Silversong frowned and bared his teeth, the migraine getting worse. "I couldn't let Ironwrath win. Not after all he did. Not after all he had yet to do. His utopia would've been built on the bones of any who opposed him. He doesn't care who he sacrifices, he has no limits. He's as ruthless as the Warden and equally insane." A sharp jab of pain struck his brain, and his grasp on Frostpaw loosened slightly. He tied more threads around the corporal for good measure.

Rime's mouth twitched, ears pulled back. He astonishingly kept himself from snarling. "None of this matters anymore. My children are in danger, and I'll gladly give my life to protect them. We can discuss our departure later, Cindersky."

"You're the one who isn't listening!" Again, Silversong barked so intensely it scratched his throat. "If you go to Thornhollow, you'll be putting Cindersky and your children in more danger than they already are!" The large exile closed his eyes and hardened his muscles, trying to suppress his obvious despair. "Rime… just leave. Leave the Four Territories behind. There's nothing for you here other than pain."

"I can't leave without Cindersky!" Rime stomped a forepaw on the ground. Strangely, one of the roses beneath him remained upright and healthy. Or had its decay been reversed somehow? No. It wasn't possible. Rime opened his eyes, and there was a resigned look to them.

"If you stay, you'll be hunted by wolves like Frostpaw. You've ripped friends and families apart, Rime. Do you really expect them to sit on their own tails and let you roam around like nothing happened?" Silversong could smell the stinging fury wafting off the frozen corporal. Those yellow eyes burned hotter than a wildfire.

Rime growled at Frostpaw. "Then I'll start by finishing him off like I did his mother! One less flea off my back!"

"No." Silversong tensed the threads around Rime, reminding the exile he wasn't in control here. The action caused the migraine to withdraw for some reason. "I won't allow it. Either you leave and return only when you're ready to answer for your crimes, or I avenge Wind's Rest and all the wolves you've killed since then. Consider this an ultimatum."

Cindersky yowled and moved to protect her secret mate. Silversong caught her limbs in his aura. "Don't!" she begged. "Tiderunner, please listen to him! Silversong, don't do it! I can't lose him!"

"Cindersky," Rime's voice cut through her desperate pleading. "I love you."

Silversong contemplated all the atrocities Rime had committed under the Heretic's command. Could Silversong really let the exile go after all the suffering he'd caused? Silversong envisioned his deceased packmates urging him to bring this monster to justice. Rime would've never given Silversong the same courtesy if their roles were reversed. Why should he be merciful? Why should he deny Frostpaw his revenge?

"I love you too." Cindersky fought against the invisible force keeping her away from Rime, fought against the threads bound tightly around her legs until exhaustion took over. Body going limp, she wavered, and Silversong untied her, allowing her to collapse in a fit of frail whimpers.

Rime ignored Silversong and hastened to where Cindersky had fallen. He lay on his stomach and licked her face, whispering softly to her as she slowly recovered. "It's all right, Cindersky. It's all right. I'll… I'll accept Silversong's proposal. I'll go far away where nobody can track me. I'll…" He flinched and struggled to contain his emotions. "I'll do it for you. For our family. You'll always be in my heart no matter the distance between us. And one day… one day we'll see each other again, my love."

Silversong tried not to feel sorry for the exile. A growth expanded in his throat and made it difficult to breathe. Perhaps justice had already found Rime, perhaps isolation would be punishment enough, and perhaps there was a chance at redemption far into the future.

"Oh, Tiderunner." Cindersky pushed her muzzle into Rime's fur. "I'll never forget you."

Rime broke away from her and stood, whining his final goodbyes. "Remind my children how much I love them. I wish I could've watched them grow. I wish we could've lived together as a happy family." He smiled at Cindersky—a bitter but tender smile. "Promise me one thing. Don't ever let our children be ashamed of who they are."

"I… I promise." Cindersky could say no more, her energy all but spent. She attempted to return Rime's smile, but her lips wouldn't budge as she slowly got up.

For the first time, Rime seemed exhausted. The anger he'd drawn upon for so many seasons now sapped the vigor from his body. He looked old and tired, like an aged bear on its last hibernation. His eyes found Silversong's, and though conflict still raged within them, Rime's wrath had dulled like a river calmed after the passing of a storm. "I can't control my corrupted beasts if they're too far away from me. For now, they'll target Ironwrath, but afterwards…"

"We'll grant them merciful deaths… which is more than you deserve," Silversong grunted, trying not to dwell on the torment Rime had inflicted on so many living beings. "Now go before I reconsider."

Rime's attention slipped toward Frostpaw, and he studied the hatred in the corporal's eyes, the unquenchable thirst for hollow revenge. "Can you guarantee a future where wolves like me don't have to become murderers to protect who they love? Ironwrath could."

"I can guarantee a better future. And mine won't be built on the bones of those who oppose me." Silversong braced himself for the return of his migraine. He could feel it coming like thunder foretelling a cruel tempest.

"We'll see, little lamb. We'll see." Rime and Cindersky shared a longing look, and like the retreating tide, the exile padded away from the single flower defying the decay. Cindersky couldn't take her eyes off him as his frame slowly blended into the shadows of the night. More than once her forepaws twitched as though she almost wanted to run after him and share the burden of isolation, but her duty to her children kept her still and silent. Rime had been right about one thing—he would never be forgiven, and if he ever returned to the Four Territories, he would face a reckoning.

Just like Silversong's one-eyed image had predicted, Rime had escaped Frostpaw's fangs once more. The exile's fate as a loner would serve as punishment for now. Silversong cringed at the spikes impaling his brain, and he released the immobile corporal.

Frostpaw landed atop the blooming flower and crushed its healthy petals. "Why?! I could've avenged her! I could've redeemed myself! I could've won my father's love!" His eyes were fragile orbs, and his face was a mixture of pain, anger, and sorrow.

"Her death was never your fault, Frostpaw. And trying to please your father after he disowned you isn't the way to go." Silversong's stomach dropped as Frostpaw growled, not at Silversong, but at the ground. Even so, it made Silversong back away. "It's time to accept the truth. Your mother is gone, and nothing can bring her back. Your duty is to the Wolven Bulwark, and right now, it's under attack!"

Frostpaw turned to Cindersky and bristled, a dangerous snarl hinting at his intent. Silversong put himself between Cindersky and the unstable corporal. "Don't. Don't do it, Frostpaw. This isn't you. This isn't the Frostpaw who saved me inside the Mountainmouth, the Frostpaw who's brave and kind and strong. Let go. Just let go for once! Please!" Silversong stepped in his direction.

"DON'T TOUCH ME!" Frostpaw leaped away, biting the air as a warning.

Silversong recoiled, a terrible weight settling into his core. His mouth ran dry as whimpers fought to leave his throat. "Frostpaw..."

Frostpaw stared off to the side, shutting his eyes and baring his fangs. "I-I was so close."

Before Silversong could think to catch him in time's threads, Frostpaw bolted through the meadow, following Rime's tracks. The darkness of the forest reached out to consume him just as vengeance had. If not for the Heretic's attack on Thornhollow, Silversong would've chased after Frostpaw.

Cindersky crouched and prepared to pursue the corporal, but Silversong stopped her. "No. The Wolven Bulwark needs us." He willed the threads to show him Frostpaw's fate, pushing through the fog obscuring the near future. The golden circle revealed a lost corporal alone among the dry plains of Stone-Guard Territory, searching for a reason to keep hunting. Revenge sustained him, but it would only lead him further astray. "He won't catch Rime. When this is all over, I'll go looking for Frostpaw. I won't abandon him to his own misery."

A vision of a collapsing spire instilled a deep fear in Silversong's heart. He looked to the distant Flame-Heart den. "We've wasted too much time here. We need to head back to Thornhollow at once! The fighting has already begun."

"I'm right behind you!" Cindersky's worried scent filled his nostrils.

Without delaying a moment longer, Silversong drained his mind of all but the drive to protect those he loved. The wind girdled the length of his body, and he let it guide him toward the Heretic.

Tonight, Ironwrath would die, and the exiles would break before the might of a united Wolven Bulwark. Tonight, Silversong would prove the Heretic wrong.

CHAPTER 27

The Battle for the Four Territories

"Keep up!" Silversong barked to Cindersky as they rushed through the remainder of the forest. "We don't have much time!"

Cindersky lagged behind, her breaths coming out in raspy wheezes. Silversong cursed and reached out to the currents of air around her, urging them to lighten her strides. Fear drove away his own exhaustion. His packmates counted on him. The Wolven Bulwark needed him. Already the golden circle showed him potential outcomes of the battle, all of them terrible. They hung there in the threads, dangling above his head as if to mock him.

The pain of Frostpaw's departure sliced his heart in two, and the desire to run after the corporal hampered his speed. He fought for a clear head. Far above, inky clouds choked the moon and thundered in response to Rime's anger. The face of the Fallen Titan had withdrawn, but the storm's wrath had yet to rain.

Silversong could hear the fighting ahead, wolves yelped and cried, barked and growled, and loud bangs interrupted the shouting commanders as the scent of blood intensified. A trembling in the ground elevated Silversong's fear to the heights of terror.

"We're almost there!" Silversong declared to reassure himself rather than Cindersky. She struggled to maintain her sprint. Without the wind to urge her onward, she would've collapsed long ago.

Flame-Heart wolves should really run more often.

He spotted the distant clearing and narrowed his eyes on the battlefield beyond it.

Finally!

His hope was ripped to shreds by the worsening earthquake. If not for his momentum, he would've been thrown off balance. Branches and leaves smacked him as he pushed through the forest's border, eyes tightly sealed against the whipping offshoots.

He planted his paws firmly on the shivering ground, his throat on fire, every passing breath feeding the burning sensation. The horror unfolding near the spire made him freeze.

Piece by piece, the earthquake was breaking Thornhollow apart. Chunks of obsidian pummeled the bloody field as the Wolven Bulwark rallied under Cedargaze and Riptide. Together, they repelled the Heretic's forces. It seemed Rime's monsters had turned the tide against the exiles. The antlered beasts surrounded the enemy from the rear, forcing them toward the defenders of the Four Territories. Bodies were scattered across the grass, but most of them had been loyal to Ironwrath in life. There he was at the centre of the cramped mass, spilling all his fury into the ground, encouraging the violent tremor. Bronzeblood had failed. The Heretic had successfully forced the Wolven Bulwark out of the spire. Still, Ironwrath had suffered heavy losses despite exposing the defenders of the Four Territories to his onslaught.

Cindersky caught up to Silversong. She leaned against him to keep from falling over and found her children battling under Scorchfang's orders. "My children! They're alive!"

"Go to them!" Silversong barked and accelerated the wind circling around them. "Motherwolf watch over you."

"Motherwolf watch over us all." She ran toward those she needed to protect.

All at once the visions of destruction ceased, and an encroaching darkness engulfed the edges of Silversong's sight, slowly creeping inward until all he could see was the Heretic. This was it. This was the end of Ironwrath. Silversong's heart shoved a prickling energy through his veins. It seared his exhaustion and weariness to smouldering ashes. He pressed on his haunches and charged forward, letting everything else sink into a pitch-black void.

Time seemed to slow the closer he got to Ironwrath. Swiftstorm and Greyhail led the sentinels at the frontlines, relentlessly harassing the throng of exiles as the Stone-Guard wolves worked to counter the Heretic's earthquake. A pleasant surprise. Silversong had expected them to have given up by now. Bronzeblood yelped as the force of the tremor knocked him into his own lieutenants, causing them to tumble to the ground. Scorchfang had taken charge of her packmates, helping them launch fireball after fireball into the opposing army. The strongest among them breathed streams of flame onto the exiles. The bitter stench of charred corpses overpowered the metallic scent of blood.

Sleet pelted Silversong's body, but it did little to affect his haste.

The grass beneath Thornhollow rotted and fused together to form long, lashing tendrils. Some wrapped around the throats of unsuspecting wolves, crushing their windpipes and thinning the number of Silversong's allies.

Whistle-Wind soldiers hurled small twisters at the exiles, and Scorchfang's loyalists lit the whirlwinds on fire—a deadly combination. The Heretic's forces couldn't keep this up forever. At every boom of thunder, two or three of them joined the dead, trampled by wailing monsters or killed in any number of ways by the Wolven Bulwark.

The exiles were fighting a losing battle. Maybe if Rime hadn't unleashed his corrupted prey upon the Heretic, they would still have a chance, but Ironwrath had doomed his cause by breaking his promise to Rime. Either the Heretic hadn't anticipated this reaction from his lieutenant, or he thought he could've defeated the Wolven Bulwark before Rime discovered his treachery.

Hazel noticed Silversong and conjured an arc of air, whipping the black strands threatening to strangle her. She howled to announce his return, and the Whistle-Wind wolves cheered his name. Some of the exiles turned around and snarled, teeth gnashing.

Silversong rounded the wave of monsters and found a gap where he could easily reach his target. He moved the circling wind to his hind paws, the currents bursting as he sprang over a group of wounded exiles. He aimed his fangs at the Heretic's neck. "IRONWRATH!"

The Heretic looked over his shoulder in pure disbelief. Before the threads could snare him, he commanded the earth to yank him away. Silversong landed where his foe had been, stretching his aura to the limit and freezing many exiles in time.

"WOLVES OF THE WOLVEN BULWARK!" Cedargaze lifted her head and barked her heart out. "CHARGE!"

"Rally to Silversong!" Riptide cried out, his lieutenants repeating the order for those behind.

Long tendrils of rotted grass collapsed and lay unmoving, and as the combined might of the Four Territories broke through the army of exiles, the slaughter began. Rime's corrupted prey gored and bashed the enemy on their way to Ironwrath, and from the other side, fangs entered throats to sever vital arteries. When an exile caught in the threads was killed, Silversong released them, lessening the severity of the coming migraine. Up above, Thornhollow leaned dangerously over them all, portions of the spire breaking off and crushing groups of unlucky wolves. The Heretic had managed to maintain the earthquake.

"Get him! Get the Heretic!" Bronzeblood ordered as his lieutenants helped him up. "He's too powerful, like Stone-Guard himself! We can't subdue the earthquake forever!"

You call this earthquake subdued?!

Swiftstorm and Greyhail were already on the job, darting around frozen exiles to avenge the Great Chain. Ironwrath smacked a forepaw down, sending blasts of earth to knock the sentinels over.

Perhaps realizing the fight was over, Ironwrath rode an earthen wave toward Bronzeblood, hoping to take out his former Chief before the end.

Silversong ran to intercept the Heretic. "FACE ME, YOU COWARD!"

The Stone-Guard lieutenants erected a thick brown barrier in front of their Chief. Within the wave Ironwrath rode, the earth wove itself into sharp spikes, shooting through the shield and impaling those behind. The Heretic demolished the weakened barrier, squishing the survivors still defending Bronzeblood.

The Heretic halted his wave directly above the Chief who'd banished him long ago. "Greetings, Bronzeblood. You've gotten bigger."

Bronzeblood submerged his paws into the trembling ground, his focus spent on dampening Ironwrath's earthquake. "It's over, Heretic. You lose again. Our victory is assured."

"Indeed, but you won't live to see it." Ironwrath commanded his wave to crash into Bronzeblood, removing the final bar holding devastation at bay.

The earth raged.

The piece of time pulsed, sending Silversong images of the disaster to come. He released the remaining exiles trapped in the threads. Swiftstorm and Greyhail had almost caught up to the Heretic. Ironwrath turned to Silversong, eyes devoid of hope, of fear. His expression said it all: he'd lost, but he would cause as much destruction as possible before death claimed him.

Enormous cracks fractured the obsidian spire, and larger pieces of it broke off to smash the victors. Many would die; Silversong couldn't save them all. He could slay the Heretic here and now, but doing so would cost the lives of loved ones. Silversong growled in frustration and hardened the upper layers of his aura, running toward his cowering packmates. Falling debris stopped short of entering the tightened threads, resuming the descent at top speed once Silversong moved far enough away.

He raced against time, saving Snowleap before a thick spike skewered her, rescuing Scorchfang from a crashing wedge, stopping a length of obsidian from falling on Cindersky and her children. The migraine struck—heavy blows to the brain. Silversong squealed and yowled, but refused to let go of the threads. The winding air around him dissipated due to the assault on his focus, but he pressed on despite the sharp pain.

"Look out!" Riptide barked in the distance.

Wolves and corrupted beasts died all around him, their bones crushed under fragments of the collapsing spire. Silversong reached his family in time to prevent their deaths, the block of black stone frozen just above their heads.

Shadowgale huddled near Cedargaze as she ordered her subjects to stand close to Silversong. Palesquall leaped into the aura, blood soaking his white face. More subordinates followed, then came the corporals, Gorsescratch and Tawnydrift among them. The lieutenants ushered the elders and the youngsters into the threads, and Silversong thanked Motherwolf most of them were still alive. The Wise-Wolves entered last, and their gushing wounds revealed how intensely they'd fought.

Shards of ice punctured Silversong's skull, his limbs shook, his stomach burned, and stinging bile oozed up his throat. He clenched his teeth and growled. "Can't… hold… much… longer…"

Legs feeling heavier than mountains, he trudged out of the trajectory of the frozen block, his packmates following and giving him fleeting encouragements. Someone was missing. Someone dear to him. Who was it? He could hardly think. The pain was too great.

Hazel… where's Hazel?!

She ran toward him, zigzagging around falling chunks of Thornhollow. A swift current carried her forward, whistling to the din of pounding rubble. One of the larger portions of the spire broke off from the main structure, plunging to where she would be moments from now. She hadn't noticed the danger.

"Hazel!" he coughed out, too weak for her to hear. His packmates looked over one another, too distracted to listen. "Hazel!" He could barely even whimper her name.

Oh, Motherwolf! Please, no!

A blast of shrill wind flew her way. No, not wind. Palesquall. It was Palesquall who charged out of the safety of the threads to rescue Hazel. He'd seen the danger too! Hope soared high then dove back into despair. Palesquall collided into Hazel, launching her away from the falling obsidian.

He took the crushing weight instead.

"NO!" Silversong wavered, breath leaving his lungs. He teetered on the brink of fainting, the loss of Palesquall too much for his heart to endure.

"Let go," his distorted voice whispered into his ears.

"Palesquall!" Silversong yelped, the golden circle weaving a string of memories across his eyes. All the games, all the fun, all the teasing, all the lovely moments of friendship… gone forever.

"Let go," again his warped voice whispered.

Silversong had stretched the piece of time to its limit. The weapon fought against his attempts to control the threads, throbbed defiantly in his gut, adding nausea to its arsenal of painful attacks. Silversong retched, hot vomit surging up his throat. Having enough of Silversong's abuse, the golden circle rode the bile up his gullet and out of his gaping mouth.

The last thing he saw before the connection broke was a familiar pair of pale blue eyes.

The threads winked out of sight, the spikes in his brain retracted, and Stormstrider's weapon rotated calmly above the contents of Silversong's stomach.

"The cycle continues," his own voice whined to him in all the wrong tones.

Silversong tipped over and landed on his side, so weak he struggled to breathe. Too exhausted to twitch a single whisker, he could do nothing as the final sections of the spire landed around him. An unnatural storm of dust blinded him to the events happening more than a tail-length away. The ringing in his ears suppressed the barking, the yowling, the wailing. How many had died…? How many did he fail to save…?

The piece of time! I need to… I need to—

The Heretic appeared in front of him, battered and bloodied, and in one swift bite, he swallowed the golden circle and took flight, Swiftstorm and Greyhail hot on his tail.

Silversong rolled onto his back and blinked out the irritating specks in his eyes. Unable to summon the energy to form a single thought, he dropped into unconsciousness.

It's time to let go.

CHAPTER 28

A Ruin of Bronze

Silversong stood at the edge of the Silverhaze Forest, the Running River roaring behind him. Only… there was no forest.

The land simply *ceased* where the foggy woods should've been, replaced by nothingness. No, there were things inside the boundless void that stretched beyond sight, twisted things no soul could hope to comprehend. Spiraling shapes mocked the very essence of life, all made of flesh and sinew, fusing together to create horrible structures of eyes, viscera, and bone. Like spiderwebs, they latched onto inorganic constructs of darkest stone, spreading far and wide like uncontained tumors. They drained all hope from Silversong while reassuring him not to despair. A strange contrast. They wanted to shelter him, to care for him, to receive him and absorb his experiences, his joy, his pain. If he stepped into the blackness, he would never return, and yet something about the idea was tempting. As tempting as licking honey from an active beehive.

He lifted a forepaw, but a sudden presence made him lower it.

A stranger came to his side, black of fur and eyes but otherwise mirroring Silversong nearly to perfection. He'd seen this… *creature* before. It took on many forms, including the one it wore now. The more Silversong looked, the more he noticed how *off* this reflection of him was. Its eyes were just slightly misplaced, its face just a bit too wide, its proportions incorrect in the most minute of ways.

An intense sense of wrongness radiated throughout Silversong.

"It is not I who is *wrong*, Silversong." The creature mimicked Silversong's voice, but like its appearance, the sounds it made were eerily inaccurate.

"Traveller…" Silversong uttered, making no effort to hide his fear.

The Traveller's gaze seemed to encompass all the warped shapes within the void. "They long to meet you. So eager."

"Why're you here?" Silversong leaned away from the Traveller, feeling as though the creature could at any moment reach out and gobble him up.

"To offer direct passage."

"To where…?" Silversong squeaked.

"Truth." The Traveller stared *into* him, and within the creature's eyes blinked countless other eyeballs tied to writhing tendrils.

Silversong broke away from the nauseating sight, panting like he'd just ran to the moon and back. "I-I need to wake up. My friends need me. My sister needs me. Oh, Motherwolf! The Heretic has the piece of time!" He remembered it all. The battle, the earthquake, the blood and crushed bones.

Oh, Palesquall! NO! Not him! Grief swelled to drown the terror within.

Even without looking, Silversong could somehow feel the Traveller watching him. None could escape the entity's gaze. "Then wake."

Silversong's eyes fluttered open, startling the two Wise-Wolves regurgitating a minty concoction into his mouth. He swallowed the chewed-up leaves and cringed at the cool trail in his throat.

"Silversong!" His mother nearly crashed into him before he could stand. She licked his face without a care for the shocked onlookers.

The Wise-Wolves moved on to others in need of healing.

His father joined in on the affection, nuzzling Silversong when Cedargaze would allow him some room. "You saved us, son. You saved our pack."

Silversong beheld the devastation the Heretic had wrought. The sun stretched its morning rays behind the clouds, colouring them orange and red. Dew speckled the blades of grass not coated in a bloody sheen. The earthy scent of the dawning day seeped through the bitter miasma wafting from the corpses scattered across the field. Thornhollow had been reduced to a single stark growth barely the size of a pine, pieces of its broken body strewn about like shattered ice, crushing the bodies of former allies and enemies alike. Many of Rime's monsters also sullied the ground, pools of rot spreading from where they'd fallen. There were so few survivors—too few.

Silversong spotted Hazel sitting between her parents and Palesquall's kin, shoulders hunched and eyes closed. Before her was a cracked chunk of obsidian, the one Palesquall had saved her from. Silversong's heart dropped, his mouth going dry, his ears falling to the weight of a crippling pain. He plodded forward, leaving his parents to follow at his tail. The survivors took notice of him, and one by one, they joined his stride to where Palesquall had died. Gorsescratch, Tawnydrift, Riptide, Icetail, Snowleap, Cindersky and her children, Scorchfang and her loyalists, and even some of the Stone-Guard wolves walked solemnly behind Silversong.

He reached Hazel, and she looked up to meet his gaze, burying herself in the fur of his throat, whimpering softly. Below her, the obsidian sheet fractured around Palesquall's crushed body, now nothing more than a pulpy mass. He'd seen the danger threatening Hazel, and he'd given his life to save her. Silversong would've done the same. He wished it had been him instead.

"Goodbye, Palesquall," was all Silversong could manage. If he whined anything more, he would shatter the shell containing his sorrow.

"I can't believe he's gone." Hazel whimpered in Silversong's embrace. There was no comfort he could offer to lessen her grief. This wound would never fully heal for either of them.

They stayed glued to one another for a long while as the Whistle-Wind wolves once again spoke their last farewells to fallen packmates. A deep howling ensued, but this time, all wolves regardless of allegiances joined the tragic tune. A numbness overcame Silversong, and he found it difficult to muster the energy to release his voice. He'd lost so much. How could he continue the climb without Palesquall's good humour? Without his silly smiles and quips?

He couldn't remember when the howling ended. He couldn't remember leaving Palesquall's corpse behind, but upon opening his eyes, he somehow found himself at the centre of the Wolven Bulwark, Scorchfang briefing him on the aftermath of the battle.

"They named me Chief," Scorchfang explained, her loyalists nodding in approval. "But Ashenfall's lackeys rallied under Sunpelt, and they took off into the forest to join Darkwave and his *Devoted*." Scorchfang scowled at the mention of Darkwave's new faction.

Riptide growled beside Icetail. "I should've had him executed for daring to desert River-Stream. I should've executed them all! They say they wish to follow the Wolven Code in its purest form, but abandoning their Chief makes them all code-breakers! Hypocrites, the lot of them!"

Icetail shared some of her mate's anger. "Indeed, but we were too exhausted from the fight against the exiles. We couldn't withstand another battle."

"Nor could we," Scorchfang added.

"They wanted you killed, Silversong," Cedargaze grunted. "Darkwave and his lackeys. They wanted to execute all the known code-breakers, which I suppose includes everyone who now supports you, son. I said if he ever threatened us again, I would feed him his own tail for a meal."

A flicker of relief lit the emptiness growing inside Silversong. At least no one from Whistle-Wind had joined the Devoted. But still, a decent chunk from the other territories had renounced the Wolven Bulwark, nearly halving it. "And the sentinels?"

Shadowgale answered. "They're hunting the last of those monsters that attacked the exiles. Abominations, the sentinels called them."

"All but Swiftstorm and Greyhail," Silversong grunted.

"Yes," Shadowgale confirmed. "We saw them chasing the Heretic toward Stone-Guard Territory."

"He has the piece of time."

Hearing it from Silversong's mouth prompted many gasps and yelps. He thought he heard a couple wolves faint in the back.

"Won't this madness ever end?" Shadowgale peered at the breaking clouds.

"I wouldn't fear too much," Silversong's tone inspired little encouragement. "The weapon is greatly weakened from my use of it. He can't possibly defeat us all on his own."

"But still…" Cedargaze whined.

"We must go after him." Silversong forced confidence and certainty into his voice. "If not to bring him to justice, then to save Swiftstorm and Greyhail."

"Yes," Cedargaze agreed, as did Shadowgale. "I won't allow the Heretic to take my daughter away from me."

"But they're sentinels!" Scorchfang bristled. "They'll join the Devoted first chance they get, adding to Darkwave's numbers."

"We still outnumber them," Shadowgale argued. "And Swiftstorm can be convinced to join our side. She'll listen to us, I'm certain of it."

Silversong wasn't so sure, but he decided not to express his doubts. "The Devoted are a problem, but pious as they are, they'll refuse to fight together as one. We have them beaten already. They just don't know it yet."

A silence broken only by the occasional murmur overcame the assembly. Finally, Snowleap spoke up. "Where's Frostpaw? You said you would bring him back."

Silversong's fur lifted to a chill.

"Cindersky is here," Snowleap whined worriedly, "but not Frostpaw."

"He..." Silversong closed his eyes, trying not to envision his poor friend alone somewhere in Stone-Guard Territory, vengeance his only company. "He's off hunting Rime. I pray he'll see reason and return to us soon."

"I pray he tears off the mongrel's hide," one of the River-Stream wolves grouched. One of Frostpaw's siblings.

So, not all of you joined your father.

"Forget Frostpaw," Cedargaze barked, commanding all ears to shoot up. "We mustn't waste more time here than we already have. The Heretic has Silversong's weapon, and we must cut off the head of the exiles before he causes more damage. All in favour?"

In short order, the Wolven Bulwark rallied behind Silversong as he led them away from the broken spire and across a stretch of yellow grass clinging to the soil. Those too wounded or too young to join the marching army remained at the ruined den to be looked after by the Flame-Heart Wise-Wolves, who'd been given strict orders to feign loyalty to the Devoted in case Darkwave came back for them. Scorchfang gave permission for Cindersky to stay behind; though she'd saved her children, all of them had fallen into a state of shock. They needed a mother's care more than anything. Amberstorm's pups would have no such luxury. All Silversong could do for them was ensure they grew up in a better time.

More than once Silversong tried peering into the future only for realization to quickly set in. Having the weapon removed from him was like losing one of the senses he'd relied upon for so long. He was *less* without the golden circle, incomplete, and he couldn't deny the troubling desire to become whole again. Would it be worse to lose his sense of smell, his touch, his sight? He shook the ponderous thoughts out of his head and focused on saving his sister from the Heretic.

The sun had burned away most of the clouds by the time the Wolven Bulwark reached the Stone-Guard border. A long and rocky descent led to dry flatlands where trees dared not grow, and far in the distance rose the largest mountain in the Four Territories: the Grimtooth, the den of Stone-Guard Territory. A fitting name for such an uninviting brown mass. According to legend, Stone-Guard himself had commanded it to rise at the end of the War of Change, and he'd declared it a home for his soldiers and their descendants.

Silversong imagined the piece of time tugging on him, and he began the downward climb into the vast plains so different from the lush forests of the upper territories. Still, something about the parched land inspired a sense of freedom. It never once curved. It never needed to. It was content the way it was. Like a wave in the open sea, the breeze could fly without hindrance, wolves could run in a straight line without meeting a single obstacle, and the brave plants—bony and lacking leaves—could sprout without the expected thirst for moisture. There was a certain beauty in the simplicity, a certain… allure.

As the mellow light of evening covered the plains in gold, Silversong detected Swiftstorm's scent, then Greyhail's, then Ironwrath's, all freshly imprinted on the ground, and he pursued the trail far into the night. The inhabitants of this territory dug out mole-like creatures to feed the army. The meat was chewy and difficult to swallow, but it was filling.

Silversong awoke to the faraway echo of a lonely howl. It sounded like Frostpaw, but he dared not trust his hope.

Hazel came to see him, her sleep disturbed by the events of the previous night. She sat beside him as glowing insects hovered above their heads. "You like him, don't you? Frostpaw."

"Yes," Silversong whined longingly, feeling no pleasure at the admission.

Hazel leaned against his shoulder. "I saw it in the way you act around him. The way your tail starts to wag without you noticing. The way you look at him. The way you smell all anxious at the mere mention of his name."

Silversong chuckled. "I guess I'm not very subtle, eh?"

"Not in the slightest." Hazel smiled, but sadness tainted her green eyes. "You've shown us the true value of working together, Silversong. And if we beat the Devoted, I think we'll break the boundaries on who we can love. I hope Frostpaw feels the same way about you, I hope he returns to us, and I hope you two can live happily together as mates."

A fuzzy feeling rushed up Silversong's limbs to heat his face. "Thank you, Hazel. I'm sorry I couldn't save—"

"No." Hazel nuzzled him and closed her eyes. "It's not your fault or mine. I'll remember Palesquall as the hero he was. I think… I think I was starting to feel a certain way about him… I think…" She shivered while trying to suppress a whimper.

Silversong returned her nuzzles and licked her gently. He wanted so much to release his sorrow, to cry out to the heavens, but he decided it would be unwise to wake the slumbering soldiers who weren't on sentry duty. "Shh. It's all right, Hazel. I'm sure he's looking down on us from beyond the stars, boasting to Motherwolf about the adventures we had together."

For the remainder of the night they reminisced about all the trouble Palesquall had gotten into, and when morning struck, Silversong put on a determined face and continued the search. Scouts reported a smaller army of wolves pursuing them from afar—the Devoted.

So, Darkwave decides to try his luck against the Wolven Bulwark only a day after the defeat of the exiles? I'll pluck out the disease before it festers again, Silversong thought grimly.

Night bloomed once more as Silversong arrived at the rim of a gorge yawning toward a distant structure reflecting the fleeting starlight. From here the unnatural formation looked like a solid mass of rectangular blocks piled atop one another, the bronze surface triumphant against all erosion. A sense of unease washed over him, his hackles rising. This was the place where Aelrion and the last of the Forgotten Ones disappeared at the climax of the War of Change. The tracks descended into the gap of tapering spires and thorny shrubs, leading toward the ruin of bronze.

Something wasn't right.

"Stay here," Silversong grunted to Cedargaze. "They're inside the ruin. I'm going alone."

"Why?" Cedargaze demanded, green eyes wide and sharp. "We came all this way to defeat the Heretic together and save Swiftstorm, and now you're telling us to stay behind?"

"I've got a terrible feeling, mother." Silversong couldn't say more. He craned his head up and stared across the gorge. "I think if you all follow me, we'll never make it out of the ruin alive."

"How can you be sure?" asked Shadowgale. "You don't have the piece of time anymore."

Silversong questioned why the Heretic had come all this way.

Why choose this ruin of all places to flee? Silversong envisioned the Heretic collapsing the entire structure atop the Wolven Bulwark.

"I think the Heretic is planning to bring the whole ruin down on our heads," Silversong explained. "It would be a last spiteful move against everything we achieved."

Worried wolves whispered among themselves, debating on the proper course of action.

"Can he do that?" Icetail shivered. "Breaking Thornhollow was one thing, but the ruin over there is made entirely of metal."

"We don't know how strong the foundations of the Bronze Barrow are after so many seasons," a Stone-Guard soldier grunted. "And the Heretic can control metal. It would be a huge risk bringing our entire force into the ruin."

"Then I'm sending an escort unit to protect you, Silversong," Cedargaze insisted.

"No, mother—"

Unharmonious howls resonated from far behind. The sounds were rough, violent, and ended abruptly, leaving no doubt as to the intentions of the approaching wolves. The Wolven Bulwark turned to the opposing force, the strongest soldiers moving to the front to prepare for the confrontation. Riptide and Scorchfang took charge of their fighters, ordering them to support one another regardless of allegiances. The Stone-Guard members looked to Cedargaze for guidance. No lieutenants among them remained.

Silversong nosed his mother on the cheek. "The Devoted have come to destroy us. You need everyone you can spare. Show them the power of wolves united."

Cedargaze stared at Silversong, the fear of losing him clear in her green eyes.

"Please, trust me," Silversong whined softly.

Finally, she relented and licked him goodbye. “Bring her back to us, Silversong.”

“Good luck, son,” Shadowgale gave him a loving nudge.

Silversong couldn’t bring himself to promise Swiftstorm’s safety. He gave his blessings to the Wolven Bulwark and made haste toward the Bronze Barrow.

I’m coming, Swiftstorm. Don’t you die on me yet.

CHAPTER 29

Ghosts of the Past

Silversong paused in the middle of the gorge, catching his breath and stirring the whirling air around his legs.

His lips were cracked just like the desiccated ground he stood on. They ached at the slightest movements, and his dry mouth begged for water. Here and there stale pools dotted the skeletal ravine, filthy and smelling of potential infection. He resumed his run under the towering spires, and it kept his thoughts off how uncomfortable he was. He had a sister to save and a Heretic to slay.

He skidded to a standstill, sending up a dusty cloud. Greyhail lay dead before him, impaled by thick blades of compressed earth. Though Silversong bore no love for the sentinel, he imagined Swiftstorm's pain and howled a solemn tune for her loss. There was nothing more to be done. He continued his sprint toward the looming bronze ruin.

He could still save Swiftstorm, couldn't he? Back in the Mountainmouth, his one-eyed image had shown him her death, but he'd also shown him Hazel suffering Palesquall's fate instead. The future could still change so long as Silversong lived to change it.

The past is a frozen pond, the future an endlessly shifting whirlpool.

He arrived under the stark glare of the Bronze Barrow, feeling as though destiny itself were leading him by a string toward his doom. The blocky structure imposed its undying presence upon the edge of the continent, its symmetrical glory outlasting the erosion of time. Clean steps led to its square mouth, still hungry since the end of the War of Change. It had devoured Aelrion and his army and had refused to cough up even their bones, and now it had swallowed Swiftstorm and the Heretic. As Silversong's claws clinked on the metallic ledges, he doubted the structure would be kind enough to release his sister from its belly, or himself for that matter.

Far behind him, the fighting began, the night lit by brief explosions, the *boom* of the impacts delayed like thunder after the strike of lightning. Silversong tilted his head at the curious phenomenon.

He panted at the top, squinting at the murky darkness waiting patiently to savour him. Etchings marked the contours of the gaping mouth, ancient-looking and without curves. He sniffed and detected the scent of familiar wolves within. Taking a deep breath, he urged himself into the cool throat of the relic.

A metallic stench overwhelmed everything but the scent of his quarry. He sniffed and padded through a rectangular corridor bearing traces of dried blood.

Please, Motherwolf, let Swiftstorm live. I can't lose her too.

The strengthening smell of his sister's fear pierced cleanly through his nostrils, and he picked up the pace despite the lack of light. Swiftstorm had tracked the Heretic down this passage, and as Silversong got closer to its end, the sound of labored breaths made his ears stand at attention.

Swiftstorm!

He continued to a massive circular chamber reaching from one end of the hollow structure to the other. He paused at the entrance, noticing the wet trail of blood leading to the centre where Swiftstorm stood, wounded and wheezing, her paws trapped in the floor itself. She would bleed to death soon without proper care. She needed help fast!

Some distance behind her loomed a closed entrance of reddish metal.

The Heretic was nowhere in sight, but Silversong cleaved to caution. He twirled his tail until he could form a tight shield of air around his body, strong enough to withstand the heaviest of blows. He charged forward.

"Silversong!" Swiftstorm gasped, coughing up a spray of blood. "Don't! He's here!"

The floor turned into a liquid state, sucking in his legs and solidifying around them, trapping him like an insect in amber. "Swiftstorm!" he cried out. He was so close to her. He could almost stretch his muzzle and—

The Heretic emerged out of the shadows, the clink of his claws sending shivers along Silversong's spine. The old exile had been cut, struck, bashed and bloodied, but the beatings had failed to fracture his confidence.

"No!" Swiftstorm's head slumped, her body going limp in defeat. Snared as she was, she couldn't even collapse to the ground.

"Release your wind," the Heretic demanded a few leaps behind Silversong.

"Bite my tail, scatfur!" Silversong clutched his connection to the raging air, ready to send it flying toward the Heretic if he came any closer.

"Do it, or she dies."

A bronze spike formed directly under Swiftstorm's belly, moving up steadily. Frigid terror lifted every strand of fur on Silversong's body as he recalled the terrible vision his scarred future had shown him. The slicing currents evaporated, his only means of defense abandoned. He hyperventilated, trying wordlessly to beg the Heretic to spare Swiftstorm's life.

She's still my sister, my family. I WON'T lose anyone else!

"Good." The Heretic sauntered over to Silversong, eyes impassive like the first time Silversong had looked upon them. They seemed to drink in the faint light emitted by the strange reddish metal at the far end. "Not so sure of yourself now, are you?"

Silversong sensed a subtle aura tickling his flesh. "Pl-please, don't—"

"No. You've shown me the folly of mercy, and now I've none to spare," the Heretic calmly stated, flexing the threads of time. Silversong cringed, regret digging a deep pit in his pounding chest. "Fascinating thing, isn't it? This weapon? When I swallowed it, I saw the wonders of a long-forgotten age—Stormstrider, the Forest Father, Motherwolf herself, the Forgotten Ones, the War of Change—all through the perspectives of those who'd previously wielded the weapon. I also saw more recent events through your eyes, no less. Your efforts at uniting the Four Territories were valiant indeed."

"I… I… I did unite them," Silversong sputtered. "I… I… I bested the Warden… I bested you!"

The Heretic pondered his defeat, breaking his unblinking gaze from Silversong. "Yes, you did."

Silversong wrestled for control of his breaths, forcing them in and out until his trembling ceased. "I ushered in a new age for all wolfkind. We have but to amend the Wolven Code."

Swiftstorm clenched her jaws and let out a rueful growl. She would come around. She wasn't entirely lost.

I forgive you, Swiftstorm!

Her actions ate at her conscience. He saw it in her eyes.

"I love you, Swiftstorm." Silversong gave his best attempt at a smile. It was neither wide nor stable, but it came from the heart, and it tamed Swiftstorm's fury.

"Touching," the Heretic grunted, facing Silversong again. "You still failed in the end. The Four Territories are a husk of their former strength because of you."

"No." Silversong straightened his posture and bristled in defiance of Ironwrath's statements. "I'm not the one who attacked Thornhollow and broke an oath made to a loyal lieutenant."

Ironwrath's mouth opened as if to speak. Nothing came out. Creases took shape on his forehead, more and more appearing until they formed a troubled frown. "You stole my destiny. My future."

"It isn't your future anymore," Silversong wounded the Heretic more than the sharpest slice of air ever could. "You're irrelevant, Ironwrath. A ghost of the past. All you can do now is fade into obscurity."

Shock found its way into the Heretic's expression, his fur standing on end, his lips curling to display dripping fangs. Silversong snarled back, knowing the Heretic wouldn't dare use the piece of time against him. Ironwrath wanted Silversong's death to be personal, visceral, real.

Come on…

Silversong anticipated the Heretic's move. He would strike at Silversong's neck, but Silversong would duck just in time to bite upward and crush the Heretic's throat.

Come on…

The Heretic considered it, then covered his fangs, backing away from Silversong.

NO! He must've seen his death in the threads!

All hope evaporated, the fear once drained now resurfacing from the depths. Silversong shook without control.

The Heretic gave him the subtlest of grins. "Do you remember our first meeting in the Silverhaze Forest, little lamb? I said given the power, I would consider returning us wolves to a state ruled by instinct."

Silversong's mouth gaped in horror, pale blue eyes flashing in his thoughts.

The Heretic continued. "Now I have the power to do so. And I have considered. Did you see him too, Silversong? The haunting presence? The pallid face drained of blood? I saw him upon consuming the piece of time. I heard the directions he was given, and somehow, I knew where I needed to go. This is where he led his army, isn't it? This is where they disappeared at the end of the War of Change. Where do you suppose they disappeared to?"

The Heretic convulsed. The invisible threads tensed and vibrated. Ironwrath opened his mouth as if to vomit, and out came the whirling piece of time, expanding larger and larger, moving away from its new master until it hovered between Silversong and Swiftstorm. The light of the shape revealed intricate carvings etched in the floor that Silversong couldn't make sense of. Blood turned to ice in his veins as the enlarged circle showed within its frame near and distant reflections of the chamber. Swiftstorm was there one moment, then gone the next, the pattern repeating as the true gateway looked further and further back into history.

See-through figures appeared in the frame, two-legged figures in shells of metal or hide or other strange fabrics. Some pointed to the shifting circle, yelling incomprehensibly at one another until a prominent silhouette strode in front of the filmy crowd, tooth of metal gripped tightly in one forepaw, a shorter, more compact object clutched in the other. The images and afterimages collided together, the ripples of the impact spreading to reveal Aelrion and his army of Forgotten Ones at the climax of the War of Change.

Aelrion's icy gaze instantly landed on Silversong, his tiny mouth opening in shock. Angara-kal and a huge hairless brute of a Forgotten One stood beside the pale figure, weapons pointed at the golden circle, at Silversong. Those at the front of the army knelt and readied their long *sticks*, aiming them at the wolves beyond the gateway.

Aelrion shouted something in gibberish. He put no meaning into those sounds, no emotion, nothing. It was just loud noise. It seemed he'd given the order for his soldiers to lower their weapons. Some looked angry and terrified, others looked resigned to their deaths. They smelled so different, so… alien. A low and triumphant howl resonated from Aelrion's side of the gateway.

Motherwolf.

Other beasts echoed the cry for victory. They were closing in on the Forgotten Ones.

Aelrion yelled something, and his army came racing through the gateway into the present, filling the empty chamber to its limit. Silversong couldn't look away. His thoughts were blank as fresh-fallen snow, and his legs were utterly weightless. The bellows and growls of ruthless beasts drew ever closer, and when the last of the two-legged pack pushed through the golden circle, Aelrion himself made the journey from past to present.

The presence that had haunted Silversong since he first consumed the piece of time stepped in front of him—a pale phantom in shining metal. Silversong's vision trembled to the intense shaking of his entire body.

The Heretic prostrated himself before the alien swarm, eyes closed. Many of the Forgotten Ones aimed their weapons at the wolves. Aelrion stopped them. An argument broke out, but he established dominance without once growling. Using his long tooth of metal, he lifted Silversong's head and peered into his eyes. The sharp and cool edge teased a little blood from Silversong's throat, staining the blade. Aelrion's pasty-white face lit up in recognition… and fear. He hid it masterfully, but it was there. The forepaw holding the pointy bar of metal jerked slightly. There was an unnatural *awareness* about the two-legged leader Silversong couldn't explain, and he wondered if the bipedal Chief was casting a spell on him.

A more primal fear preyed on Silversong's lesser frights. He couldn't move. He couldn't blink. He couldn't breathe.

Aelrion spoke once more in the meaningless language of the Forgotten Ones. Was he speaking to Silversong? Did he think Silversong could understand him? Silversong could no longer rely on the piece of time to translate this nonsense. The pale creature smelled of blood, grime, and metal, and he had the likeness of a soul who'd escaped death but was unafraid of facing it. A tired predator who wouldn't sleep until all his prey was hunted.

Silversong broke his gaze from the ashen-haired leader, trying to make himself look as harmless as possible. Aelrion removed the blade from Silversong's throat and spoke to some prominent two-legged figures. Lieutenants, perhaps?

Silversong stayed still, frozen helplessly as the Forgotten Ones slowly withdrew from the chamber, Aelrion leading them into the light of a distant future from their perspective. The piece of time tensed, flickered, vibrated, frayed, then dissipated into nothing, its power fully spent.

Too shocked to speak, too confused to think, Silversong could do nothing but watch as the Heretic moved to stand at his side. "And so our ancient enemy returns to an age that has forgotten it. The curse of sentience can't be shared between us and them. In their conquest, they'll return us to the simple beasts we were always meant to be. Your victory is a hollow one, little lamb. I've corrected the course of the future. Yes, this was my true purpose all along. I see it now. Breaking the Wolven Code, dominating the Four Territories, healing a corrupt society… these are nothing compared to this greatest of deeds."

"You're… you're insane!" Silversong tried to growl, but it came out as a whimper.

Ironwrath turned to Swiftstorm, allowing a smile to stretch his mouth wide. "How I wish I could've killed the Warden. I can't deny how badly I wanted to make her suffer. I suppose I'll have to indulge myself another way." In a panic, Swiftstorm attempted to yank herself free of the floor.

The Heretic cocked his head up, and the bronze spike beneath Swiftstorm drove itself into her stomach. The ground released her, the sharp point lifting her entire weight. She screamed in agony, her piercing wails reaching a crescendo as the metal penetrated her spine. A sickening crack echoed throughout the chamber. She spasmed once, muscles hardened, then her body hung limp on the spike. Silversong yowled and closed his eyes, thrashing and pulling. Nothing worked. The Heretic still had him thoroughly confined.

A void swallowed his heart. His head whirled. His legs buckled. He couldn't distinguish one emotion from another as they were all sucked into a growing hole inside him.

"I'll be waiting for you outside. I would prefer to fight you on even ground. Don't delay too long," the Heretic whispered.

The floor pushed Silversong out until he stood completely free. He opened his eyes.

The Heretic was gone.

Silversong blacked out.

How much time had passed? Swiftstorm now lay in a pool of her own blood, the spike retracted. On leaden legs, he trudged over to her. She looked up at him, eyelids fluttering, her lower body completely paralyzed. As the final vestiges of her life leaked away, she smiled at him—a loving smile, a sisterly smile.

Then she was gone.

All Silversong could hear were his own breaths. His surroundings winked out of existence. He was alone. The fear, the rage, the pain, the sadness… the void squeezed it all together into a single flame fighting to stay alight. The choices were clear: give up, or fight. Smother the flame and surrender to the void… or feed the fire, the withering light.

Heat soaked into him, seething, smouldering, fuming. A frothing torrent tempered the surge, and he woke up. His flesh prickled, his fur bristled, his frown bulged over burning eyes, and he turned to the corridor leading outside, fangs bared.

He had a dim awareness of sprinting out of the ruin. He blinked, and the Heretic was down in the gorge waiting for the confrontation. Silversong caught a strong wind, divided the current into several winding swirls, then leaped for Ironwrath's throat.

Silversong soared, his slicing air breaking apart the Heretic's launched projectiles. Ironwrath zipped backward, dodging the deafening impact of Silversong's landing. Dust billowed like smoke, the bloody moon spectating the duel between wind and earth. Distant bangs sounded from where the Wolven Bulwark fought the Devoted, but Silversong's eyes stayed locked on his adversary. Nothing more needed to be said between them. One of them would die today, and there was comfort in such simplicity.

Spikes formed beneath Silversong. He jumped out of the way before they could impale him like they had Greyhail. Silversong whipped his tail sideways, unleashing an arc of air so powerful it carved through several spires, bringing two of the smaller ones down on Ironwrath. He halted them, throwing one, then the other at Silversong. Maneuvering the wind and hurling himself to the right, Silversong evaded the crushing blows.

The ground softened and pulled his paws under. Silversong concentrated, forcing the air to hack away at the conjured quicksand. He kept running so his enemy couldn't snare him, all the while dodging boulders and towering heights of earth. He couldn't withstand this onslaught forever. Soon he would lose. He inhaled until his lungs begged him for mercy and blew out a strong blast, shearing a hail of brown blades into clumps of harmless debris. On a wave of dry clay, the Heretic rode, more projectiles shooting out of the stirred soil.

Silversong willed all his wind downward and used it to propel him onto one of the spires. The Heretic's wave increased in speed, crashing into the base of the formation and threatening to knock Silversong off. He hopped onto another platform as the spire on which he previously stood crashed to the ground, broken to pieces and absorbed into the Heretic's deluge.

Silversong leaped from spire to spire, narrowly escaping the Heretic's earthen tsunami. The prickling energy in Silversong's veins began to fade, exhaustion slowly taking over. His opponent was a master at weaving earth, a force of nature Silversong couldn't hope to rival alone. He gritted his teeth, flinging sharp wind crescents whenever he could spare an attack, putting all he'd learned over the seasons to the test. Boulders flew to shield the Heretic from the cutting slices. Silversong cursed, leaping off his platform onto the head of another spire. The Heretic commanded its brittle neighbor to smash into it. Silversong yelped as the impact threw him to the ground.

Amid the panic, clarity struck. Silversong caught the currents of air around him and moulded them into a mighty swirl. The whirlwind ejected him out of the Heretic's reach and drilled straight through a weaker spire before delivering Silversong onto a more stable one. Ironwrath's wave flowed inward, growing taller and taller the narrower it got, lifting him until he faced Silversong directly.

Cracks formed all over Silversong's platform. Twirling his tail, he conjured a massive vortex and launched it at the Heretic, but the exile jumped onto a nearby tapering formation, abandoning his tumultuous wave to the wrath of the wind.

The enormous cloud of dust thickened in several places, condensing into heavy orbs of compressed particles. They rotated around Ironwrath, gathering speed. It was over. Silversong couldn't possibly deflect them all.

A shard of frozen water, foul and filthy, pierced the Heretic's neck. He yelped, stumbling backward. Silversong looked down to where he thought the projectile had come from, eyes popping, heart racing, tail twitching.

"Frostpaw!" Silversong cried out the name of the one he loved, elation and confusion jolting through him like lightning.

Frostpaw's yellow eyes were brighter than the moon, and just looking at his resolute face fed Silversong's determination not to give up. "Did you see Greyhail's body?"

"Yes!" Silversong barked.

"Lure the Heretic there!"

"But why?!"

"Just trust me!"

Leaving no time for questions, Frostpaw took off toward the dead sentinel at an impressive pace for a River-Stream member. The Heretic recovered from the unforeseen attack and concentrated on breaking Silversong's spire. He jumped right before his platform erupted, scrambling onto another high surface then hopping to the next one, following his ally toward Greyhail's corpse.

He came back for me!

Though his chest heaved and his muscles burned, Silversong couldn't give up now. He had to keep moving. For Frostpaw, for the Wolven Bulwark, for himself. Renewed motivation warded off his exhaustion and dampened the aching pain in his limbs.

The Heretic pursued Silversong more intensely than ever. Boulders rained from above, tiny blades of natural metal zoomed forward, some nicking Silversong on the legs, and snakes of dust slithered to blind him. Each spire fractured soon after he landed, exploding into rubble which then followed the Heretic. Silversong dropped onto a lonely platform close to where Frostpaw stood, forepaws rubbing the ground near Greyhail's corpse.

Silversong turned back to his previous platform. The Heretic bristled atop it now, his fury greater than a thunderstorm. All the debris he'd gathered from the broken spires hovered on either side of him, transforming into thick blades poised to shoot at Silversong.

"Whatever you're doing, Frostpaw, do it now!" Silversong barked.

The hail of earthen blades descended on him.

He caught a strong updraft, shaped it, compressed it, wove it into a whooshing barrier that sliced to dust the deadly volley. The Heretic concentrated, growling at Silversong. The sharp points almost made it through, but the shield of wind barred the brutal assault. Silversong's focus waned, exhaustion creeping in again. As a final act of defiance, he pushed the cutting barrier outward, flinging all the missiles every which way.

Water erupted below—a splashing flood. Silversong blinked.

A huge tendril of clear liquid reached for the Heretic and caught him. He thrashed within its grasp as it lifted him off his platform and brought him down to the ground in a bone-breaking *WHACK*. There was a spring of some kind beneath the dry gorge, the final remnant of a once mighty ravine, and Frostpaw had exposed it.

The Heretic coughed up a spray of water, dazed and stunned in front of the gushing hole. He craned his bleeding neck to look at Silversong.

Silversong conjured a fearsome whirlwind and wove it around him. He jumped off his platform and somersaulted, the powerful currents accumulating at his tail. Just as he came down, he released a thunderous wave to smite his enemy.

Ironwrath closed his eyes.

The boom of the impact shook Silversong's eardrums as he landed. When the dust settled, the Heretic was no more. In his place, a large watery crater remained.

Silversong finally allowed himself to catch his breath. "It's done. Fade into obscurity." His legs trembled so much he thought his bones might shatter. Frostpaw came to his side and helped him stand.

"I sensed a flowing body of water here when I was looking for you," Frostpaw explained, puffing and rasping. "I feared for your life when I saw Greyhail's corpse."

"You came back." The initial pain of Frostpaw's departure dissipated, and Silversong allowed himself to smile.

"Someone has to look after your rump." Frostpaw smiled back.

Silversong fought through the gnawing fatigue to ask his question. "But… but how…?"

"Long story short, I realized what really matters to me. Who really matters to me." Frostpaw tenderly licked Silversong's wounds, extracting gasps. "I spotted one army pursuing another as I was leaving Stone-Guard Territory behind, then I confronted Chief Riptide as the Wolven Bulwark was preparing to face off against the Devoted."

Frostpaw peered at his forepaws and shivered, baring his teeth. "Yeah, he briefed me on my traitor of a father and his new faction of fanatics. I said I would go search for you, and my Chief gave no objections. I'm sorry I abandoned you, Silversong. I'm such a terrible friend."

The whimpers started. Silversong gently licked the corporal to reassure him. "No, Frostpaw, you're a good friend. You made the right choice in the end." Frostpaw trembled against him. "Shh. It's okay. It's okay."

Frostpaw stared into Silversong's eyes, their noses touching. The scent of fear took over. "Silversong, you won't believe me, but I saw an army of two-legged creatures in the gorge while I was searching for you. I watched from a distance. It-it was like something out of a legend!"

The roots of dread entangled Silversong's heart. "As a last spiteful move, the Heretic used the piece of time to bring the Forgotten Ones from the past into the present. Where were they heading, Frostpaw?"

"WHAT?!" Frostpaw bristled, ears shooting up, hackles stiffening.

"Where were they heading?!" Silversong demanded, breathing heavily and startling his companion.

Frostpaw looked to where the Wolven Bulwark was, dead quiet in the night. Smoke drifted up in thinning trails above the gorge, but there were no more explosions, no more flashes of light, nothing.

Motherwolf's mercy.

"Come! I'll explain everything later!" Silversong barked, forcing himself to run in the direction of the Wolven Bulwark.

The meagre wind he could still rely on in his wearied state offered little relief, and the closer he drew to the Wolven Bulwark, the more he realized how thoroughly the Heretic had doomed wolfkind.

The tales parents told to frighten their pups were real. The Forgotten Ones had returned, angry and vengeful, and there existed no better outlet for them to vent their rage than the descendants of those who'd hunted their kind into extinction long ago.

In the back of his mind, Silversong could almost picture his one-eyed future shaking his head in disappointment.

CHAPTER 30

Vengeance of the Forgotten

Fearing for the Wolven Bulwark, Silversong hurried out of the gorge alongside Frostpaw.

The gloom of the night couldn't shelter Silversong's eyes from the aftermath of the massacre. The scent of blood wafted from everywhere, accompanied by the frantic yelps of the dying. After witnessing Amberstorm's murder, Palesquall's death, and Swiftstorm's gruesome end, the feeling of loss was a hollow one. The storm of emotions had already passed, leaving behind a gaping pit that could only grow bigger.

Frostpaw rushed to the wounded, but Silversong couldn't raise a single paw. The Heretic had done far worse than break the Four Territories, he'd condemned them to the wrath of the Forgotten Ones.

Darkwave's forces had been completely decimated, the sentinels too. Thick red streams leaked from small holes all over their bodies, the wounds far too deep to patch. Many had been slashed, cut, bashed, or punctured by a variety of unnatural weapons. The Wolven Bulwark was in a slightly better shape, but only dozens remained of its once vast number. Soldiers of all ages lay strewn about like fallen leaves—older rookies, subordinates, corporals, lieutenants.

Shrill yelping sliced through the night whenever Scorchfang cauterized a grievous injury. Gorsescratch and Tawnydrift helped the Wise-Wolves gather the nearest medicinal plants for swift use. The healers all aided one another, no longer bound to serve only their packmates. A Flame-Heart subordinate choked as

Moonwhisper eased something into his throat, Mistyfur put pressure on the wounds of a surviving Stone-Guard corporal, and a skinny Wise-Wolf instructed Chief Riptide to keep his hacked off forelimb submerged in the soil.

Icetail licked her mate tenderly on the neck. "Oh, Riptide. It's all right. I'm here."

A dazed and worried look was the Chief's only response, his eyes sliding back to his maimed leg.

The healer tending to him pressed on the bloody soil. "You're a tough one, sir. Don't you ever think less of yourself because of one missing limb. Why, Stone-Guard himself was a legend during his time. The most powerful of Motherwolf's generals despite being a cripple. You'll get through this."

Snowleap returned carrying a clump of dry plants in her mouth. She dropped the medicine before two working Wise-Wolves and hurried to where Frostpaw stood, sniffing him all over and whining her thanks to Motherwolf. She spared a few sorry looks for her father.

Silversong found his parents, relief flickering through him. They were giving orders to a couple lieutenants. Cedargaze whipped her head around, nudged Shadowgale, then padded over to Silversong. His mother was missing an ear, blood trailing down the right side of her cut face, though her wounds might've been simple scratches for all the attention she gave them. Shadowgale appeared unscathed in comparison, but as he approached, Silversong could see in his father's eyes how shaken he really was.

Hazel spotted Silversong too. Leaving an injured sibling to the care of her family, she ran toward him and nearly knocked him back into the gorge. She immediately began licking his muzzle. Her wounds looked relatively minor, and only a few new gashes stained the charred side of her face.

Thank Motherwolf you're alive!

Cedargaze's remaining ear flopped low upon noticing the absence of her daughter. "Swiftstorm…?" She emitted a high-pitched whistle.

Hope kept Shadowgale from whimpering. He looked around, trying to locate Swiftstorm among the survivors.

"Dead." The bitter emptiness spreading throughout Silversong lowered his voice to an emotionless whisper.

Shadowgale dropped to the earth, choking on his grief and shaking his head. Cedargaze froze, breath catching in her throat.

Silversong looked away in shame. "I'm sorry. I just wasn't good enough to save her."

Something pressed against him. Not Hazel. His mother. She buried her face in his fur and whimpered, holding nothing back. "You're not to blame for any of this, Silversong."

Silversong wasn't so sure. He'd stolen the piece of time from the Heretic. He'd failed to master the weapon. He'd failed to predict this awful fate. His one-eyed future had been right. He should've listened to his own advice. He should've let the Heretic…

… NO. He'd strived to unite the Four Territories, and he'd done it. He'd beaten the Warden, the exiles, and the Devoted, though his victory had demanded a heavy price.

Oh, Palesquall, Swiftstorm… I'm so sorry.

He shared some of his mother's whimpers, hiding under her frame, trying to disappear. She sheltered him as if he were a pup. At this moment, he couldn't care less about the potential judgment of others. Some of the pain had to leak out. His father joined them, and they mourned together under the fading moon.

I'll miss you, Swiftstorm. I know you would've chosen family over the sentinels in the end. I know it.

Time slipped away from him. His whimpers stopped, then started up again, over and over until sorrow filled the emptiness within. Opening his eyes, he saw Frostpaw standing over his father's body, his one remaining sibling waiting tentatively behind him.

Silversong heard his dearest friend grunt, "your treatment of me was never fair. I was your child as much as the others, and you rejected me. I hope Motherwolf accepts you into her den, because I intend to confront you there one day. Then we'll have ourselves a long discussion about family. Farewell, father."

All around, frightened whines and whispers livened the night.

"The spirits of the Forgotten Ones have come for revenge."

"They showed up out of nowhere."

"Those loud bangs were so awful."

"We only survived by running away and hiding."

"Some of us had to play dead."

"Darkwave was foolish enough to fight them."

"Where did they go?"

"They'll return eventually. I'm sure of it. We must prepare."

"We must pray to Motherwolf for guidance."

"There're too few of us remaining to stand a chance."

"How…? Where did those monsters come from…?"

Too many had died for proper rites to be given individually, but the survivors mourned their losses all the same. A more formal ceremony would have to be planned for the fallen, and Silversong hoped wolves of all territories would participate. Shared grief was better for healing.

The shy rays of the morning sun peeked over the horizon, shining light on the devastation caused by the Forgotten Ones. Silversong removed himself from his mother's comforting fur and stepped back to see the entire Wolven Bulwark watching him, expecting answers.

"The Heretic is dead, and the piece of time is gone," Silversong explained, throat aching and fatigue tugging him toward unconsciousness. "He trapped me in the Bronze Barrow and used the weapon to open a gateway connecting the present to the end of the War of Change." None of the wolves could even bring themselves to gasp. "He invited the last of the Forgotten Ones into our time. The Heretic is the reason they vanished in the Bronze Barrow so long ago, and he's the reason they're here now. He used up all the remaining power of the piece of time to do this. One final insult to the Wolven Bulwark."

He was back in the dim chamber again, watching Swiftstorm wail as the bronze spike impaled her.

He snapped out of it, wincing and breathing heavily. "After that he… he…" Frostpaw stepped forward and put his forepaw atop Silversong's. They locked eyes. "After that I only managed to defeat the Heretic because Frostpaw found me in time."

Most wolves tried to make sense of the revelation and failed. Silversong struggled to make sense of it himself, and he'd been there to witness the return of the Forgotten Ones in person. Some of the wounded had died during the night, and those lucky enough to have survived had the look of despair about them, already anticipating another attack from the two-legged monsters.

Silversong had nothing more to say. He could think of nothing more to say. No inspiration to give. No hope to embrace. Frostpaw moved back, and the void returned.

“What do we do now?” Riptide limped forward, one of his forelimbs ending in a stump. Icetail stayed by her mate’s side in case he lost balance.

Everyone had the same question in their eyes, causing Silversong to give a hollow chuckle. How could they look up to him after all this? He sighed. “We go back to the Saltshore. There’re enough resources in River-Stream Territory to go around, and all of us put together, we’re barely enough to form a single pack. We’ll never recover if we remain rivals. Staying true to the Wolven Code now means certain defeat. All former boundaries must be uprooted, and laws must change. Only by working together can we dare to hope for a better future.”

“And the Forgotten Ones?” Scorchfang asked, still visibly shaken from the attack. Most of her injuries had already been cauterized. “If they return and see they missed some of us…”

Worried yelping came from the more inexperienced fighters.

They would return. Silversong knew it for a fact. “You’re right, Scorchfang. We better get moving before they come back. We’ll prepare a proper defense at the Saltshore.”

Silversong’s muscles ached badly. *So tired. I hope they bought it.*

The plan wasn’t a complex one by any means, and more than a few questioning glances were thrown his way by the senior lieutenants, but if they had any objections, none were voiced, and when Silversong woke up in the middle of the night to do his business away from the watchful sentries, he silently slipped away from the Wolven Bulwark and ran.

It shouldn’t be too difficult to locate Aelrion’s trail.

The Forgotten Ones were clumsy and neglected to hide their movements. Each one smelled unique, and each one looked very distinct. Finding Aelrion’s pack would prove easy, but killing him…?

Quite another matter entirely, but I’ll solve the issue when I get there.

Aelrion feared Silversong. The leader of the Forgotten Ones had seen something in the threads of time. Something that had stayed his blade in the Bronze Barrow. Something about a wolf in the sun, burning, but never dying. Whatever that meant, it gave Silversong the hope he needed to keep going.

The Forgotten Ones were perhaps the greatest threat the land had ever seen, and this time, there were no Titans to stop them. Would cutting off the head of their army be enough?

Well… maybe there's one Titan I can rely upon. How about it, slimy tentacle monster? You still owe me a favour, don't you?

It pained him to leave everyone behind—his loved ones especially—but he couldn't watch anyone else die, and if he did nothing, Aelrion would come back for them all sooner or later.

Silversong looked over his shoulder, stomach sinking. One of the sentries had spotted him!

"Pricklethorn!" Silversong cursed and seized the flowing air around him, willing it to enhance his speed. He was now among the fastest runners in the Four Territories. Nothing could catch him. Nothing could—

He splashed in a cool pond, tripping on a submerged stone and falling muzzle-first in the wet snare. Shaking out the water in his ears, dazed and soaked, he connected himself to the passing breeze and leaped out of the pool.

The black surface stirred, bulged, then snatched him out of the air, freezing him in a humiliating position.

A River-Stream sentry! Just my luck!

"L-listen," he stammered, hanging like a pup caught by the scruff, "I-I was just—"

"Out for a late-night stroll?" Frostpaw's face came into view, the cloudy sky turning his blue coat black. He looked furious, hackles stiff and tail straight.

"Frostpaw!" Silversong squirmed uselessly in his frozen prison. "Let me go!"

"Why? So you can run off and chase ghosts?" Frostpaw tightened his grasp around Silversong, drawing out a whimper.

"Just one ghost." Silversong's eyes darted to where the wolves slept. None of the other sentries had noticed his disappearance or Frostpaw's absence yet.

Frostpaw stared at the ground, ears drawn back and tail drooping. "I'm sorry about Palesquall and Swiftstorm. Their deaths weren't your fault, and it tears me up inside knowing how badly this must be hurting you."

A whimper almost made it out of Silversong's mouth. His heart became suddenly very heavy. "I…"

Nothing remained of Frostpaw's scowl. "Please, listen to me. Throwing your life away for vengeance won't solve anything. You taught me as much." His eyes showed only a deep concern for his friend.

Silversong tried not to think about all he'd lost. "This is different. I'm not hunting the leader of the Forgotten Ones out of my need for vengeance. I'm hunting him because it's only a matter of time before he returns to finish us off for good. We won't be able to run or hide then. Even the Titans feared him during the War of Change. He'll destroy everything we know if we let him live."

Galdreth put him up to this. Aelrion is the hero destined to return the Forgotten Ones to glory. The power he wields is too great. He must be stopped.

Frostpaw shook his head and laughed. "And you're going to face him?! Alone?!"

"Uh… yes?" Silversong thought about revealing the surreal experience he'd gone through after first swallowing the piece of time, but Frostpaw wouldn't understand.

Frostpaw paced side to side, muttering to himself about how crazy a particular friend of his was. He stopped, ears pricked and whiskers twitching. His frown loosened a bit, and he peered up at Silversong. "You know, this reminds me of when we first met."

"I'm even in the same humiliating position as last time," Silversong remarked.

"Exactly." Frostpaw smiled, eyes fixed on Silversong as if waiting for him to realize something. "You were ready to do anything I asked, right?"

"Only because you threatened me!" Silversong glared, recalling something about being thrown into a boiling geyser.

"But you would've done anything to keep me from hauling you off by the tail, right?" Frostpaw's knowing gaze unsettled Silversong to the core. "Such as letting me tag along on a potentially fatal mission?"

"Yeah, probably—wait." Silversong gasped in astonishment. "No. No. NO!"

Frostpaw's smile grew wider. "Yes. Yes. Yes."

EPILOGUE

A Future to Conquer

Three days since humanity had faced certain doom in the Bronze Temple.

The way out has been sealed. Galdreth was mistaken. We're trapped, and the enemy is nearing.

Three days since Aelrion had accepted the death of hope.

The beasts are howling for blood, eager to finish the purge.

Three days since a golden circle had connected the present to a distant future.

Galdreth's ultimate plan has come to fruition at last.

Three days since Aelrion had encountered the silver wolf, the one he'd seen burning in the sun, refusing to die.

The fight isn't over yet.

The event replayed itself in his head over and over again, and each time he shuddered upon thinking of the silver wolf. He brought a gloved hand to his steel breastplate, feeling a phantom pain in his chest. Why had he not killed the wretched animal? Its eyes… blue like the deep ocean itself. He'd seen those eyes before, seen the fear in them. Those eyes had belonged to children just before they were ripped to pieces by gnawing fangs, mothers who wailed as claws dug into their hearts, fathers who screamed as the beasts began their rampage, slaughtering indiscriminately. How then could a wolf's eyes remind him so of humanity?

And that old wolf who bowed to me? I suppose I spared it because somehow it gave humanity a second chance. Did it understand the consequences of bringing us here? Did it open the gateway intentionally? Probably not.

Aelrion thought for a while, recalling how wise the aged beast had seemed to him.

What about the beaten wolf trapped in the floor itself? The answer was simple. *What would've been the point of killing it? It probably died of its wounds after our departure from the Bronze Temple.*

Then there was the silver wolf, the one whose eyes had seemed so… human.

How could I not hesitate?

When he'd marched his army out of the gorge, an enormous pack of wolves had blocked the way forward. While they fought amongst themselves for whatever reason, Aelrion had seized the opportunity to put his soldiers into formation and break through the tempest of fangs. He'd killed easily enough then, firing and slicing and felling beast after beast until the cowards ran and hid. Had those wolves also carried the same humanity in their eyes? The same intelligence?

What does it matter? It's us against them. They made that abundantly clear by trying to eradicate us.

He'd given the wolves a taste of retribution. If they understood this concept, if they'd somehow gotten more intelligent, all the better. They wouldn't soon forget the crimes of their ancestors now.

Aelrion fingered the darksteel object in the leather holster strapped to his waist. A *revolving pistol*, Galdreth had called it. A weapon of the future. Aelrion gripped the smooth handle of his melee weapon. He preferred the blade to these more advanced killing tools. The sword offered a fluid elegance a firearm foreswore. Still, he owed his gratitude to Galdreth and his blacksmiths. Because of them, most people here were equipped for melee *and* ranged combat, even those far too young to be considered adults. Everyone needed training. Everyone had to fight, for the beasts wouldn't spare a single soul no matter the age.

Aelrion sighed and walked out of his tent. The Highguards in their gilded armour saluted him—right hand to the chest—as he passed into the crisp air of the grey ridge. Dawn was about an hour off, but his orders had already been passed down the chain of command. The lower-ranking men and women broke up the camp and prepared for the long journey south. Clerks, quartermasters, and cooks bustled about. The lieutenants delegated duties to their subordinates after brief inspections. The captains oversaw battle plans and scrutinized different maps, trying to figure out just how far into the future they'd been brought. Aelrion would've liked to know himself.

More than a few centuries at least.

Five thousand strong. The last remnants of the once Great Nations, all brought together in one stirring pot, and Aelrion wielded the spoon. A mighty spoon it was.

Adania, Kinwyr, Uktabar, the Stormlands, and the Northern Kingdom. Once these nations would've been at each other's throats, but the threat of extinction had united them all under Aelrion's guidance. Galdreth had worked tirelessly to make it so. So many cultures, religions, and beliefs in one place, all contradicting each other in some way, and yet this war had glued humanity together rather than divide it further. The enemy had underestimated them.

Aelrion questioned whether this mutual alliance would continue, now that mankind had evaded extermination. Would the nations and the numerous factions within them return to plotting and quarrelling against one another? Would they reawaken prejudices once put to slumber? A nagging voice at the back of his head warned him not to deny the inevitable.

I won't let this alliance fracture. The nations must remain united under a common goal. But why? Why must it be I who leads them? Perhaps there was no answer. Perhaps this was just the way things were. Galdreth had drawn Aelrion here because the piece of time had deemed it the only way to preserve humanity. The wolves had somehow gotten their filthy mouths on Galdreth's weapon and blundered inside the Bronze Temple by linking the present to the future, or the present to the past, depending on how one looked at it. Galdreth had foreseen it all.

I misjudged you, my friend. I'm sorry. It all made perfect sense. Galdreth had met every requirement for this outcome to happen. But few as they were, could Aelrion rebuild humanity's presence even now? Could he return the Great Nations to their former glory as Galdreth had hoped he would? Could he usher his species into a new age of peace?

The clouds brewed lightning in their viscous layers, briefly exposing two figures strolling toward him. One was the Spearsage of Harzima, a region of Uktabar once renowned for its production of explosive powders. The other was Warlord Ripolasch, leader of the Kinwyrian survivors. He towered over most men, and his hairless scalp marked him a fierce warrior among his people.

Aelrion raised a hand so his Highguards could stand at ease, then walked toward his brethren in arms, giving each a deferent nod. "Angara-kal, Ripolasch. I apologize if my move orders woke you up so early. The enemy's situation hasn't yet been assessed, and I would rather not get complacent."

Angara-kal's intense brown eyes betrayed no fatigue. Alert as an owl, she reminded him so much of his mother, though the Spearsage was a fair bit younger and far darker. "The early sandraptor often catches the sleeping snake, Crownless One." A thick accent slurred her Common Adanian. The mechanical spear Galdreth had forged for her was attached to her girdle, and her rifle was slung across her back, freshly oiled by the smell of it.

Ripolasch yawned, his great big mouth wide enough to swallow a hare whole. The many scars decorating his rough face stretched at the movement. "Bah. You could wake me up in the mid of night if it means slaughtering more beasts. It was amusing watching those wolves back there squeal and squirm." He laughed, deep voice rumbling out of his thick throat. His iron armour clinked, and his enormous double-bitted axe bobbed in its loop.

A few soldiers turned their heads at the sound of such mighty laughter. Most of them no longer smiled, for their smiles had been smothered by the horrors of war. A chuckle was a rare occurrence even among the more optimistic groups.

Aelrion couldn't blame Ripolasch for his bloodlust. Aelrion too had been submerged under the dangerous tide of vengeance three days ago. All the humans who'd been tortured, burned alive, mauled to death or murdered in a hundred other brutal ways had smiled upon him that night.

"There's more retribution to be served, Ripolasch. In due course," Aelrion said, one hand gripping the base of his sword, the other clenched into a fist to keep it from shaking. When had that started?

His memories dragged him by the feet to the screeching children as wolves tore into them, to the vines and roots dragging his thrashing soldiers into the earth, to… to…

Oh, Arieth…

"Hmph." Ripolasch grunted, yanking Aelrion back to the present. "Maybe along the journey south we'll find some good sport, and none of that cowardly shooting business. I'm yearning for a real fight. Maybe those saberfangs still roam Kinwyr, eh? They always make for fun opponents."

"As I informed General Mezrek and the other leaders, we keep a low profile," Aelrion repeated, hardening his emotions into stone. Angara-kal nodded approvingly. "We've no clue if the wildgods are still lurking about. Should we encounter any, we must take them by surprise."

Ripolasch cursed in Kinwyrian.

An immortal life can still be felled. Aelrion had heard Galdreth's quote from one of the senior Adanian officers. If the wildgods still lingered here, Aelrion would find a way to dispatch them.

Angara-kal's eyes swept across the misty peaks, jagged against the gloomy skyline. Behind them lay the Stormlands, the birthplace of Aelrion's mother. The Cloudfoots were among his army now. After escaping the Great Deer's treachery, their Chieftain had sworn himself to humanity's survival. They all had. Peoples who'd never once seen eye-to-eye had thrown aside their differences for this grand cause. If humanity triumphed in the war to come, perhaps peace could finally be achieved between the nations. A lasting peace.

The shadowy reflections of a terrible future haunted Aelrion's mind, a future where humanity eventually destroyed itself. He would ensure that never happened.

For the first time since leaving the Underground City, the solemn Spearsage smiled. "I am eager to travel south to Adania. The home of King Galdreth Zeken. I always wanted to see those apple trees he talked so much about. The hillsides so green they would shame an emerald."

Ripolasch snorted at the mention of Galdreth. The battle-hardened warrior hadn't forgotten Adania's conquest of Kinwyr orchestrated by one of Galdreth's ancestors.

Aelrion focused on the task at hand. "I'm afraid there's no time for sightseeing. We must reach Aralor, Adania's fallen capital. Galdreth said he preserved many blueprints there depicting humanity's future innovations and achievements. We'll use the capital as our base of operations and prepare for the coming war. We'll reconquer the planet and remind the beasts that humanity's flame is not so easily extinguished."

The two leaders shared their reports and marched off to oversee the movements of their forces. Frigid gusts battered the camp, blowing supplies out of arms and stirring swirls of dust. People yelled, workers cursed, and soldiers on break found whatever shelter they could while gulping down their meals. Goosebumps pulled at Aelrion's skin. He strolled to a cliff looking out over the southern end of the Northern Kingdom, the Province of Berethen. The farmsteads and cozy villages were no more. Nature had risen from the ground to devour even the memory of civilization.

So much history lost, forgotten.

His guards shuffled behind him, letting a sure-footed newcomer through. Aelrion turned to see Chieftain Waktalik bring his arms across his bare chest and flex—a formal greeting to acknowledge an equal. Aelrion returned the gesture, though his armour reduced the effect. "Chieftain. The clouds bring us rain today," he said to the boom of thunder. The guards kept a close eye on the Stormlander, hands near blades that would do no good against a Knifedancer like Waktalik.

"The clouds shall cry tears of anger for the injustice done to us, Atek," Waktalik said in an even thicker accent than Angara-kal. He could've spoken gibberish, and Aelrion still would've found the Stormlander's voice pleasantly smooth and calming.

Waktalik had called him *Atek*, meaning *Chieftain* in the Stormlander tongue. Aelrion supposed a *king* and a *chieftain* were interchangeable concepts to a tribesman. He knew some of the language from his mother, and he still cherished the name she'd given him, his *true* name.

The Chieftain wore little clothing, his brown skin bare for the land to see. Why shame your body by hiding it? That wasn't the Cloudfoot way. In their society, lack of apparel meant higher status. The wise warrior had to earn the right to display their flesh. Tassets of malleable yet steel-strong wood served as his only protective gear, and an animalistic mask of the same material hung from his waist. A simple tattoo on his forehead marked his position as Chieftain—a horizontal blue line overlayed at the centre by a white circle. Ivory knives were strapped all over him for easy access—the Cloudfoot weapon of choice. His long ashen hair was braided. Two braids flowed down his chest on either side. A longer one traced the length of his spine and ended at the small of his back. If Aelrion had been a true Stormlander Chieftain, he would've braided his hair in much the same manner.

“Yes, and when our struggle is over, they shall weep tears of joy,” Aelrion said.

The Chieftain frowned, closing his eyes and connecting himself to the mountains, the sky, the grass below and the plains beyond. He seemed aware of things he couldn’t see, things he couldn’t hear. He let the roaring winds direct his body like it was a lonely blade of grass, swaying this way and that. “Balance is in turmoil. Water and fire clashing. Two trees locking branches, each trying to strangle the other. Who shall win? Who shall wither?”

Aelrion closed his eyes and opened himself to the land as the Chieftain had—a trick his mother had taught him. No… *landspeaking* was far more than a simple trick. He became a piece of the land itself, like the land was a piece of him. He sensed the mountains and their history, touched the clouds and their moisture, reached to the distant rivers and the faraway trees, *saw* their every movement, their memory. The drafts of wind showed him where to lean, where to go.

“We triumph. We must,” Aelrion answered, and to him his voice was distant yet loud as the thunder above. “Who now can stand against the might of humanity?”

He opened his eyes, balancing himself upon his connection to the land, his sight greatly enhanced, his awareness keenly sharpened. Something moved far below—two shapes entering the storm’s wrathful gaze, striding on waves of grass.

A pair of wolves stopped beneath the ridge, craning their heads up at the grey heights. The larger of the two squinted at the soldiers moving about while its companion somehow found Aelrion straight away, blue eyes narrowed under a determined frown.

Follow me if you must. Next time, I won’t hesitate. Aelrion stared down at the silver wolf, warning it not to continue its futile pursuit. *You’ll find me no easy foe. My fate isn’t to wither, but to win.*

Destiny draws us together. Two different souls from two different times.

Thunder announced the start of a new war.

Let humanity’s hour of triumph begin.

The journey continues in

The Crucible of Pain

Book Three of

A WOLF IN THE SUN

PREVIEW:

The Crucible of Pain

CHAPTER 1

Silversong and Frostpaw

Silversong couldn't escape the Heretic's thundering voice, couldn't escape the grasp of the metallic floor.

"You stole my destiny. My future," Ironwrath repeated over and over again.

"It isn't your future anymore," Silversong could barely utter the frail whisper. The pressure was closing in.

Swiftstorm stood before him, equally trapped and bleeding from dozens of fresh wounds. Hatred burned in her green eyes, burned hot for Silversong. "You're no brother of mine," she growled.

"I love you," Silversong whimpered.

A bronze spike formed under Swiftstorm's belly, and the Heretic's smile stretched wide. "How I wish I could've killed the

Warden. I can't deny how badly I wanted to make her suffer. I suppose I'll have to indulge myself another way."

"NO!" Silversong cried out.

The bronze spike drove itself into Swiftstorm's stomach, lifting her entire body as she thrashed and wailed.

CRACK!

The metal broke through her spine. She spasmed, muscles hardening. The Heretic released her, she collapsed to the floor, and then she was gone.

Silversong couldn't move. He was too weak. Too powerless.

Swiftstorm lifted her head to look at him, eyeless sockets twitching, her rotting corpse reanimated and oozing vile liquids from old wounds. "You should've listened to yourself back in the maze of madness, brother. You should've let the Heretic consume the piece of time," she drawled.

"I… I couldn't!" Silversong protested as Swiftstorm shambled toward him, maggot-white teeth dripping a putrid substance.

"Now the road before you leads only to one destination." Her mouth gaped wide, too wide. Her bloated tongue reached out to taste him, breath hot and foul. His body wanted to recoil, but terror kept him frozen solid. "PAIN."

Her jaws clamped down on his throat, tearing from him a large chunk of bleeding meat. He opened his mouth to scream, but the pain was so great it demanded utter silence.

Swiftstorm swallowed Silversong's flesh, slurping up the blood dripping from her mouth. "You taste good, brother. So sweet and innocent."

She moved in for another bite.

The air pushed itself out of Silversong's lungs, jolting him awake. He looked around in a panic before remembering how to breathe. He focused on the cool night, on the raindrops tapping the ground outside of the little dug out den, on Frostpaw watching him, worried and anxious.

At least I'm not alone.

"Are you all right, Silversong?" Frostpaw's voice, a gentle breeze to Silversong's ears, evoked a swell of comforting chills.

Silversong peered into his friend's bright yellow eyes—stars lighting the surrounding darkness. He closed his mouth and swallowed, thinking about how to respond. "I'm… I'm fine, Frostpaw. It was just a nightmare."

"You're having those too, eh?" Frostpaw stared at his forepaws. Silversong leaned against him for comfort. "I dreamed the Four Territories were burning. The Forgotten Ones returned to finish us off for good. The Wolven Bulwark broke before their might, and all hope faded."

Silversong's mind lingered on the breaking of Thornhollow, on Palesquall's crushed body, on the Heretic inviting Aelrion and the Forgotten Ones into the present, on the devastation they inflicted. "The Four Territories… the Wolven Bulwark…" Silversong shook his head, "they're already broken, Frostpaw. The Heretic won. I'm fighting for all wolfkind now. The War of Change never ended. It was only postponed."

Frostpaw licked Silversong on the cheek. "Then let's finish it together. After we slay the leader of the Forgotten Ones, we can go home and begin to heal."

Silversong wondered if they would ever return to the place once known as the Four Territories. Would they be welcomed back by the remnants of the Wolven Bulwark? The question was on the tip of his tongue, but he decided to return Frostpaw's affections instead of asking it aloud. His friend's fur was still damp from the long day journeying in the ceaseless rain. Climbing the ridge during the storm had been a tough endeavor on its own. Tracking the Forgotten Ones through unexplored terrain without getting spotted had been even more difficult. Aelrion was driving his army forward at an impressive pace for two-legged creatures, and more than once his scouts had almost sighted Silversong and Frostpaw, forcing them to linger behind and away from danger.

Thunder growled within the clouds, and the rain poured harder. Did the moon and stars never shine here? Silversong took in a whiff of air, but the earthy scent overpowered all other odours. He stood and stretched, the possibility of more nightmares driving him away from sleep.

"We heading out?" Frostpaw yawned, slowly getting up.

Silversong turned to his friend, taking his time to appreciate Frostpaw's loyalty to the cause. "I was just going out for a stroll. You know… to clear my head."

Frostpaw yawned again and blinked moisture into his weary eyes. "If we're both awake, there's no use delaying the pursuit, is there?"

Once, Silversong wouldn't have denied the opportunity to sleep next to Frostpaw. In truth, the desire tugged at him even now, but there were more important things to be done, and the more they waited, the more Aelrion's strength increased. The hunter had to close in on the prey before the prey became the hunter.

"I guess you're right," Silversong whined, walking out into the cool and rainy night.

His eyes strained to make sense of his surroundings. The eternal shroud above choked all moonlight, and the reach of the stars failed to pierce the storm's defenses. Everywhere he looked, the grass leaned one way and then the other, swaying wherever the breeze wished. In no time at all, he was dripping wet and fighting off shivers. Frostpaw emerged out of the hole dug out in the small mound behind him, standing close to Silversong.

Sharing their body heat, they sniffed for the lingering scent of the departed army, detecting it after a brief search. Even the constant dampness couldn't hide this swarm of strange odours. The Forgotten Ones had stopped here during the day, and some of them had buried their waste in a poor attempt to throw off their pursuers. They should've dug far deeper.

All throughout the night, Silversong and Frostpaw followed the trail, snacking on whatever odd berries they could find in the sparse bushes bordering a lonely pond. Frostpaw almost stepped on a huge insect, causing it to emit a wailing cry as it took off into the rain. It looked like a cricket, though it had at least a dozen limbs and multiple transparent wings. And had those been eyes growing all over its body? It was all very bizarre. Hopefully the Forgotten Ones had poor hearing, otherwise they would be alerted to the location of their stalkers.

"Do you think it's strange how empty this place feels?" Frostpaw asked a while after the cricket incident. "Other than that cricket-thingy, I haven't seen a living soul here besides us and the Forgotten Ones."

Silversong thought for a moment and agreed. "Yeah, something's off. The large prey of Whistle-Wind Territory would've jumped for joy if they could graze such lush fields, so why isn't there any prey here at all?" The more Silversong thought about it, the more an unexplained sense of dread took root in his heart. "Let's focus on the mission."

The scent trail took them over shivering mounds and through long stretches of open field where no creature dared to roam. Pools of water dotted the ground and satisfied Silversong's thirst. Frostpaw bathed himself in one of them, cleaning spots the rain might miss. Silversong hopped in too, thankful for his companion's offer to wash his coat. The courage to sleep again found Silversong just as the sun cut a bloody gash through the thinning clouds. Red on bluish-grey, the dawning light crested the distant peaks and brought relief to his eyes. Now he could see much further than before.

The land dipped into a sparse forest of leafless tress, oddly symmetrical and bearing the likeness of different beasts. One was eagle-headed, another resembled a fox, a raven, a bear. These weren't regular trees. These were shaped and carved by the Forgotten Ones in a bygone age. Moss and lichen slowly creeped up the wooden heights, and those already fallen had long surrendered to decay. A morning fog soaked into the air, obscuring everything beyond the strange formations.

Up close, the *trees* were far more impressive, and the creatures they depicted seemed to be looking down on the two wolves straying further and further away from home. A narrow ray slipped through the clouds and stabbed Silversong in the eyes. As he turned away from the light, he thought he saw the outline of rotating threads. He panted, opening his mouth to seize the piece of time and make everything right.

The illusion lasted until Silversong blinked again. The threads were never there. The piece of time was gone, its power drained to the fullest. Even now the impulse of using the golden circle was strong, and the guilt of not being able to predict this outcome ate at his conscience. He should've been better. He should've found a way to beat the Heretic while also preventing so much destruction.

"Hey." Frostpaw's voice made Silversong's ears shoot up. "If something's bothering you, let me know, all right."

Silversong looked over his shoulder and forced a smile to appear on his face. "Don't worry about me, Frostpaw. I'm fine."

Frostpaw's wide eyes pierced the thickening fog. "But if you're not… don't keep it to yourself, okay? It's just you and me out here, and if one of us is feeling hopeless, we have to be there for each other."

Silversong's smile became a genuine one. "I'm happy you're here, Frostpaw."

Frostpaw walked up to him and nudged him on the side. "Someone needs to look after your rump."

The memories hit him without warning: his sister torturing him, Palesquall crushed under an obsidian sheet, Swiftstorm impaled by a bronze spike, the wolves of the Wolven Bulwark indiscriminately maimed and slaughtered. Silversong froze, and his breaths ran short.

"I…" Silversong choked on a whimper. "They're gone, Frostpaw. Palesquall, Swiftstorm… they're all gone. I let them all down."

He'd tried not to think about his losses during the journey here. Maintaining a tough and stoic demeanor had been a mistake, it seemed. He'd only fed the strength of his sorrow, and now it crashed into him like the river's wrath breaking through a beaver's dam.

"Oh, Silversong." Frostpaw nuzzled him, breaths hot on Silversong's face. "None of this is your fault. The Heretic is responsible, and no one else. Do you understand me?"

Silversong broke away from Frostpaw, head spinning in circles. "No. No, I could've prevented all of it. In-in the Mountainmouth, I could've—"

"Silversong. Breathe." Frostpaw placed a forepaw atop Silversong's, pressing down slightly. "Breathe."

Silversong opened his mouth and let the cool air rush into his lungs. He regained some semblance of focus and buried his muzzle in Frostpaw's neck. "I'm sorry."

Frostpaw rested his chin atop Silversong's head. "You've nothing to apologize for. Like I said, none of this is your fault."

"But it is." Guilt gripped Silversong by the chest and wouldn't let go. "In the Mountainmouth, in the maze of madness, I saw a future version of myself, one-eyed and scarred."

Frostpaw backed off to look Silversong in the eye. "Yeah, you mentioned that during the moot."

Silversong continued. "He showed me a possible outcome if I let the Heretic consume the piece of time. Frostpaw… wolfkind was at peace, united under the Heretic as one mighty pack, the Wolven Code shattered and forgotten. Wolves weren't forced into separate groups based on the Blessing they controlled. They could live freely and…" Silversong's heart pumped faster as his gaze lingered on Frostpaw, "and they could love who they wished."

Frostpaw opened his mouth to whine something, closed it, then exhaled. "Silversong…"

"I stole from us a good future, Frostpaw," Silversong admitted, encouraged by his own guilt. "And I brought only suffering to the Four Territories."

Frostpaw's bulging frown startled Silversong. "Enough. I won't hear this nonsense from you." He came within a whisker-length of Silversong's face, breaths parting the fog. "You also united us as I recall. The Heretic's grudge against the Wolven Bulwark was no fault of yours. Besides, how can you be sure the Mountainmouth wasn't simply playing tricks on you?"

"It was too real to be a trick—"

"And if you think about it," Frostpaw interrupted, "the Forgotten Ones were always meant to return. In the outcome where you let the Heretic win, they still would've found a way into the present, otherwise they would've all been slain in the Bronze Barrow at the end of the War of Change. We would've been in the same situation then as we are now."

Silversong thought about it for a moment. Frostpaw was right. The Forgotten Ones were always meant to return, even in the future where the Heretic won. How could they have disappeared in the Bronze Barrow so long ago if no one brought them into the present? The guilt still clung fiercely, however, unconvinced of the argument. "At least we would've stood a chance if the Heretic led us."

And who would've opened the gateway to bring the Forgotten Ones here? It would've happened eventually… but how?

Frostpaw's eyes wandered off to the side. "There's no use obsessing over hypotheticals. We live in the here and now, and as it stands, we have a Forgotten One Chief to slay."

"There's something else, Frostpaw." Silversong's legs trembled, his courage dwindling by the breath. "I fear as though I'm being led by a thread toward this one-eyed version of myself. I-I can't really explain it, but… it's like all of this has already happened before, and there's no escaping my ultimate fate."

The fog seemed thicker and more stifling for some reason. Above, the scowling face of a wooden deer stared at Silversong.

Frostpaw still managed a smile, small though it was. "Try not to lose an eye then."

The absurdity of the answer forced a chuckle out of Silversong. "You're right, Frostpaw. Silly me. All I have to do is make sure my eyes stay right where they are."

Frostpaw snorted, his smile fading. "Look. Even if this… one-eyed version of yourself wasn't an illusion conjured by the Mountainmouth, and even if it was telling the truth, we have other priorities in front of us. Take our mission for example. The Chief of the Forgotten Ones threatens not just us wolves, but all descendants of those who fought for the Titans during the War of Change. No one is safe from wrath and retribution. We solve this problem first, then we can worry about your future."

Hardly the answer Silversong was hoping for, but again, Frostpaw was right. Aelrion had to die. As much as the pale Forgotten One deserved his revenge, Silversong had to ensure the safety of those he cared about, those he loved. His one-eyed future, inevitable or not, paled in comparison to saving this realm from Aelrion's designs.

Silversong pressed down on the grass to keep his limbs from shaking. "Since when did you become so wise?"

Frostpaw touched his nose to Silversong's. "A fruitless pursuit among the plains of Stone-Guard Territory has a way of changing you, I guess."

Silversong licked Frostpaw on the mouth. "Thanks."

"For what?"

"For being here." Silversong licked him a few more times.

Frostpaw giggled. "Same goes for you. Now how about we chase some Forgotten Ones?"

Silversong agreed, and together they pressed on through the carved forest, leaping over fungi-infested logs while following the winding trail of their two-legged quarry. By the time they reached the edge of another slope, evening rays poked searing holes in the clouds. Far into the distance a rainbow arced through falling droplets, the vibrant colours partially obscured by a massive tree—the largest one Silversong had ever seen. Its black leaves tickled the borders of the sky, and its bony branches, pale as death, ignored the commands of the breeze. An odd feeling burrowed into Silversong's core, a not-entirely-unfamiliar one. Even from so far away, the sheer size of the tree made his stomach perform a variety of peculiar movements.

"Motherwolf's milk…" was all Frostpaw could manage.

"Indeed." Silversong gaped at the colossal monstrosity. How could such a thing even come to be?

The scent of the Forgotten Ones was strong here, and their tracks clearly led toward the unnatural thing. Silversong's hackles stood on end. He met his companion's uncertain eyes, hoping to find in them the courage he lacked. Frostpaw smoothed his raised fur, the expression on his face resolute. Silversong nodded and began the descent. He wouldn't allow his doubts to persuade him off the trail.

There was only one way forward, so why hesitate? It was a question Silversong had to ask himself more than once as he got closer to the tree. Even its shadow—a spidering mass of darkness upon the swaying grass—gave rise to a glacial sense of dread.

If Aelrion walked here, so must I.

The paw prints of the Forgotten Ones slowly broke off around the freakish tree, all save one steadfast pair.

I know you'll let nothing block your path.

Though Silversong's fear tried pulling him back, he pushed onward just as Aelrion had. If Silversong tucked his tail so easily, how could he hope to face the bane of all beasts?

I'm coming for you, Aelrion. As the moon chases the sun, so too must I chase you.

An invisible force pressed against his body, watched him from every direction. A presence of many eyes. It peered into his thoughts, scrutinized him down to the marrow of his bones.

From the depths of his mind echoed his own twisted voice.

"*You can't escape the circle.*"

About the Author

Coltrane Seesequasis is a young fantasy writer of Willow Cree heritage who grew up in Gatineau, Quebec. He first began his writing journey on long bus rides to school where he would alleviate the boredom by daydreaming of fantastical worlds, noble heroes, and unwavering villains. Eventually, he put those ideas to paper and started writing stories of his own with the hopes that they would one day morph into something more than just a passion. *The Threads of Time* is the second book of the series A Wolf in the Sun, which follows a young wolf called Silversong, in a fantasy world similar to our own. Inspired by a love of nature as well as myths and folklore that challenge the limits of creativity, Coltrane joins a new generation of writers, adding his voice to the immersive genre of fantasy.